Dear Absent Friends

By

Anthea Ingham

Published by New Generation Publishing in 2015

Copyright © Anthea Ingham 2015

First Edition

The author asserts the moral right under the Copyright, Designs and Patents Act 1988 to be identified as the author of this work.

All Rights reserved. No part of this publication may be reproduced, stored in a retrieval system or transmitted, in any form or by any means without the prior consent of the author, nor be otherwise circulated in any form of binding or cover other than that which it is published and without a similar condition being imposed on the subsequent purchaser.

All characters in this novel are entirely imaginary and bear no relation to anyone I have met at the bridge table or elsewhere.

www.newgeneration-publishing.com

Chapter 1: The Opening Bid

I want to draw you a picture. Well, I'm cheating a little because I'm peeping at one of the many photos that John took on his new camcorder. He likes all that stuff, while I am really rather a Luddite. Still, technology has its uses because I am squinting at this little neon textured square to refresh my mind and show you who we all were, and why Lady Prettyman was so disliked, and why any of us (including John and me) might well have murdered her.

Is this a whodunit? I don't know. John says I am writing it to show how clever we were, but he is wrong; actually, we were incredibly stupid – the answer was staring us in the face the whole time! I suppose, really, it's about a lot of different things: the relationship between John and me; and how people who appear on the surface to be quite ordinary, in this case a number of bridge players, in fact, live the most peculiar lives and have the most extraordinary secrets. And, of course, the game of bridge comes into the story as well; but in case you are not interested in bridge you can skip those bits.

Back to the picture: we are all hanging about in Reception at *Il Sole*, a second-rate hotel on Lake Como, waiting to be allowed in for dinner, (taken early so we can get stuck into a good long session of evening bridge). However, you can see from the photo that no one's heart is really in it. We are only the runt of the party, by virtue of the fact that we are scheduled for the Birmingham flight, while the majority who elected Gatwick and Manchester have already gone.

There is nothing worse than the last hours of a holiday when everything is really finished, you have a plastic bag full of smelly boxer shorts and are fed up with eating pasta. That is, I suppose what Lady Prettyman is saying, not, I mean about the smelly knickers, but about the food.

"If you think I'm paying for all these supplements," she is saying lowering and glowering like a great craggy cliff over the desk, "you're quite mistaken. The food has been dreadful, and the service abominable. My room is a disgrace, and the meals are never on time." She senses that the girl is not responding to her. "Here, you just look at me when I'm speaking to you. Do you know who I am?"

The girl gives Lady Prettyman the look of studied insolence that Italians, especially the women, are so good at, and then focuses her attention back on the computer. Lady Prettyman is livid. She is dressed tonight in baby blue: blue sequined top, blue skirt, shoes with blue bows and a blue ribbon in her hair. She looks, if possible, even more hideous than usual. John and I used to argue about Lady Prettyman when we were idling about at the bridge table or in the bar and her ladyship hoved into sight. John maintained that she was the ugliest woman the world had ever known. I said I'd once seen a docudrama about Neanderthal man. John said this was irrelevant, and that, on reflection, Lady Prettyman was more like the Abominable Snowman.

I suppose the best way to describe her is like a man in drag: a huge bristly face, a pendulous lip, a sallow complexion and an enormous, slightly crooked nose; all exacerbated by her penchant for squeezing her eighteen stone into little girl clothes. Now it wasn't just a question of her ugliness, after all, nobody can help that, but the fact that she was so extremely rude and unpleasant, and her huge ugly cantankerous body was a kind of outward expression of her inner nastiness.

"Here!" She continues, leaning her great elbows on the desk. "I'm talking to you. Stop looking at that computer and pretending you don't understand English. Do you want to keep your job?"

We gaze listlessly on; we are used to Lady Prettyman's tirades – and to a degree we agree with her, the bridge holiday was not top of the range, the food has been poor and the rooms grubby. But suddenly we prick up our ears, her ladyship has changed tack. Tubby has appeared on the scene and we look forward to see him once again in the firing line.

"Where have you been? You're never here when you're wanted. How can you just stand there doing nothing while this girl... Stop twiddling your thumbs!"

Tubby is the only person I have ever seen who actually does stand and twiddle his thumbs; round and round he twiddles, his small fat face suffused in foolish placatory smiles, his round little body swaying to and fro in time with the twiddling. We are all more interested now, and prepare to take a sadistic interest in Tubby's humiliation at the huge red hands of his hideous wife.

And when I say 'we' who do I mean? I'm looking for guidance from the photo. The Macalisters have just come in from the bar and stand in an awkward group; Mrs Macalister, Isabel, is a woman one imagines to have been extremely good-looking in her youth, perhaps beautiful. She is also, I suspect, quite bright, certainly a good bridge player, and we used to wonder how she ended up with him, Mr Look-at-Me, with his 'artistic' clothes and after-shaved fragrance – that we thought, (John and I) probably hid more distinctive smells. He had, in fact, once enjoyed some success on a Children's Television programme and had subsequently made a living as a bit-part actor and an adviser on things dramatic to schools who were unfortunate enough to have to listen to him. "Ah," he exclaims, "we are about to partake of our last meal, our own veritable Last Supper," looking expectantly round for the audience appreciation he so seldom merits.

"I suppose you see yourself as Jesus Christ," mutters their daughter Janet, standing apart from them, her hair scraped back into a pony tail and anger on her face. You can see (I look now at the photo) that she is old to be accompanying her parents on holiday; she must be over thirty, and one senses that there is something wrong with Janet, as she stands there, silent like her mother, but angry, unable or unwilling as she has been all though the holiday, to communicate with anyone except her bridge partner, Lewis, across the table. Trevor Macalister runs a careless hand through his grey hair, which he wears long, and addresses his wife:

"What would you like to drink, darling?" He speaks loudly, particularly enunciating the word 'darling' so we can all see what a fine, husbandly fellow he is. She says something so quietly that he has to ask her again.

"Aha, a Campari, the very flavour of Italy…" He looks towards Janet, he seems to lose his accustomed manner with her; it is as if she intimidates him. "Janet, can I get you a drink?" I feel he would rather not ask, but he wants us to see that although Janet is so unresponsive, he has just the right paternal touch. But Janet turns her back and stares out of the window. Despite its other shortcomings, the hotel does have the most wonderful views, and we have, over the fortnight, seen the lake in all its moods: gentian-blue and kindly in the morning, pools of red and amber when the sun goes down, black as treacle and bedazzled with lights at night; grey, dolorous and full of Debussy on the odd stormy day. Notwithstanding, the battle at the desk rages on.

"Well, are you going to tell this Signora or Signorina or whatever she calls herself where she gets off, or not?"

"Well, my dear," Toby twiddles, "I think…"

"*You* think! That'll be the day."

Tubby's fat little cheeks are suffused in sorrow. Wickedly, we are all slightly in hope that he is about to cry. We are, however, to be disappointed: Lady P., whom it must be admitted is pretty quick off the mark, has noticed Sammy coming to her aid.

"Ah! It's you. And about time, too. Let's hope *you* can get some sense out of this girl! God, I never thought I'd prefer a black to my husband."

Sammy is gorgeous, so smooth, in every way, wonderful face, wonderful body. John once asked him where he bought his clothes. 'Savile Row, Sugarplum,' he'd replied, and laughed his wonderful laugh, a huge laugh that not only encompassed his own body, but all of us; making everyone in his midst feel that the world was a better place for Sammy. Much was unknown about him; where did he disappear to at night – when he had finished scoring up the bridge, and sorting out the myriad of little problems, like bed-time whiskeys and disappearing silver pens, dietary requirements, and so on? What did Sammy do when he wasn't working as a tournament director, where did he get his money from, and had he really had all the waiters, as John insisted?

And now, how did he feel when Lady P. accosted him in her aggressive language.

"Sugar plum, he said taking her arm, "you are going to buy your Sammy a large vodka tonic to comfort him for the thought of losing you." And he led her off towards the bar blowing a kiss to the grinning receptionist. Tubby stared after them bemused: why couldn't he do that?

"I hope he makes her pay," said Carol to Simon, "although I am afraid I think that's unlikely. I do dislike meanness, but I suppose that's because I have a generous heart. I'm afraid our Lady Prettyman… Well," she sighed affectedly, "it's not for me to comment."

Simon blinked nervously from behind his big glasses, but didn't reply. Lewis turned his back and looked fixedly out of the window. I guessed that having spent the fifteen years of his life prior to retirement as the headmaster of a minor public school, encounters with awkward parents had left him skilled at avoiding involvement in such discussions. Perhaps of all of them on that holiday, Lewis was the person I found it easiest to get on with: I found him courteous, good-humoured and rather clever – and a good source of information about our fellow guests. John and I don't always share the same opinions about people – as this narrative will demonstrate – and John liked him less than I did. He added that he didn't think Lewis cared for either of us much either, but even he had to admit Lewis had made a good job of partnering the difficult Janet; occasionally he even brought a smile to her discontented face, and they made a formidable pair at the bridge table. He hadn't, in fact, partnered her at the beginning, as Sammy had given him Carol, presumably wanting to partner the younger Janet and Simon together. We none of us knew what had happened, but it had been all change after just a few days. Lewis got Janet and Carol got Simon.

What can I say about Carol? She was a rather a plain, middle-aged women with blue-rimmed glasses and an assortment of frilly blouses. She gave the impression of knowing more about you than you would perhaps have liked, and her comments (spoken in a little-girl voice) always seemed to contain some subtle barb. Actually, it was bad luck on Carol getting Simon, because Carol was on a husband hunt, and shy, tongue-tied, twenty-seven year old Simon was no match for her. He tended to look scared to death.

Poor Simon! There he stands in the photo, so self-effacing you can hardly make him out. I think he had the most unmemorable face of anyone I'd ever met: pale, small-featured, mousy haired, and all you ever noticed were his great big glasses, with blinking eyes behind them. And then he was so diffident – dreadfully hard work to make conversation with, and I'm afraid both John and I had rather given up trying. Lewis told us that he was a teacher at some prep school and John and I used to wonder how on earth he coped there.

Carol has moved on to Tubby to have a dig about Lady P., and she pipes up in her sweetest voice: "Your poor wife gets very upset, doesn't she? I expect you'll be pleased to get her back home. You must have had a very difficult holiday." She smiles a bright, lipsticked smile.

"Oh yes, yes... I mean no," twiddles Tubby; he's not a great conversationalist.

"I sometimes think she hasn't enjoyed her holiday very much?"

Lady Prettyman has been particularly unpleasant to Carol throughout the holiday, commenting on the frilly blouses ('did you buy a cut price lot?'), and unhesitatingly attacking Carol's rather average bridge skills ("I can't stand playing against beginners.")

Trevor Macalister returns from the bar, bearing his wife's Campari and what looks like a double scotch for himself.

"Here we are, my darling." The lustrous-haired Italian girl at the reception desk is laughing with one of the waiters, handsome Gino. John, and I, and undoubtedly Sammy, think Gino's a bit of all right. The Italian girl obviously does too; she tosses back her hair and I see that Trevor Macalister has noticed, and throws her one of his own carefully cultivated smiles – one that says, "Look at me, I am an actor!"

Sammy leads Lady Prettyman back to Tubby, laughing his big laugh. She has been won over. She turns to Tubby, "I didn't get you a drink," she says, "Samuel took all my money."

Sammy laughs uproariously, "Lady P. and I have expensive tastes," he says.

Janet is standing by the window, staring out furiously; she is wearing her jeans and a tee-shirt; she never dresses for dinner. I go over and try to make conversation. I shall not go away from the holiday without making one more effort.

"I've been meaning to ask you; John said you were at Bristol, the University, I mean, weren't you? I used to live there in the nineties.…" She looks at me, but doesn't reply. I persevere, blundering on, "I was wondering if we might have been there at the same time, have some memories in common." I smile foolishly and Janet looks at me as if I'm an idiot, understandably.

"I shouldn't think so. I wasn't there long; I didn't finish the course." She looks past me round the room as if she is expecting someone, and then heads off to the bar. John is laughing at me from the other side of the room; he knows I regard myself as a bit of a charmer and enjoys it when I fail. I give him a well-you're-not-doing-so-brilliantly-yourself look as he stands offering Simon a bowl of crisps while Simon is shaking his head. John is relieved however, by Carol who has apparently come back to bully Simon over bridge tactics. I can't make out Simon's expression because I am too far away, but I see a sort of drawing back on his part.

"Ah Simon, we must have a little talk about our play. I think we might try 'Astro' tonight."

"Yes, if you like."

"After all, it's our last time, here."

"Yes." The sound of relief is palpable.

Carol smiles. "But I am sure we shall stay in touch. I always stay in touch; friends are so important to me."

I go over to join Lewis at the window. "It looks as if we're about to go in to sample the last of *Il Sole*'s pasta. I can't say I shall miss it too much, can you?"

"No, but it's been a pleasant enough fortnight – in most respects. Have you enjoyed it?"

"Oh yes, we've both enjoyed it, but I'm afraid we haven't covered ourselves with glory. Ah! We're going in. May I sit next to you?"

"Certainly. We can commiserate with each other over all the slams we've missed making."

It was spoken most politely, but perhaps John was right, Lewis didn't particularly relish our company.

We bridge players have our own special corner and are waited on by handsome Gino. During the bulk of the time we have not been allowed to sit by the view; presumably GrandSlam Bridge negotiated some particularly sharp package, and only now on the eve of our departure are we to be given this privilege.

The lake is particularly lovely just now; the sun has gone and the night has descended with that suddenness that marks the Mediterranean. The last ferry is about to leave and the remaining passengers are disembarking. In the semi-darkness they cease to be ant-like tourists, but attain the gravitas of travellers embarking on a new, perhaps final, journey; those that go out over the waters by night and never return. The lights of the bar across the bay reflect in the dark waters, and the mountain that reaches down to the water's edge so reassuringly by day, now assumes a menacing air."

"You're thinking a load of crap about that lake," says John who knows me unfailingly.

"Shelley was drowned on a night like this," I retort, but John whom I imagined probably wouldn't even have heard of Shelley, surprised me.

"No, he wasn't, he died at sea in a storm, not in a lake." He looked very beautiful in the evening light, and I wished we could sod the pasta and go to bed. I haven't described John, have I? All I want to say here is that he is shortish with masses of curly brown hair and greenish eyes. He is forty-one; I am sixty-one. Enough said.

"Where is my wine? I had the bottle specially marked; one of those waiters has had it. Am I to put up with this? Well, am I, Tubby?"

Sam is easing everyone into chairs and smoothing ruffled feathers.

"Lady P., are you going to honour me with your company, make my last night for me?"

"I know what Tubby reminds me of, I've been trying to think of it all holiday," says Lewis offering me some stale bread. "A small owl."

There is a commotion at the end of the table: the Skorskis have arrived late from their last minute bargain hunting. Claire, long, lanky and unlovely, is clutching what looks like a hundredweight of pasta under each arm, and Karl holds what seems to be some unmentionable part of a pig, wrapped up unwholesomely in a kind of netted stuff.

"Cheaper," Claire is saying, "cheaper than that place in the Piazza." And, because she talks tautologically, she adds: "That place in the Piazza is much more expensive. Karl and I went to that strada that goes behind the cinema, I had my eye on it from the second day, so did Karl; he knew it would be cheaper there, same as me. I said to him: 'Salami will be cheaper there,' and Karl said 'Eez cheaper,' and in we went. Not straight away, mind, let them come to you, that's my motto. Here," she accosts Janet, "how much do you think we paid for this?" Janet shrugs and looks away. Karl places three pieces of stale bread in the small bag he always has with him. Janet and her mother exchange glances. Interestingly, Janet is not angry with her mother; there is a fondness there, and they appear to share a sense of humour. John and I sometimes think Janet has come on the holiday for the sake of her mother; but at other times we've wondered whether her parents have brought her to get away from some horror at home.

Karl Skorski looks furtively about him and helps himself to wine that someone else, certainly not he, has paid for. His wife is now brandishing a huge bunch of ribbons, also a bargain, although what she can want them for, I cannot imagine, certainly not for her hair which is short and greasy. Karl examines the knives on the table.

"Testing them for sharpness, just in case," says John to me. And indeed Skorski looks for all the world like an assassin, a stage villain, dark and menacing – except that he is only about five foot two, which rather detracts from his sinister appearance when he stands up. But now, sitting among the knives, you wonder if he would like to sharpen them up for someone. He is also a very silent man, but perhaps that's because his wife says everything twice. We none of us know what his nationality is, it has never been mentioned. It is generally believed that he cheats at bridge.

"Are you drinking my wine?" Lady P. bellows down the table at the miniature assassin. "… And you needn't pretend you can't hear."

Claire bristles. "Don't you speak to my husband like that. I won't have you speaking to Karl like that!"

"I shall speak just as I like to you or your husband, particularly when he is stealing my wine." We all look up; we fancy a pleasurably unpleasant situation is evolving.

However a huge laugh bounces down the table, ricocheting off each person. "My word, you are a one, Lady P. I'm going to top up your glass and mine… there we go… and we'll all drink a toast to the loveliest group of bridge players I have ever met!" Warfare has been postponed.

We have finished our tepid spaghetti starter, a bit of yesterday's main, and await the next course. It smells of fish, and is a greyish colour, but it could contain a number of things – including botulism. John gets up and goes outside, not to gaze at the lake, but to have a fag; Janet is already out there with hers.

"Glad to be going?" John asks her, without expecting an answer. Instead she turns a tear-stained face towards him and mutters, "No, I don't want to go back – ever." Then she drops the cigarette, grinds it viciously with her espadrille and returns to eat her spaghetti salmonella.

Eventually we finish and drift into the Bridge Room; it

will be an anticlimax after the previous night when the full party was present, the winners announced and prizes given. John and I could never decide whether Sammy fiddled the scoring or worked it out assiduously.

Now I'm taking you into the Bridge Room. This time I don't have a photo to prompt me, so I'm working from memory. The first thing, no, that's inelegantly expressed – the first people we saw were Bethan and Megan, and yes, they really were called that. I wondered why they hadn't joined the rest of us for the last meal; it was not like them to miss meals – a fact you would appreciate if you were ever to meet them in the flesh – and flesh is the operative word: they were huge, enormous, vast, both of them, indeed it would be difficult to say which was the larger, for when they lay by the pool the sun-loungers sagged equally and the stomachs rippled and wobbled with equal abandon; and what was terribly nice about them was that they simply didn't care. They were perhaps in their late fifties, but I really don't know, they had a sort of agelessness about them, as if they had always been so, and that the end of the world would find them leaning companionably side by side: "Could you reach me the knitting pattern, Bethan?" "It's under your chair, Megan." Bethan was the dominant one (John and I had discussed the possibility of their being lesbians, but thought the logistics argued against it). Bethan was a great talker and spoke with a strong Welsh accent. Megan's voice had more of a lilt to it; she was shy, with a face of great sweetness and would gaze trustingly while you spoke.

Anyway, we were going to join them at their table and make up the four, because we liked them and they played a friendly game of bridge – which is not to say they weren't good players, they were both pretty good, particularly shy Megan, but they praised you when you won and didn't gloat when they beat you. However, we weren't quick enough, they were joined by Simon, pale behind his big glasses and Carol full of frills and smiles,

"Oh, Bethan, you haven't given me that knitting pattern,

and you promised… I did like that cardigan you were wearing."

"Takes a lot of wool."

"Not for me, dear, I'm only a little one." Which wasn't strictly true, but I suppose it was comparatively true. "I'll pop round to your room and pick it up after the bridge."

"No," said Bethan firmly, "I'll drop it into your room."

"Are you pleased to be going home, Simon?" asked Megan quietly. Sweet-natured and somewhat reticent herself, she saw the shyness in Simon and was eager to assuage it.

"Yes," His bright little eyes blinked nervously, "I've met some nice people. I shall miss them, but..."

"You won't be missing everyone, then," said Bethan nodding her head in the direction of Lady P., and moving her eyes in the direction of Carol. She didn't much like Carol, which was probably why she hadn't bothered with the knitting pattern,

"Oh, it's not really goodbye," said Carol, "I shall be keeping in touch with everyone, shan't I, Simon?" Simon said nothing, but didn't look as if he found this comment particularly reassuring.

"Shall I shuffle the cards for you, Bethan?" Bethan had arthritis and couldn't shuffle, so Megan used to do it for her.

We'd managed things badly, all the tables were taken except Lady P. and Tubby's. Nobody wanted to start the last evening being insulted. She was towering over the table in all hideousness, and Tubby was fidgeting with the cards opposite.

Now I probably haven't explained enough about Lady P. and Tubby: you see Lady Prettyman wasn't just an ironic nickname invented by us, but she actually was a lady, I mean she possessed a title and it was 'Prettyman'. Now you might think that if you were big and ugly and unpleasant you might prefer not to be called Prettyman, particularly when the opportunity was there to change it. For Tubby was no knight of the realm, and his surname was Smith (it never occurred to us that he had any other Christian name than Tubby), so when Lady P. married him she had in fact become Mrs Smith. But here was another amazing fact: Lady Prettyman had been married before! How on earth had she managed to net one husband, let alone two? We were indebted to Lewis, who was excellent at winkling out information on our fellow bridge-players and had put the burn on Tubby when Lady P. was at her daily session with the hairdressers. Apparently Lady P.'s father had made a fortune, being an early innovator of the low-flushing lavatory, and died leaving Marjorie, as she was called, a fair bit of money. Eventually a deal had been struck with what Lewis termed 'a poor thing', a totally useless individual with no money and a nebulous sort of job whose only asset was a title inherited from an equally useless and impoverished father. But beggars (unlike buggers) can't be choosers, and they were wed. Who got the best of the deal Lewis didn't discover, but probably Lady P., for the titled husband was killed, appropriately enough in a Lamborghini, on which he had spent the last of the money. So he was out of the game, but she was left in – with the title. Now Lady P. had developed a taste for matrimony, and with no taste or presumably any capability, for doing a job, she was now up against it, since even if she did have the title, she had very little money. So, this being long before the age of computer or other sorts of dating, she took to advertising in a magazine, and not meeting with much success on the first few adverts had one put in permanently; Lewis reckoned it might have been for years. Anyway, it appeared that Tubby himself coveted the state of matrimony, (John and I thought there might have been speculation on his virility at work), saw the advert and reckoned Lady P. was as good as he would get. And perhaps he was right, for Tubby was no Adonis: short, round, bald and bespectacled, and on top of which, he was foolish and thumb-twiddling, fussy and rather pompous; John and I agreed we had never heard him say one interesting thing – that is, before this night I am about to describe. Anyway they were married, and one would prefer not to speculate on the events of the wedding night; and Mrs Marjorie Smith went on calling herself Lady Prettyman, a handle to which she was no longer strictly entitled.

Now Tubby was busying himself shuffling the cards:

"What are you doing them again for? You've done them once already."

"You can't shuffle them too much, my dear."

"Course you can; you've probably changed our luck now."

This 'luck', the mention of which brought a grin to Lady P.'s face that made her look even more horrible than usual, was a reference to the fact that she and Tubby had won the tournament and received fifty pounds-worth of M&S vouchers, a bottle of champagne and a rosette at the previous evening's awards. And, as much as John and I were loath to admit it, both Lady P. and Tubby who was an irritatingly slow player, were pretty good. (In case you are wondering where John and I came in the tournament, all I will say is that we weren't *quite* bottom.)

"Not luck, my dear, our skilful play," ventured the avid shuffler, looking to his wife for approbation.

"*My* skilful play." She looked up, "Ah, I told you our luck had changed, we've got the poofters."

Well, if Sammy could put up with racist innuendos, and Karl could endure being called a thief, I reckoned John and I could put up with being called poofters. I smiled and sat down. John sat down, but he didn't smile.

A huge gust of laughter as Sammy stood up.

"Ladies and gentleman, this is a sad night and a happy night..." (more laughter). "Sad because this is our last night together... talking of which, may I remind you that the minibus leaves for the airport at the terrible hour of 4.30, that is 4.30 a.m. as you know, and if you insist on it being 4.30 p.m, well, I'm very afraid you won't be on the plane with the rest of us. The minibus will be outside the hotel foyer at 4.15. to enable the driver to get all the cases and bottles... oh, yes, I know all about those bottles packed away! If you have any questions... I can see you do, Carol – catch me during the evening. I said it was a happy time, didn't I? And that's, ladies and gentlemen because we're going to play bridge.

Now, because there are only three and a half tables instead of the fifteen we're used to, and because it's our last night, we're going to play rubber…" Sammy holds up his hands… "Now, no arguments, just deal and play. When you've played a rubber – a penny a hundred, settle up, shout out 'Table up' and give first chance to whoever is sitting out. No bidding boards tonight, I've packed them all away, so chat as much as you like. Bonne chance!"

A general muttering ensued, Carol was heard to say "I hope everyone pays up; sometimes some people can be a teeny bit forgetful." Lady P. remarked that she wasn't going to do any sitting out, and Janet looked round frantically, her eyes red and tearful, but Sammy had us under control; none of us, not even Lady P. dared disobey Sammy. Like bingo players our eyes were cast down and concentrated on the cards before us.

We were however disturbed by the Skorskis, coming in late once again:

"I expect he's been packing up the knives and forks into his suitcase," said Lady P.

I invite you to view us from above – take an aerial view, as it were. There's Sammy in front of the computer screen, half an eye on it, half packing everything away. Although he does everything properly, indeed expertly, you can see that he's conscious of the fortnight coming to an end and his responsibilities slipping away – little did he know that they weren't! Not even Sammy can see into the future.

Let's have a look at the table where Lewis and Janet are playing against her parents. Trevor is declaiming and overbidding. Isabel has passed. Lewis passes and Trevor opens a spade. Janet looks at him with loathing and goes two clubs. Isabel passes. Lewis goes two hearts, and Trevor bids three no trumps, which Janet doubles and Trevor, with much aplomb, redoubles.

"You'll find that a rather difficult contract, darling," says Isabel lightly, and Lewis leads a heart. She is right; Lewis and her daughter clock up fifteen hundred points.

"Bad luck, darling," says Isabel in a resigned voice.

"Bad distribution," says Trevor. "All I needed was a couple of finesses to come off, and I should have been home and dry."

"Balls," says Janet, "you should never have been in no trumps, you didn't have enough points. You should have shut up."

"I think we are all tired; we have probably had enough bridge for a while," says Lewis diplomatically. "Ah, look, there's Gino for our drinks orders."

The drinks orders are not only for now, but some people order them to go up to the bedrooms afterwards. Lady P. had initiated the system and quite a lot of the others had thought it not so bad an idea. Gino would take the orders and one of the waitresses would bring them up. Ordering was done discreetly, so one could never be sure who had strong liqueurs sent up, but John and I guessed Janet and perhaps her mother, probably Carol, and of course, Lady P. – but not Tubby, who didn't drink: 'I have to be careful at my age,' although what he had to be careful about, nobody knew. But we all thought that if we had been married to Lady P. we should not have been teetotal. The Skorskis didn't have drinks sent up. "Have you seen the prices? Have you seen what they charge? We have our own supplies, we bring it with us, a bottle of gin from the Duty Free lasts us the fortnight." John and I emulated them – although one bottle of gin certainly didn't last the fortnight.

John and I are doing very badly against Tubby and Lady P. It is partly my fault, but mostly John's. We have already lost the first game.

"I don't wonder you came bottom of the tournament," says Lady P. blowing her nose triumphantly and examining the contents in an unsavoury handkerchief.

"We didn't come bottom," says John who is unafraid of Lady P.

"As good as," she replies, " deal them out, Tubby."

We lost the next game as well. John doubled and instead of taking him out, I left the double in, so we had doubled

Tubby into game.

"Damn fool play," said Lady P. Tubby did his sums:

"That's £1.65p from each of you."

John banged down a pound, "That'll do." Ever cowardly, I put down a fiver.

"Table up!" roared Lady P., gathering up the money, and not offering any change.

Megan and Bethan got Lady P. next. Poor shy Megan was terrified of Lady P. and her play, which was usually very good, inevitably went to pieces at the sight of her lowering face.

"Back to sheep-dipping tomorrow?" asked her ladyship. This was a reference to Bethan's smallholding which she farmed with a mysterious son known as 'Big Irfon'.

"No, we don't dip until June; I should have thought a lady of your superior knowledge would have known that." Unlike Megan, Bethan wasn't in the least intimidated by Lady P.

"Marjorie is a town-dweller," says Tubby, fitting in a quick twiddle, "she is ah... an urban person." He senses the drawing up of battle lines and is anxious to be on his wife's side when the trumpets sound.

"I'm not urban. I don't know what you mean, I was brought up in the country. If anyone's urban it's you."

"Shall we cut for dealer, then?" asked Bethan. "We don't want to sit yattering all night." Megan looked nervous – I know because John and I were sitting out, waiting for another table to finish.

"Hold your cards up, Megan. I don't want to see them; I'm not Mr Skorski." This was a not unjustified reference to Skorski's bridge habits. Poor Megan, she would have done anything not to have had to play the hand, but there was no escape, she had good cards and Bethan was supporting her, so four spades it was. Even so, it wasn't an easy hand to play. Tubby was void in spades and Lady P. had four, so when Megan went to play from dummy, she touched the queen before changing her mind and playing the ace.

"Tournament director!" roared Lady P., but Sammy was nowhere to be seen, "bloody man's never where he's wanted.

Well, you'll have to play the queen now, and I put my king on."

"Don't be ridiculous, "said Bethan. "My partner can play any card she wants"

"It doesn't matter," said Megan, "Lady Prettyman is quite right, I shouldn't have hesitated. I'm sorry, I am afraid I'm not a very good player." And then to compound her crime she played a club instead of a spade.

"Revoke!" roared Lady P. "That's two extra tricks."

Bethan opened her mouth to protest, but must have caught sight of Megan's face, because tears had started and were rolling down the rolls of flesh. We didn't see the outcome, because Janet's parents, having lost the rubber, had gone to play the Skorskis, and we went to join Janet and Lewis. Janet was in a strangely excitable mood.

"I beat him, I beat him – I got him two off doubled twice!"

"Indeed you did, or rather we did. May I have a little credit for my winning six of diamonds?"

"Yes, you were brilliant, really brilliant, "Janet was smiling at him, and in spite of the scraped-back hair and the shapeless top, you got the feeling that if she made any effort she might be rather a pretty girl.

"Shall I deal? "I asked "We are playing pretty badly tonight, so don't be too brilliant, Lewis."

"One of us is playing badly," said John; he hadn't forgiven me for leaving the double.

"Sorry," said Janet looking round vaguely, "I have to go outside for a minute. I need a fag."

"Good idea," said John, and got up to go with her, but Janet had gone; whatever it was she was going for, she didn't want John; but he went outside anyway; nothing stands between John and a cigarette.

So Lewis and I sat and observed Lady Prettyman and Tubby who were joined by Carol and Simon. Sammy must have drawn off Megan and Bethan who were sitting together at the end of the room; Bethan had her arm around Megan, one could imagine the 'there, theres, my lovely,' that were going on.

Carol was pointedly saying nothing to Lady P. and brightly addressing Simon:

"No silly finesses, Partner!" Simon made no reply, but Lady P. did; she wasn't going to miss any opportunities for rudeness on this last night. She leant her great man's body over the table, the lip hanging more pendulously than ever:

"It's not just your partner that makes silly finesses. If you hadn't been such a fool in that slam last night, you wouldn't have come down the bottom."

"Marjorie's quite right, you know," said Tubby the sycophant.

"Well," said Simon smiling nervously. "I think you deserved to win really."

"Do you?" asked Carol, "do you really, Simon, I'm sure I don't; we were very unlucky with distribution."

"That's what they all say," said Lady P.

"Oh, all who, may I ask?"

"Bad players. Deal out, Tubby, we haven't got all night."

"I hope you are not calling me a bad player." Both Simon and Tubby sat silent looking unhappy, until at last Simon mumbled,

"I'm sure … um, um … Lady Prettyman didn't mean that."

"Marjorie can't resist a joke," said Tubby.

"I am afraid I fail to see anything amusing about insulting people. And…"

"No sense of humour either," added Lady P.

"And…" Carol's voice became shrill and the voice lost its veneer of refinement: "At the club at 'ome, I have just won the Rosemont Bowl."

I looked across the table waiting for John to come back, and caught a little smile on Lewis's face. I thought he was enjoying seeing Carol put down. As I mentioned, he had initially been paired with her, but had subsequently switched to play with Janet. How and why the exchange had taken place, I hadn't liked to ask – pleasant and urbane as Lewis was. Indeed, at this moment he looked the very picture of the elderly gentleman: strikingly, but not nattily dressed, and wearing a claret velvet jacket and ivory shirt that looked as if it had just been taken out of the case. I thought he made a striking contrast with myself who, at the end of a fortnight looked like the before picture of an advertisement for some particularly powerful washing powder. Even John looked a little less cool than usual. But as I was saying, one felt that Lewis was ultimately a very private person, one with whom liberties could not be taken, and perhaps, I thought, Carol's play or personality had in some way displeased him.

"Ah!" he exclaimed, "here's Janet and John... just like the old fashioned reading book."

As Janet came back into the room, I saw her mother glance up.

"Darling," Trevor interjected, "are you going to play a card?"

"I'm so sorry; of course."

"Better now," said Janet, but she didn't look it.

We lost the rubber against them – not entirely my fault: how often do the opposition have five of your trumps, all in one hand? Carol and Simon however, won against Lady P. and Tubby.

"Perhaps some people aren't such bad players after all," trilled Carol full of smiles.

"Table up," roared her ladyship. We watched as the Skorskis made their way to the table.

"Bloody Poles," said Lady P.

"Ladies and gentlemen," announced Sammy, "we must make this the last rubber because we have to be up very early tomorrow."

John and I didn't bother finding another table; we had had enough, so we missed the epic battle between the Skorskis and Lady P.

Chapter 2: The Death of Lady P.

"You've packed," I said. "That was very good of you, John."

"You're trying to sweet-talk me. You played rubbish bridge."

"I know. Are you still cross with me?"

He was standing on the balcony (£7.00 a night supplement), smoking and staring out at the lake, but suddenly he turned and smiled; John has a particularly winning smile that makes you forget how grumpy he can be.

"Oh Mark, bridge is only a game!"

And he chucked the cigarette into the lake and we went to bed. There is something about a last night that makes me feel sentimental and romantic, and I was enjoying sharing these sentiments with Mark. In fact I was very much engaged in giving expression to them when suddenly there was the most god-awful banging on the door, which then burst open. (We never locked it; John has a thing about fire.) And here, of all people, is Tubby – advancing towards the bed quite oblivious of anything going on, waving his arms and shrieking. Initially it was difficult to get a handle on what he was saying – not just because of its unexpectedness, but equally on account of natural embarrassment – but it seemed to consist of "Majorie! Heart attack!" And "Help! Help! Help!"

Now John has much greater presence of mind than I, and anyway I think he was in a more suitable state. I remember him jumping out of bed and covering himself with the towelling robe.

"I'm coming. Keep calm, Tubby, I'm on my way."

Tubby could have found no-one more suitable to take charge of the situation. Not only is John extremely sensible, he is also quite unflappable, which was just as well since Tubby past the comfort of thumb-twiddling, was exhibiting symptoms of hysteria and he started trying to drag John towards the door.

"Come on, come on! She's dead! I know she is!" and his voice rose in a fretful – and, dare I say it, comical squeak.

I followed - when I had put on some trousers. Their room was in the next corridor, just around the corner from ours, which is, I supposed, why he had burst in on us rather than anyone else.

It was a scene from a nightmare: the monstrous Lady P. lying across the bed, her body contorted and her face frozen in a sort of screech of pain; her eyes huge and bulging in her hideous face.

"Do something," shrieked Tubby, "stop it all." John, with his ear to her chest and his hand on her wrist then turned to me, shaking his head.

"You got your mobile? No? I'll ring reception…no, on second thoughts, you ring from our room, and get Sammy. It's all right, Tubby."

As I fled on my way I could hear Tubby wailing "It's not all right, she's dead, Marjorie's dead."

Rather than ringing I went down to Reception in the lift. I could hardly think at all and I doubted I would find Sammy who usually disappeared at night. However, I was in luck, he was returning from whatever he had been doing and was half way through the revolving doors. I was torn between him and Reception, but opted for Sammy.

"Sam, Lady P.'s had a heart attack, I think she's dead."

It was the first time I had seen Sammy fail to laugh when faced with a crisis.

"Where is she? Who's with her? Keep your voice down."

"John…Tubby… She's dead."

"All right, I'm coming; just a minute."

I hung around wondering whether I ought to go back up, stay put, or what.

"Go on up, "said Sammy, "but quietly, Mark. And don't talk to anyone. Stay there until I come."

So I went back up and knocked on the door. John had tidied up a bit and had Lady P. covered with a sheet. The irreverent thought crossed my mind that she could never be rude to anyone again, not even Tubby who sat in a corner and wrung his hands instead of twiddling his thumbs.

"Oh Marjorie," he kept saying, "my little flower."

I thought then how strange love is: how could anyone call huge, rude pendulous-lipped Lady P. 'a little flower', and then I felt somewhat ashamed at such a callous thought, because there she was, her enormous body covered with a sheet, obscured like a great mountain in a tactful mist. I couldn't think of anything to say to Tubby, and John had either had enough of trying to comfort him or was wearied by the heaviness of death; he sat by the bed, staring ahead of him in silence.

We seemed to remain frozen there interminably like the figures on Keats' Grecian Urn. Poor Marjorie! And how strange that having only been known as Lady P., she had now become Marjorie; death having robbed her of her titles and all the vain trappings of life.

At last there there came a tapping at the door, so quiet that we almost missed it, despite our silent wait for Sammy. It was Tubby who called out,

"Who's there? What do you want?"

It wasn't just Sammy, it was the manager whom I dimly remembered seeing once when Lady P. had been creating at Reception. He was small dark and unremarkable, and the third man looked exactly like him, could have been his brother – which, in fact, we were to learn, he was. He went to the bed, pulled the sheet back, looked, shrugged and replaced the sheet.

"Si, è morta, è vero, Stefano."

A moaning from Tubby.

There had obviously been discussion between Sammy and the two brothers; some sort of decision had been taken.

"I thank you," said the manager, whom we now knew to be called Stefano. "I detain you no more; you are fatigued and must sleep before early departure, yes?" Sammy went over to Tubby:

"Stefano's brother is a doctor; he will see to everything." I didn't think he looked much like a doctor – but there, what do doctors look like? My own GP is a tiny little girl who looks about sixteen. Sammy, a new serious Sammy, turned to me.

"I'd rather we didn't say anything to the others – there's

no point, it'll just upset them." Actually, I thought he was wrong: nobody would be upset by the news of Lady P.'s death; in fact for some it would provide a very pleasing close to the holiday, but somehow I didn't feel I could put this into suitable language, and found myself nodding. John said nothing.

"Yes, it is better to say nothing," said the Italian who might or might not be a doctor.

"You give your words," said Stefano looking from John to me; it wasn't so much a question but an order. He was looking at John. For a moment John hesitated, I know him so well, I could see he might obstinately argue the toss. However, he shrugged.

"I shan't say anything."

Sammy was holding Tubby in his big warm arms. We left and I put my arm around John as we walked back to the room.

"What an awful…"

"You heard what the man said," said John shortly. "We don't talk about it." He took off his towelling wrap and got into bed.

'Grey' is how I would describe that half past four in the morning when we assembled, waiting for the elderly hotel minibus that would take us to the airport. There was a general feeling of mist and misery; in the first place it was damned cold – even Lake Como is cold in those small hours – and, besides, the summer had ebbed away. As we stood there, a small huddled band, it was as though we watched the summer's retreat. Death had brought an end to the easy living of the warm days. And yet nobody knew about this nocturnal visitor, and it seemed to me there was a strange innocence about these ignorant people, even now looking forward to the business of getting back to grips with their regular lives.

Bethan and Megan sat opposite one another, each occupying a whole sofa; wrapped in identical woolly coats, and resembling two huge mountains wrapped in mist. Lewis stood apart in beautifully cut grey trousers and a light grey jacket. He looked impeccable, as ever; He was joined by Simon, pale and fey behind his enormous glasses, but even Lewis wasn't inclined for company at that hour, and he turned abruptly away. The Macalisters stood together; she, in spite of the earliness of the hour, as elegantly turned-out as ever, in a long grey cashmere jacket; her husband, on the other hand, was far from elegant, loud and officious he was doing something unnecessary with the cases.

"All present and correct," he remarked looking round as if for applause. I thought he looked peaky; the early morning obviously doesn't favour actors any more than the rest of us, I thought. Janet was standing alone. No one seemed inclined to talk. Reception had been covered by a metal grill which added to the feeling that we were all awaiting some sort of custodial sentence.

"I'm going out for a fag," said John; even John, who, to my eyes at least never looks less than astonishingly handsome, was the worse for wear with his hair sticking up in little tufts.

Then Carol arrived towing an enormous puce-coloured case.

"Wakey, wakey, everyone," she cried merrily. "What a lot of sleepy-heads you all look."

If she wanted to make us all react, she certainly succeeded. Simon visibly jumped, Lewis shook his head violently and turned his back, but Janet went so far as to mutter, "Why don't you shut up and fuck off?" Her mother raised an arm in a remonstrating sort of way, and John went off for his fag.

"Goodness me, what a lot of cross-patches." But she had changed the atmosphere; people shuffled around, looked at the iron grille and checked their watches. I wondered when someone was going to ask where Lady P. and Tubby were – and what I ought to say if the question was addressed to me, since for reasons I couldn't quite fathom John and I were sworn to secrecy. But I couldn't help wondering what the reaction would be if I said, "Oh, didn't you know? Lady P. is dead."

My thoughts were interrupted by the arrival of the Skorskis, and at that point I realised the cunning of Sammy. Clutching rugs, an assortment of plastic carrier bags and her husband, Claire was visibly the bringer of tidings:

"Well, it's no use waiting for Tubby, I say; it's no use waiting for Tubby. He's bad with his stomach, got a bug."

"Bad viz 'is stomach," echoed Karl, for some reason peering into his little bag, which even now he kept close beside him.

"Got a bug, getting a later plane, not coming with us, I say they're not coming in the minibus. Sammy says not to wait for him either, just get on the bus. I said they'll have to pay for another flight, they'll make them pay again, that's what I said, didn't I, Karl?"

"Zose were your verds, yes."

"Got some sort of stomach upset; don't know about her, I expect she's all right. Don't know why Sammy can't come, but I expect GrandSlam Bridge will refund his fare. I expect he'll get his fare paid, though it's not easy getting your money back. We tried, didn't we, Karl.... several years ago, not last year, and they said... well, of course they don't say anything really."

How clever Sammy had been! He had purposefully primed Claire Skorski to impart a bowdlerised version of events, knowing that she would have the effect of boring everyone into indifference. Indeed if Claire Skorski had first-hand knowledge of the Queen's assassination, I don't think anyone would have listened.

As it was, only Carol remarked that she was surprised Lady P. didn't leave Tubby to fend for himself. "I can't," twinkly smile, "see her as Florence Nightingale, I am afraid." But nobody liked Carol either and so beyond the odd, "Well, I hope old Tubby's all right," from Bethan and a treacherous "Yes, so do I," from me, nobody evinced any further interest in the absence of Tubby and his wife. But while I was admiring Sammy's cunning, I also got to wondering why? Why did it all have to be hushed up? A woman had had a heart attack; admittedly a woman nobody liked, and admittedly a number of people would not have been heartbroken to learn of her death, but surely it was worth a mention. Didn't death rather remove one from the sphere of petty hatred? Why was Sammy so anxious to hush it up? I could see that the hotel manager might prefer not to advertise a sudden death on his premises, particularly bearing in mind the quality of his food, but why should Sammy care?

Anyway my musings were curtailed. The glamorous young woman from Reception appeared, looking, it must be said, rather less glamorous than usual at 4.00 a.m. She glowered at us, any veneer of courtesy that had been offered during the course of our holiday, erased. Presumably someone had got her out of bed, as opposed to getting her into bed, and detailed her to get us into the minibus.

"You please leave now. No, you must carry your own valigie; the porter is sleeping. You wait outside now."

So we went outside and stood in the cold with our own valigia and waited to be despatched to the airport.

"Well, that's the last we'll see of our old friends," I said.

I usually get things wrong.

However, once in the plane, just after the revving up of the engines, which always makes me nervous, I felt like talking to John about Lady P. and Tubby and the mysterious behaviour of Sammy.

"Poor Tubby," I began, "he was so distraught, wasn't he? Perhaps he really did love her, after all…"

"Poor Tubby! My arse!" said John. Then he added:

"Tubby did her in."

"What!"

John often surprises me, but this took the biscuit. I leaned over him absolutely amazed at what I was hearing.

"What do you mean?" I grabbed hold of his arm, even oblivious to the roar of the engines. "What are you saying? Do you know something… Tell!"

"Ssh! Don't go shouting out all over the plane; we'll talk about it later."

"But…"

"And I shouldn't eat that lasagne if I were you. It looks deadly and we don't want another fatality, do we?" John never eats airline food. He settled back to read the in-flight magazine, and proved to be unmoveable on the subject of Tubby.

In the taxi home I pleaded again, but John remained obstinate.

"Nope, I'll tell you when we get home."

And he did.

We got back home in the afternoon, (the house is nice, Victorian rectory, quite tasteful). We have a sort of ritual when we get back: I gather up the mail, give it a cursory glance, John tours the house checking up, then he pours us both a drink and we sit at the breakfast bar and see what Mr. Postman's brought – but today was different.

"Tell," I commanded. John, as so often, had a change of mood.

"Not much to tell, really."

But I had lived with John for eleven years and if one accepts the adage that in any couple there is one who loves and one who is the recipient of love, John was, I suppose, the recipient, but equally, I could manage him as he couldn't me, because I had learned the benefits of infinite patience. I went over to the corner cupboard and got out a tin of foie gras that we had brought back from a holiday in Uzès.

"Of course there is," I said and put the tin in the electric tin opener. Nothing happened.

"It would help if you put the power on," he said, and as the tin began to turn he started to talk.

"As soon as we got in the room I could see she was lying in an unnatural way, at an unusual angle, she was contorted as if ... well," he seemed to reconsider as he spread the paté on his toast, "I suppose, it's no fun dying of a heart attack either, but it looked worse than that. And then I saw the glass fallen over by the side of bed and ….."

"It smelled of almonds," I said. "It was prussic acid!"

"No, you read too many detective stories… Shall I make some more toast?"

"No, no, I'll do it. Well what was odd about the glass if it wasn't the smell?"

"Well there *was* a funny smell, but it wasn't almonds, and the drink was a sort of cloudy – at least, what was left of it was. The glass was lying where it had fallen; she must have just taken a sip and that had been enough. I could smell it on her body."

"Did you pick it up?"

"I did not. I didn't want my finger prints all over a glass of poison."

"Yes, well, but if Tubby had made her drink it, surely he would have picked it up and washed it out and well, cleaned her up too? He wouldn't have just left evidence like that lying round for anyone to find!"

"Yeah, I know, I thought that… Toast's ready. Is there any more butter?"

"I suppose," I said, "he must have panicked. I mean, we know how pathetic Tubby is. Say he screws himself up to finish her off, everything goes according to plan – but there she is dead, and suddenly he realises the enormity of what he's done."

John pulled a face; he finds it irritating when I use what he regards as pretentious words. But he was forced to agree.

"Yeah, yeah, that's what I think. He suddenly gets scared, panics, and runs to us."

"Why us?"

"Well, we're on the same corridor – just around the corner. He's seen us going into the room and he knows where we are and he goes for the nearest help, in the hope that she's not dead after all. Perhaps we'll tell him everything is going to be all right."

"So what are you saying?"

"Well, I think, like I say, he panicked. There she was dead. He thinks 'must tell someone and make them think it was natural' – but he didn't go for the manager, did he? He didn't go rushing downstairs demanding a doctor; instead he gets the two of us, plants the idea of a heart attack, and expects both of us to go haring off to make it all official while he clears things up."

"Why didn't he clear things up straight away?"

He considered.

"Paté's lovely. Because he panicked. Don't forget Tubby's used to doing what he's told, not thinking for himself. So now she's gone he needs to ask someone else what to do… Or perhaps he meant to own up, and then chickened out. Perhaps he thought we would both go for the manager, and then he would clear things up."

"Perhaps. Alternatively, listen," I have thought of something rather brilliant: "He wanted to try us out, see whether we would buy the heart attack, and if we didn't, enlist our help."

"Could be."

"But then, I'm not sure that Tubby is quite so subtle."

"Subtle enough to plan to murder her – I mean what a good time to choose, just as we're all going home, with everything in a muddle. He must have been hoping the death would get sidelined in the general bustle."

"John?"

"Yes?"

"When did you think all this?"

"Well, more or less straight away, I think."

"Why in God's name didn't you say anything?"

"Well," he helped himself to the last of the paté. "I nearly did, but I wasn't certain – and you can't go accusing someone who is weeping and wailing over their dead wife, in case they haven't done it. But the more he 'my little flower-ed' and wept and wailed, the more I thought he had done it, and again I was going to say something, but then you and Sammy and people turned up, and the opportunity kind of passed. So I thought: leave it to them, let them sort it, nothing to do with me."

"But you thought he'd killed her?"

"Was sure he had."

"But you can't…." I tried to marshal my thoughts. "You can't literally let people get away with murder."

"Well," he paused and looked thoughtful. I love it when

he looks pensive and does the Rodin Thinker bit. I don't know if I've mentioned – well, I am sure I have, but I'll say it again, John is very beautiful and forty-one, whereas I am sixty-one, and not at all beautiful (although I wasn't so bad once). But for some reason – and I've never discovered what that reason is, he loves me. I digress.

"Well, I've thought about it a lot – all the time since we left really, and no, people shouldn't get away with murder, of course they shouldn't, but the world's a better place without Lady P. She was a total bitch to pretty much everyone, and I can't see anyone missing her. I don't suppose GrandSlam Bridge was the only place that she got up people's noses; I should imagine she managed to upset everyone wherever she and Tubby lived, and…" He could see I was about to interrupt with my Ladybird Book of Ethics. "Honestly, Mark, I couldn't see what there was to do. I mean, I didn't know for certain Tubby had killed her, and I thought if I started making a fuss, we wouldn't get on the plane because we'd be down the carabinieri shop. And, furthermore…"

"That sounds like one of my words!"

"'Plus' then, I could see that I wouldn't get anywhere. It was perfectly clear that Sammy, like me, didn't want any trouble – I imagine people getting themselves murdered when you're Tournament Director doesn't look any too good on your CV; then the hotel guy didn't want any fuss, and most of all Tubby didn't want any fuss. As it is, he'll have to live with what he's done for the rest of his life. That's punishment isn't it? In the end I think I did the right thing." He looked at me, a bit on the defensive, I thought, and I wasn't prepared to quite let him off the hook.

"Depends what you mean by right."

"Thank you, Mr. Nietzsche. Now why don't you do something useful like sorting out the post?"

I could have gone on arguing about it, but I didn't; I put the plates in the dishwasher and followed his example.

"That's the end of that, then," I thought – and so it would have been, if I'd not gone up to London a few weeks later to buy some naughty DVDs. No, no, don't worry, nothing nasty, just something to while away an autumn evening, if we got bored.

Chapter 3: Sammy asks a favour

It happened like this: I was at a bit of a loose end and had gone up to town. I'd taken a look round The National Gallery, where I always go – I like the Flemish stuff, and then moseyed on down to this shop in Soho where I picked up a couple of DVDs. As I was leaving, I noticed two things simultaneously: a) that it was pouring with rain and b) there was Sammy – looking extremely well and elegant.

"Hello, Mark," huge laugh. "Fancy meeting you!"

"In such an unexpected place, too!" I said with a little irony. I had always suspected Sammy's tastes might include the offerings of emporia like this one.

"You look fit," I said.

"It's the sushi; I always live off sushi when I come back," he beamed seductively. "It gets me into shape. Hey, look at that rain!"

I looked. There was a lot of it.

"Let's go and have a drink," he said. "There's a place just opposite."

We charged across the road, Sammy gracefully skimming across, me narrowly missed by a bus, and went inside. It was called *Tomorrow*.

The bar staff of both sexes seemed to be dressed in little more than leather thongs – well, I exaggerate, they wore a bit more than that, but not a lot.

"I'm glad I've seen you," said Sammy sitting down and flashing a beautiful signet ring. "I've got a favour to ask."

My mind began to run riot: the murder had been discovered, Sammy was under suspicion... an accomplice to Tubby... and, oh God, John and I were accessories after the fact... What was this favour, what lies must we tell, what...?"

"It's Tubby."

"Yes, I know, "I blurted out. "It wasn't a heart attack at all, Tubby killed her!"

"I wish he had." said Sammy. He gestured at a black

leather Thong. "Two vodka cokes, please." I stared at him goggle-eyed.

"Sammy, what on earth do you mean?"

Vodka in one hand, a smoke in the other, his eye upon a thonged youth, Sammy began his story. Here's the gist of it.

As soon as I had told him about Lady P.'s death, Sammy's suspicions were aroused. Lady P. complained incessantly about everything, but she had never mentioned a heart condition. Interestingly, he was pretty sure Tubby *had*, which was why he didn't drink. Now, Lady P. had been going on at Tubby all night, and Sammy reckoned he had finally had enough, put his heart tablets into her goodnight glass of whisky, and finished her off. Sammy's reasoning had been much like John's: nobody suffered by her death, but to make a fuss was going to cause a lot of trouble. Sammy's own position, it turns out, with GrandSlam Bridge was somewhat precarious ("we've had one or two disagreements"), there were also reasons (Sammy didn't specify) why he didn't want any hassle from the hotel manager, a man he knew rather well, although again he did not specify why – "A few little favours, man," was all he offered. So Sammy put the manager in the picture – or rather the picture as Sammy saw it, and the manager's reaction was as Sammy expected, knowing all too well that once package holidays get wind of anything unsavoury, they start cancelling like billyho. So then things moved quickly: the manager found the brother, who actually *was* a doctor ('of sorts,' added Sammy), who in typical Italian fashion lived in the hotel annexe, and they decided that they would hush it up; the brother would provide a death certificate – natural causes, and arrange to have the body brought back. However, this proved rather more complicated than the conspirators had anticipated: to get the paperwork done for bringing the body back required three doctors, and even though Italy is "a shit hole of corruption," as Sammy put it, this looked too difficult even for Sammy, the hotel manager and the doctor brother to orchestrate.

So the upshot was that they suggested Sammy persuade Tubby to have the body cremated locally – and from there on, all would be plain sailing. Sammy used his powers of persuasion, and found Tubby willing to go along with whatever anyone suggested – through fear and guilt Sammy thought at the time; and the body was cremated two days later, Sammy presiding. "Man," said Sammy looking at his empty glass. "He didn't even bring the ashes back. I was shocked."

"What did he do with them?" Sammy inverted his glass and held it up to indicate a pouring action.

"Put them in the lake. He *said* she had once mentioned something about wanting to be buried in Italy." After which Sammy packed Tubby and himself on a flight, and dumped the grieving widower at Birmingham Airport.

"I had another tournament to direct, and I honestly wasn't sorry to see the back of this man – not literally, you understand." Sammy concluded his account with the customary burst of laughter, but tinged this time with some element of bitterness.

"But," he continued, lighting another cigarette, "I was wrong."

He hadn't been back more than a week when he received a letter that had been sent to him care of GrandSlam Bridge. "Damn lucky he hasn't got as far as email, and nobody – well, only the select few, have my mobile."

"A letter from Tubby? What did he say?" I asked. I could hear the rain pelting down outside, I felt warm and cosy with my vodka and coke, and was longing to hear why it was that Tubby wasn't a murderer, and what his letter was all about.

"Tubby said..," Sammy took a judicious sip, "and I can't help but admit that he had a point, that he had been in shock and not able to think things through properly, and that he had been... what was the word he used? I know 'scurried' into making decisions. He's a little squit really. Actually, he didn't mind the speed at which it had all happened; what he minded, once he had had time to think it all over, was that he realised we all thought he had murdered Lady P., and had been trying to protect him from 'those carabin people.'" Sammy indicated to a different Thong that his glass needed replenishment. "He was really indignant, he kept saying 'how could you think I had murdered my little flower?'"

Sammy took delivery of another glass, I'm not good with spirits and held back – also I suspected I should be paying, and as John rightly says I am a bit tight over rounds.

"Can you credit him calling that old bitch "my little flower"?"

"Yes, he called her it that night, when she was lying there."

"So…" Sammy looked round for another Thong. "When he had finished going on about that, he started on something else…" Sammy leaned forward, "I'm not at all sure he's as stupid as we all thought."

"You may be right; he wasn't a bad bridge player. What was this new tack?"

"Well, seeing as he hadn't murdered her, obviously someone else had…"

"Hang on a minute," I said. "He told us she'd had a heart attack, why should he change his mind? I mean he was the person who used the words 'heart attack'…"

"I'm coming to that. I'll have another vodka and coke – you're paying aren't you, Mark?"

"It's a pleasure, Sammy."

He looked round. "Nice place, Mark."

"Yes, yes," I said, "carry on."

"He said he'd had time to think and could remember things he hadn't thought of before when he was being 'scurried.' He went on to say…"

We watched while our drinks were put down, I was wondering how much all these vodka and cokes were going to cost, particularly when this last one was handed to us personally by Chief Male Thong.

"What did he say?"

Sammy paused impressively: "He said his wife had drunk poison."

"Well actually," I said eager to add my surprise shot. "That's what John thought."

Sammy was unimpressed. "It's what we all thought. But

then he said something else: he said he knew who'd done it."

"He knew who'd done it?" I got terribly excited and between the vodkas and the Thongs and the story, the words came out more loudly than I had intended.

"No need to tell everyone, Mark.

"Who was it?" I whispered.

"He wouldn't say; he wanted to meet up and tell me all about it."

"Didn't he give a hint?"

"No."

"Does he want this person arrested? I mean why doesn't he go to the police? He's safe back in England now."

"No, he doesn't want anyone arrested, he just wants..." Sammy gave a hoot of laughter, "he just wants them to say sorry. And he wants me to organise it all."

I began to see why Sammy was cultivating me. It clearly wasn't just the vodkas.

"You mean," I said, "that you intend off-loading this 'organisation' on to me?"

"Sort of."

"Actually?"

"Yes."

I sat considering this and was struck by a thought – I suppose I'm not terribly quick on the uptake. John is, but it takes me a while to digest things.

"Now, Sammy... I'm none too sure about the position of Tubby in all this. Just because he starts accusing other people of murdering his wife, it doesn't mean that he didn't do it."

"True."

"And, in fact, I put a case to you: someone discovers Tubby's done it and starts blackmailing him, so he sort of pre-empts them by throwing the guilt on someone else."

"Now listen to me, Mark. In the first place nobody in this world is going to find any proof. For a start, the death certificate has been signed by three doctors. Stefano got two of his mates to add their signatures."

"But you said the difficulty of getting the body out of Italy was due to getting a lot of signatures."

"There is a difference signing for a body that's going to be cremated the next day, and a whole body travelling to another country in an aeroplane. Anyway, Mark, it was all signed and sealed."

"All right."

"All that remains of Lady P. is inside Lake Como's fish. Nobody is going to be able to pin anything on Tubby. Anyway, how would you do it? Go back to 'The Hotel Sole', and say, "Excuse me, Signor Manager, I think someone murdered one of your guests a few weeks ago. Please may we send in the carabinieri to investigate?"

"Well..."

"You can bet your bottom dollar if the doctor's his brother, the Chief of Police is his father."

"Mmm... and you think Tubby really is innocent."

"I do, and looking back I can't think why we thought a little twit like him was capable of it anyway."

"Who do you think did it then?"

Sammy threw back his head and roared. "That's what you're going to find out."

I must admit the role of detective rather appealed to me. I saw John and myself working in tandem: John, of course, the Dr. Watson to my Sherlock, Pascoe to Dalziel, Bunter to my Lord Peter. However I didn't intend letting Sammy get away too lightly; after all, I already appeared to be paying for seven vodka cokes.

"Why don't *you* do it?"

Sammy became evasive, but I gathered relations between him and GrandSlam were none too rosy, and he didn't want the Tubby affair on top of everything else. Furthermore, he didn't like hassle.

"I'm a working man, Mark, not a gentleman of leisure like yourself. You'll enjoy it. It's a privilege."

"Hmm."

"Just be nice to Tubby, listen and nod your head, and then hush it all up. Tell him anything you like, but don't let him anywhere near a police station."

"I don't want to do anything illegal," I said a tad

nervously. I have always been a little in awe of the police; even carrying the dodgy DVDs got me worried."

"My dear Mark, with a face like yours, how could anyone suspect you of anything?"

I felt rather miffed. Although one likes to be thought of as honest, there is something rather humiliating about being told you have the sort of fresh-faced look of a country bumpkin. Particularly when your companion is a black hunk.

Suddenly Sammy became businesslike; he clicked his fingers for the bill.

"I'll email you names and addresses of everyone, in case you have lost the original list and have to go and visit, but don't forget it's all Tubby's fancy, nobody gets put down for anything. Just get Tubby off my back. A small favour, Mark."

He handed me the bill. "Now off you go. You pay at the desk. I think I shall just stay and, er, finish this drink."

After I had paid £93.81 I glanced back, Sammy was entering some sort of inner sanctuary where I imagine even thongs would be superfluous. I didn't leave a tip.

Chapter 4: Tubby

The following day John came back from work with a John Lewis bag.

"For you."

It was a deerstalker hat.

"I couldn't afford the violin."

John had, of course, instantly perceived the extent of my ambitions. Initially he had been somewhat dismissive of the whole thing: yes, he could entertain the thought that Tubby was not a murderer, he could also imagine a number of alternative assassins – "including you, Mark." I countered by pointing out he had got to Tubby's bedroom before me, so if anyone was implicated it was he.

He could see why Sammy didn't want to be involved – he added that he suspected that he had off-loaded a lot of hassle on me by appealing to my vanity, and was now laughing even more loudly than ever. But, at the end of the day, he couldn't really see what could be achieved, or indeed what it was that Sammy actually wanted me to do. It looked like a lot of trouble. "And there isn't even any money in it." John, as I say, regards me as somewhat tight-fisted.

However a murder-mystery is an intriguing thing, and I know John well enough to wait and look for signs of interest. And sure enough some hours later he enquired when *we* were going to visit Tubby. Of course, I didn't take him up on this – some subtlety is needed when dealing with John. I merely replied *we* would go as soon as *we* had Tubby's address. And indeed, Sammy was as good as his word and a list of addresses arrived – appended to the cryptic remark; "you should have stayed longer in 'Tomorrow'!"

Tubby lived in Warwickshire about a hundred miles from John and me, and I casually asked John if he wanted to come. As I am retired, I could go at more or less any time, but John would have to arrange a day off.

"Shall I phone Tubby and see if he will have us on

Thursday?" I asked, and to my surprise John smiled brightly and agreed. I was beginning to suspect that he saw himself in the role of Master Detective as much as I.

After this promising beginning I was all fired up for my phone call to Tubby. This however was not equally encouraging. I got though to him all right, but he couldn't seem to understand what I was talking about.

"Hello, Tubby... Mark Hadley here. Do you remember me?"

"No."

"From the bridge holiday, GrandSlam Bridge, I was wondering how you were?"

"Who did you say?" I could sense anxious thumb-twiddling. "Who are you?"

"Mark Hadley."

"Oh are you one of the poof... I mean I think I know who you are, but which one?"

I was forced into saying between gritted teeth, "The old one." Needless to say John found this hilarious.

"Oh!"

"I was wondering how you were."

"Ah well, I have a lot of worry, a great deal of worry." I could sense a positive crescendo in the twiddling.

"I am sure you have, Tubby. That's why I'm ringing. I've been talking to Sammy."

"Who?"

"Sammy, the Tournament Director."

"Well, I'm in the bathroom now, you'll have to get off the phone." He hung up.

I felt dispirited, I turned to consult John.

"He didn't seem to like me mentioning Sammy, I'm sure he won't want us interfering." But John was more upbeat;

"Of course he will. He's just on the loo at the moment."

"Do you think so?"

"Yes. People always ring when you're having a crap."

I thought about it and decided he was right. My second call some hours later was more successful. I intimated that Sammy had confided that Tubby was worried, but Sammy himself, although there was nothing he would have liked better than to come along and solve Tubby's problems, was unfortunately tied up.

"Tied up?" he asked suspiciously.

"Well, busy. And he thought that I might be able to help."

"Why?" This was a difficult question to answer. I took a flier:

"Well, I was very fond of Lady Prettyman."

Could he, would he swallow this? He did.

"Yes. She wasn't appreciated, you know. And now in her demise…" I thought 'demise' was exactly the word Tubby would choose. "There has been," Tubby cleared his throat, "muddle, injustice, FOUL PLAY." He paused, and it occurred to me that Tubby's motives in stirring this whole thing up, might well be less about clearing his name, and rather more about becoming the centre of interest for once in his life. To have a secret that no one else knew about, and to use it to intrigue and tantalise; I thought I would play on this.

"I was most shocked by what Sammy intimated to me, and thought if I could help, come and hear all about it…" I thought I would stick to the singular pronoun, I didn't want to alarm him.

"What could you do?" On the whole, I thought Tubby's question rather astute. I prevaricated. "I should like to come and see you. I can easily drive down."

"I shouldn't be able to give you a meal." Mean old sod, I mouthed at John.

"Oh, I shouldn't want anything to eat."

"That's all right then." He paused impressively, "This is top secret, of course."

"Absolutely." At last I was able to be truthful, "Sammy stressed that the whole business must be dealt with as quietly as possible."

On the way down John and I discussed what Tubby's house would be like. (Such discussions were to become a feature of future trips we would make to other unknown houses). John thought seven bedrooms at least, and I stipulated for a minimum of three acres based on the name 'Fairlawns.' But it became increasingly obvious as, obedient to the wonderful Satnav (I have no sense of direction at all), we neared Small Wotton, and that a nineteen- fifties estate was a strange place for a stately home.

"I can't see Lady P. living here," said John doubtfully. "Are you sure you've got the address right?"

"Ah, yes, of course!" I said as we parked outside a very unprepossessing semi. "Don't you remember Lewis said that Lady P.'s first husband had squandered all the money? Any money there was actually came from Tubby."

"I wonder if Tubby knew that when he married her," said John thoughtfully.

"You're still not convinced that Tubby didn't murderer her, are you? Do you see him taking a belated revenge for finding he'd got her without any money?" He gave me a look.

"Just a thought, that's all."

We walked up the path which ran alongside some rather withered Busy-Lizzies, each resembling a small Tubby: florid, fussy and rather uninteresting. The door was painted an unattractively dull green, and there was a large picture window beside it, and behind some not particularly clean net curtains, we could discern the fumbling figure of Tubby.

He was smaller and stouter than I remembered, pinker and more fluffy, like a baby owl who suspects one of its brothers is about to push it out of the nest.

"Well, here you are," he said without much enthusiasm; a comment that I was wondering how to reply to, when John reached out and patted him on the shoulder.

"How are you doing, Tubby?" Unlike me, John's awfully good at things like this.

"People say a lot of things," replied Tubby enigmatically, and I wondered whether the neighbours, of which there were an awful lot on the estate, might have been harbouring the same suspicions as the rest of us.

We stood awkwardly in the hall and Tubby looked accusingly at me.

"You didn't say *he* was coming." I imagined 'he' meant

that John's name had slipped his memory.

"I've come to help," said John politely.

"Ah," said Tubby.

We continued to stand in the very narrow hall, which appeared narrower than it was because of three rather large and ugly oil paintings of some cows, some ships, and a large, plain woman in period dress, not unlike Lady P. I supposed they constituted the remains of Lady P.'s squandered wealth.

"Shall we go and sit down?" asked John, gently propelling Tubby through a door.

The sitting room was pretty unattractive, but Tubby had made it quite comfortable. I say Tubby, because I had the feeling that things had been re-arranged now he was on his own: a chair very near the fireplace, with a table on each side and a pouffe for his feet.

He had said we wouldn't get any lunch, and I now suspected we wouldn't be offered any coffee either, since the remains of a mugful sat on the table beside his chair.

I started saying something inept, a sort of amalgam of being sorry, being pleased to see him and how cosy the room was. Neither John nor Tubby looked impressed. A silence fell. Suddenly Tubby burst out.

"I know what you must think of me, allowing Marjorie to live in a house like this. Unworthy of her, but no money, no money."

"I think it's a very nice house," lied John. "Lovely pictures." Another silence fell and I was wondering how to get Tubby started on the subject of murder when an absolutely terrifying thing occurred, probably the most terrifying thing I have ever experienced. Even more terrifying than the sight of the dead Lady P. arched over the bed.

A familiar voice shrilled out from what must have been the kitchen: "Tubby you're a fool!"

The voice of Lady P.!

When you hear someone say 'he went white', you think it an exaggeration, but John really did turn white, (I did too, he told me afterwards); we both leapt to our feet and gawped and looked towards the kitchen in horror. What was there?

The cry was repeated: "Tubby you're a fool! Tubby you're a fool!" We lurched towards the kitchen door.

A large green and red parrot regarded us maliciously from its cage. Tubby came stumbling in after us, fished a towel out from behind a chair and thrust it over the cage.

"Marjorie loved Albert, he said, "but I'm not keen on him myself."

We returned to the sitting room. I felt grumpy, as if Tubby had played an April Fool's day trick on me, so I addressed him rather more brusquely than I had intended.

"What's all this about a murder."

I could feel John wincing at my lack of subtlety.

"Oh dear me," said Tubby. "Nobody said anything about a murder. More a mistake, I'm sure. I don't want anyone arresting me for libel."

"I'm sure you're quite safe with us," said John, "and it will do you good to get it off your chest."

"Well, it will, it will, "said Tubby, but it was difficult to get him started.

"If only I hadn't been scurried!" he began plaintively.

Eventually, amidst assertions and retractions, and expressions of shame and indignation, a sequence of events leading up to Lady P.'s last hours began to emerge.

After the bridge had finished they had gone back to the bedroom and Lady P. turned the television on ("very loud, she always liked it very loud"), and settled down to watch it while imbibing her 'goodnight whisky.' Gino had left this in his customary fashion on the shelf outside the door, and Tubby who didn't drink ("alcohol has never suited me, oh no"), went off to have a bath. Later, Tubby emerged from the bathroom, but retreated straight back in again when he saw the bedroom door was open, and Lady P. obviously engaged in an energetic row with the figure outside. When he emerged again with his dressing gown on, he saw a hand thrusting a glass at his wife and he heard the words,

"And I hope it kills you, you vicious old bitch."

And Lady P. had replied (with dramatic irony, I thought), "It'll take more than a glass of whisky to finish me off, you miserable Welshie." Then she slammed the door. Tubby had timidly enquired what had happened.

"Bloody Bethan complaining that I had upset her darling little Megan. Well, at least she produced some more whisky. Turn off the box and the lights – no, no leave mine on, Tubby, you fool. I've still got this to drink." And as Tubby went to sleep, she was sitting up in bed with the glass and a magazine.

According to Tubby, he was woken up by some terrible choking noises, and a cry of something that sounded something like, "Oh God, my heart!"

By the time he had put the lights on ("it always took me a little time to find the switch"), Lady P. was dead.

"She said 'my heart' – I'm sure she specifically mentioned her heart!" I felt this was important. Tubby looked nonplussed. "Well, she must have done, mustn't she? That's why I thought it was a heart attack."

"Did she have a bad heart then?"

"Poor Marjorie always had a lot of things to worry her."

I felt I hadn't made a lot of headway, but I persevered.

"You didn't think at the time she had been poisoned?"

Tubby looked smaller and rounder and more owl-like than ever. "I didn't think at all, I just knew my dear one was dead."

I didn't like to ask what made him think she was dead, but John did.

"Her back was all arched," he said, his eyes filling with tears. "She didn't look . . . attractive any more."

"Well!" I thought. Either he was a brilliant actor or, well, what? I suppose beauty is in the eye of the beholder...."

"Didn't you notice the glass on the floor with the spilt whisky?"

Tubby looked reproachful. "I was only concerned about my wife."

"Then you went to fetch us?" asked John.

Tubby nodded sadly.

We were gentle, but we did give him a sort of 'third degree'. When did he begin to think she had been poisoned?

Why had he said nothing about Bethan at the time?

It was difficult to get anything wholly coherent out of him. He had been – he seemed greatly attached to the word – "scurried." He had tried to say something, but Sammy and the two Italian men had frightened him, and in the shock of it all, he hadn't thought particularly about Bethan's words. People often said nasty things to Marjorie. And then everything happened so quickly; the doctor gave him an injection to make him sleep. "I never thought about the plane." And they had taken the body away. Then the next morning they had been nasty to him, even Sammy, and they'd told him it would be difficult to take her back to England, and he had better have her cremated.

"They said they were thinking of me, but I don't think they were," said Tubby indignantly. "They were afraid people would cancel their holidays if it got out that there had been something funny." But when he thought about it, he decided Marjorie would quite like "being in the lake", as he put it, "because we had been happy there." He had tried to say something about Bethan and the poisoned whisky, but they had been "very unsympathetic", and reading between the lines, I thought, decidedly intimidating. The upshot had been that Tubby was moved to another hotel, and Lady P. was cremated the following day. Tubby signed some forms, disposed of Lady P. in the lake, and was "scurried" on to a plane back to England.

Everything had happened so quickly that he couldn't get his thoughts together. (I imagined all the thumb-twiddling that had gone on.) Sometimes he thought one thing and sometimes another. Perhaps she hadn't drunk any whisky; perhaps it *was* her heart, and perhaps, after all, he had imagined Bethan's words. The television had been on full blast, and as time went on – I could imagine how it was – life became quite comfortable for Tubby. Neighbours who hadn't spoken to him for years brought him delicacies and were pleasant to him, and it was easy to talk about a 'heart attack.' It was only when Mrs Appleton from two doors had started dropping some hints –

"Not that *she* thought anything," explained Tubby. "But she thought she ought to mention to me that one or two others ..." I could just imagine La Appleton.

And Tubby began to worry. "I thought I should know the truth," he said. "I don't want to make any accusations," he added nervously. "After all, I might be sent to prison for libel!"

I thought there were more serious sentences that he might be subjected to. But he seemed to have accepted the idea that John and I had come with the purpose of clearing his name.

"You'll see to it, then?" he concluded. Exactly how he meant us to tackle "it" didn't seem to interest him. Perhaps he envisaged us having a nice cosy chat over the bridge table with Bethan, in which we said something like, "Three No Trumps and by the way, Bethan, just wondering, did you poison Lady P.?"

There didn't seem much further mileage to be got out of consulting Tubby as to ways and means, so we said we would see what we could do, or rather John did, and we made moves towards leaving. He hadn't offered us any coffee or indeed any thanks, and the whole visit had been rather depressing. I tried to feel sorry for Tubby, but he cut such a feeble figure standing there in the hallway under the picture of the Lady P. look-alike that I felt nothing but irritation.

As we went out of the front door, he must have gone into the kitchen and taken the cloth off the cage, for Lady P.'s voice shrilled out: "Tubby you're a fool! Tubby, you're a fool!" It pursued us right to the car; perhaps he found it reassuring.

"What are we going to do?" I asked as we got into the car. (John's. It's a BMW, of course).

"Stop at the first decent pub and have a bloody good lunch," said John.

"I didn't mean that, I meant . . ."

"I know you did," he replied, "but you have to get your priorities worked out. I need a great big juicy steak."

When John sets his mind to something he usually gets it. 'The Black Dog' wouldn't have been one's first choice for gourmet dining, but there was nothing wrong with the steak.

There was something about the sight of the meat that was conducive to discussion; whether it was the blood issuing forth which focussed our minds on the question of murder, or whether it was the fact that we were simply ravenous, having not had so much as a biscuit at Tubby's; whatever it was, as we picked at the chips, we picked over our various courses of action.

"Of course," said John, "the easiest way out is to do nothing – just tell Tubby that he misheard Bethan and, jolly sad, but that Lady P. really did die of a heart attack."

"But we're not going to do that."

"No," John admitted. "But it won't be easy. If we go and visit Bethan, we can hardly arrive at the door and say, "By the way, dear, this isn't just a social call. We're rather hoping you'll confess to the murder of Lady P.""

"I'd imagined a similar conversation taking place over the bridge table. But it's not as clear-cut as that, is it? Just because Bethan hands her a glass of whisky, it doesn't mean she intended to poison her. And actually we don't know that it *was* poisoned."

"I think it was."

"But you don't know for sure."

" You get a kind of feel for these things."

I thought the comment unconvincing, but let it pass."Okay; well, perhaps we just engage Bethan in idle chat and see how she reacts."

" Like 'Have you committed any good murders, recently, Bethan?'"

"Hang on, wait, John. If she *is* innocent, she won't know Lady P.'s dead – let alone murdered. We can introduce that very subtly."

"Subtly, you? What was it you said to Tubby? "What's all this about a murder?"

"I'm going to have some more wine, "I said. "I'm not driving."

The waitress came over and asked if everything was all right? I didn't feel she cared very much. Once she'd gone,

John said:

"If you were going to poison someone, would you give them a glass of Scotch and then say loudly, 'I hope it kills you'?"

"Probably not."

"On the other hand," said John helping himself to my chips, having finished his own, "It doesn't look good for Bethan. I mean Lady P. had already drunk her usual 'goodnight whisky', so it wasn't that that finished her off."

"Could it have had delayed effects?"

"I don't think so, because she's affected as soon as she drinks this second lot of whisky. So it looks as if it's Bethan's whisky that does for her – whisky that Bethan has brought specially."

"I just don't see Bethan in the role of murderer," I said, " and now I'm going to have the Caramelised Apple Tart." John had the Baked Alaska. But that was about as far as we got that day.

Chapter 5: Welsh cakes

The following Saturday we went to Wales. We had made careful plans about the route, but still hadn't worked out how we would broach the ticklish question of murder.

We had a very nice time getting there. We had gone to Hay on Wye, bought a lot of books: I, a copy of Dorothy Sayers and John some Agatha Christies 'to get us into the right frame of mind', and we stayed the night at a very good hotel, and then set off through the Brecon Beacons. I must say the scenery was stunning: mountains lowering at us through a sort of purple mist and wonderful streams rushing and trickling down to the road, black-faced sheep and great swathes of sky and loneliness. I thought it was rather wonderful. John, who is less affected by such things, said grimly that living out here would make him suicidal rather than murderous, and I replied primly that I had never thought Bethan was a murderer, and everyone was deemed innocent until proved guilty in a Court of Law.

"That's our strong point in dealing with Bethan," said John. "That nothing will ever come to a Court of Law, and nobody's interested in involving the police because nothing can be proved. It's all to put Tubby's mind at rest."

"It depends what you mean by 'all'." John didn't reply because what we both rather wanted was for Bethan to indicate she was guilty – but it didn't seem very likely that she would cheerily pipe up "Oh, Lady P.? Yes, I bumped her off, you know. Of *course* I'm delighted for you to tell Tubby." But one never knew, and as I said rather hopefully to John, "luck might be on our side."

"The only thing that's on our side are these wretched sheep," said John, coming to a halt.

"Not just on our side," I added as the whole flock came into view. There was nothing for it, but to turn off the engine and wait. I have never seen so many sheep, nor any animals that moved so slowly. People talk about 'following like sheep', but it didn't seem to me that they these sheep went in for any following; they were only too happy to wander off on some idiosyncratic quest of their own. I mentioned this to John and he agreed. He went further, he said they did it on purpose to hold us up.

"We shall be late," I said. "She might think we aren't coming and go out somewhere. Shall I ring?"

"Go out? Where would you go in a place like this?" Another hundred sheep went past.

It had fallen to my lot to contact Bethan and I hadn't made a very good job of it. John, who had been listening, said afterwards that he had never heard anyone lie so badly. I didn't think I was too bad. I said we were spending a few days in Wales and could we pop in – we had seen her address on the list at GrandSlam and it was on our route. I could see now why she had asked suspiciously where we were going, were we heading for the top of Calder Idris? I said that John was in charge of directions and it was no good asking me. I just liked Wales, and no, I hadn't been there before. I liked the idea of it. Anyway, she seemed to come round and was very welcoming, and said if we came in the afternoon, she would give us a real feed. This sounded much more promising than Tubby's invitation. Then I had felt guilty: it seemed rather craven to eat her Welsh cakes and try and pin a murder on her at the same time. But John said if she was guilty it would serve her right, and if she wasn't, it would be nice for her to have some company – he didn't imagine you had too many people dropping in when you lived in the middle of nowhere. John doesn't really do rural.

It really was in the middle of nowhere. Even the Satnav gave up and told us we had reached our destination – when we patently hadn't, unless it meant a lopsided gate tied up with a bit of barbed wire and what looked like miles of mud. Closer inspection showed there was a pot-holey sort of track going through brownish grass. John got noticeably more grumpy; his car means a lot to him, and already the right side was covered in something with the look of dung about it, and the wheels were coated in yellow mud, and to cap it all, it was coming on to rain which suggested that the track ahead was likely to contribute further to transforming the car into something very agricultural.

"Pity we didn't bring your car," said John. "Yours always looks like this." I was miffed.

"I don't think that's quite true."

"Well, we won't argue about it."

"I'll pay for the services of Mr Super-Clean," I promised. Mr Super-Clean is an expensive, and in my view, swindling car-valeting service that John favours.

"Inside as well?"

I glared at him.

So we travelled a long way – a couple of miles, I should think, down this track, neither of us commenting on the suspension-damaging potholes. The farmyard, when we got to it, was little better. We got out and John inspected the damage in silence. I wished he hadn't chosen to wear the designer shoes that he'd bought for a hundred and eighty pounds (in the sale).

However, after we had negotiated the greenish puddles and other noisome areas, things improved – at least for a bit. Bethan appeared at the door, even vaster than I remembered, swathed in an enormous woolly jacket, doubtless the fruit of her labours, both with the sheep and the needle.

"What a shame about your shoes," she commented as she led us inside. "Never mind, I'll put them on the range to dry off." It says a lot for John that he smiled and said thank you nicely, but he kept them on – and, as it happened, it was fortunate he did.

Bethan was eager to know where exactly we had been staying, and couldn't understand why we had taken this particular route. "But you should have gone through Clent," she kept saying.

"But we wanted to eat your tea," replied John. Bethan liked that.

She led us through an enormous stone-flagged kitchen, untouched by the demands of the twenty-first century, or even the twentieth. There was a huge Belfast sink with a single tap, and a range which was unlit. I could see why she had the woolly coat; it was absolutely freezing. However the parlour was a different kettle of fish, a log fire roared away and a table was set before it with the most scrumptious spread I have ever seen: sandwiches, (ham, egg and cheese), scones (butter, jam and clotted cream), sponge cake, fruit cake, ginger cake, Welsh cakes (of course), and a trifle waiting on the sideboard.

"Irfon will eat up what you can't manage," she remarked. Irfon was the son; we'd forgotten about him.

"He looks after the sheep, does Irfon; he's good with the sheep. You should see the prizes he's won for his Blackthorns. Does all his own butchering too."

I remembered she had referred to him in Italy as 'Big Irfon'. Somehow I rather wished she hadn't mentioned this particular aspect of his farming skills.

As the cakes went down, we talked about farming and the Welsh countryside and speaking Welsh, and the problems with lambing. I was full of tea and cake, and the fire blazing away made me feel comfortably sleepy, and increasingly I felt disinclined to broach the subject of murder. Judging from the flushed state of John's face (he was sitting right next to the fire) he felt much the same. But unexpectedly, Bethan provided an opening.

"Shall you two boys be doing any more GrandSlam bridge?"

"I don't know," I said. "Shall you?"

Bethan's answer was vehement.

"We shall not. Excluding your good selves, we did not enjoy the company. There was one person in particular I shall not be sorry never to see again…" (I sneaked a look at John to see whether he appreciated the ambiguity of the comment.) "Poor Megan was made very unhappy."

John spoke softly, "I don't think you can have heard."

"Heard what? Has something happened to her?"

I digested this, Wasn't Bethan a bit quick off the mark with this question? On the other hand if she *had* murdered Lady P., would she have made a point of going on about her?

"She's dead," said John. He's not one to mince his words, but I gave him credit for provoking a response. Bethan's reaction was interesting: a smile passed over her lips.

"I should not like to be in her shoes when she meets her maker."

I thought of Lady P. at the bottom of Lake Como, and reckoned that her shoes were probably an irrelevance by now.

"How did she die?" I was very cunning:

"She had a … collapse. Interestingly, you may well have been the last person to see her. Tubby says that you came to see her in her bedroom that last night and …"

The change in Bethan from cuddly Mother Wales to Lady Macbeth was immediate. She stood up, quite quickly for one whose movements were somewhat hampered, and knocked over John's cup of tea.

"Now look you here … I knew it! I knew there was something funny about you coming here and not going over Clent. Why have you come? To accuse me of murder, is it? Calling me a murderess, is it?"

"No, certainly not! I merely …"

"Well, you go and get the police, then! Go on! Go and call the police!"

She opened the door as if there was a uniformed unit standing ready in the freezing kitchen.

"You come here, eating my food…" She looked accusingly at John who, it must be said, had been eating solidly for the last half hour – he can be immensely greedy, "… doing Irfon out of his tea; eating like a starving creature; enjoying my hospitality, and secretly plotting to lock me away!"

"No, no, Bethan. I only said…"

"Well, you can get out of my house now before I set Irfon on you. Accusing me! Wait till I tell Megan, you wait … Go on, get out!"

John looked as alarmed as I felt, as she banged her large arthritic fist down on the table.

"You sneaking little poofters! I tell you one thing, I'm bloody glad she's dead, God forgive me, and I shouldn't mind if you joined her."

We reached the door. Usually John and I are very polite, but it didn't really seem appropriate to thank her for the cakes.

"Get out before I call Irfon!" and these parting words took us both through the door, as a mental picture of some sort of Welsh Heathcliffe rose before us. We fled though the freezing kitchen and at the door she bellowed after us:

"If you're looking for someone to frame – although what business it is of yours I don't know, I should be looking at one or two others. Oh yes, there were a few people walking around that night, like your friend Lewis and that Janet – why don't you go and ask them a few questions, Mr Policemen? I should think there's no shortage of people for you to pin her ladyship's murder on. Just remember there's a law to stop people going round accusing other people of murder, and you can tell Tubby, too, that if I see him around here, I'll put him in the sheep dip." The door slammed.

"I'm glad I kept my shoes on," said John.

In the safety of the car we had time to reflect. It was hard to judge whether we had met with any success or not. On the one hand Bethan had reacted very violently to my innocuous remark, which might mean that she was guilty and, having considered herself quite safe, was now caught on the hop. On the other hand she might have been entirely innocent and merely exhibiting a very natural indignation. It didn't, however, look as if there would be too many more opportunities for pursuing the conversation.

As we drove back down the track in the pouring rain, mud squelching over the tyres and splashing up the sides of the car, we saw a very small man walking past with a dog; he must have been all of five foot two.

"I bet that's Big Irfon," said John.

Neither of us felt inclined for further conversation.

Chapter 6: Elsinore

John did not want to stay in Wales; in fact he went further, he said he would never go to Wales again. So we drove straight home listening to the radio in an attempt to put murderers and murderesses far from our minds. Then we went to bed. The next day however we felt more bullish and we settled ourselves into the conservatory, a recent and rather unexpectedly expensive addition to the house. But it is comfortable and nicely conducive to conversation, so you must imagine us stretched out on two basket lounger chairs with a pot of coffee and some croissants, trying to decide what to do next.

"Is Bethan guilty?" I asked melodramatically.

"No idea."

"But what do you think?"

"I think she was pretty cross. Mind you, I would be, if I'd baked a great tea, and the people who sat there scoffing it then accused me of murder."

"We didn't; that's why it was so odd that she assumed that we were."

"You did say…" John did a wildly-exaggerated imitation of my subtle comments, "you were the last person to see her alive."

It was time to change the subject.

"The priority is to report to Tubby," I said. John hooted.

"And what will you say?"

"Ah, well… I shall say we had a… ah … an inconclusive meeting with Bethan."

"And Tubby will ask you when you are going to have the conclusive meeting."

"I shall say a date has not yet been fixed. Actually, I thought it would be better if you spoke to Tubby."

"I thought you might. Now let me tell you what I think." Thoughtfully he exerted pressure on the top of the cafetière, "I think we tell Tubby we are sorting things out, but we can't do things in a hurry. If he asks, we say we haven't seen

Bethan yet, as we're organising dates to go and see all the suspects."

"All the suspects? I didn't know there were any others."

"Lewis and Janet, of course; the two people that Bethan said she saw wandering about."

I was amazed, not only that John had taken Bethan's parting words seriously, but that he was interested in continuing with our 'investigations'. I thought he would have thrown in the deerstalker. I suppose that's why I love John so much – I never quite know where I am with him.

"You've got the list of addresses that Sammy sent. Where do they live?"

"I haven't got the list here, but I know where Lewis lives because he told us. It's a village somewhere near Worcester. Hopefully Janet won't live too far away. I mean, she probably doesn't, because they both got Birmingham flights."

"So did Megan and Bethan," I said, and nobly got up out of my basket chair to find the list. It turned out that Janet and her parents lived near Banbury. We didn't really want to do Worcester and Banbury in one go, so we opted for Janet; then there was the question of whether to forewarn them or just 'drop in'.

I was for forewarning. "We don't want to go all that way for nothing."

But John liked the idea of the surprise element. "We'll start off and ring up when we're half way there, then hang up if they're in. Then we won't have wasted too much time."

"But we shall have wasted time – and petrol, all for nothing."

"Well, we'll find somewhere for lunch and then ring again."

"But even if they are in they might have gone out by the time we get there."

John sighed. "Don't be so difficult. We'll go on Tuesday."

He got up with the air of one who brooks no argument. "Now I'm going to ring Tubby, seeing as you've wimped out."

I listened with baited breath, but John came back to say

there was no answer. He rang Tubby again later but there was still no reply. "Your turn next," he said.

"All right then."

But I got no answer either and I gave up after three goes.

At ten thirty on Tuesday John called the Macalister household. Almost immediately the familiar self-satisfied voice replied,

"You have reached the residence of Trevor and Isabel Macalister." (I noticed that he placed himself first and no mention was made of Janet). "I apologise," continued the histrionic voice, "for the fact that neither of us can reply to your most valuable call in person; we should be most gratified if you would call again later."

"They're out," I said and added unhelpfully. "I thought they would be."

"We'll go on anyway," said John. To my surprise it seemed that he really had got the detective bit between his teeth. And as it happened he was proved right; half way to Banbury we tried again. This time Isabel Macalister's pleasant voice asked how she could help us, and I rang off.

"Let's play the 'what sort of house do they live in?' game." I said, "I mean we weren't right with Tubby, in fact we couldn't have been more wrong, but as for Bethan…"

"It's not too difficult to spot a sheep farm," said John. He is often grumpy in the mornings. "Does the house have a name?"

I consulted my piece of paper. "'Elsinore'!"

"That's bloody Denmark!"

"I suppose once he must have played Hamlet. I imagine Trevor would like people to remember that fact. I wonder what it's like? Do you think it *is* a castle? I can imagine gothic turrets. Perhaps even a drawbridge!"

"No," said John, "she's too sensible. It will be modern, detached, begonias at the front and a ding-dong bell; sort of medium posh."

"Inside?"

"Inside there will be hundreds of photos of him in various

bits of theatrical regalia."

I was partly right about the outside, more right than John, as I pointed out to him. While it wasn't a castle, it was pretty big, mock Tudor with casement windows and plenty of lawn. Trevor's voice-overs must have been quite lucrative.

John rang the bell: it went ding-dong, ding-dong, and John gave me a look, but before he could crow, Trevor came to the door.

"Holy Jehosaphat! If it isn't my two old friends from GrandSlam Bridge!" He made an elaborate gesture of surprise, throwing up his arms.

Isabel's voice was heard calling from the kitchen: "Trevor, is it Janet?"

With rather less elaboration he shouted back, "No, it isn't."

Isabel appeared. I reflected again that she must have been rather beautiful when she was young. Even now, with delicate features, high cheekbones and fine dark hair, she retained an air of elegance, despite being rather less well-turned out than usual. Still, I reflected, we had caught them on the hop.

As ever she was charming and smiled, but I felt our presence was probably a disappointment. Well, it was a disappointment for us too, if there was no Janet.

"John and Mark, how nice! I thought…"

"Ah the dour cast of thought," Trevor smiled at us as if expecting us to congratulate him on being able to bring out a snippet from – I felt sure he would say – 'the bard'. I suspected either he didn't want to talk about Janet or he wanted us to ask about 'Elsinore'. We didn't.

Nothing daunted, he continued to spread his arms expansively: "Come in, come in, and tell us what brings you to these far-flung parts."

I didn't think Banbury was that far-flung, but wasn't going to argue about it. Also, I needed to remember what excuse we had decided on for calling. I couldn't remember exactly what we had agreed. I left John to do the talking.

"Well, we will come in," he said, "just for a moment." As

we were conducted into the sitting room, he added craftily: "We had to come this way *on business* and thought we would drop by with a bit of news." I thought this a master-stroke, but was a little resentful that John had been saving it up and hadn't told me."

"And what kind of business might that be?"

Isabel looked embarrassed, "Please, Trevor, I am sure whatever it is, it is not at all *our* business." She smiled; she did have a wonderful smile. "Let me get you some coffee."

"That would be very kind," I said.

"Or should I hear the news first?" she asked, halting on her way to the kitchen.

I took a deep breath and John and both spoke together like a kind of comedy duo.

"Lady P. is dead."

"Poor woman," said Isabel and went out to the kitchen.

There was a pause and then Trevor remarked in a man-of-the world tone: "I lack my wife's charitable nature, I fear I shall not be covering my head with willow boughs nor again with myrtles." He flung back what I am sure he would have referred to as 'his mane'. Actually he looked older than I remembered – older, I thought, than me, and he didn't look terribly well; his skin had a yellowish tinge that wasn't suntan – or there again, I thought, perhaps it was; I could just imagine him on a sun bed topping up his tan. John was right about the photos, anyway. There was also a large leather-bound album on a side table, entitled 'MEMORIES'.

"Now, sit down, make yourselves at home. Elucidate this mystery! Was she simply ill, or can we imagine murder by the hen-pecked husband, or the spontaneous attack of a goaded waiter? Or perhaps …" he looked at us, I thought rather shrewdly, "revenge for a particularly venomous bridge hand! Or have you even…. no, no, no, surely you have not come to accuse one of us of assassination?" He hid his face in mock horror at the suggestion – which he himself had raised. Now, why, I asked myself should he say that? After all, nobody has made any suggestion of foul play ... yet.

I noticed that the china figures on the mantelpiece were

semi-naked female pre-pubescent figures, given a sort of spurious respectability by masquerading as the three graces.

"I'll tell you about it, shall I?" said John. This time it was not the brainchild of John alone, but a joint premeditated effort, a sort of bowdlerized account that omitted Sammy (too complicated), us (too incriminating), and Bethan (too libellous), and threw the ball back firmly into Tubby's court. We had bumped into Tubby in London...

"Where you were on business again?" asked Isabel, quietly returning with the tray. I couldn't decide whether she was being sarcastic or not, but I reckoned she was pretty sharp.

John smiled and continued his story. Tubby had, he said, told us that although he had at first thought Lady P. had died of a heart attack, as indeed the doctors had, later he began to think he had not seen things clearly, presumably because he had been in shock. "Tubby remembered various odd things," John concluded "for example, a glass with its contents spilt on the floor...".

"Hah, prussic acid! The smell of almonds," said Trevor putting two spoonfuls of sugar into his coffee. "I told you it was murder."

"Why did he tell you all this?" asked Isabel. She was, I reflected very much more astute than her husband.

"I think he just wanted to talk it through," I said.

"Did he think someone had put poison in her drink? One of the people in the Bridge party?" Whether or not Trevor was taking the suggestion seriously, Isabel certainly was.

"He thought it possible."

"Well, each and every one of us – your good selves included, I daresay, would cheerfully have finished her off," said Trevor, who obviously didn't imagine himself as a suspect. "Isabel, our guests have not been offered chocolate biscuits."

"I am afraid you ate them all," said Isabel. She continued: "How could anyone have poisoned the drink, if she had it in her own room?"

"Tubby could have, and I don't blame him – poison for a

poisonous woman," commented Trevor, looking round for our approbation as if he had said something clever.

"But he'd hardly have raised the subject if he *had* murdered her," I said.

"But how did the poison get there?" continued Isabel.

"Apparently it was in her 'goodnight whisky'." Which of course wasn't strictly true because she'd already drunk that, but it seemed unnecessarily complicated to explain.

"Well then, one of the staff must have done it," said Trevor. "They disliked her as much as the rest of us."

I must admit I hadn't thought of that. Indeed, my thinking had been very limited and gone a bit like this: 'Tubby did it; oh, not Tubby. Bethan then; oh, maybe not Bethan. Someone else mentioned by Bethan; who were they? Janet and Lewis!' Not perhaps the most sophisticated of reasoning methods, but John had obviously got there ahead of me, as he often does.

"The thing is," he said, "if it was one of the staff, why did they wait until the last night? She'd have been out of their hair by the next day."

"I suppose," said Isabel slowly – she didn't drink any coffee, but sipped at a glass of water. "I suppose someone intercepted whoever was bringing up the drink for Lady P., and swapped the glasses, one of the GrandSlam bridge people."

I was amazed at Isabel's dogged interest, particularly in the face of her husband's fairly blunt unconcern, but, then, I imagined few things interested Trevor that didn't relate directly to Trevor himself.

As it was, he laughed. "I hardly think so, darling. It's not likely anyone would intercept Gino, or whoever was carrying the tray, and say: 'Scusi, I want to swap this glass.' Besides, how would anyone know it was for Lady Prettyman? Lots of people had 'goodnights', as you, my dear, know."

This was obviously a dig. I wondered if she drank too much, but Isabel clearly kept her secrets to herself – and so would I if I'd been married to Trevor. But actually, I thought, he was right, and it was something John and I had avoided discussing. If it hadn't been Bethan, how on earth had anyone managed to substitute a poisoned glass on to the tray?

"Gino didn't take up the drinks," was Isabel's calm response. "That was the waitresses' job. Gino had other things to do."

"Well, "I said craftily, "did you see anyone of our party wandering around near Lady P.'s room?"

"As we have no idea where her room was, we can hardly say," he replied, rather edgily, I thought.

"It was 238. We were just around the corner. Was that anywhere near you?"

"No, we were 307, on the floor above. I imagine she must have been over on the other side; certainly not near us."

"But you might have seen somebody wandering around?"

"We had better things to do than spend our time spying on our fellow guests. We left that to the Skorskis," said Trevor, and although he added a jovial laugh, I rather thought he was ruffled.

"The Skorskis?" But we were not to be enlightened on the subject of their espionage.

"We saw nobody," said Isabel. "Shall I take your cup, John? Mark? But I do rather wonder at your coming here to tell us this, particularly as you say the doctors were satisfied that Lady Prettyman died of a heart attack. Has Tubby, for some reason, appointed you as unofficial investigators? If he is worried, surely his best course of action is to go to the police."

"Oh he didn't want to do that," I said hastily, worrying that once again things might turn out unpleasantly. "He just wanted to satisfy himself that it had been a heart attack.

"I thought you said that there was evidence of poison."

I was beginning to feel out of my depth.

"I rather agree with my wife. Why doesn't the fellow ask his own questions, eh? Quite frankly I can't see what business it is of yours." said Trevor. He had spilt some coffee on his shirt and began dabbing at it in an irritated sort of way. I felt a nasty premonition that this was going to turn into the Bethan scenario all over again.

"Well, you know what Tubby is," said John coming to my

rescue. "A bit of a chocolate teapot."

Isabel's face illuminated briefly with a smile. "I like that description; I shall remember it." Then her tone changed. "All the same, I find it rather unsettling that on your unofficial mission undertaken on behalf of Tubby, you appear to make the Macalister family the first port of call."

"Very peculiar," agreed Trevor.

"Well, as I told you," I said unhappily, "we had to go to Banbury and thought we'd drop by. Quite frankly…" I could feel my 'quite frankly' had a mendacious sound, "to see if you had any ideas as much as anything else. And…" I played my trump card, "actually you weren't the first port of call; we went to see Bethan in Wales."

"Good Heavens, I should have thought her a most unlikely suspect?"

"Beware the Welsh bearing gifts," commented Trevor sententiously. Isabel stood up and picked up the tea tray.

"Well, I can't imagine any of us will learn very much after all this time, particularly if, as you say, the ashes are in Lake Como. I think you had better tell Tubby to forget all about it."

"Let sleeping dogs lie," added Trevor.

Isabel stood up and paused. Perhaps, I thought, she had studied dramatic timing with her husband.

"Janet will be so sorry to have missed you."

It was meant as a signal for us to leave and I heaved a sigh of relief that unpleasantness had been averted. Isabel was so much more the master of things than her husband, I thought, wondering not for the first time, how on earth she had come to marry him? I also wondered how we were going to get hold of Janet; after all, it had been Janet that Bethan had accused of wandering round at night and it was Janet we had actually come to find out about.

"Yes, I'm sorry to miss her," said John standing up obediently. "Janet and I often met outside the Bridge Room to have a cigarette."

"What is she up to at the moment?" I asked, trying to sound casual, but failing dismally, as could be seen by the guarded response of her parents.

"What do you mean?" asked Trevor sharply.

"She's in London," said Isabel quietly. "She has started a new life there." It was said in a way to suggest that the conversation was over and no more questions were to be asked. However, I wasn't going to be defeated so easily.

"What is she doing there? Isn't she a bio-chemist?"

"She is in retail," said Trevor shortly. "Retail."

There was a pause. It struck me that Trevor always seemed to lose his sang froid whenever Janet was mentioned.

"It was so nice of you to call and give us your news. We must have a game of bridge sometime," said Isabel leading us towards the door. I could see the use of 'your' and 'sometime' was her way of disassociating the Macalister family from both the murder and its dubious investigators.

"Could you give us Janet's phone number?" asked John boldly as we went into the hall.

"I am afraid not," said Isabel coldly. She was clearly furious.

"Furthermore," said Trevor extending a minatory arm (I imagined the stage directions, 'addresses with angry authority'), "the last thing our daughter would wish is to be mixed up with your extremely dubious detective activities. In fact," he lowered his voice ('exerts quiet authority'), "one rather wonders what you yourselves were up to on that fateful night." I laughed a conciliatory laugh, but evoked no response from either.

"Well, thanks for the coffee," said John.

"I am so sorry there were no biscuits," said Isabel who had recovered her composure. "I'll pass on your good wishes to Janet. You must excuse me, I have things to do." And she disappeared in the direction of the kitchen.

"How do you like my castle?" asked Trevor, who insisted on accompanying us to the car. Perhaps, I thought, he was anxious to emulate his wife and part on good terms, or perhaps he was simply unable to resist a little boasting. "Bought it from the proceeds of one or two little films I made back in the seventies."

Neither John nor I enquired as to what they were.

Looking back I saw Isabel regarding us thoughtfully out of the kitchen window, looking, I thought, like Tennyson's Mariana in her moated grange. I wondered whether Trevor minded her being so much more interesting than he was, but then I thought that perhaps he didn't consider she was.

We had a discussion about it in the car.

"Why do you think they clammed up about Janet? I mean, there was no *way* they were going to let us get in touch with her. Do you think they might have thought she was involved with it – the murder, I mean? Or is it just that they just don't want anyone getting to her? You know how odd she was; perhaps she's had a nervous breakdown or something, and they don't want people prying."

"I don't actually think she is that odd," replied John. "I think she just doesn't like *him*. Well, I'm with her there, and I reckon all she needs to put her on course is a bit of the other; she had that look to me."

"Did you glean this information from your fag-smoking activities?"

"No, she never said much, but I felt she had things on her mind."

"What sort of things?"

"No idea. Talking of fags, can you reach into my jacket pocket?"

"What did they say she was doing?"

"Retail."

I looked blank.

"She's working in a shop," said John, "that's what retail means."

"Wonder why?"

"Dunno."

"He's an awful man, isn't he?"

"Yes, but he's not a murderer."

"Isabel could be. I mean she looks as if she might have been a bit of a femme fatale once."

"The sort you would have fancied before you decided where your interests lay?"

Unlike John who has never been anything but gay, I had spent my younger years primarily chasing after women. I always felt that John rather disapproved, and I tend to feel uneasy when John refers to my past, but as far as I was concerned, all my life had been spent waiting for him to come into it.

John lit up, "God, that's better."

"And she's got brains," I continued determinedly. "Look how she handled us."

John smiled. "We weren't hard to handle; we carried on like a couple of idiots. We need to get our act together a bit more, before we try anything again."

"You mean before we go and see Lewis? Well, we won't have to pretend to him; we can tell him the whole story. He's more of a kindred spirit."

"I don't mean Lewis, I mean the rest of them."

I turned and stared at him, (he has a charming little mole on his left cheek).

"All of them?"

"We've started; we may as well finish. Bethan hasn't done it…"

"Probably not."

"Trevor and Isabel probably haven't, and we don't know how to get hold of Janet, so we may as well try the rest."

"I never thought you would be interested."

"No, nor did I, but I am. I'm stopping for petrol. Have you got your plastic?" And he says I'm the mean one!

Chapter 7: The Gingerbread House

"I think we ought to contact Tubby," I said. "I feel we ought to tell him something."

"I thought we'd agreed to leave him for a bit."

"I feel we ought to say something."

"Why don't you ring him, then, while I make some coffee."

"He won't answer," I said crossly, "I've tried three times."

"I'll try this time," said John. And of course, just to make me look foolish, Tubby answered immediately.

"Yes, hello, who is it?"

"Hello, Tubby. It's John Page here."

"Who?"

"John Page. Mark and I came to see you about… um … your wife."

"Oh?" Tubby didn't sound very interested.

"I thought you might like to hear how we have been getting on." There was a pause.

"I'm going away for a few days. I'll ring you when I come back. I don't expect you've managed to find anything much out yet." And the phone went down.

"I find that very odd," I said indignantly, "don't you? One minute he's all in a state: writing to Sammy and putting us on the trail, and now he sounds as if he couldn't care less."

"Perhaps someone's got at him," said John.

"Bethan!" I exclaimed. "It must be Bethan."

"Or Trevor and Isabel," said John grinning, "rushing down there to put the frighteners on him the minute we've gone!"

"Well, I think it's very odd," I said obstinately.

"If he's going away somewhere, he'll be busy packing and won't want to bother with it until he comes back."

"I wonder where he's going?"

"God knows. Perhaps he was being kidnapped."

"Do you…?"

"Mark, stop being a prick. Forget about Tubby. Are we

going to see Lewis?"

He sat down and poured coffee. I brightened up; the thought of an outing, particularly one with John, always puts me in a good mood. I have quite a bit of time on my hands, being retired, but it's not just that. I adore doing things with John.

"Definitely, I think we should go, but I'm sure he's not guilty."

"You would think that."

"Why, because I like him?"

"You like him more than I do, but then I don't have so much in common with him. Going out to have a fag."

I knew what that was about. John is an engineer and I am a retired publisher, and he thinks that makes a kind of discrepancy between us, and that it matters. Actually he is quite wrong – as I am always telling him. In many ways John is much sharper than I, certainly more streetwise, and while I feel my many years among books were of dubious value, I have no doubt of John's contribution to society. And, while I am largely happy to idle my time away at home, John has been repeatedly promoted and holds a very responsible job. Still, there is, or rather, was this sense on his part that people like Lewis and I with our (largely useless) degrees were somehow members of a secret club from which he was excluded. So I remained silent and let him go, and when he came back in, he was more cheery.

"What reason are we going to give for calling? We didn't make a very good job of our last lot of excuses; Bethan and Isabel both thought we were liars."

"I'll think of something," I said. And I did; I thought of it as I watched him walking down the path to his car ("some of us have to work"), admiring his retreating hips in the expensive designer suit I had bought him for his birthday.

Going to Lewis' was very much more pleasant than going to Bethan's or Trevor's, or indeed Tubby's, but then we knew it would be. Going down I raised (again) the 'what house?'

question.

"I can't play because I know," said John. "He told me."

"What did he say?"

"He said he lived in a gingerbread house."

"Ah."

We went through some beautiful countryside on one of those perfect early autumn days when everything seems to have a shimmer of gold about it. We were heading for an expensive ceramics place entitled *The Rustic Potters* where I had suggested John might commission a specially thrown pot for my birthday. I lost no time in choosing one. John gave it an ungracious prod.

"Good thing I've got six weeks to save up," he said as he got out the plastic for the deposit. I smiled demurely, thinking of how much John had paid for his shoes (now ruined at Bethan's farm).

"Birthday presents always make a hole in the pocket," I replied smugly, "and anyway, you must admit it gave me a perfect excuse for ringing Lewis." I enlarged on my cunning: "He knew all about this pottery. All I had to do was talk about buying pots, and then I slipped in a bit about needing his advice on something – appealing to his vanity…."

"*His* vanity?"

"… and Bob's your uncle, there was an invitation to lunch."

"I hope you didn't give anything away. We need the element of surprise."

"I was the soul of discretion."

"That will be a first," he said as he folded up the receipt.

The village where Lewis lived was in the Cotswolds, not a self-conscious, touristy sort of place, but rather charming, reached through narrow lanes amidst fields of late buttercups and moon daisies. Even John who claims to have zero interest in the natural world was impressed.

"I can see myself living there," he commented as we passed a mellow old rectory with roses climbing over it. We came to a small hamlet with a Norman church.

"That's a wool church," I commented knowledgeably

(having looked it up in Pevsner). John replied that sheep farming was not a subject he wished to discuss, but here was a pub called the 'Jolly Farmer' and he was quite prepared to discuss that, but I said no time to stop because Lewis was expecting us. We drove past a duck pond and were stared at by some unfriendly-looking geese.

"I hate animals," said John.

"They're not animals; they're birds."

"I hate them too; that parrot of Tubby's nearly did for me." I was about to protest that it was probably quite a nice parrot, when he added: "And you! I've never seen anyone look so frightened when it started screeching out…" John did a rather alarming imitation: "'Tubby, you old fool!'" But before we could argue about who had been the more cowardly, John took a sharp left and came into 'Turn Again Lane', but we didn't need to turn again because there was Lewis's gingerbread house.

It was exactly like the pictures you see in children's picture books: a tiny little half-timbered thatched cottage with a neat little sign on the tiny gate: 'Gingerbread Cottage.'

"I wouldn't mind living here, either," said John, "although not with Lewis." He parked the car by the side of a grassy bank, well, a ditch really, and we got out and walked up the path. There were a mass of gold and blood-red dahlias and the last of what must have been stunning hollyhocks engulfing the tiny house. I wondered whether it really would be Lewis who came to the door, or if he had metamorphosed into a wizard, or even the Gingerbread Witch. It was, however, unmistakably Lewis in a pink linen shirt and a pair of creaseless linen trousers. His face was wreathed in smiles and, as always, he had the scrubbed air of one who has just emerged from his ablutions. He seemed genuinely pleased to see us – which, I must say, made a nice change.

"I've put us in the garden; it seems a shame to be inside."

He led us through a dark-beamed interior. I caught a glimpse of a portrait of a girl in a white dress as we passed the sitting room, and of a tartan-lined dog basket lying under a kitchen table – which, I was delighted to see, groaned with lunch goodies.

The garden, which was a little piece of heaven, all crazy-paving punctuated by beds of rosemary and mint and Michaelmas daisies. Beyond, lay a wide field, dotted about with three huge old oak trees. A rather mangy-looking golden retriever lay dozing in the autumn sun; I thought he rather failed to match his master's elegance. Perhaps Lewis guessed my thoughts because he commented:

"This is Sergeant. He's coming up for fourteen, so he's a very old man and has an excuse for dozing in the sun. I'm afraid I emulate him with less excuse."

I looked nervously towards John and hoped he wouldn't give expression to his views on animals, but he was on his best behaviour.

"You've got a nice spot here, Lewis."

"It's quite beautiful!" I added giving Sergeant a cursory pat. I wouldn't say my views on animals are as extreme as John's, but I'm not wild about dogs.

"I'm so glad you like it. It was my wife's idea, so I can claim little credit."

This was an eye-opener. John and I had assumed that Lewis was a closet gay, but as he had been the headmaster of a minor public school, it was something he kept quiet about.

"I... she doesn't play bridge, then?"

Lewis smiled, "I have been a widower for some years."

John, who is so much better than I at knowing how to do the right thing, touched him gently on the arm.

"I'm sorry about that, Lewis."

But Lewis was a private man, much more given, I think, to eliciting information from other people than volunteering it himself, and he did not proffer any acknowledgement.

"I have opened a rather pleasant bottle of Sancière, I thought we would have a glass or two before we eat."

"John's driving," I said happily. In fact I felt very pleased with life, having glimpsed a lobster salad as we came through the house.

We told him about the expensive pot and made desultory conversation until Lewis asked us if we had seen any of our old friends from GrandSlam Bridge. This was, of course, just the opening we wanted, and whether under the influence of the Sancerre, or the sunshine, or the sense of tranquillity induced by the gentle snoring of the dog, we began, well, I must be honest, *I* began to pour out the whole story and then John began to chime in.

Lewis looked rather taken aback at our effusions, and held up a headmasterly hand:

"May I suggest that one of you – say Mark tells the story from the beginning, and then," he smiled at me, "John can fill in anything you may have forgotten."

It wasn't for nothing that Lewis had been a headmaster! I described our night-time summons, the death of Lady P., Sammy and Tubby and our visits to Bethan (although cowardice made me omit her reference to the fact that she had mentioned Lewis), and our interview with the Macalisters, but the more I talked, the more I felt like a fourth-form boy trying to explain what he had been doing behind the bike sheds. I felt how feebly we had gone at the whole business, for Lewis sat there, free from comment, but nodding from time to time, as if he read much more from my words than I had intended him to. John felt it too, because he didn't even bother adding his contribution when I finally came to a halt. He simply smiled at Lewis and said, "We've been pretty crap, haven't we?"

Lewis regarded the meadow beyond the garden, and John and I looked too, just in case the solution to it all lay amongst the buttercups. Then Lewis smiled judiciously. "I wouldn't put it as strongly as that, John. I think perhaps the problem is that you have not worked to any particular system." I felt about thirteen.

"Now," said Lewis standing up, "I hope you like Lobster Thermidor; it seems to go rather well with these early Autumn days. I suggest we eat first and then discuss what is, after all, a most intriguing business, and one which I think it very brave of you to undertake."

I felt better – at least fifteen.

"I will go and bring out the food... no, no, sit and admire

the view, it will only take me a minute."

It took him more than a minute, but it was worth waiting for.

We forked in the succulent white meat, avocado salad and garlicky potatoes, but we all knew it was a delicious respite before the serious business began. And after the strawberry shortcake and the San Aguir, (all creamy and melting), Lewis began

"Now," he said, "let's start from the beginning. Question one: what time exactly did Tubby come and wake you up?"

"Maybe half eleven, quarter to twelve."

"A bit later, I think," I interrupted. "It was after twelve when I bumped into Sammy at reception."

"And you didn't see anybody else, by which I mean any of our party or the staff – apart from Sammy, the manager, and his brother?"

"No."

"Now, John, can you describe exactly what you saw while you were in Tubby's room, while Mark had gone for Sammy."

John screwed up his face and his eyes had that far away look which makes him so handsome.

"Well, there was Lady P. slumped over the bed with her back sort of arched and a trickle of vomit coming out, and there was Tubby going "Oh, Marjorie" and……."

"Then you noticed the glass? Where was it exactly?"

"Lying on its side on the floor, at the top end of the bed, as if she'd dropped it, and there was a sort of damp patch where the rest of the stuff that she hadn't drunk had come out."

"And what did you do?"

"I left it there."

"Why didn't you pick it up?"

"I didn't want my finger prints on it."

"So you thought there was something odd about it?"

"Well, I suppose I did, but what with Tubby moaning and carrying on I had other things to think about." Lewis nodded; there was no knowing what he thought.

"Let's move on, allow me to re-cap: the hotel manager didn't want any trouble and he and Sammy – and I must say I find Sammy's behaviour rather reprehensible here – managed to persuade Tubby to get his wife's body cremated and return to England?"

"I think Sammy thought what John thought, that there wasn't a lot to be achieved by stirring things up." For some reason I felt anxious to defend Sammy.

"A woman had been murdered," remarked Lewis mild-ly.

"I didn't know that for sure and nor did anyone else," said John indignantly. "It wasn't as if she was lying there with a dagger through her heart."

"But you said you were suspicious."

"Well, it's a bit different when you're there in the middle of the night and the general consensus of opinion is to say nothing. I daresay I wasn't thinking too clearly and I daresay you wouldn't have done either." Lewis let this pass.

"What do you *think* happened?"

"Don't know," said John, "we've probably thought about it too much. I mean, I don't think Bethan poisoned Lady P., because you don't say "I hope it kills you," if you want to get someone to drink something nasty."

"But there again," I chipped in, "why did she get into such a fury if she was innocent?"

"The important thing," said Lewis, "is to establish how and why Bethan had the glass in her hand. It wasn't Lady P.'s ordinary 'goodnight whisky'; she'd had that, this was a second glass that someone somehow had got into her hands. Don't you think you should ask Bethan how she came by it?"

"I don't think either of us want to talk to Bethan again just at the moment," said John.

"It's perfectly plausible that someone stopped her and asked her to give it to Lady P.," I added.

"One of the staff?"

"Yes, but the staff never spoke to the guests, and anyway why bother poisoning Lady P. when she was going away forever as far as they were concerned the next day. And one of our party could hardly hand a glass of poison over with a casual, "By the way, I'm not too keen on Lady P.; will you poison her for me?"

"Perhaps I was being a little simplistic," admitted Lewis. ("Ha!" I thought.)

"Someone could have left it outside the door," said John.

"What, on the floor?"

We all shook our heads.

"Perhaps it was Tubby after all," I said.

We all three fell silent. The sun was descending into the buttercup meadow; some swallows gathered on a telegraph wire, and a comfortable peace descended. I felt I could sit here forever.

"Do you mind if I have a cigarette?" John asked.

"I would rather you didn't," said Lewis. "I gave it up when my wife died – a sort of apology for her cancer." A look of great sadness crossed his face – I suppose he was in his late sixties or early seventies, and at that moment he looked an old man. But the look didn't last. He leant forward.

"You said Tubby was in shock and did what he was told. It wasn't until he got back and the neighbours start gossiping, that he started putting two and two together, and it struck him that he had been – what is the colloquial expression … ah! 'stitched up'. Then he contacted Sammy because he didn't want the police involved, but he did want to find out the truth. Have I got this right?"

"Absolutely," I said.

"Hmm, I wonder what Tubby intends to do with the truth – if he finds it?"

"I don't think he wants to do anything – he just wants to know."

Lewis pulled a face.

"If someone had killed my wife, I would not only move heaven and earth to find out who had done it, I should want to see justice done."

"Yes," said John who was less in awe of Lewis than me, "but you're not Tubby, and it would be pretty difficult to pin anything on anyone without a body."

"Habeas corpus," I said helpfully, but neither looked

impressed.

Lewis continued: "Then Sammy handed it all over to you... Have you contacted him again?"

"Sammy? Well, no," I said, "he made it pretty clear that he didn't want any further involvement. Anyway, I think he was going to Tunisia to do another bridge holiday."

"And Tubby?"

"Oh! Tubby! Well that's rather strange, we can't get hold of him," John grinned. "Mark thinks Tubby's been murdered, done in by Bethan, or kidnapped by Trevor!"

"No, I don't," I said indignantly. "You suggested that. Actually, I don't think anything melodramatic has happened."

"No," said Lewis thoughtfully, "Tubby was such an ordinary sort of fellow, the sort of person you imagine going through life with very little of moment occurring – and yet extraordinary things *have* happened to him. He married Lady P. for a start, and then finds her unexpec-tedly deceased, and is even now, I suppose, a sort of accessory after the fact..." he looked first at John and then at me rather keenly; he had very piercing eyes, "...as of course, you are yourselves."

A note of acerbity had crept into Lewis' voice. I felt, as a schoolboy, it would not have been pleasant to have been summoned to his study, and I found the words 'accessory after the fact' rather disquieting.

"For the sake of argument," he continued, "we assume Tubby wants to know the truth. Was his wife murdered, and if so, was it Bethan? Now, what exactly..." (I had begun to dislike Lewis 'exactlys.' They implied that this was very little exactitude in John and my way of proceeding) "... did Tubby say about Bethan?"

"He thought she said, 'Here's your whisky and I hope it kills you.'"

"While she was standing at the door? Oh, Look there are two red admirals!"

We looked, and somehow the sight of the butterflies sunning themselves seemed to remove the whole business into the realms of fantasy.

"But you didn't ask her?" said Lewis reproachfully. "You

went all the way to Wales and you didn't ask her?"

"Ask her what?" I said tetchily. I was getting rather tired of being told off. "And," I added spitefully, "we were rather thrown by her accusations about *you.*" Lewis frowned.

"About me? You didn't mention that."

"Well yes – and Janet…. wandering about."

Lewis looked thoughtful. "What did she say?"

"She said she saw you and Janet wandering about that night."

Lewis held up his hands in mock horror: "*Sighted wandering about at night!* Now there's a sign of guilt if ever there was one! Obviously Janet or I must be the murderers… Were we working independently or in collusion, I wonder? I hope you have your handcuffs at the ready to make a citizen's arrest."

"Shucks, we forgot them!" smiled John.

"Where was I wandering about, I wonder?"

I felt rather foolish. "I'm not entirely sure. We didn't ask."

"And Janet?"

"Again, we didn't ask."

"And was there anyone else wandering about?" I smiled foolishly.

"We didn't ask," said John. Lewis gazed out over the meadow, into the far corner where it disappeared into a copse.

"Bethan was right; I was wandering about that night, about half eleven. That is why I asked you what time Tubby woke you. I may well have gone past Tubby's room, although I can't vouch for that, as I don't know what number room he occupied – but, of course, you have to take my word for that. Perhaps I'm lying; perhaps I had a glass in my hand, saw Bethan standing outside, and handed it over to her, asking her to give it to Lady P. I imagine I'd have said something along the lines that the girl at the bar had forgotten Lady P.'s order, and I'd said I would bring it up as I had to go that way."

"Did the girl at the bar really say that?"

"Oh, Mark," said John, "of course she didn't."

"You must verify your facts," said Lewis. "You only have to ask Bethan; you could ring her now, if you like. I'm just going in to make us some tea. Would you mind Earl Grey?"

"Can I help?"

"No, thank you, John, just sit there and ponder my guilt – or alternatively, ring Bethan!" We did neither.

When he returned, he brought tea in a silver pot complete with silver jug, sugar basin and tongs. There was also a large, sticky cake."

"Did you make it?" I asked.

Lewis laughed, "One of the better things about being a widower is that there are always plenty of ladies feeling sorry for me, or, alternatively, looking for an excuse to further their acquaintance with me. A widower is an easy target. I have a constant supply of cakes," he sighed, and looked uncharacteristically angry. "I would rather be left alone."

"So why *were* you wandering about?" asked John.

"Actually, it's quite simple. I had had a couple of drinks in the bar with Simon and walked back with him to his room. I don't think he's a drinking man, so I thought I ought to be sure that he got back safely…"

"I know what Mark is thinking," interrupted John."

"What am I thinking?" Actually I was annoyed; I felt he had interrupted Lewis when he may have been going to say something else.

"You are thinking," said Lewis, "and John must be too, otherwise he wouldn't have mentioned it, that I am not the murderer after all, and that the murderer was Simon – who killed her in a drunken rage."

"He's hardly the type," argued John, who hadn't had much time for Simon. "He wouldn't have the balls."

"Actually, I'm not so sure," I said. "It's the shy, introverted ones who bottle things up that crack in the end. I mean Simon has been simmering with hatred for Lady P….."

"Except that he hadn't," said John, "because, if you noticed, she hardly ever had a go at Simon."

"For a very good reason. Now, can I offer you another piece of this cake?"

"What reason? And yes, please." I held out my plate.

"Are you ready for the bombshell?"

"Yes!" For once John was as eager as I to know the truth.

"Simon had paid for Lady P. and Tubby to go on the holiday!"

"No!"

"Why?"

"Because he's her nephew."

"Nephew! Simon?"

"Well, not exactly a nephew, but a cousin once removed." Lewis smiled at our surprise. "Let me put you in the picture. Simon has quite recently been left rather well off by the death of his father – a distant scion of the enamel urinal manufacturer who fathered Lady P. He got talking to Lady P. at his father's funeral and mentioned that he had booked to go on this bridge holiday. Apparently she said, in her usual charming manner, that seeing as he was about to find himself rather well off, he could pay for her and Tubby to go as well. So he said yes."

"But why? Why on earth should he?" I was astounded.

"Because, basically, he's a good chap, and apparently Lady P. had been kind to him as a boy... Yes, I know it's hard to imagine and no, Mark, I don't think he polished her off to prevent further calls on his purse. I think he acted out of gratitude or just plain kindness in paying for her; he told me that she had once been really pretty wealthy, and he felt sorry to see her looking down at heel. So, now he had got a bit of money he thought, 'well, charity starts at home', and wrote out a cheque. As I said, basically, he's just a good chap – which, incidentally, I've heard corroborated since, because I know the headmaster of the prep school he teaches at. Simon's not the greatest teacher in the world, but he's kindly and sympathetic.

"Well!" I said. A red admiral had settled itself on the tablecloth and was trying to extract nectar from an embroidered rose.

"What did you talk about, you and Simon?" asked John unexpectedly. "I didn't know you were particularly matey.

Why were you drinking with him anyway?"

"Simon's a hard person to get to know," said Lewis slowly. "I've always rather prided myself – I suppose through my job as headmaster, on being able to understand people – and their motives. Send a boy to my office, I could generally work out what was going on in his mind, see to the bottom of the problem. Take the bridge holiday; I'd got a notion about most people there: the Skorskis – he with his little bag and his cheating, she with her repetitive garrulity, Lady P. with her rudeness, and so on, but Simon was something of a cipher. So when he happened to leave the bridge room at the same time, I thought this is the last chance to find out what makes him tick."

"And did you?"

Lewis laughed, "Well, no, not really, but I did find out that Lady P. was his cousin!"

"What else did you talk about?"

"I think you're a more thorough interrogator than Mark, John! What else did we talk about? Let me see… it is a few weeks ago, you know. I must have asked him about his school – which isn't far from here, and I got the impression that he had a bit of a problem with discipline, but that he tried to do his best. Very conscientious, I thought. Oh yes, we talked bridge; normally he's not a very good player, but we discussed that hand – do you remember, when North opened two no trumps and South had ten hearts, and he came up with the correct bidding – which I must say Janet and I signally failed to do… But I did most of the talking; he is painfully shy – which was why I bought him a couple of g and ts, but even after that he didn't volunteer much. When we had exhausted the subject of teaching, there didn't seem much else to say; as you suggested earlier, we didn't really have a lot in common."

He paused. "Well, if you want to worm out my secrets, you had better go and see Simon; he's only nine or ten miles from here – the school's called Heathward House, but… On second thoughts, I think it would be kinder to leave it for a week or so, because they've only just gone back for the

Autumn term and I imagine it'll all be a bit much for him at the moment. As I say, I think he has a good deal of trouble with discipline. And of course, something you may not have thought of, assuming that he didn't bump off Lady P. – and I must admit I share John's views over Simon's capabilities as a murderer, he may be rather shocked to hear of her death."

"He may have heard already through his family." I said.

"He may... but I didn't get the impression they were close. I think that funeral where he met Tubby and Lady P. was the first time he'd seen her since he was a child."

We had stayed longer than planned. There was the first sensation of chill in the air, and the sun was nothing but a rim over the meadow.

"You are probably right; we won't bother Simon today."

"Your reason for coming to visit me was that you wanted advice, but I suspect you came to see if I was the guilty one – after all I had been seen *walking about at night*! Oh, and what was my motive?"

"We hadn't given that much thought," said John.

"Perhaps you will be able to think of one on your way home."

"No," I said, "we didn't really think you'd done it, Lewis. We really did want some advice."

"Hmm," he gave me an old-fashioned look, "I suspect that like most people who ask for advice, you really prefer your own way of working."

"No, really, we would value your advice, wouldn't we John?" John grunted; he's not a person who likes being told what to do.

"Well, if you are going to continue with any success, you do need a plan. I think this rather dilettante way of proceeding must stop."

"Go on, then," said John.

I wondered whether, had Lewis been gay, John would have fallen for him. Or maybe, I thought, that was why John didn't particularly like Lewis – he secretly fancied him!

"This is what I suggest: you didn't find out much from the Macalisters, so go and see Janet – but you must have a list of questions, and write up notes of your interview afterwards."

"It doesn't sound much fun," I said, "and how are we meant to get hold of Janet?"

"Janet has a mobile."

"Ah! And you have the number?"

"I have it somewhere because I remember her giving it to me at the bridge table that last night, but I honestly don't know what I did with it; I only took it as a matter of courtesy. I didn't imagine our paths would cross again. A disturbed girl, a good thing she got away from those parents. I'll have a good search around and let you have it."

"Okay," said John, "so who do you recommend we should see next?"

"What about the Skorskis? After all…" Lewis' face creased into a smile, "he certainly looks like a villain – when he's sitting down!"

"I was thinking of Carol next," John said.

"I think you'll be unlucky there."

"Why?"

"I remember her saying she was off to Tunisia; another bridge holiday, I believe."

"I don't know how people can afford to keep going on bridge holidays," said John, for whom money was still rather a sore point after the purchase of my birthday pot.

He paused, "And come on Lewis, what else? You look as if you want to say something." As I'd thought, John was getting rather irritated at having to accept all this advice.

"I don't mean to come the headmaster at you both, but the habits of a lifetime are hard to break and I think you should address two issues, first: be guided by probabilities – pace John's suspicions. It does seem to me that Lady P.'s probable cause of death was a heart attack; after all, doctors, even Italian ones, don't sign death certificates lightly. But if you really think she was poisoned, my money is on a member of staff wanting to give Lady P. a nasty surprise, possibly misjudging the dose, and handing Bethan the glass. I'm sorry to disappoint you, but I don't really see any of our fellow guests cut out for murder - as unpleasant as Lady P. was, and much as they might have enjoyed the result."

"What's the second thing?" asked John bluntly. I knew that like me, he suspected Lewis was probably right, but didn't want him to be.

"Well, since you ask, it's this: I have a pretty broad back; you develop quite a thick carapace as a headmaster, and I don't mind too much when you come to accuse me of murder. But you have already managed to upset Bethan and, by the sound of it, the Macalisters, and although I'm not familiar with the laws pertaining to libel, I think you should be a little more careful if you intend carrying on with your enquiries."

He looked rather seriously from John to me, "Don't you think?"

We were both silent, and I felt that Lewis would not have made either of us a prefect this term.

Chapter 8: Simon

John lit a cigarette and for some time we drove in silence, both chastened by Lewis's last words. Then John spoke, quite suddenly,

"Why don't we go and see Simon? It's almost directly on the route, only about six miles away, and it would save us coming all this way again."

"Lewis said to leave him until…"

"That's why I'm saying let's go now."

"Do you think Lewis has some reason for stopping us going, then?"

"No, not exactly. But I kind of feel I'd like to do something he had told us not to do, like making a rude sign behind his back. I'm not really a member of his fan club and I get a bit tired of that look he gives us – what's the word?."

"Supercilious."

"Could be."

"Well after all, he was a Headmaster."

"Well, he's not one now, and I don't like being treated as if he's caught me wanking behind the bike sheds. Shall we go?"

"I rather think we said we wouldn't."

"I can't see that it matters what we said; it's nothing to do with him whether we go and see Simon or not. Anyway, if we're going to go, we have to turn off in a minute, so make up your mind."

"Well, he *was* a headmaster and he obviously knows about pressure on staff at the beginning of term, and Simon's hardly the toughest guy I've ever met. I think we ought to respect that."

"Because he's a wimp?"

I could see that this wasn't so much about of cocking a snook at Lewis, but more about whether I adhered to Lewis sort of values or jettisoned them in favour of John's more pragmatic ones; in other words it related to the question of our disparate personalities. He took his eyes off the road for a moment and looked at me.

"Well?"

"Alright, John, we'll go."

He sighed and stopped the car, then turned to me and said, "We don't have to go, Mark." And of course, I said, "Yes, I think we should go, I think you're right." He touched me gently on the shoulder, "Not if you don't want to." John can be very sweet.

"Come on, let's go." So we went. And against all Lewis' injunctions about working from a plan, we prepared no questions; somehow it seemed too much like hard work.

"I regard us as inspired amateurs," I said.

"Amateurs alright," said John.

We drove up a long avenue of limes and the scent wafted through the windows. After a minute or so, a large Palladian villa came into sight: HEATHWARD HOUSE PREPARATORY SCHOOL (*Boys and Girls Entered for all Major Public Schools*).

"I'm glad I didn't go to a posh school," said John parking next to a Merc and looking critically at the board.

"You might have had a nice headmaster like Mr Lewis."

On closer inspection the school looked in pretty poor nick, the roof looked as though it could do with a few million spent on it, and one of the stone lions outside the front door had lost its nose, which seemed to indicate the general state of the place.

"There doesn't seem to be anyone about," said John. "We should have thought it was no good calling at this time – look it's nearly seven o'clock."

"John, it's a boarding school."

"Looks more like a prison to me." John disapproves of privilege, although I notice he is not always so averse to a bit where it concerns himself.

"Go on, ring, then." The bell didn't seem to work so I hammered with my fists.

Eventually a middle-aged woman whose face was framed by an enormous blonde beehive hairdo, appeared at the door in a navy uniform with a badge saying 'MATRON'.

"Yes?" She regarded us suspiciously.

"I wonder if it would be possible to see Simon Johnson?"

"People don't usually visit after teaching hours. What do you want?"

"Simon Johnson," said John briefly.

"Poor old Simon, what's he done now?" said Matron.

"Nothing; we're just old friends."

"Oh, well, perhaps you'll cheer him up; he always gets into a bit of a state at the beginning of term. The children play him up, I'm afraid."

John looked a bit shame-faced; Lewis had obviously been right after all. Seemingly, though, Matron had decided we were bona fide, and ushered us along a corridor chattering away in quite a friendly manner: she hated the beginning of term too, and here she was on her own, it was a very lonely job etc.. I wondered if she had designs on John – or even me!

She led us to a staff room that was grubby, and smelled of stale cigarettes. "You'll have to wait here. He's on dorm duty and there'll be the usual sort of chaos going on. I'll let you know when he's finished. What name did you say?"

She looked round the room critically and raised her voice. "All right there, then, Cuthbert?" Waiting for no reply, she made for the door, her beehive leading the way like a Davey lamp.

Cuthbert emerged from clouds of foul-smelling pipe smoke, an old bloke something like a picture of Father Time or God, sitting at the far end smoking away (John looked pleased), and doing a crossword. He looked up in a not unfriendly way.

"Arbuthnot-Jones. No use talking to me, I'm stone deaf. Smoke if you like, can't do with all this PC stuff. Where I come from PC meant Police Constable. Don't do much teaching now…"

"Hardly surprising, "said John

"Eh?"

"We've come to see Simon Johnson," I shouted, thinking this a golden opportunity for gathering some background information.

"Who?"

"Simon Johnson."

"Ronson? Don't know him."

"Johnson," we yelled together. Arbuthnot-Jones regarded the dusty air as if he would catch motes of sound, and perhaps he did, for when I had given up expecting any further response, he remarked, "Oh young Johnson. A poor stick, bit namby-pamby, but come into some money, they tell me. Wish I had. Doesn't have much to say for himself, no use saying anything to me anyway. I play a game of three-handed bridge with him and Matron. I make the most terrible mistakes, teehee!" The old fellow laughed gleefully, "I say diamonds when I mean spades, but they don't mind. Matron has her gin and Johnson doesn't get a word out anyway... Mind, other people here do, though. I see them complaining about me, but I can't hear a word they say; makes them mad to see me sitting there beaming. Do you know, if I come back in another life, born again, I should ask to be born deaf, don't have to listen to a lot of fools."

He returned to his crossword and John lit up. I could find no suitable occupation and even caught myself about to adopt Tubby's thumb twiddling. I stared round at what was a pretty uninspiring room: a duty roster and a calendar showing August (it was September), a pile of telephone directories and a football shirt labelled STANNINGS lying on a broken chair. I felt for poor Simon forced to spend his days here. I supposed that his shyness and inadequacy doomed him to such an existence. Perhaps inheritance would make his life a bit easier. Perhaps he could leave. Why didn't he leave?

Nobody spoke. A daddy-long-legs dangled in a corner, shrieks of children being silly wafted down from above. Then Arbuthnot-Jones looked up from his crossword.

"Can't do nine down; 'He entertains work from eternal springs'. Four letters, should be easy."

"Hope," said John. (He's good at crosswords, but not as good as me!) But his words were not heard; instead Mr A-J began seemed to want to revert to Simon. At first I thought we would hear nothing new, but then he chuckled.

"Dark horse, young Simon Johnson. Bit of a soft spot for the ladies, I think – and has a bit of success too. Never think it, would you? But there's a very attractive young lady…"

Unfortunately we were to hear no more, as Matron chose that moment to re-appear. She looked with affection at our elderly friend.

"You still here, Cuthbert? I'll bring your sandwiches in a minute." But meeting with no response, she turned to us, or rather to John – I think she fancied him. "Come with me, duckie. I've told Simon you're here. He was very surprised – couldn't think who you were for a bit."

She led us along an endless scuffed corridor and up a staircase, talking as she went.

"I'm taking you up to the prep room because he's on duty and he's not allowed to leave them until lights out. We all work very long hours here. Mind you, I shan't spend much longer here; I've had enough of this place – I should think Simon has too, the kids play him up rotten… Listen!"

We listened; a chorus of childish voices shrieked something that sounded like: 'Simon, Simonetta, we're coming to getcha." And Simon's voice, hesitant and resigned, pleaded:

"My name is Mr Johnson; please don't call me…"

Matron stuck her head through an adjacent door:

"And you can shut up, William Tyler, or I confiscate your tuck box." Silence fell and Simon emerged; in the school setting he looked even younger, smaller and more vulnerable than I remembered. He smiled nervously from behind the familiar huge glasses.

"I'm sorry….I, er…"

"Take them into the Prep Room, Simon," said Matron impatiently.

"Oh, oh yes, of course…"

"You couldn't spare a fag, could you?" said Matron, looking at John. "I'm right out and its miles to the village – and Cuthbert's only got his pipe."

"Have the packet," said John. Matron beamed and took it without any pretence of hesitation.

"You're a star; you can come again anytime."

We went into a small scruffy room smelling of chalk and old trainers and stood there in silence. When John and I are in company he usually prefers me to initiate conversation, basically because he is shy, but also because he prefers me to be the one that makes the silly mistakes. So now we all three stood there, everyone, it seemed, waiting for me to say something, Simon not even having the courage to ask us to sit down, just looking round, smiling rather foolishly. There were, in fact, three incongruous chairs that looked as they had once belonged somewhere rather better, but had gravitated to the dreary Prep Room to spend their last days there before they collapsed. John sat down on a sort of scarlet satin throne, and I seated myself with care on an enormous oak affair, leaving a thin rickety chair for Simon. I decided it was time for business.

"I hope you don't mind us popping in on you unexpectedly like this, Simon..." I didn't give him time to comment, "but we've just been having lunch with Lewis and he wondered whether you had heard the sad news? We thought you must have done because... (I thought this a rather clever way of introducing the fact that we knew that Lady P. was related to him) of course, she was family."

Confusion and then comprehension were expressed on Simon's face.

"Oh yes...yes, poor Auntie. Tubby wrote to tell me."

Presumably, I thought, before he'd started getting worried about it all.

"He didn't say much, only a line or so, but I wrote, of course I did. I didn't really know what to say... he just said a heart attack, and the funeral was over... I thought he might have asked me to go... I didn't know she had a bad heart; I think it must have happened soon after she got back to England. I mean, she seemed fine when we were on holiday – and we were told it was Tubby who had got ill that night. They missed the plane because of it."

John and I exchanged glances; I felt it was time for John to take over.

"Your aunt died in Italy. Didn't Tubby say?"

"Italy? I don't understand."

"Yes, she died the last night. Sammy didn't want to upset people so he made out that Tubby was ill. Of course, if he'd known you were related, he would have told you."

Simon sat down and said in a bemused voice.

"My aunt died during that last night. My aunt?"

"Yes, and there's something else Tubby didn't tell you…" John was obviously going for the brutal approach, he had never much liked Simon, "Tubby doesn't think now she did die of a heart attack. He thinks it might have been something else."

"Something else?" Simon's eyes, surprisingly bright behind the enormous black glasses showed consternation. "What do you mean?" He paused, then he burst out, "You're saying she committed suicide? No! I'm sure she wouldn't have done that. No, no, she liked living, she…"

"Not suicide," I said and, rather conscious of being melodramatic, added "Murder. Tubby thinks someone may have murdered her…"

"But…he didn't say so in his letter, I mean, how… what happened? I don't understand!" He got up and started walking about.

"Well – and of course, this mustn't go any further, Tubby thinks her whisky was poisoned."

Simon turned and stared at me, the eyes behind the glasses huge. "But how? How could…? I mean how could anyone get poisoned whisky to her? How? Oh God, oh poor Auntie. Oh no, I can't believe it!" He looked at me and there were tears behind the glasses; he was naturally fair skinned and now he looked quite white. "Not Auntie, not her." He sat down with tears literally streaming down his face, and the rickety chair nearly gave way under him.

Well, I thought, if he's acting surprised, he's a very good actor; I had never seen anyone look so shaken.

He sat there with his head down, and then he lifted it and took off his glasses and without them he looked defenceless, like a child. While he was still in shock, as it were, I told a glib story about bumping into Tubby, how Tubby didn't want any trouble … just the truth … impossible to convict anyone …and so on.

He looked up and asked in his thin little voice why we were involved in it? This question had also been posed by the Macalisters, and I found it a difficult one to answer. After all, why were we involved? I could hardly say idle curiosity.

John however – as so often – came to the rescue.

"He knows we get around a bit, see a few folk playing bridge, thought we could put a few feelers out."

"What do you mean, 'a few feelers'? Find out who did it? Is that why you came? You thought I'd murdered her?" He wasn't angry, just puzzled, and the tears still steamed up his glasses.

"No, mate, we didn't," said John stoutly, "but we thought you might have an idea who did. It isn't just you we're asking, we saw Lewis this afternoon…"

"You've been talking to Lewis?" He paused. "Have you been talking to other people as well, about me?" Suddenly he seemed to get angry. "Who else have you been talking to?"

"Oh, nobody much," lied John. Like me, John obviously thought mention of Sammy, Bethan and the Macalisters was probably not helpful at this stage, "and we haven't been talking about you at all, only about your aunt, just for the record, to see if we could get any ideas." There was a pause. "Well, have you got any?"

"No," he looked hopeless, "nobody would want to kill her."

It hardly seemed a suitable moment for saying that most people who had ever met her, would happily have volunteered to polish her off. John, however, was less punctilious.

"Come on now, Simon, she wasn't that popular."

"I know," he said, dabbing ineffectively with his fingers at the wet patches on his face, "I know people thought she was … difficult, but that's not a reason to *murder* anyone! And, you see, I remember her when I was a child – we used to go and see her when she was married to her first husband, and it was all very grand. She had a lot of money, you know, and he, her husband, Uncle… what was he called…? I can't remember. Anyway, before he spent it all and got killed, she wasn't so … She was in love with him. Well, I don't know, I mean I haven't been in love…"

Arbuthnot-Jones's words flashed across my mind: 'Dark horse, young Johnson, dark horse. Bit of a success with the ladies, smart young girl…' Looking at Simon now, I found this very hard to believe. Perhaps Arbuthnot-Jones's eyesight was as bad as his hearing.

Simon replaced his glasses, and with them back on his face, he seemed more composed.

"She was very kind to me. I can remember…it's a bit embarrassing, I was about twelve and the other kids had been calling me names and …things, and I think Mummy might have said something about it to her, and she… I can see her now coming out of their dining room – it was very dark in there and I used to be frightened – and she shouted at me, 'Come here, you!' You know the way she has… had, and I was very scared, but she made me go and stand by her, and I remember thinking how big and ugly she was… And she said, 'Don't take any notice of them, Simon. Looks aren't everything, you know, look at me, I've done all right'… But of course she hadn't because her husband – Raymond, that was his name – spent all her money. Anyway, then she gave me ten pounds – ten pounds! – and it really cheered me up and I didn't feel so bad then. So when she wanted to go on this bridge holiday…"

"You coughed up?"

"Yes. I thought I owed it to her. But instead of doing her a good turn – I killed her!"

"What?" John and I must have spoken in chorus.

"Well," he seemed oblivious of the impact of his words, "if I hadn't sent her to Italy she would still be alive, wouldn't she. Nobody would have poisoned her. She'd still be alive."

"Ah," I said. I think we were both a bit disappointed that he wasn't making a personal confession.

"And you don't have any idea who it might be…? After

all, she upset quite a lot of people on that last night."

"Did she? I don't remember."

"Yes. Bethan and Megan…"

"Oh, but they were very nice. I don't think…"

"And Carol? What about Carol?"

He hesitated, but only for a split second, and then he said carefully, "No, I'm sure she wouldn't have done a thing like that."

"And what about the others….the Skorskis for instance?"

A visible tremor ran through him: "Why do you mention them? Why do you bring their name into it?"

"Well, they were part of the bridge group, weren't they?"

He looked relieved. "Oh, them, oh yes…. I mean, no, I don't think they would have…"

Suddenly he brightened up. "Perhaps it's all a mistake." He wiped his nose and looked thoughtful. "That's what it is, a mistake."

"No," said the unforgiving John. "Someone poisoned her. Where were you on that last night?"

"Me?" He stared at John.

"Yes, you."

"Well, when do you mean?"

"After the bridge, what did you do?"

"I had a drink with Lewis, but...," he tried to look fierce, but only succeeded in looking scared, "I don't see why you should ask me all this. Who told you to?"

"Tubby, like we said." John had no patience with Simon at all, but I did have some sympathy. After all, he was clearly pretty traumatised by the news of his aunt's death, and this was making him even more irritatingly nervous than usual. I thought he deserved a little kindness.

"We're only asking questions so that Tubby will get a clearer picture of everything."

"Oh," he seemed a little happier. "Why doesn't he ask all this himself?"

"Because he's upset."

He nodded.

"Yes, poor Tubby, he must miss her dreadfully."

"And probably," I said, "it was one of the hotel staff that did it – your aunt wasn't very nice to them."

"Oh no, I am sure none of them would have done that. No, no." He sounded very decided. I was surprised. I'd have thought that latching on to this idea was a very convenient way of shifting the blame away from the bridge party as a whole – and away from Simon in particular, but he didn't seem to want to do that.

"And what did you do after your drink with Lewis?"

"I went to bed. In fact, Lewis walked me to my room because I was a bit tipsy. I hardly ever drink, just a half a glass of wine sometimes."

"Half a glass!" John's voice was infused with scorn.

"Did you see anyone wandering about on your way back to your room?"

"I don't think so, but I don't think I would have noticed. I *was* a bit tipsy."

"You would have noticed Bethan. You couldn't miss her. Did you see Bethan?"

"Bethan?" He looked taken aback. "Why should I see Bethan?"

"Was there anyone in the bar?" asked John, "while you were having your drink?"

"Oh yes, lots of people."

"Belonging to our party?" I asked, patiently.

"I can't remember… I think Janet came in. Yes, that's right, she looked very worried."

"No one else? Lewis said Carol came in."

"Oh! Yes, I don't know…" He rubbed his hair which he wore very short. "Please, I think I should like to be on my own now."

He looked up at John pathetically. "It's very kind of you to want to help, but I don't understand." His eyes looked strange and wet behind the glasses and he repeated, " I don't understand …any of it."

We took pity on him – or rather I did; John had just had enough; we told him not to be too upset and to keep the whole business to himself. Then we left. As I turned and caught a last sight of his slight figure huddled in the rickety chair, I couldn't really imagine him having either the wit or the guts to poison anyone. And as we walked down the corridor we heard naughty children's shrieks, then a cry of "Simon, Simon…" and an eight year old head peeped out and, seeing we weren't the expected quarry, quickly withdrew. John opened the door and four boys in four beds regarded us as if butter wouldn't melt in their mouths.

"Listen, you" said John, "don't you go playing up Mr Johnson tonight. He's had a bit of bad news and he doesn't need any hassle from you lot." He shut the door.

"That was good of you, John."

"I hate rich kids," he said.

As we walked back past the staff room, we could see Arbuthnot-Jones sitting there fast asleep. It occurred to me that we ought to ask him about Simon's so-called girlfriend, but somehow it didn't seem appropriate, and anyway he wouldn't have heard.

As we approached the front door we saw Matron through an open door in what I suppose was her office; the television blared out and she was lying on the sofa with a bottle of gin on the table next to her, clouds of smoke billowing out. She turned and waved. "Come up and see me sometime, boys," she called.

We beat a hasty retreat.

Chapter 9: We have unexpected visitors

The next morning a very surprising thing happened over breakfast. John was eating the egg and sausages which he always cooks before going off to work. We had done a lot of discussing since our visit to Lewis and Simon, even more than we had done since my first meeting with Sammy in Soho. I liked the feeling of togetherness it brought, because although we were close, we tended to live rather separate lives. It's what we thought best when we first set up house together, but for me this desire for separateness is a pretence, and I could cheerfully spend all my time with John. I'm sure this is why I wanted to continue what I called 'our investigation,' even though we might be getting into deep waters.

We did, in fact, see our way a little more clearly now: we would have to be careful that no-one else thought we were accusing them of murder, something we had to date handled rather badly and, as Lewis said, we must begin working with some sort of plan – though what sort of plan we couldn't really decide.

Over breakfast we talked about our suspects. We pretty much dismissed Isabel and Trevor, not because we thought they couldn't have done it, but because we had no idea what they had been doing that last night – we had forgotten to ask! However, we decided that we definitely *did* need to go and see Janet – but we would have to wait until Lewis found her phone number.

John didn't altogether trust Lewis, and thought we shouldn't have taken him into our confidence, but why should Lewis who had spent his life dealing with difficult parents, and had appeared unruffled by Lady P.'s rudeness, suddenly decide to murder her? And, indeed, he had seldom been the butt of Lady P.'s remarks because of all of us, bar Sammy, he dealt with her the most diplomatically.

And then there was Simon. He had certainly seemed very surprised and upset, but could that just have been an act? If so, it was a very good one and, anyway, we both doubted that he had it in him to put on such a show of grief if he didn't feel it, let alone carry out the business of murder. And there again, what was his motive? Simon, we thought, must have been the only person in the world who was actually fond of Lady P.

And what about all the other 'old friends', those as yet unvisited by Watson and Holmes? Carol was probably the person Lady P. had been rudest to. She was not a pleasant person herself, but did her endless prying into other people's business make her the sort of person who wouldn't be too particular about taking matters further? But murder?

Then there were the Skorskis – whose very name seemed to alarm Simon. Now that was odd. *She* wasn't very sinister, but he certainly was – or would have been if he had been a foot taller! And he certainly cheated at bridge. But, as John pointed out, cheating at bridge doesn't make you a murderer.

Then there was Janet with her mysterious nocturnal wanderings, whose whereabouts nobody knew. Simon said she had come into the bar looking worried and Bethan said that she had seen her running down the corridor. Had Janet some reason for wanting to get rid of Lady P.? Janet was odd – possibly unhinged? Had she done it while the balance of her mind was disturbed?

"But," pointed out John, waving a piece of toast at me, "we talk about all these people, but we come back to the same question: how did anyone actually get the glass of poison to Lady P., if it wasn't Bethan?"

I nodded; at the end of the day it was still Bethan who had handed over the glass. Really the most obvious suspect *was* Bethan – unless Tubby was lying about her, but why should Tubby lie? Why, in fact, should he stir the business up at all? Was it all some kind of subtle double bluff on Tubby's part? But then, there was nothing very subtle about the thumb-twiddling Tubby. And why did he now seem uninterested in the whole business? Really there was no getting away from the fact – Lewis had been right, we needed to talk to Bethan. I suggested a phone call.

"Saying what?" asked John buttering the last piece of

toast.

"Perhaps saying we were sorry she had misunderstood what we were saying and, er, could we come and see her again and er…"

"Yes?"

"Actually, John, I don't think you're being terribly helpful."

"Well, I don't fancy going all that way down to Wales and have the dogs set on us."

"She didn't set the dogs on us."

"She threatened us with Irfon"

"He was about five foot two."

"Mad."

"How do you know?"

"Sensed it." He stood up and ran his hands under the tap. "Anyway, I must go."

And just as John said these words and was drying his hands on the kitchen towel, our attention was caught by a taxi drawing up on the road outside. It stopped and nothing happened, no one got out, and it was too far to see who was inside.

"We've got visitors," I said.

"*You* have," said John, "I've got to go to work."

"Oh! John, wait!"

We both stared. The passenger door opened, but whoever was inside seemed unable to extricate themselves. Then the taxi man got out, and we saw him bend down and brace himself to help. A figure was coaxed out. We stood goggle-eyed.

"Jesus Christ!" said John, "It's Bethan!"

But he was wrong: it wasn't Bethan, it was Megan!

We stared in disbelief as the enormous figure of Megan began lumbering up the path. She was dressed in a huge brown tweed suit (Welsh wool), which somehow had the air of being her best, and she was carrying a suitcase.

"She's come to stay," I said.

"Oh, blimey," said John, "thank god I have to go to work!"

Megan pursued her course heavily and doggedly up the path; she bore a set expression on her face as if she was on the way to execution, and didn't appear to notice the two of us staring rudely out of the window. I went to let her in.

"Megan! What are you doing here? What a lovely surprise!" She stared at me in silence, tears glistening in her eyes. It occurred to me that everywhere John and I went we seemed to make people cry.

"It's a surprise, but it's not lovely, dear God, it's not," said Megan. What between the tears and the stentorian breathing from the effort of walking up the path, I thought I had better get her inside.

We settled her into a chair, but she wouldn't be separated from her suitcase which she held on to tightly.

"I'll make you a cup of tea, love," said John touching her arm gently. (I felt a ridiculous frisson of dislike for Megan; I am always jealous of those John treats with tenderness). She shook her head sadly.

"No, no tea, they'll give me tea at the station when they want to make me talk. I've seen it on the telly."

"Megan, love, what are you talking about?" He crouched down at the side of the chair. I could see this was one of the days that John was not going to be in work on time! She looked down piteously at John, her whole vast body wobbling with emotion.

"When I tell them I did it; I murdered her."

Now she looked directly at us, regarding first John and then me, and I thought that once, before she became fat and middle-aged, what a pretty woman she must have been. Even now, if you disregarded the rolls of flesh around the chin, you were struck by her smooth and creamy complexion and large vivid blue eyes. They didn't *look* like the eyes of a murderess (although as John was to comment later, 'what do you think murderesses' eyes look like, then?') and there was something appealing and defenceless about her.

"Rubbish, said John, "of course you didn't."

"I did," she sounded indignant, "it was me, not Bethan. I want you to take me to the station and then I can confess."

She stirred in her chair, but it was rather low and the attempt was too much for her.

"We don't think either of you did it," I interjected.

"And even if you did, no one's going to the police, because, whatever happened, no one can prove anything. And anyway; it was only Tubby muddling around, and now he's lost interest."

Megan looked up as if a little reassured, but then her face assumed its resolute look again.

"It was me."

"Now Megan, "said John, "I'll tell you what's going to happen: I have got to go work, but Mark's going to look after you, and you're going to tell him all about it – once you've had a nice cup of tea."

Poor John, it did seem hard to have to go to work at this point, just when Megan was going to talk. There were, I reflected, some advantages to being old and retired.

I made tea and I saw Megan's eyes wander to John's remaining sausage and linger about the toast rack.

"I didn't have much of a breakfast," she said. "They don't know how to make a decent bacon and eggs in England." She paused, "And I don't expect I'll be eating a Welsh one again."

She might be about to confess to murder, but she was still a large hungry lady. I headed for the kitchen.

While Megan ate her breakfast (her second lot of bacon and eggs, as it transpired), she started to open up. This was more or less what she said.

She was very tired of Lady P. and her rudeness and she thought it was time she was taught a lesson. So she filled up the glass from the bathroom with whisky, and stirred in three of her heart tablets, and then she waited for Bethan to get in the bath, then she walked up to Lady P.'s room on the next floor and handed her the whisky.

"I told her I hoped it would kill her. I didn't really mean it; I just wanted to teach her a lesson."

I sat considering this, and had some toast and marmalade

myself. It seemed transparently obvious that the story had not the slightest ring of truth about it, and had been concocted, I felt sure, to save Bethan. I picked on some salient points.

"But you and Bethan didn't drink, Megan. Where did you get the whisky from?"

"Bethan and I do have the occasional drop. Lord forgive us, we had a small bottle in the room." I felt that might be true.

"Did Bethan tell you about our visit?"

No, not Bethan, Irfon had told her when she visited the next day. He said that Bethan was very upset. Irfon used to go and fetch her twice a week so she could spend the day with Bethan at the farm, and he'd told her in the van. She had tried to talk to Bethan, but Bethan hadn't wanted to talk about it.

"She's very private, is Bethan," she concluded, and looked a little wistfully at the newly emptied toast rack.

"Well, Megan, if you did it – and I know you didn't – I can't think why you didn't come out and tell Bethan you had done it. If you didn't want her falsely accused, that is."

"That's why I've come now."

"Did you tell her you were coming?"

"No, but I told Irfon."

I was struck by another thought.

"But it couldn't have been you, Megan. Tubby said that Lady P. had told him specifically…" and here I wagged my finger to emphasise my point, "that it was Bethan she had spoken to."

Megan had an answer for that.

"Lady P. often called us by the wrong names, and it's not only her. People often get us the wrong way round, not being familiar with Welsh names. And it was dark in those corridors with those automatic sort of lights that switched off every couple of minutes. A great nuisance they were."

I wasn't convinced, but thought I would leave that for the moment. When had she decided to come and tell us, and why hadn't she gone to the police at home if she was so determined to tell the police?

She had spent the day with Bethan, and could see that she

was clearly upset, so when Irfon had taken her back home she had decided to come down by train, spend the night at a B&B and then come and confess it all to John and me so that we could take her to the station and explain everything to the police.

"But I told you, Megan, there's no question of the police being involved. Nobody wants to know – not the Italian police, not the hotel, not the English police, not even Tubby now."

Megan looked unconvinced. "He might change his mind."

"Well, even if he does, there's no case to answer. Lady P.'s ashes are at the bottom of Lake Como." Then Megan said a funny thing.

"They're always suspicious of someone who's been involved with police matters before."

"Have you been had up for murder, then?"

I smiled; I have never seen anyone look less like a hardened criminal than Megan.

"Oh no."

I thought she might explain her enigmatic remark, but she was silent and I suggested we adjourn to the sitting room, proposing that she might be more comfortable on the sofa. Actually, I rather feared for the chair.

I didn't know what to do or what to say, I wished John was here. He saw to the heart of a thing, saw what needed doing, what requirements other people had, and how these requirements should be dealt with, whereas I was pretty clueless in these matters, and here I was, saddled with Megan, without the faintest notion what to do. Would I really have to take her to the police station? And, if so, how on earth would I begin to explain everything: Sammy, Tubby, our visits to the Macalisters, to Lewis and to Simon? Nor did I relish the thought of describing to some young constable the night when it all happened when Tubby summoned us to his room. I thought of Lewis's 'accessories after the fact.'

Furthermore, Megan was obviously innocent, but she seemed to believe that Bethan wasn't. Well, perhaps she was and perhaps she wasn't, but it would all become extremely nasty and confusing once either of us tried to explain it all. For the first time, I began to wish that I had never met Sammy at the shop in Soho, and never started the business at all. All John and I had done was to upset people and make them cry – all about something that couldn't be proved anyway. I felt hopeless; in fact I felt like crying myself.

"I always have a cup of cocoa about eleven," said Megan wistfully. "I don't expect they let you have cocoa in prison."

I went and got a saucepan out and crashed about in the kitchen, I felt irritated with all this talk about prisons. I even began to worry about whether John and I could find ourselves getting banged up too.

"I think I'll go and powder my nose." Having come back ("better now,"), Megan clutched her cocoa and seemed inclined to relax. I sensed the urgency of her need to go and confess at the police station was beginning to recede.

"No one ever had a better friend than Bethan," she mused. "You can't imagine the things she's done for me."

Sitting opposite with coffee (I am not a cocoa lover), I wondered whether it would be politic to ask what things.

"Bringing up Irfon, as if he was her own."

"Oh! I thought…."

But what I thought and what Megan was about to tell me were forgotten in our shared amazement at the next turn of events: an ancient Morris Minor braked loudly outside, reversed to park in front of the house, and in the driving seat could be discerned an enormous purple shape – revealing itself as it emerged as Bethan.

"It's her!" murmured Megan in a voice of wonder – presumably here was a new manifestation of yet another of the extraordinary things that Bethan had done for her friend. However, I felt that Bethan's doing of amazing things was unlikely to favour me; I was scared to death.

"Perhaps *you'd l*ike to let her in," I said, and Megan positively nipped off the sofa, spilling cocoa over the (rather nice, pale blue) carpet unheeded. I went and got a cloth, rather relieved that mopping up the cocoa offered me a good excuse for *not* going into the hall, and would conceal my agitation. But, cloth in hand, I listened avidly.

"What on earth are you up to, you old silly sausage, coming all the way down here when you've not been out of the village on your own for three years, and on some madcap scheme, Irfon said! How did you know where they lived?"

"We exchanged addresses one day by the pool, don't you remember?"

"And why come all this way to see bogus old Sherlock there? Oh, my dear one." This was followed what sounded like kissing and crying noises and Megan's voice.

"Oh, I was so frightened, Bethan, getting on that train and then the trouble getting the taxi man to find me somewhere to stay, and the price you wouldn't believe, and then getting here, but they've been very kind, I told them…." Here her voice was lowered and a long muttering ensued.

"You what?" A shriek of incredulity.

"Well, I didn't want the police thinking it was you because of the… you know …. other."

I crept forward to catch what this 'other ' might be, but my subtlety was lost by the sudden appearance Megan's vast bulk thrusting in its way in through the sitting room door. Clad in an enormous purple garment the like of which I have not seen before, Bethan behind gave vent to a loud and terrifying "Ah!"

Alarmed as I was, I was still conscious of my duties as host.

"Good morning," I said loudly, twiddling my cloth for courage. "Would you like some coffee, or would you rather join Megan in some cocoa?" Bethan took up a stand by the sofa.

"Oh, I shan't be stopping." But I noticed her eyes stray in the direction of the chocolate biscuits. I decided it was time to be masterful.

"Please sit down. I think it is time for us both to be quite open."

"There was nothing open about you creeping up to Bryn Maw along with your fancy man, and accusing me of murder and upsetting Megan so she has to travel two hundred miles and come and perjure herself. Megan – who's not left the village on her own for three years!"

"Nobody's accusing anyone of anything. Lady P.'s remains are in the bottom of Lake Como, and even if there was a murder – which I doubt, nobody could possibly prove anything. The only person who wanted to know was Tubby, and even he's lost interest now."

Bethan looked unimpressed. "You could have saved yourself a journey to Wales, then."

I took a gamble – I like to think I have a certain amount of charm. "But we would have missed the best tea in the British Isles."

For a moment there was silence and then Bethan gave a grudging smile, and helped herself to a chocolate biscuit. Megan, seeing the smile, smiled too, and I added my smile to the general pool.

"I think I'll have that cup of cocoa now," she said when we'd all had enough of the smiling, "and you can tell me what you have been up to."

"Very well," I replied, and determined to capitalise on the feeling of good humour, I wagged my finger at her. "But you must tell me what you were up to, too."

"You drive a hard bargain, boyo."

So, having made another vat of cocoa, I told her from the beginning about meeting Sammy and then, with great trepidation, repeated what Tubby had said. So imagine my surprise to see her nod her head.

"He was quite right," she said, "I did poison her."

But Megan was having none of it. "Oh, Bethan, you didn't. I did."

"Don't be so bloody silly, love. I gave her that glass of whisky, so I poisoned her."

I began to see light.

"But you didn't put the poison in it in the first place?"

"Course I didn't. I've had quite enough dealings with the police in my time to want to get in trouble for that old bitch."

This second mention of 'trouble' was interesting, but I thought it was better to concentrate on the matter in hand.

"Did someone give you the glass, then?"

"Now, Mr Sherlock Holmes, I'll tell you what happened, seeing as you can't work it out for yourself." There was a faint muttering from Megan who seemed loath to relinquish the role of chief culprit.

"And you can be quiet, my girl. You're in enough trouble from me imagining I was guilty in the first place. Now here I am… Megan's in her bath and I'm remembering the knitting pattern I'd promised to that nasty Carol. Now I don't think she wanted it for a minute; what she wanted was to come and have a snoop round our room, nosy bitch that she was, but I said I'd give it to her, and give it I would. I always keep my word; I'm a great believer in that, aren't I, Megan?"

Megan conceded this to be the case.

"So I thought I'll go along and give it to her, otherwise I shan't remember when we have to get up at five, so I put my dressing gown on and along I go and find her room; and a long way it is, right over the other side and – like I told you back at the farm – I wasn't the only one roaming in the gloaming, and gloaming it was with that corridor light going off every ten seconds or so…"

"Who did you see?"

"There was the Headmaster man, I can never remember his name…"

"Lewis."

"That's right, Lewis."

"Was he on his own or was he with Simon Johnson?"

"I didn't see Simon. Mind you, you never noticed him anyway, poor weak lad, and then I almost bumped into that Janet, not all dowdy with her hair scraped back like usual, but with it all loose, hanging down her back, rushing along the corridor as if her life depended on it. She had a bottle in her hands, now I come to think of it – could have been whisky – and a minute or so after, there was her father going down the corridor as if he was looking for her."

"He wasn't her father," said Megan. I hadn't known this and was about to enquire into it further but Bethan was on a roll.

"Well stepfather or whatever he was, a nasty bit of work, if you ask me. Mind you, there were plenty of unpleasant people in our party."

"I hope you aren't getting at me, Bethan."

"That remains to be seen," she replied darkly.

"And then what happened?"

"Well I get to Carol's room and knock on the door. In fact I knock twice, quite loudly…"

I could imagine!

"… But she wasn't there, or if she was, she wasn't answering. So I think to myself, so much for wanting that knitting pattern, and I shove it under her door. I expect she's gone on one of her little night visits, I thought to myself."

"Night visits?" Here was yet more intrigue.

"Yes," continued Bethan, without answering my question, "so I set off back, thinking what a waste of time, but then I get to outside Lady P.'s room…"

"How did you know it was hers?"

"Because she was forever saying, 'Make sure they take up my goodnight whisky, Gino, Room 335,' – never a please or thank you, of course. And I thought to myself, well, this won't be a wasted journey after all… I'm never going to see this woman again, except tomorrow morning, but even she will be half asleep then, so I'll give her a piece of my mind now while I'm all fired up; tell her how she's made a misery of this holiday for Megan, and for a few others as well – and, as I stood there sort of composing my speech, along with the goodnight whisky comes…"

"Gino!" I interjected brightly.

"No, not Gino," replied Bethan. "Seems to me you do too much jumping to wrong conclusions, and I daresay Gino was otherwise engaged."

"Who, then?"

"One of the girls from the bar, I imagine…"

"Which one?"

Which was the one who had dared to take poison to Lady P.? I cast my mind back, but couldn't really remember any of them, just an amorphous pool of Italian womanhood who carried trays and stood patiently saying, "Si, Signor." And what an indictment of me that was!

However I felt less guilty when Bethan said, "Oh I don't know, they all looked much the same really, but I seem to remember this one was blonde. And anyway the light had gone off again, and I asked her to go and do the switch – I never could find them – and she muttered something in Italian and pointed to the door. I don't think she wanted to face that old woman inside."

" She wanted you to take the tray inside to Lady P.?"

"Yes, and I took the glass off the tray so she wouldn't have to come back after she'd done the switch, and off she went; the light came on, and I hammered at her ladyship's door."

"What did you say to her?" asked Megan spellbound. "You never told me."

"Well, to tell the truth, I let rip and afterwards I felt a bit ashamed of myself. I've got a temper on me, you see, it lands me in trouble."

I could vouch for the temper.

"So I put it to the back of my mind. Then, the next morning someone said Tubby had been taken ill, but I didn't know anything had happened to Lady P. I didn't know she'd died until you came to the farm." There was a pause. "It does seem funny to me, the way it was all hushed up by Sammy, and, of course, while I don't like to hear of people meeting sudden deaths – well, not usually, there are exceptions, mind, but I can't say I'm sorry she's at the bottom of the lake. I should think Tubby was delighted to stop twiddling his thumbs and tip her in. Speaking for myself, I should think if anyone did her in, it was him. And I, for one, couldn't blame him."

"You shouldn't say that, Bethan," said Megan shocked.

"Oh, you're too soft-hearted, love. She's no loss to anyone."

I was trying to absorb all this so that I could repeat to John, and to make some sense of it.

"I suppose," I said slowly, "that one of the staff she'd

been rude to, did it – perhaps not meaning to kill her, just to upset her stomach or something."

Megan said nothing. I think she was trying to work out if she should still be claiming responsibility for murder, or whether the moment for this had passed. Bethan, however, was having none of it, and made the same point that John had made when we first discussed it: why should they wait until Lady P. was going? What was the point of landing themselves with a lot of trouble, just when they were about to be shot of her?

"Someone gave the glass to the waitress – one of the GrandSlam bridge people, no doubt in my mind," said Bethan.

I thought how interesting it was that Bethan didn't want to pass the blame onto the staff at the hotel – which suggested to me that she was innocent and, being blameless, was only too happy to cast suspicion on one of her own party. Or perhaps, like us, she thought it was more fun if one of the people she had sat cheek by jowl with every night for a fortnight at the bridge table, had done it. But, at the risk of being a killjoy I had to point out (having already been through this with Lewis and John) that it was unlikely anyone would want to run the risk of being recognised as the person who gave the orders.

"Pooh," said Bethan, "by the time it all came out, everyone would have gone, and it wouldn't have been in anyone's interests to try and drag us all back from England. Then you've got the issue of identifying which girl had been carrying the whisky – staff come and go, and the hotel would be sure to get rid of whoever it was, if they thought there was likely to be any unpleasantness."

"I still think it would have been too great a risk; most of the people in our party were pretty distinctive and, after all, Tubby might well have made a fuss."

"Him!" I hadn't heard such scorn since John had reiterated Simon's 'Half a glass of wine!'

I turned to Megan. "Can we take it that you have retracted your confession? I mean you don't really want to go down to the police station now?"

"Of course she doesn't," said Bethan.

I thought they would probably decide to go at this point. Bethan had exonerated herself – always assuming I believed her, which I did – and she had exonerated Megan. However, neither seemed in the least inclined to depart.

"You've made things very comfortable here," said Bethan, having a good look about her. "I've never been keen on leather, but I must say I find this reclining thing is very pleasant. Nice view you've got out the back too."

She placed a cushion behind Megan's back and set about getting au fait with our investigations.

"Now, who else have you two been visiting to accuse of murder?"

It was now late in the morning and I got out the sherry. There was no demurring, and I thought the part of Megan's story that had related to the presence of a bottle of whisky in their room was probably true.

I started by telling them about our visit to the Macalisters.

"I don't much care for Janet's father, Trevor," I said when I had detailed the account.

"He's not her father," said Megan quietly. "Isabel told me she was widowed when she was quite young and left with Janet to bring up on her own. It was only later that she married Trevor."

"I wonder why she married such an awful man – she must have been a good-looking woman," I mused.

"Well," said Bethan, "he was quite a celebrity, you know. He did that children's programme, and one or two films and made some money doing the talking for advertisements – what do you call it?"

"Voice-overs?"

"Very likely. I daresay having been on her own and trying to bring up a child, she liked the idea of having a bit of money, going to the odd glamorous party and so on. Expensive clothes she had, didn't she Megan? Lot of cashmere, and that doesn't come cheap."

Suddenly we were all friends. Megan reclined on the sofa and Bethan had settled herself into my recliner with her feet up. I wondered how long they would stay.

"Of course, you must talk to Janet," said Bethan. It seemed to me that now she was getting quite interested in it all, she had no wish for the quest to be curtailed. And I felt pretty sure that she had not been responsible for poisoning the whisky, even though, of course, her story was quite uncorroborated.

"As I say," Bethan continued, "I saw her rushing down the corridor with Trevor obviously looking for her."

"I wonder where she was going?"

We all three shook our heads.

"Let's hope Lewis comes up with her number," I said.

I described our visit to Lewis.

"Fancy him living in a house like that," said Megan. She obviously had a child-like appreciation of things. She continued, "I think he was very upset by his wife's death. Cancer, I seem to remember he said it was. He must have idolised her; you should have heard him talking about her – talked and talked, didn't he, Bethan, that afternoon when the bridge was cancelled and the three of us went and had a cup of tea together. He even asked us into his room – he was next door to us – he had a photograph of his wife in a frame, all dressed in white.

"I couldn't see anything so special about her myself," interjected Bethan. "Fancy bringing a framed photo with you on holiday. Of course, that was why he disliked Carol so much."

"Why?" I couldn't see the connection.

"We oughtn't to say, really, should we, Bethan?"

"I don't see the harm." I was all ears.

"Well it was Megan, not me, who heard because I was asleep."

"What happened, Megan?"

Megan didn't seem to mind telling. "Well, Bethan was asleep. It must have been quite late, and only the second or third night of the holiday because Lewis was still partnering Carol at bridge. We'd thought Sammy had put them together because they were nearer in age, and partnered Simon and

Janet because they were the two youngsters…"

"Not that young," said Bethan, "Janet won't see thirty again. Though I'm not saying that he wasn't matchmaking; look you, stranger things have happened on bridge holidays."

I wondered if either Megan or Bethan had dreamed of meeting Mr Right at *Il Sole.*

"There I am lying awake…" continued Megan, warming to her tale.

"Megan doesn't sleep well…"

"And I heard a knocking on Lewis's door. Then I heard the door open and Carol's voice. I can't remember exactly what she said, but it was something like, "I thought you might be feeling a bit lonely. I know what it's like being on your own, so I've come to offer…" And she never did say what it was she was offering."

"I think we can all guess, don't you, Mark?"

"What did Lewis say?"

"I have never heard anyone so angry! He was very gentlemanly as a rule, but he told her plainly to get out – and he called her a very rude name which I wouldn't like to repeat, and said something I didn't quite catch about the good name of his wife. I could feel that anger coming right through the walls..."

"Megan's very sensitive to emanations."

"… And Carol was very upset. 'Well, I'm sure,' she said, 'I was only being kindly. I shan't be bothering you again. You can keep your precious wife.' She slammed the door and I heard her footsteps going away. And the next day there was Lewis partnering Janet, and Simon got Carol."

"Wouldn't have been much point trying her tricks on Simon," said Bethan. "Not much red blood there, I'd say. And she must be fifty if she's a day, and Simon can't be more than mid-twenties. Though I think she tried to get her own back on him for missing out on Lewis. She was forever niggling at him, and he always looked scared to death of her. But of course he was a poor player, - not much good at anything, really, poor soul."

"That's not what Mr. Arbuthnot-Jones said." And I told

them about my visit to Simon. They couldn't get over the fact that Simon was related to Lady P., and even more impressed by his paying for her holiday.

Then Bethan asked, "What time does your young man get back from work?"

I said he was usually back about four.

"Then I tell you what we'll do; we'll all have a nice game of bridge."

I was somewhat taken aback; the day was clearly going to be full of surprises.

"What about getting back?" I asked. "It's a long way."

"Well you've got a few bedrooms here, I daresay. Megan has her suitcase and always has a spare nightie, and we're much the same size. We wouldn't mind spending the night here." And so of course I had to ask them to stay.

"And now I think I should like a bit of lunch – and so would Megan, I daresay. She looks as if she's fading away."

I looked at Megan and we all laughed. Then I took them out to the Italian restaurant down the road. They ate as if they had not seen food for a year.

Over the meal – I was going to say we 'picked over the events as we picked over the food', but there was nothing picky about Bethan and Megan; they *loved* their food. I persuaded them to start with a plate each of antipasto, although I think they would really have liked spaghetti followed by spaghetti. We discussed our favourite suspects.

"I think it could have been that Gino," said Megan, her tongue loosened by the chianti. "You know that good-looking waiter that was always chatting up the other waitresses."

"Perhaps," said Bethan, "Now I come to think of it, Lady P. used to shout at him quite rudely about her goodnight drink – 'I don't expect to have to wait …' and so on."

"I thought we agreed it wasn't a member of staff," I reminded them.

"Well, who do you think, Mr Cleversticks, now you've decided it wasn't Megan or me?"

I didn't say that I hadn't entirely crossed them off my list – since neither had an alibi, but for something to say, I offered the Skorskis. Megan's baby blue eyes grew round, "Oh, do you think so?"

"No, not really," I was forced to admit.

"Don't you be so sure," countered Bethan. "Remember how rude she was to Claire on that last night, and how there was that row. And he's foreign."

"Oh?" I said. "That must have been after John and I had left – we didn't stay to the end. What happened?"

Bethan was only too pleased to put me in the picture, and I could well imagine the scene. I now retell it - with a little artistic license.

Apparently Carol and Simon had just won the rubber against Tubby and Lady P. and the Skorskis who had been sitting out, waiting for the 'Table up' shout, went over to play against Lady P. and Tubby.

"I never thought I'd have to spend my holidays playing against woofters and the dregs of Eastern Europe," remarked her ladyship as she saw the Skorskis setting off in her direction. Unfortunately Claire Skorski heard. "Hey what's that you're saying? I said what's that you're saying? Are you trying to be offensive? Are you trying to insult me and my husband?" Lady P. was entirely willing to enter the lists, there being nothing she enjoyed more than a good cut and thrust, no holds barred.

"Why don't you just sit down, stop talking for a change and make a bid, I don't want to be sitting waiting all night and nor does he." She jerked her head towards Tubby, and her huge lower lip wobbled aggressively. Karl Skorski's face registered nothing, but he took a firm hold on the little bag that accompanied him everywhere.

"Who knows what murderous thoughts were in his head," said Bethan.

Tubby started shuffling the cards, he always spent ages shuffling; I suppose it was the next best thing to thumb-twiddling. But Claire had got her dander up;

"I'm not sure I want to be sitting down at this table. I say, I don't want to sit down at this table, you may be a ladyship but manners maketh man, that's what the saying says, and you have the manners of a pig." She leant over the table and added "Honk, honk." A faint smile hovered over Karl Skorski's lips.

"'Onk," he corroborated. "I too say 'onk."

"Tournament Director!" roared Lady P. and Sammy came over. He looked a little strained, but managed the usual prolonged burst of laughter that rolled over the top of insults and broke like a great wave to drown them.

"Now," he said, "let's deal out a goulash and have a bit of fun. Come on Karl, you sit down …"Taking him by the arm and pushing him into the chair, "and you, my darling…" (this to Lady P.) "deal 'em out, two lots of five and one of three, and you, young Tubby, keep them all in order."

Peace was restored momentarily, but not for long: the goulash hand had produced a bizarre distribution and Karl hesitated a long time over his call of six hearts. When Claire passed, Lady P. again summoned Sammy: Karl's hesitation had given information to Claire, the game was unplayable.

"Are you accusing my husband of cheating again? Are you saying we spend our time cheating?"

"If the cap fits. It's not the first time he's been called a cheat, I'll be bound, nor the last, I should imagine."

Karl stopped smiling at this point and his furrowed face assumed a menacing air. He stood up, looking every inch his five foot two, and Claire threw her cards into the middle of the table. Tubby could be seen trying to pluck up courage to do something – and failing. People began to look up from their play to see what was happening and the whole thing threatened to become very nasty indeed. However before things could become violent, Sammy arrived on the scene.

"All change," he said. "Musical chairs time."

There was no resisting Sammy but Claire offered a parting shot:

"If there's one thing I'll be glad about tomorrow, it'll be never seeing you and your silly little husband again. In fact, the world would be a better place if nobody saw you again, I say if no one saw you again." And gathering up her husband and his bag, she went muttering off.

Then Sammy had a word with Lewis and laughed him and Janet across to the table. Apparently Janet had sat there scowling, but Lewis, as ever, had been most diplomatic, asking Lady P. whether she was packed and ready to go, and whether they were looking forward to getting back.

"Well," I said, "so it could have been the Skorskis after all." I could imagine him wielding a knife and smiling a sinister smile.

"It could have been anyone," said Bethan, "even you, Mark!"

Before I could protest, the waiter brought their spaghetti. Megan's face lit up.

"May we have some more bread, please?" asked Bethan.

After lunch Bethan made Megan go for a nap, ("she's not strong") and the sound of her snores combined with the after effects of a good lunch engendered a feeling of warmth and confidentiality between Bethan and myself.

"What shall you tell Tubby?" asked Bethan, "now you don't suspect Megan and me?"

"I'll tell him what you told me – that a waitress handed you the whisky and hence it must be one of the hotel staff, not you – or indeed any member of the GrandSlam Bridge party. And there will be an end to it."

"Do you think he will be happy with that, lay it to rest like?"

"Quite frankly I think he's lost interest."

"It seems odd after he was in such a taking about it, writing to Sammy and seeing you two. Do you think…" She leaned forward wobblingly, she had taken Megan's place on the sofa) "do you think he's been got at? Someone's told him to stop?"

"Well, John and I wondered that, but the only person who might have done so was you," I ventured daringly. "We hadn't told the others, then."

Bethan laughed, it was a rich pleasant sound.

"Well, it wasn't me," she replied comfortably and her eyes closed. Then they opened again. "Was it really true what you said about the parrot, speaking like Lady P.?"

"Absolutely."

"If I was Tubby, I'd ring its neck." She pondered, "I tell you something else odd; if the whisky was poisoned, where did the poison come from? There's not many people go on holiday with a packet of poison in their case."

"Megan claimed she had used her heart tablets. I suppose someone might have done that."

"There, that proves she didn't do it. Megan has a wonderful heart, she doesn't need heart tablets."

"And you?" I asked daringly.

"Nor me. You don't run a sheep farm with a dicky heart."

"Is Irfon looking after it while you're away."

"Yes, he's a wonder with the sheep, is Irfon."

"Bethan...." I'd been plucking up courage to ask ever since we had been sitting so cosy together, "tell me about Irfon. Is he your child, or Megan's?"

All sorts of emotions crossed over her face: surprise, sadness, anger and finally resignation; unlike Megan, Bethan could never have been a pretty woman, her face was long and forbidding, her nose snub and her hair wiry, but it was a face with character. It belonged, I felt, to a person who would get things done and see them through. She sighed deeply and prepared herself for speech, an exercise which involved re-arranging the cushions on the sofa.

"I thought you would ask me in the end, but you're not to go telling people. It seems to me, young Mark..." (I must have been ten years older than her) "... you don't know when to keep your mouth shut – going about all over the country, accusing people of murder." I thought this a little unfair, but I had to admit that neither John nor I had shown much discretion in our enquiries.

"Your secret is safe with me, except I shall tell John; I don't have any secrets from John." She looked at me with a keen look; there wouldn't, I thought, be much use hiding things from Bethan.

"Nor he from you?"

Now it was my turn to sigh and reflect.

"I hope not, Bethan," I replied at last. But I was conscious that John was forty while I was sixty-one, that he was still very handsome and I, well, I was past my best. How did I really know that John worked the hours that he said he did? Was he faithful to me, or did he have other lovers? I never asked; I said to myself that it was because I trusted him, but perhaps it was really that I preferred not to know. Perhaps Bethan sensed something of this because she leaned over and patted my arm.

"There, there, life's a difficult business, we must make the best of things."

And then she began her story. Told in her lilting Welsh accent, it sounded like a legend of long ago. Essentially, Bethan was pushed into an arranged marriage. She was an only child, and her father's farm was contiguous with that of his cousin, so it made sense to join up the two farms. Bethan was no beauty and the son had little to recommend him, but both families thought it a satisfactory solution. Even Bethan herself had no wish to move from the farm, and had no real objection to getting married. Her mother had died of cancer during her teens, and her father died shortly after her marriage. Her husband was a morose man who kept himself to himself and the marriage was not a happy one. Bethan was miserable and lonely, seeing little of anyone but a girl from the village, Megan, who came to help in the house and with the chickens. After a while, it became apparent that the girl was pregnant – and terrified.

Under Bethan's concerned but direct questioning, it gradually emerged that the husband had been abusing the girl for some time. Shortly afterwards, he suffered a fatal accident on the farm; he had fallen into a 'gulley'.

Bethan did not explain the word 'gulley', and I dared not ask about its nature. However, bearing in mind Megan's earlier words about the police, I could only surmise, although it did not appear that any charges were laid. Some months later Megan produced a son, and Bethan adopted him at Megan's wish.

"As I say," Bethan concluded, "life is never easy."

Now I could see why Bethan was particularly sensitive about Lady P.'s mysterious death, and any associated 'trouble.' The revelation also suggested to me that I would do well not to incur Bethan's anger again – although, of course, she might have had nothing whatever to do with her husband's untimely death.

"Thank you for telling me, Bethan."

I think I expected that a discussion would ensue but I was wrong.

Bethan got up. "And don't you go talking about this to Megan; she doesn't like it talked of, and nor do I. And now I think we should be getting ready for the bridge. Where do you keep your card table?"

And so it was that when John came back from work, he found Megan, Bethan and me seated at the bridge table with the cards ready spread out. I haven't often managed to surprise John, and on the few occasions I have, he has managed to conceal his surprise. This, however, I won hands down. I can see his face now.

"I… er… why, er…?"

"I thought we'd have a nice game of bridge," said Bethan.

"Sit down, John," I said. "I've already dealt for you."

We picked up our cards. Nobody mentioned Lady P. or murder or anything else.

John and I played extraordinarily bad bridge, my excuse being that our minds simply weren't on it. Megan and Bethan, however, played extremely well; it was as if the day had performed some sort of catharsis for them, each behaved as if they hadn't a care in the world. We played rubber bridge and they won by 3,000 points, and at ten pence a hundred, they garnered £3.00.

They decided not to stay after all. ("Megan's never happy in strange houses"), and they set off, intrepid into the night, in the ancient Morris Minor. They didn't even 'rage against the dying of the light'.

John and I had plenty to talk about.

Chapter 10: Facienda

Like me, John decided that Megan could never be a serious contender in the murder stakes, and he was inclined to exonerate Bethan – in spite of this being the second mysterious death in the record of her life.

"It's got to be one of the hotel staff," said John, but I could tell he would like to be persuaded it wasn't. It would have been awfully disappointing to settle for the hotel being the culprit, and, anyway, we would never know which of the staff it was. Now we had got the bit between our teeth we wanted to pin the murder on someone we knew.

"I would much prefer it to be a GrandSlamite," I said.

"Let's go and see the Skorskis, then. It's interesting about their barney with Lady P."

"I don't suppose you've had any more thoughts about the poison, have you John? Nothing has jogged your memory? You haven't recognised the smell?"

"I've had other things to do, Mark, I haven't been sitting round all day gossiping."

I felt rebuked. "I tell you whom I feel sorry for in all this."

"Who?"

"Carol." John looked amazed.

"I'll tell you why: she goes on that bridge holiday looking for a husband or even a harmless bit of the other. She's partnered with Lewis – a likely prospect, but she jumps the gun and goes offering herself too early. Her chance is gone altogether, and she lands poor little Simon, who she could eat for dinner."

"I don't feel sorry for her at all; I thought she was a right bitch."

"Well, we ought to go and see her. Oh, we can't, she's gone on a bridge holiday, Lewis told us."

"Well, you could check it out, she might not have gone yet or she might be back. I can't think how she can afford to keep going on bridge holidays." In case John started reflecting again on the money other people had at their disposal (while all his went on pots for people's birthdays), I asked "What was her job?"

"Retail," he replied. "Interesting – that's how the Macalisters described Janet's job now. And that's odd, too; hasn't she got a degree in biochemistry or something? What's she doing working in a shop?"

"I suppose because she didn't finish the course… Hey, John! Biochemistry – Janet would have known about poisons." But John was still being grumpy and wasn't prepared to be impressed by my brilliant new idea; he merely suggested that I could check that out, too.

"I can't, not unless Lewis comes up with her number."

"Get on to Lewis then."

"Oh, you are a Mr. Bossy Boots," I said, but I knew it was really because he was annoyed at having to go to work. He might miss all the excitement.

"Remember what Lewis said about being systematic. In fact, I'm going to write you out a list of things to do…"

"Facienda," I said in my irritating academic way.

John wrote the list. He substituted the 'a' with a 'u' and added a 'k' after the 'c'.

Then this was what he wrote:

1. Ring Lewis – and if he's got Janet's number, ring her.
2. Email Sammy and tell him what's going on.
3. See what Tubby's up to.
4. Try Carol.
5. Arrange appointment with the Skorskis.
6. Anything else you can think of.

I rang Lewis, thanked him for the lunch and asked him whether he had Janet's number. He said he hadn't been able to find it, but would keep it in mind. He sounded a little less gracious than usual, and it struck me that I ought to have written to thank him for the lunch. As an ex-Headmaster these things probably mattered greatly to him.

To turn the conversation into other channels, I told him about the advent of Bethan and Megan, but as we had disregarded his advice, I didn't tell him about our visit to

Simon. I was afraid he'd still not quite forgiven me for the unwritten letter, because instead of showing delight at all I had elicited from the Welsh ladies, he merely commented, "I think it possible you are a little precipitous at crossing either off your list." Now it was my turn to feel grumpy, but I didn't want to argue over it, so I simply said he must come and have lunch with us very soon and perhaps we could make it into a bridge. We left it like that. But I still hadn't got Janet's number.

Then I did Task Number 2: I sent a long email to Sammy with a synopsis of everything we'd unearthed so far. However, I did this more to please John than anything else; I didn't expect to hear from Sammy again. I saw him as a great mover-on-er and an avoider of hassle. Having offloaded the Tubby business on to our shoulders, I couldn't see him taking any further interest in it.

Next I rang Carol, not expecting to get a reply, so I was somewhat thrown when I heard the familiar little-girl tones and wondered what on earth I was going to say?

"Oh hello, Carol…. this is Mark Hadley, do you remember, from the holiday? I have been … er ringing round some of the people we met at GrandSlam Bridge with rather sad news…"

"Oh yes, very sad, I know. Poor Lady Prettyman."

I was amazed, but then less so, remembering how she wormed secrets out of everyone. However, I had to ask, "Oh, how did you know?"

"I went to a bridge week-end and heard there. She wasn't a favourite of mine, but I grieve for her sad demise."

Demise. That was Tubby's word.

"Who told you?" There was a pause.

"The Macalisters. I'm afraid you rather upset them – and, of course, he does have a heart condition so really, I think, perhaps a little thoughtless… but then I am unusually empathetic. And they have so much worry about with little Janet. I'm afraid she may have taken what I would consider to be a very unfortunate course of action – although my lips are sealed, poor girl… So I'm not sure it was wise of you to bother them, but I'm sure you have learned your lesson and that will be an end to it. You have to be so careful, don't you, when you talk about death…? I shan't repeat the 'm' word that you mentioned – after all, we do have the little law of libel in this land, don't we? I do hope you haven't run any risks. I am always very careful what I say, although I find so often people confide in me, and share so many of their little secrets."

"Well, I…"

"I am afraid you must excuse me; I'm getting ready for Tunisia, my next GrandSlam. Dear Sammy is directing it, so I shall feel I'm among old friends. Give my love to John. I hope he's being a *good boy*… It must be worrying for you… being so much older. Young people will have their fun, won't they? Byee."

Down went the receiver. And to think I had felt sorry for her! John was right, she was a bitch of the first order – although I grudgingly had to admit she had a point about being careful.

I made myself a cup of coffee and sat down to mull it all over: the Macalisters were still upset, were they? Well, perhaps it would be diplomatic to write a thank-you note for the coffee. What was the sub-text of Carol's warning about being careful when you talk about death? Was she intimating that the Macalisters might consider suing me for defamation? Or was she warning me off asking *her* any questions? Aha, yes, and hadn't Bethan said Carol wasn't in her room when she went with the knitting pattern? She might well have done it!

I put together a scenario: Carol, failing to have it off with Lewis and insulted by Lady P. feels the need to vent her frustration. She waits and watches for a waitress carrying whisky, distracts her and substitutes a glass of poison. I could see as a hypothesis it lacked conviction, particularly as the original good-night whiskies would already have gone up, but I might just be on to something. I would mention it to John when I had got it into shape.

Then I composed a letter to the Macalisters:

Dear Trevor and Isabel,

Thank you so much for inviting us into your beautiful home and entertaining us so royally last Thursday. I do hope neither of us said anything to upset you. I, in particular often express myself badly, and I expect I blurted out all sorts of stupid things. I do apologise. Anyway, it seems most likely that member of the hotel staff was responsible for providing the spiked drink which resulted in the tragic event I mentioned.

It would be fun if we could all have a game of bridge. Would you care to come over here? We might make a day of it. Do let me know.

John joins with me in sending warmest wishes. We both hope Janet is enjoying her new life in London.

Yours,

Mark Hadley

I was rather pleased with this, particularly the bit about 'the spiked drink'. I did, however, hope they wouldn't take up the offer of bridge.

Then I sat down and thought about what to say to the Skorskis. Lewis was quite right: one must have a proper plan. But what? So I rang up without making one; I felt I was always better on the spur of the moment – well, actually, I just felt lazy! The phone was answered immediately and I recognised Claire's voice, but I was disconcerted, to say the least, by her response;

"Hello. Dear absent friends. Dear absent friends." I didn't regard myself as a friend exactly, and anyway I hadn't said who I was, but, admittedly, as far as Claire Skorski was concerned, I was absent. I paused, wondering how to reply. Irritation came into her voice.

"Hello? Do you have an appointment? Have you made an appointment?"

Little fragments of memory began to coalesce in my

brain, but I couldn't marshal them into a whole.

"No, no, Claire, this is Mark Hadley from GrandSlam. Do you remember me – and my partner, John?

"Oh, you should have said! Why didn't you say? What can I do for you? Is there something I can do?"

"Well, actually, Claire there is. John and I are visiting friends in Bath and we have to come practically past your door. So… we were wondering whether we could stop off for a cup of tea…" I took a gamble, "next Wednesday."

"What sort of time? What time do you think you'll you be coming past? I'll have to check with Karl; I'm not sure what Karl has on."

"And," I said holding out the bait, "I've got some rather sad news."

"Sad news? What's happened? Has something sad happened?"

But I was too wily to satisfy her curiosity, and I negotiated a slot for the following Wednesday.

"And you'd better come round the side, don't use the front door. Come round the side." Once I'd hung up, I sat and racked my brains for the meaning of 'Dear absent friends', but they evoked no memories.

So then I phoned Tubby, but he wasn't in, so I went off to play bowls with Jeremy. (Jeremy is my good deed, he is a sort of Arbuthnot-Jones and it cheers him up to get out, even though I'll swear he can't see the bowls.)

I tried Tubby again when I got back, but there was no still answer.

Chapter 11: Some dear absent friends

John couldn't throw any light on 'dear absent friends' either, but he thought it unlikely that the Skorskis had many of them. I said I disagreed; I felt that many, if not all the Skorski's friends might be absent.

The Skorskis lived in an Edwardian semi in rather a shabby sort of road on the ouskirts of Bath. I was longing to creep up to the front door and have a peep through the window to see why we had to go round the side, but before I could do that, Claire appeared as if by magic from some back entrance.

"Here you are," she said, "here you are." We couldn't deny it, and allowed ourselves be led into a sitting room. It looked comfortable but shabby: a couple of sofas covered in knotted rugs, and on the walls a number of kitsch pictures of kittens. There was also a picture I hadn't seen for a long time: 'His Master's Voice' – a faithful dog listening to an old gramophone. In a corner of the room was a basket with a poodle curled up in it. We seemed doomed to encounters with dogs, and we both gave it a wide berth.

Out of another door Karl emerged, I thought he looked rather more imposing in his own environment; at least five foot three and less sinister than I remembered. Surprisingly, too, for a man who had remained so silent at *Il Sole* and whose most noticeable venture into conversation had been (as reported by Bethan), "I too say 'oink,'" he seemed prepared to talk. John went off to the kitchen, supposedly to help Claire with the tea, but actually to have a snoop round, and Skorski told me at length about a hand he'd recently been dealt which contained thirty-six points and how, in spite of missing the king of hearts he had managed to make a grand slam. I imagined him taking a peek at the opposing hands.

"What's their name, then?" asked Claire returning from the kitchen with John in tow. "What are they called?"

Both John and I were confused by the question. I looked at the poodle, but it offered no help.

"Your friends," said Skorski., "the friends who you visit, they 'ave a name?"

"Rooney," said John promptly. I may not have mentioned John is keen on football.

"Steven Rooney? We know Steven and Alice Rooney, clients of ours, weren't they, Karl. The Rooneys; you remember the Rooneys?"

"No," said John, "Greg and Mary."

"Greg?" said Claire pensively. "This Greg, where does he live? Which side of Bath does he live…?"

"North-east," said John, a little irritably I thought.

"I doubt you'd know them," I broke in, "they have only just moved."

"Vere 'ave they moved from?"

"Southend," said John finally, and before the geography of Southend could be brought under discussion, he asked, "have you heard about Lady Prettyman?"

They hadn't, and both were riveted. Even Claire was silent, absently filling up her own cup and forgetting about the rest of us. John presented a bowdlerized version, omitting any mention of our nocturnal involvement, or of the complication of Megan and Bethan, or our visits to Lewis, Simon and the Macalisters. He had, it seemed, met up with Tubby who had told him that his wife had died, and then confided that he thought she might have been poisoned. No sooner had he uttered the word 'poisoned' than Karl was on his feet.

"So," he said, "so, everyvere eez ze poisonings."

This sounded interesting, but Claire made him sit down and shut up, by the simple expedient of poking at him with the spout of the teapot. John continued explaining: someone had replaced Lady P.'s whisky with a glass of poison, and although it was too late to find who had done it…

"Always too late," remarked Karl sadly, but he was mindful of the spout.

Tubby, so John was saying, was worried by the whole business and asked John to ask any *innocent* people – like the Skorskis – that he happened to meet, if they had any ideas.

And, as we were going to see our old friends (I thought he was going to say 'dear absent friends') the Rooneys, Greg and Alice, recently moved from Southend to north-west Bath...

"You said north-east before," interrupted Claire.

"West," said John unperturbed, "....and had they seen anyone walking about or behaving suspiciously that night. Had the Skorskis, in fact, seen anything?"

Claire and Karl were like the Inquisition: no question was left unasked, and every question was posed three times, twice by Claire and once by Karl. Actually, to be fair, they asked all the questions that we had avoided asking because we didn't know how to go about finding the answers: what member of staff had been on duty that night? How had the poison got into the glass? And so on. So we repeatedly said we didn't know. I couldn't help thinking that the Skorskis would have made a much better pair of detectives than John and I.

Some questions we were able to provide fairly reasonable answers to. Tubby hadn't taken any action in Italy because he had been in a state of shock and hadn't been able to think straight. He believed Lady P. would have wanted to remain in Italy – or perhaps he was simply such an idiot that he could be persuaded into believing that to be the case. More difficult to answer was why we hadn't yet spoken to people like Megan and Bethan: "Thought we would start with people like you that we *know* are innocent," said crafty John.

Finally there was a respite from the interrogation and Claire remembered the amaretto biscuits that she had bought three packets of in Italy, but added that they might have gone stale, so she went off to get another cup of tea and the stale biscuits.

The dog remained unmoved.

One of the good things about the Skorskis was that, unlike the others we had visited, who had shown anger, in varying degrees, at being singled out for attention, Claire and Karl seemed quite unaware that they should in any way have incurred suspicion. Indeed, they were thoroughly enjoying sharing the role of detective, and were not the slightest bit resentful of our presence.

I asked Karl if he had any information about suspicious poisoners, as he had remarked on the subject of poison earlier, but he merely shook his head and said nothing.

While Claire was in the kitchen we heard the phone ring, and her reply:

"Oh, yes. Yes, what loved one? What size? The price would depend on the size. Also the type of finish – glossy or matt, what …?"

I looked over at the dog basket, and I met John's eyes. He had obviously sussed out before me that there wouldn't be too much tail-wagging from our dear absent friend in the corner. I blinked and came back to the matter in hand.

"And did you see anything that night, Karl?"

"No, I zee no tings that night, but I zee tings other nights."

"What tings, things?"

Claire came back loaded with tea and information.

"Karl saw all sorts of things; any amount of things. Tell them, Karl! Tell them what you saw."

The Skorskis' room had been admirably placed as a lookout post since it was situated at the top of a stairway that overlooked both floors below. Also, it seemed that Skorski was often at his post, gathering information; he claimed he had prostrate trouble and, as the toilet in their room made a lot of noise, he preferred to go down the corridor, so as not to wake Claire. I thought there was probably a grain of truth in this, but thought it likely that, just as he couldn't resist peeking at people's cards, he also kept a wary eye on their nocturnal habits. And there ensued a great list of people who seemed to be given to walking about at night, long after the bridge had finished when you might have imagined them to be safely tucked up in bed. He had often seen Sammy, and Janet; he had also seen Lewis, and on one occasion he had seen Carol - "dressed all in black," interrupted Claire, "a black negligee."I exchanged glances with John. This must have been the occasion when she had gone off to seduce Lewis.

"How did you see all this?" asked John "when the

corridor lights were never on for more than a couple of minutes?"

"I zee enough. There were often many peoples walking about."

"But not on that last night" I said deflatingly. I was rather tired of his smug air.

"No," he agreed, "I zee nozzing that night because all peoples sleeping, must be rising early." He returned to his previous catalogue: on no occasion had he seen Bethan or Megan, and the Macalisters also seemed to keep to their room.

"What about Simon?"

"No, I do not see 'im, but once I zee something ve-ery interesting."

"Yes?" We all looked up – except the chap in the corner.

"One night, I see a very beautiful girl leave 'is room."

I thought this *was* very interesting, but John was not particularly impressed or, perhaps like me, he was beginning to feel irritated by Skorski.

"I shouldn't think you could see very clearly," he said. "If I remember, his room was two storeys down from yours on the first floor."

Regretfully, Skorski was obliged to admit that he hadn't seen very clearly.

"Then how do you know this girl was beautiful?"

"I see she 'as long gold hair 'anging down 'er back, and she walk swinging 'er 'ips from side to side." He got up to demonstrate; Claire was not impressed.

"Sit down, Karl, don't be standing there looking silly."

"So you didn't recognise her? She wasn't a girl you had seen about the hotel?"

He shook his head sadly, but the expression 'hair hanging down her back' seemed familiar. Where had I heard that before? And who was this girl? Simon seemed about the last guy in the world to attract women, but Arbuthnot-Jones had also made a comment about girlfriends. I wondered if Simon was spending some of his newly-inherited wealth on a call-girl or two.

"So, Claire," I said "if Lady P. was murdered, who do *you* think might have done it?"

But Claire became defensive: you had to be careful when you talked about murder, I say you have to be careful. Karl however was less discreet.

"Tere eez a person that Claire and I do not like; someone we think is not a nice person; someone who would be 'appy murderer."

I was all agog, but just at that moment the phone went and Claire disappeared into the kitchen; "Hello. Dear Absent Friends. Oh, I'm sorry to hear that, that's very sad." Then the voice dropped to a murmur, but afterwards John swore that he heard the word 'crocodile.' Nor was Karl to be drawn without his wife's say-so. But on returning Claire was brisk and to the point.

"That Carol," she said, "her with the black negligee." I said I couldn't see that black nightwear was a crime.

"It eez not that, though that eez not nice clothes for lady; I would not like my wife to wear such clothes. No, it eez zee smiling and zee prying."

They both embarked on a long, complicated story, and what with Claire repeating everything and the vagaries of Karl's speech, it was difficult to build up a picture of events, but what seemed to have happened was that Claire had gone to sleep by the pool and Karl had made one of his many trips inside to visit the lavatory. On his way back, he had seen Carol hurriedly putting something back in Claire's bag – possibly a business card.

The nub of the problem for the Skorskis seemed to be that they hadn't wanted people on the bridge holiday to know the nature of their business. Perhaps they had met with hostility or even unseemly mirth on a previous occasion. Anyway, Claire went on the defensive.

"You see we run a legitimate business; we perform a service. If you had a nice little dog you would want to keep him by you always, like our Fifi here. We like him here, and there's others too who like to keep their friends. Yes, many people who like to keep their friends with them."

"Eez very skilful business."

"But not everyone appreciates it; some people are funny when they know what you do – and then they expect you to do it for nothing."

"Eez very expensive material; cost money."

"So when we are on holiday, we don't say much about it. We rarely tell anyone." What seemed to have happened after the handbag incident, was that Carol tended to drop hints, make out she was going to say something, and then draw back.

"Always she eez smiling."

"But that doesn't mean she would commit murder," said John.

"Eez a woman with no pity. That Lady vas rude to 'er, like she was rude to all peoples. I see that Carol did not like that, she want to puneesh 'er. She would like to pour poison into 'er glass; she would be smiling, smiling."

"Not that we are saying she did; don't think that. We don't say anything, do we, Karl?"

"Of course not," I said, "you have been very discreet."

The phone was ringing again; business was obviously good, and it was time for us to go – the Rooneys of north-west Bath would be wondering where we had got to. Karl said it was a pity we had no time for a game of bridge. So with a nod in the direction of Fifi and the uttering of thanks and promises not to pass their suspicions on, we took our departure.

On the way home we discussed the visit.

"I couldn't live with that Fifi in the corner," said John.

"Do you think she'll stuff Karl when he goes?"

"The trouble is," said John angrily hooting at a dithering pedestrian, "you never know whether anyone is telling the truth. I mean the Skorskis come across as relatively straightforward, but then you remember he cheats at bridge and makes out he doesn't understand English whenever it's convenient. So you don't know whether to believe him or not."

"Well, he didn't say much of use anyway – oh damn, I meant to have another go at him about the poison."

"Poison?"

"Don't you remember he said 'alvays ze poison."

"I wonder," said John, "what he used to carry about in his little bag – I didn't see it today, did you?"

"No. Probably his instruments of taxidermy."

"Come on, Mark, he wasn't likely to be doing any elephant stuffing on holiday."

"No, but I suppose he could have had some, I don't know – chemicals? with him? If so, he's the only person who had the means of poison all handy."

"Perhaps," said John meditatively, "it wasn't Claire's bag that Carol went through, perhaps it was Karl's, and she found some poison or something and that was what she threatened to talk about."

"Yes," I agreed, "you could be right, because I don't remember hearing her drop any hints about the stuffing."

"It's a pity we can't talk to her," said John opening the window and lighting up. How long has she gone to Tunisia for?"

"I didn't ask."

"Can't see you making Chief Constable." We joined the motorway and lapsed into silence.

"Do *you* think Simon had a hooker in his room?"

"Well I can't see him being great on the pull, can you?"

"Hang on, you know Karl said the girl had 'hair hanging down her back?'"

"Did he?"

"Well at the time I thought it sounded familiar and I couldn't think where I'd heard it before. I just knew I'd heard someone say that recently – and I've got it. It was Bethan talking about Janet. She said something about her rushing down the corridor with her hair all loose and hanging down her back" .

"What are you saying?" asked John, patiently.

"I'm not sure, but suppose Simon and Janet were having an affair…"

"Come off it, Mark!"

"Well, supposing they had something, some secret and…"

"Yeah, yeah – and she went to his room in the middle of the night with her hair all loose to plot the death of Lady P. Very likely."

"Well," I said, hurt, "it's easy to sneer."

"Yes, you're right, sorry," he patted my hand, and grinned. "Yes, there could be some connection – if only because you never saw them talk to each other! Very subtle. A deep plot."

"But Janet didn't seem to talk to anyone, just stood about smoking and looking miserable. And she and Simon did partner each other for those first two days – before Carol blew her chances with Lewis and Sammy swapped them round. They could have come to some agreement in those first two days; in fact *they* could have asked Sammy to swap partners; we don't know that Lewis was the one who asked – so it would look as if they had no connection with each other."

"But, Mark, there wasn't any motive. Simon didn't have any motive, and I don't think Janet was bothered by Lady P. – *something* was bothering her, but we don't know what, and it doesn't look as if we shall ever find out, as Lewis hasn't produced her number. Why don't you phone him again?"

"I don't feel like it at the moment; he didn't sound very jolly the last time."

"Well phone Tubby then. Let's see if he's got any more interested."

"What, now?"

"No time like the present."

"What shall I say?"

John considered. "Just say we've done a lot of detective work and we'd like to come and discuss it with him."

"Why don't you do it?"

"Because I'm driving this car."

There is a kind of pragmatism about John that you can't argue with. I fished about for my mobile.

"Better use mine," he said. "You won't have charged

yours." He has no high opinion about me and modern technology.

"Hello? Hello, Tubby? This is Mark Hadley. How are you?"

"Oh hello. Yes I'm well, very well, yes. I… um…"

"John and I have been very busy…"

"Yes, yes, I quite understand; much too busy over all that silly business, I should think, had quite forgotten I'd asked you."

I thought this was a bit much. "We've been busy on your behalf – talking to people.."

"Oh dear, oh dear, no, no, much better forgotten. Marjorie would have wanted it forgotten… Don't talk to any more people, please. I don't want anything done about it. In fact…," I could sense the little man puffing himself up, "I forbid you to talk about it." I was pretty cross.

"Well we've been to a lot of trouble on your behalf, Tubby."

"And don't call me Tubby. My name is Laurence."

"Well, you never told us that before."

"Yes, well, it's time to move on now. Goodbye to you."

The phone went down.

"He's been got at," said John.

"Yes, I think he has, but by whom?"

"That," said John, exhaling the last of his cigarette, "is the billion dollar question." We drove on in silence, shattered by the mental effort of the day.

"Which would you rather have in your house," I asked, "Tubby's parrot or Skorski's Fifi?"

"I think I'll just settle for you," he said.

Chapter 12: The DAFS

Over the next few days we discussed, and discussed, and discussed. It seemed as if Tubby – or, I should say *Laurence*'s injunction to call a halt to the investigations had in fact spurred us on. We discussed it in bed, we discussed it over breakfast, and John even turned the sound down on the television so we could discuss it over the football, so you can see it had become a matter of some importance to us.

First of all we discussed who had put the frighteners on Tubby. It didn't seem to make much sense, since, as John pointed out, it would be more effective to put the frighteners on us, because we'd been far more active in the matter than Tubby. And, we thought, more likely to meet with success than Tubby.

"Perhaps the murderer knows that Tubby has a piece of evidence that he doesn't know about, doesn't realise is significant – something he hasn't told us." I was rather pleased with this.

"So the murderer makes a journey to Banbury to remind Tubby what this significant thing is and to tell him to say nothing about it."

"Well, not exactly."

"What then?"

"Ah!" I said, "perhaps Tubby *did* murder Lady P., but in collusion with someone else, and now this someone else is frightened …"

"Don't be silly! Why would Tubby ever have stirred it all up in the first place – writing to Sammy and so on."

"Guilt. Horrible, gnawing guilt."

"Then why go accusing Bethan?"

"Because he secretly wanted us to find out the truth… Yes..," I was on a roll now, "and now he suspects we are on the trail…"

"But it *was* Bethan who handed over the whisky."

"Red herring. Tubby had secretly prepared another glass of poison."

"Why did he need an accomplice then? And can you see Tubby as a murderer?"

"You could that night. You told me that he *had* murdered Lady P.. Ha!"

John ignored this. "Why didn't he to go to the police, then? I can't see much point in his badgering Sammy and telling us to go questioning Bethan."

"Perhaps Bethan was his accomplice: they had been seized by a huge passion for each other, and plotted the whole doorstep whisky thing."

At this point John turned up the volume on the television.

"Go and see him," said John when the match had finished. "Go and see Tubby."

I wasn't too keen on this suggestion. "He might not be there; he never seems to be at home."

"You won't have lost anything."

"But you'll be at work." I added pathetically, "I don't want to go on my own."

John grinned.

"Afraid of Tubby? Well, I can't hold your hand all the time."

But that, of course, was the problem. I wanted him to hold parts of my anatomy all the time – but I suspected that such a feeling was not mutual. Young men soon weary of old men's cloying desire for manifestations of love. I remembered Carol's words *Give my love to John. I hope he's being a good boy....it must be very worrying for you, being so much older than him; young people will have their fun!*

I sighed heavily.

"Cheer up," he said, "it's not that bad."

"No." But I thought that it might be.

So I did what I was told, drove the seventy miles to Tubby's house, walked up the path and banged on the door. There was no reply, so I banged again, and there was still no reply; but such is the irrationality of the human condition that having stated at the outset that he wouldn't be there and having my hypothesis confirmed, I now firmly believed he *was* there.

My imagination took wing: I saw him lying in a heap of blood, a dagger through his heart. I saw him, his body contorted like that of his wife, a glass of poison spilling over the flowery carpet. I wondered if I should break in or call the police.

As I stood there, pondering on my preferred course of action, I became aware that I was observed. A pair of little girls with two long black plaits apiece and a big bouncy ball between them, had suspended their play in the garden next door and regarded me with friendly expressions on their faces. I wondered how many insults they must have endured while Lady P. was their neighbour. I was a little disconcerted; I am not awfully good at talking to children – but I like them better than dogs or parrots.

"I wonder if you could help me, I am looking for Tubby… I mean Mr. Smith."

The two little girls looked at each other and became convulsed with giggles. They found the mention of 'Tubby' very funny indeed, but were clearly nice, well-brought up young girls and they pulled themselves together and said that they thought he had gone on holiday. One child volunteered that she had seen him get into his car with a big brown case and a new suit – "not the old one he used to wear, with the legs too long. He looked very smart and he had a big blue tie."

"He didn't look worried at all?"

"Oh no! He looked very happy. He didn't used to."

"When his wife was alive?"

They nodded solemnly. An older boy arrived on the scene, obviously told to keep a brotherly idea on the little girls in face of this possible paedophile. He regarded me silently, but I was undaunted:

"Have *you* seen Mr Smith recently?"

"He's gone on holiday."

"When was that, could you tell me? I'm a friend of his and I'm surprised he didn't tell me." The boy was a smart cookie and said what was my name, then. I gave him my rather horrible grandad smile, but it must have convinced him because he said it was about mid-morning, the previous Wednesday.

Then deciding that I wasn't much of a threat he added, "in his new car; he's got a new Golf – silver."

One of the little girls said, "Shall we tell him about the parrot, Deepraj?"

But Deepraj intimated that such important news was best relayed by himself. He placed himself squarely before me: "Did you know he had a parrot?"

I said I did, and I also knew that it could speak just like Mr. Smith's's wife. My credentials were obviously approved, and one of the little girls (they must have been twins) said they called her 'Ugly Lady'. The small boy frowned at this unnecessary interruption and said she was dead and people couldn't help what they looked like, and look at them. The little girls looked cross and started throwing the ball to one another again. I felt we were getting away from the main topic.

"Tell me about the parrot." I said. They all started speaking at once and the little boy gave me a man-to-man look in the face of female interruption.

He held up his small hand to assert his authority but the little girls were not to be silenced

"We could see the parrot, it was a green parrot…"

"With a red beak."

"From our kitchen window and when they had their window open…"

"And ours was open too…"

"We could hear it saying…" Here the little boy took over, and puffing out his cheeks he bellowed: "Tubby you old fool, Tubby you fool." He liked doing this and he went on doing it for quite a long time.

"It said other rude things, too," said one of the twins, "but I can't tell you because we're not allowed to say those words."

"And then before he went on holiday, we couldn't see it…"

"We could see the cage."

"And then I saw…"

"We all saw, Parminder and me saw, too…"

"Mr. Smith came out to the garden…"

"And he'd got the parrot all dead with its neck all funny…"

"He dug a hole with a trowel but he wasn't very good and it wasn't big enough, he needed a spade thing, and then he dug…"

"A big hole."

"He put the poor parrot in the hole. Parminder cried, but I didn't."

"And he didn't even put flowers or anything there."

"Parminder and me think he buried Ugly Lady there, too."

Deepraj looked judicious. "Such things are possible," he said.

"And then he went on holiday looking happy."

Suddenly they all stopped talking and looked at me. I felt some response was called for.

"Perhaps he didn't like the parrot," I said feebly. But a woman's face appeared at the window and Deepraj said, "excuse me, please. We must go now," And he gave each girl an encouraging shove.

It was time for the suspect paedophile to return home and report back. He had travelled a long way.

"What did you find out?" asked John from the comfort of the sofa upon my return home.

"He's killed the parrot," I said sinking into a chair.

"I don't blame him; I should like to have killed it myself. What did he have to say?"

"Nothing."

"Why not?"

"He wasn't there."

"Didn't you ring first?"

"Obviously not."

"Why not?"

Nobody likes to be told they've been foolish, particularly when they know it. I glowered at him, and John found it tactful to change the topic of conversation, so he went back to the parrot.

"I should think he's wanted to do it for years."
"Shows he doesn't mind killing," I said brightening up.
"Perhaps it died of natural causes."
"Pining for its mistress."
"I wonder where he's gone."
"In a hole in the ground."
"Not the parrot – Tubby."
"Perhaps he's gone back to Italy to escape from whoever it is who's put the frighteners on him."
"I wonder why he looked so cheerful and was all dressed up in his best."
"Perhaps he was celebrating the parrot's death."
I couldn't think of a better reason.

Our prime suspects changed from day to day, often triggered off by contact from members of GrandSlam Bridge, whom John and I had taken to calling 'our dear absent friends' or 'DAFS' for short.

On Wednesday came a letter from Lewis that made him into suspect No 1, at least in John's eyes. This was the letter:

Dear Mark (and John),

I am glad you enjoyed the lunch and the WI cake.

I am sorry I have not been able to locate Janet's phone number. It is remiss of me to be so careless; I pride myself on not losing things, so perhaps this is a lesson to me. Could you ask her parents for it, or would you feel embarrassed?

I hope your detective work goes well, although I fear the truth, as the proverb goes, lies at the bottom of a deep well!

I contacted Simon the other day and played the most extraordinary game of bridge with him, the brassy school matron and an old teacher called Arbuthnot-Jones – did you meet him? The matron had only played whist with her parents as a child, and Arbuthnot-Jones couldn't tell his diamonds from the hearts. We started by playing Chicago, but it seemed better for Simon to partner one of them and I to partner the other. It was quite fascinating since one didn't have a clue as to what either Arbuthnot-Jones or matron meant when they bid, so A-J's four hearts could equally well mean that he had no hearts but high diamonds, and Matron invariably echoed what her partner bid, whether she had any points or not. I once found myself playing four spades with my sixteen points and Matron's Yarborough, and Simon found himself in five diamonds with his partner's void. But as matron often trumped her partner's tricks and A-J often revoked, it was often possible to make an impossible contract – rather like playing poker. I wonder whether we should patent the game and let the craze sweep the bridge world.

Best wishes to you both,

Lewis

P.S Has John got the handcuffs ready for me yet?

John was ready to read a lot into the letter:

"Notice how he doesn't give us any help at all? I bet he *has* got Janet's number – and did he get anything out of Simon? If he did, he's not saying. But he makes sure he drops in that he knows *we've* seen him."

"But what was his motive?" I didn't actually favour Lewis as prime suspect.

"I haven't thought of that yet, just give me time." John let the remote control hover briefly over some young athletes flexing their muscles (we were watching the Olympic Games), "and yes... Look how he tried to put the blame on Megan and Bethan."

"He only said we shouldn't cross them off the list."

"It's the same thing. And cunning, as we can see from those games of bridge. I shouldn't wonder if he didn't polish off the parents of boys at his school when they complained, and I suspect him of fiddling the school accounts. I can't see him affording that house on a teacher's salary."

The trouble with John is that you never know when he's being serious.

On Friday the question of Megan and Bethan came under scrutiny when we received an enormous parcel from Wales by Special Delivery.

"It's got a very strong smell," I said heaving it into the kitchen and removing the outer wrappers. "It seems to be packed in ice."

"Perhaps it's the body of Irfon."

"Or the ear of Earfon." We both thought this was rather funny and merited a vodka tonic.

"It does say 'Produce of Bryn Maw, Proprietor I. Reece.'"

It *was* a body, or rather half a body, but not Irfon's, nor indeed Bethan's or Megan's, but that of a sheep; it was a whole side of Welsh lamb. It was extremely big; in fact it took up a dominant position in the kitchen and left very little room for either of us.

"Very suspicious, sending us this," said John. "I see it as a bribe."

"Or a coded message," I said sarcastically. I wasn't prepared to entertain the idea that my dear friends Megan and Bethan were other than pure as the driven.

"Is there a message? What does it say?"

I poked about among the wrappings and found this:

Dear John and Mark,

Bethan is sending this from both of us to say thank you. It's really from her, but I always write her letters. We had a lovely time with you and have been talking about it ever since. Have you found the murderer yet? As you guessed, it wasn't us.

Love, Megan and Bethan

P.S. The lamb is from the farm. Irfon took it to be slaughtered yesterday.

"I knew Irfon would come into it somehow," said John. He gazed at the side of lamb leaning against the fridge. "What are we going to do with it?"

"I don't know. Doesn't it have to be sawn into pieces?"

"Butchered."

Neither of us are very handy, but Gillian next door is a big strong lass, and in the end she chopped it up in return for a leg. We had roast lamb that night and shoulder the next; the rest went in the freezer because there's only so much lamb you can eat in a week.

As we sat down over the roast and a good bottle of claret, I was forced to concede: "It does seem a large thank-you present."

"Yes," said John, his mouth full of succulent lamb, "you'll have to write a long letter."

"I see you cast me in Megan's role."

"No, she only writes short ones."

"Do you really think it's some sort of bribe?"

"I think," said John selfishly finishing up the red-currant jelly "that it's their way of saying they don't want any further investigation."

"Mmm."

"Don't speak with your mouth full."

"I, personally, trust both of them," I said having swallowed it down with a slug of wine. But John was not so easily convinced.

"I wonder exactly how Bethan's husband died. He gets Megan pregnant – and then falls down a gulley or something. It sounds like murder to me."

"We don't know that; she just said 'an accident.'"

"...And if she can push her husband down a gulley," continued John undeterred, "she can certainly kill Lady P."

"Well, she wasn't charged."

"I don't know too much about farming and all that, but isn't death kind of common on farms? I mean, there was Irfon at the slaughter house only a few days ago. And it was in Wales. Maybe death isn't such a big deal there."

"If you are saying Welsh women make good killers, as a

remark it has the merit of being both sexist and racist."

"Welsh women *farmers*."

"Well farmers are a beleaguered minority too."

"And Bethan had a motive: her beloved Megan being attacked."

"Actually, I do find their relationship odd," I mused. "Shall I open another one?"

John nodded assent to both my comment and the bottle: "Yes, you'd expect Bethan to hate Megan – having her husband's child and all that. Why didn't Megan bring it up – and why did she give it to Bethan?"

"Well, she did explain a bit: because of … what had happened, understandably Megan didn't want the baby, and decided to start a new life. She left the area and went to Cardiff, but later she came back – I imagine to see how Irfon had turned out. Presumably she'd stayed in touch with Bethan, and they just got friendly again. And I suppose there was this kind of bond between them – perhaps Bethan feels guilty for taking the baby and this makes her protective towards Megan.

"Funny people, the Welsh."

"But I don't see that any of this has any bearing on Lady P.."

"You never know."

But we put the Welsh on hold and went on to consider the others.

Frankly, we couldn't see much mileage in the Skorskis although John presented an interesting theory:

"The Skorskis are doing all right with their animal stuffing…"

"Taxidermy."

"Their pet stuffing – but say what old Skorski wants is a real challenge: cats and dogs and crocs aren't enough for him, what he wants is a real human being."

"To replace Fifi."

"Definitely, and when Lady P. keeps slagging him off, he thinks 'Ah, gotcha, I'll do her." He looked thoughtful, "I'm not sure if he was aided and abetted by Tubby, but I think it likely."

I said as a theory it certainly had the merit of originality.

We considered Simon. John hadn't much time for Simon. "Wimp, non-entity, nothing in his trousers."

"Well, by all accounts he's something of a Lothario."

"Eh?"

"Romeo, stud – that what Arbuthnot-Jones and Skorski implied."

John hooted. "Well I don't see Arbuthnot-Jones and Skorki as expert witnesses, do you? If it happened at all I should think he was paying for it. Anyway, supposing he is capable of more than three no trumps, what's his motive?"

"Ah, I've thought of that; I've thought of a motive."

"I'm going to have a fag." I frowned, house rules forbade smoking indoors. "In the garden – when you've told me."

"Well, you know all that business about how kind she was to him as a child? Well, it's not terribly likely, is it, from what we know of her? What if she had been perfectly vile to him as a child, and when he came into his money he thought he would pay for the holiday and get his revenge."

"Seems a bit of a waste of money. Why not do something cheaper?"

"Like what?"

"I don't know – send her a box of poisoned chocolates or something. Anyway I don't think he did it, because it seems to me that what he said about her being nice to him as a kid was true. If you think about it, he was about the only person she wasn't rude to."

"Grateful for the holiday you mean?"

"And all that boo-hoo-hooing when we told him about the murder. Do you really think he had enough about him to put it all on?"

"No," I said, "If I'm honest, I have to say I never saw a man so surprised and upset in my life."

"I'll go and have my fag then."

"The most obvious suspect is Carol," he shouted out from behind a pot of dead fuchsias. "She was always wandering about at night trying to seduce people…"

"Only once."

"She was a bitch, and it's not just me that thinks that. You didn't like her, despite your short- lived bout of sympathy, and nor did Lewis, and I shouldn't think Simon did – she was always criticizing his play, and the Skorskis thought she was quite capable of it…"

"Because she was unpleasant doesn't make her guilty and, anyway, Bethan was willing to lend her a knitting pattern, and the Macalisters didn't say anything against her. And she wasn't *always* wandering about. Do hurry up and finish that fag, I'm freezing."

"She poked about in Claire Skorski's bag."

"That doesn't make her a murderess. In fact, I'd have thought she was the sort of woman who preferred to insinuate at things she knew, rather than take any action. I'd say it was the power of *knowing* that thrilled her. We ought to talk to her."

"Well we can't, because she's in Tunisia being looked after by Sammy or some other lucky Tournament Director. We'll have to wait until she comes back."

"And we can't talk to Janet either. What do you think about Janet?"

John looked thoughtful – he looks very handsome when he's thinking; more handsome than when he's stuck gawping in front of the football.

"I liked her – I know she was always sulky and miserable and rude to her dad."

"Stepfather."

"Right. I'm ready to come back inside now. Seems to me you ought to tidy up this garden a bit, ready for your expensive new pot."

I ignored this comment – I am supposed to do the garden, but I'm really more of an arm-chair gardener, and I take the view that in the Autumn things die down naturally ready for the next year.

"I wonder why she disliked him so much. Trevor's a pain, but a harmless pain I should have said."

"Wanker," John dismissed Trevor and returned to Janet,

"but you kind of felt if she stopped being miserable about whatever it was she was miserable about, she could be nice. Besides, she was a smoker and I always like a smoker."

I ignored the gibe: "I must say, I can't see any reason why she would want to do Lady P. in. I don't think she was remotely bothered by Lady P.'s rudeness. And I don't see Trevor committing murder off-stage, and as for Lady Deadlock…."

"Who?"

"Isabel; she's like Lady Deadlock in 'Bleak House' – mysterious, and rather beautiful. I can imagine her with all sorts of dark secrets."

"I wouldn't know about that." John likes to make out he's a Philistine, which he isn't, but he does it to annoy me when he thinks I'm being pretentious, "and apart from the fact that you fancy her…" John never let me forget that I had once lived a rather hetero existence.

"Oh, John! She's as old as I am… but of course, you still fancy me so I suppose she could be in with a chance."

"For an old man you certainly fancy yourself."

I smiled and reverted to Isabel. "She probably married Trevor for the money, but we don't know much about it."

"That's just it, isn't it?" said John in frustration. "When it comes down to it, we don't know anything; we just play a silly guessing game without having the faintest idea about who was where or when, or anything at all. It's pretty obvious to me that none of them did it, that the chances are it was one of the hotel staff… Yes, yes, I know we said why wait till the last night. Well, probably they thought she'd get ill on the plane or something – and if it was one of them, we'll never know anything more." He turned and looked at me defiantly, "So we might as well forget the whole thing."

It was a blow; I had loved doing all this with John, but it obviously hadn't meant so much to him if he was happy just to drop it all.

"Is that what you want?"

He came over and put his hand on my arm; John so often knew what I thought.

"No, I'd like to work it all out, of course I would, but we're so useless. We need to know things like what time people were out of their rooms – and where their rooms were and..."

"Sammy put the rooms on the list."

"Yes, but who knows if 20 was next to 21, or whether 21 was down a different corridor or in another wing? Anyway, Mark, I do really think it was one of the staff."

It was then I had what I thought was a brilliant idea.

"We could find out."

"How?"

"We could go to the '*Sole*' for a long week-end."

"When?"

"This weekend. Now it's off-season, it's sure to have vacancies."

John began to mutter about not being able to get time off, so I added.

"I'll pay."

"Everything?"

"Except the booze – we'll go halves on that," I put in quickly.

John got up. "Let's see what flights we can get." He can find anything on the computer.

I didn't know what a disaster was in store.

Chapter 13: *Il Sole*

Italy was a fiasco from the start. In the first place, the flight was delayed by two hours, and when we did finally get on the plane, we all had to get off again due to some engine problem or other. Then, when we got to Bergamo we had missed the transfer, and I had to shell out huge numbers of euros for a taxi. We were both pretty tetchy by the time we got to *Il Sole* – and we were too late for dinner. John likes his meals and I could seem him looking round for something nasty to say; I didn't have to wait long.

"The only good thing I can say about this idea of yours so far is I haven't had to pay for anything." I too, was tired and quite equal to him in the nastiness stakes.

"I shouldn't think that comes as any novelty to you."

There was a different girl at Reception, so no detecting could be done there, and the room had neither lake view nor double bed – both of which I had requested. So, hungry and tired we went to our separate beds where we lay and watched Italian television in silence. It is a measure of how bad the television was that John actually turned it off. We drank our bottle of duty free vodka and fell asleep.

The next morning it got better. We ate generous platefuls of fresh bread, salami, cheese, cake, fruit and yoghurt and felt more bullish. And when John had had a couple of fags he was prepared to be almost human.

"What's the master plan?"

"I thought we'd have a look at the rooms: see the layout and so on. Look…" I waved some sheets of A4 at him, "I've even got paper."

"And a pen?" asked the Sceptic.

"That too," I replied smugly.

"Won't the cleaners be about? We'll look like idiots creeping down corridors and peering at doors."

"Not if we look purposeful."

"Well, alright; we may as well get on with it, then; it's not as if it's a day for a nice trip on the lake, is it?"

It wasn't; you couldn't see the lake at all through the driving rain. It was also extremely cold – something neither John nor I had packed for.

"I'll start with the fourth floor, outside Room 401, which was where Skorski did his spying from. You go up to the first floor to… let me see… 209, where Simon's room was, and I'll see how much I can really make out. Then I'll come down and join you."

John looked unimpressed, but did as he was told and I went up in the lift to the fourth floor and after initially going along the wrong side (421-488) I found myself outside Skorski's room. I peered at the gothic numbering and identified it as 401. I looked down to see John below and discovered, pleasingly, that Skorski's vantage point provided a surprisingly clear view. I waved enthusiastically to John who took no notice, so I did a few pointless sketches, just to show him that I was taking the matter seriously, even if he wasn't, and then I went down in the lift to reconnoitre with him.

"Skorski probably could have seen Simon's lady friend quite clearly."

"What – with the corridor lights going on and off with the timer switch?"

"Perhaps he just got lucky."

"So what?" said John.

"So nothing, just checking. Now I am going to establish the position of Bethan's room and Lewis' room."

"Why?"

"Just to see if Megan really could have overheard Carol propositioning Lewis. Bethan told us the rooms were next door to each other."

John wrapped his arms round his sweaterless body and tried to instil some heat by rubbing his arms. "What's that got to do with anything? Anyway you can't tell unless you go into the room."

Suddenly I lost my temper.

"Why do you have to be so bloody negative all the time?

I'm cold as well. Okay, probably everything is a waste of time. Yes, probably most of what I have done all my life is a waste of time, because that's what you're saying, isn't it? Everything I do is sad."

"I've had enough of all this, I'm going elsewhere."

"Oh yes? What are you going to do on this beautiful sunny day? Go and have a nice sit outside at a café in the pouring rain?"

"No, I shall go back to my single bed, get into it to keep warm, smoke lots of fags and watch the football. I'll carry on doing that until I get bored and then I'll think of some other way to enjoy this fantastic holiday." He went stumping off.

I watched him down the corridor – the tight hips and the curly brown hair, feeling absolutely miserable. John is moody, even depressive, he has been ever since I first met him eleven years ago. When I first experienced it I thought it added to his charm, but I was quickly disillusioned; his moods start with grumpiness, then they degenerate into silence, and then – the worst – the only way he can rid himself of it is lots of sex. Previously, in the early years I had been able to provide that, but familiarity breeds discontent and more recently I wonder if he looks for it elsewhere. I don't think it would occur to him that this might affect our relationship, or affect whatever it is – love, affection, lust? – that he feels for me.

I wish I could feel the same – I have never been promiscuous since I met him; I suppose I got that out of my system in the years before, but I suspect, for John, that it is something that he needs. And now, as I gazed at his retreating figure, the old fear of losing him returned. I could not imagine life without him. I looked out at the lake, or what I could see of it, "I might as well join Lady P.," I thought.

I pulled myself together and took my bearings. GrandSlam Bridge had originally contained eighty or so bridge players, the majority of whom had left on the Verona to Heathrow flight the day before. The rest of us had been pretty scattered about. I was still determined to walk round the hotel, seeing where each of the DAFS had been – quite why I thought that important, I don't know. Perhaps I just wanted to be doing, so as not to think of what John might do when he got tired of the football, or what he might feel like doing when he got back to England.

I got tired of waiting for the lift and walked back up to the fourth floor, which left me quite exhausted, but I walked on past Rooms 418 and 419 which had been occupied by the Macalister parents and by Janet. It first struck me what a lot of rooms there were in the hotel, and then how odd it was that Bethan had seen Janet rushing along the *first* floor. Where was she going? There were some staff rooms, but who else from GrandSlam was on the first floor beside Bethan and Megan and Lewis? Could there have been something going on between Janet and Lewis? Was this why Lewis claimed he couldn't find her phone number? They were happy enough playing bridge together; indeed, now I came to think of it, it seemed that Janet had been at her most relaxed in Lewis's company. Was *this* why he'd got Sammy to switch partners?

Had he made up the business about Carol? Oh no, that was real because it was corroborated by both Skorski and Megan, but still – maybe he had had the hots for her, or indeed she for him. But why did she look and act so miserable all the time? Plus there was the fact that Lewis had this thing about his wife. But maybe he just fancied a bit of the other and thought Janet might provide? Okay, there was a pretty substantial age difference, but there, I reflected sadly, look at the age gap between John and me. Still, I wasn't going to brood. I would revisit the next floor down – the one where Tubby and we had been.

I consulted my list and found that Carol had also been on our floor, but further down and round the corner: she was 338 and we were 330. I followed the corridor towards our old room, which took a fair old time because most of the rooms were 'junior suites' with a sea view, and took up twice as much space.

I got to thinking about Simon's shelling out for Lady P. to have a room with a suite. (I knew how expensive they were because John and I had had a little disagreement over this, and had compromised by having 'sea view with balcony'). He must be very kind really, I thought, but then it occurred to me that it was more likely she had just demanded it, and Simon had been too scared to refuse. Or possibly – I stopped and drew a meaningless sort of sketch to show John how efficient I was – Simon had had some sinister motive for proffering the holiday, though this didn't seem very likely.

Then, just as I stopped to have a peer at the door of Lady P.'s room at 333 a cleaning lady emerged from it. She looked at me suspiciously and I hurried on back down the corridor to our old room at 330 and stared earnestly at the door, although what I expected to see there I have no idea .Then I went down in the lift and walked along the corridor that had accommodated Bethan and Megan in 126, and Lewis in 127. These doors didn't seem very interesting either.

Now I had done them all, except Sammy's. And, being Sammy, he had not included his own room number on the list.

I felt John was right; I had learned no more than I could have done sitting comfortably at home reading the list.

I did not feel inclined to go back to our room and watch the beautiful game, so although it was still very early, I thought I'd go and have a drink in the bar – something warming. And going past Reception, I saw that the original girl was back, presumably she worked the day shift. I thought I would do some cunning sleuthing.

"Buongiorno, Signora."

"Good morning." She said without looking up, obviously feeling – quite rightly – that it would be a waste of time talking to me in Italian.

I capitulated. "Do you have our passports: Hadley and Page?"

"I will see. What is your room number?"

I nearly said 330 and then remembered that we were now "126."

"I can give only your passport, Mr Page must take his himself."

"Fine," I did an adult version of my Granddad grimace that had proved so successful when talking to Tubby's neighbours. "Do you remember us from the Bridge Holiday last August?"

"No."

"I remember you," I said gallantly, "the girl with the beautiful blond hair."

And as I said it, it crossed my mind that it could have been the receptionist in Simon's room. On the other hand, looking at her it seemed unlikely.

She shrugged, unimpressed.

"We have many people staying, I cannot remember them all. It is a big hotel."

It certainly is, I thought, remembering my slog up the four stories, but I hadn't finished. "Something very sad happened at the end of the holiday: a lady, one of our party died."

I thought I saw a glimmer of concern cross her face; I was wondering what construction to put on this, when she replied.

"I can be sad only about one lady who dies, my mother who dies last month."

I felt I wasn't really being very successful. "I'm so sorry."

She shrugged again,

"Tell your friend his passport is here." I was dismissed. I did not feel it had been a successful encounter.

I went to the bar and ordered a Strega. I thought it might take some of the chill out of the day. I was told do sit down and the barman would bring my drink. I chose a chair in the corner by the window and peered out. I could see nothing but wet glass. A boy came over with the drink.

"Grazie."

The boy looked as unimpressed as the Receptionist, so I abandoned my linguistics and asked: "Is Gino still here? I didn't see him at breakfast."

The boy shrugged. "Non parlo inglese," he said.

I gave up and settled to trying to read a copy of *La Stampa*. There seemed to be a lot of words I didn't know, like all of the first ten pages. I wondered about John, whether he was still glued to La Religione, or whether he was about to embark on a series of private exploits about which I should not ask. The Strega was making me feel warmer, and I thought a second one might improve things further. However, while I pondered, a second drink was set down in front of me and I looked up, delighted that John had come down anxious for a reconciliation.

"Buongiorno, Signor 'Adley. You like very much the Strega, I think."

It wasn't John putting on a funny accent; it was our old friend the hotel manager. Now here was an interesting turn up for the books. I could only think that the Receptionist had told him that there was an English guy asking awkward questions.

"Bongiorno, grazie, si. Molto gentile, mi piace la Strega."

Like the others he obviously thought our conversation would progress more fruitfully in English.

"I also like the Strega." He raised his glass, "In bocca lupo."

I thought 'up yours' would not be a suitable reply, so instead smiled in a feeble sort of way. While I waited for him to say whatever he had come to say I had a good look at him. I wanted to think that he looked devilish or even shifty, but actually he looked quite pleasant and rather jolly, unthreateningly short and well-dressed in what was probably a designer suit (though I'm never sure about things like that. John would have known).

"We meet in 'appier times," he smiled.

"I'm sorry?" I wasn't going to help him.

"I think you 'ave forgotten the colpo del cuore of the contessa, 'ow you say attack of the 'eart. That night of sadness." He looked at me with gentle rebuke.

I wasn't going to be fobbed off; I plucked up my courage and blurted out: "Actually since returning to England her husband isn't so sure it was a heart attack: he thinks her death may not have been an accident." Okay, Tubby, I thought a bit guiltily, you may not want any more investigations done, but tough luck!

"Il povero! The poor man, 'e is 'nel sciocco', in shocking.

I tell you, Mr 'Adley. Everything is done con proprietá. There are examining, not one, not two, but three doctors, and the certificate was signata; Mr Smith 'ave a copy, but I give you another one for 'im, if 'e 'as lost it. It is easy."

"Hm," I thought, "you don't mention one of the doctors was your brother and the other two a couple of mates who'd been slipped a backhander or two." But he had called my bluff, and what was the point in asking for another certificate?

"I don't think that will be necessary." I plucked up my courage again.

"You see, Lady Prettyman was taken with a seizure after she had accepted a drink brought by a member of staff."

He looked a little less benign. "Your friend did not say that to me, 'e mention only the 'eart."

"I think, as you say, he was in shock."

"As I tell you, the doctors examined 'er. I think the doctors are knowing more than a sad 'usband." I said nothing: John always advocates the power of silence.

"He 'as perhaps informed the police that 'e 'as worries?" I felt the sarcasm.

"Well, no, not yet." He called my bluff again.

"It is a good idea; 'e can ask the English or Italian."

I thought of Tubby's impassioned cry: "Don't do any more talking to people!" and I dared not reply boldly. I settled for a weak "Perhaps he will."

The manager patted me on the arm. "I will be frank with you, Mr Hadley: I was surprised that Milord Prettyman did not wish to take the body of 'is wife to England…" I felt facts were being manipulated. Surely Tubby had been told to have her cremated here?

"If 'e was worried, he could take the body back 'ome, and 'ad autopsia, but 'e said only 'e wished for her to be incinerated, and then 'e throw the ashes….." and here he did a representation of a man hurling a javelin "nel lago. 'Ere in Italia we are not so hurry to get rid of our relations. Maria at Reception, 'er mother die last month, she spend three weeks to make a grand funeral for 'er mother." He looked at me, his eyes full of reproach.

I felt he had been very clever; not only had he shown himself willing to provide the only possible proof – the certificate, he'd also called my bluff in offering the police, and finally, ever so subtly hinted that if there was anything dodgy about the death, it was Tubby who was responsible. To top it all, he had also managed to imply that the English as a nation were unfeeling and in all probability corrupt. I couldn't compete. I gave my 'granddad grimace'.

"Now we talk about more 'appy things. Tonight we 'ave a specialitá dinner. Our guests must pay, but because we are old friends, I ask you and Mr Page as my guests." I immediately saw this as a bribe, and not a very tempting one. "You are very kind, but I think we will go out tonight."

He shrugged: "I think you make mistake – but come vuole. If you are eating not in the 'otel, I recommend la trattoria dei Leone; you will get a good meal there."

"Thank you."

"And now I must leave you. If you 'ave worries, you come see me again, but I think I 'ave… 'ow you say, put the worries to bed." He smiled, got up and shouted something to the boy behind the bar. As he left a third Strega appeared in front of me.

"Put it down to my room number," I said.

"There is nothing to pay, Signor."

I finished my drink and wondered what I should do next – I felt it was best to avoid John at the moment. There were two things that I decided to busy myself with:

1. Find out if Gino was still about, since he was the person responsible for organising the 'goodnight' drinks, and say something to him. (But what?)

2. Go to the Bridge Room and try to envisage that last night and see if I was reminded of anything.

I thought it best to do the Gino bit casually over a meal, so I sought out the Bridge Room. It was not conducive to evoking memories: the decorators were in and the room had become a sort of repository of all the furniture from that particular corridor: beds, chairs, bedside tables, dressing tables, every bit of furniture you could imagine stacked up – even the bridge tables piled carelessly on top of each other at the end of the room. I gazed, but little came back to me.

Somewhere by that cheap and shabby dressing table Lady P. had sat with Tubby fatly opposite her, busy insulting people. I tried to imagine her: what was she wearing? A sort of shiny blue top with a blue bow in her sparse hair, below which her eyes glinted and nose obtruded and her pendulous flabby lower lip expelled loud and hurtful comments: Karl Scorski an illegal immigrant, John and I poofters, Megan and Bethan fat Celts, Trevor a failed actor… For a moment I saw her quite clearly, an obnoxious smirk curling about her lips as she bawled out some new insult. But she was no more. Lady P. and all her clamouring were now only the tiniest bit of Lake Como. I thought of Saint Augustine comparing a man's life span to that of a bird flying into the Feasting Hall and out the other side, returning to the blackness from which it came. I saw tiny fluttering wings. I felt I should like to cry very loudly.

If I had brought a coat I could have gone for a walk and tried the effect of wind and rain in dispelling the gloom – but I hadn't, and it seemed foolish to go out and get wet in order to buy a coat in order to stop getting wet. But what was the alternative? There didn't seem much choice. I could sit in silence in the bedroom while John watched the football; sit accepting bribes in the bar; or continue staring at the piled-up furniture in the disused Bridge Room.

I went out, got wet, sat and had lunch in my wet clothes, and finally bought the cheapest (hah, that was a joke) jacket I could find to go back to the hotel in. I walked through driving rain. On the way back I bumped into John who had had the same idea, except that he had bought an umbrella as well, and whereas my jacket which was obviously not intended for the monsoon, now resembled a reject from the Oxfam shop, John in a belted hip length affair under his umbrella looked remarkably smart; this compounded my depression. He gave me a poke with the brolly and pointed in the direction of the hotel.

"What's it called again?"

"*Il Sole* – The Sun."

"Ah." He glanced up at the thick grey clouds. I thought he was about to set off again, but he paused and remarked, "I thought we might as well have a good meal tonight, so I've reserved a table at a good restaurant."

"Lions," I said. John looked surprised.

"How did you know?"

"I have second sight."

At least we were talking again. We did not refer to our investigations during the course of the afternoon, but returned to our room and lay on our single beds watching an Italian soap opera, only a little of which we could understand – and even less, once we'd polished off a couple of bottles of Chianti. John fell asleep.

At the ristorante I felt more jolly. John too, seemed more cheerful after his sleep, and I began to hope that, after all, he wasn't fed up with our relationship, and didn't mind me being old and apparently somewhat shabby ("did you fish that jacket out of the lake?"). Perhaps he did love me a little, and wouldn't go off and shag lots of younger and smarter men, and in the end everything would be all right.

Over the antipasto (*parma e melone* for me, and John had a plate of all sorts of nice-looking bits I wished I'd had), I told him about my morning's work. John listened in silence, stuffing in bits of artichoke.

"What do you think?" I asked finally, and because he remained concentrated on tasty bits of octopus I started on a Janet theory: "Do you think she was having an affair with Lewis?"

"No; and I don't think she was having it off with Simon either."

"Well, what *do* you think?"

"Let's get this straight. You went round all the rooms and found nothing. You went to the bridge room and saw a lot of furniture. You didn't speak to Gino, and the manager bought you a couple of stregas. I think you had better call it a day."

Put like that, it didn't sound a great achievement.

"It was a bribe," I said defensively, "he was trying to buy my silence."

"What was he trying to stop you doing?"

"Well, I..."

"I don't think it was a bribe at all; he just wanted you to go back to England saying what a comfortable place The Sun is, with a nice friendly manager."

"I think it was a bribe."

"Not much of one."

"I think that was only part of it." I paused impressively, " I think you'll find there is no charge for this meal."

"I doubt it," said John. He was, of course, right. It came to 215 euros.

The next morning at breakfast I decided to address the Gino question and I picked the prettiest waitress, remembering how much of Gino's time was spent flirting with female members of the staff.

"Scusi, Gino è qui adesso? Voudrei parlarlo."

The girl giggled. Presumably at my Italian, and answered in perfect English.

"No, he is no longer here. He has left the hotel."

"When was that?"

"Non lo so." But pressed, she said maybe a month ago – shortly after the departure of GrandSlam Bridge, in fact. I gave John a 'See-how-clever-I-am' look. Where had he gone? The girl shrugged

"Wherever there is an easy woman."

This did not seem a very satisfactory reply, but it was all I was going to get and she stood waiting for a tip. I gave her my last five euros.

"You see," I said excitedly to John, "Gino was obviously got rid of as soon as possible – either he went of his own accord, or the manager got rid of him ...so he couldn't give evidence. It must have been Gino."

"Well, that's that sorted, then. Now we can forget it all. Let's see if we can get an earlier flight home, I can't stand much more of this rain."

We couldn't; so we sat around at Bergamo airport for

hours. And on the plane back we had a row. Of course, I should have left the topic of Lady P. alone for a bit, but just because the week-end had been such a disaster, I wanted to show that it hadn't been a complete waste of time.

"Of course," I said brightly, "there's one suspect we haven't considered."

"You?"

"No, I have an alibi – as you do."

"Who, then? The manager? I thought you had decided it was Gino."

"No – Sammy. You know how up-front racist Lady P.'s language could be. Sammy always acted as if he didn't mind – well, perhaps he did mind, minded so much that he decided he'd get his own back?"

"What has triggered off this exciting new theory?"

I didn't like the sarcastic tone of his voice, but I ignored it.

"The fact that Sammy didn't include his own room number on the list. For all we know he might have been next door and managed to pop in and…"

"How would he have done that? Keys are different for different rooms, you know, that's why they have them."

"He might have had a master key as Bridge Director."

"Then, why does it matter where his room was?"

"Well, I think we should seriously consider Sammy. "

John remarked "What a load of crap."

Thinking about it afterwards, I realised he was, in fact, referring to the plastic meal in front of him, but he said it in such a way that I took it to refer to my theory.

I exploded. "It's so easy to sit there sneering, I notice you doing it all the time now – anything I say sneer, sneer, sneer."

"Yes, and it's easy to keep inventing ridiculous theories with no evidence. Thinking about nothing else, becoming obsessed with something that you can never find the answer to, anyway."

A fat woman over the aisle leaned forward; she sensed a row and didn't want to miss a moment.

"Better than not doing anything at all, just holding yourself apart, pretending to be interested in other things, making the point that anything I'm interested in is beneath your contempt." The woman leaned in closer; I glared at her, "Excuse me, this is a private matter."

"Then I shouldn't go shouting about it at the top of your voice, if I were you."

John sniggered, and we both fell silent, aware that the point at issue was not necessarily the case of Lady P., but equally the fact that I was 61 and wanting us to do everything together, and he was 41, a whole generation younger than I, and not ready for that – perhaps never would be ready, and perhaps after all, there wasn't any 'us'.

Chapter 14: The Gospel according to John

I thought it was time I contributed my bit.

Mark says I'm depressive – well, I suppose I am, a bit – but not half as much as he is! Yes, he's right in a way: I get fed up, and then I go to town a bit and have a good time, and then I put it behind me – I'll re-phrase that, and settle back down with Mark. But it isn't all plain sailing. You see I do love him – a lot, as it happens – but he's an old man and I'm only 41. Then again, he's the one with all the degrees and things. When I met him first and we started living together I used to say when we met people: "This is Mark, he's the clever one and I'm his bit of rough." But I stopped saying that after a bit because although Mark has degrees coming out of his ears and I left school at sixteen, I've done pretty well since then.

The thing about Mark is – he likes to succeed; he's used to success – well, he got me, didn't he? And he gets miserable when he doesn't have things sorted, and when he gets miserable he gets really miserable. Now I could see that he wasn't going to get anywhere with all these 'investigations'. We'd been playing detectives for nearly a month and it was clear to me that now was the time to put an end to it. After all, Tubby, for whatever reason, had told us to stop, and as far as I was concerned a surprise email from Sammy (Mark's latest suspect) clinched it: 'Great time in Tunisia – glad all your investigations finished. Sammy.'

I couldn't see any reason *why* he should say that it was finished, because we hadn't said so, but it was good enough for me, and I said to Mark to forget it all. He went very quiet and I could see he was upset and reading all sorts of meanings into what I'd said – like our relationship is finished, or you think I'm boring going on doing the same things, blah, blah, blah? Really he was identifying success in the investigation with the strength of our relationship and if that's the way he saw it, then there *wouldn't* be much of a relationship if we went on investigating the way we had been!

Anyway, the result was, we kind of agreed not to talk about it any more. So, when we ate the next shoulder of lamb we didn't mention Bethan, and we went on pretending things were exactly as they were before Lady P. – except of course, they weren't, and I could see Mark was thinking everything had gone wrong. But everything *had* gone quiet on the detective front: the Macalisters had never bothered answering Mark's invitation for bridge; we heard nothing from either Simon or Lewis (although Mark had written to Lewis suggesting a game, saying that we played a better game than Matron and Arbuthnot-Jones); the Skorskis were too busy stuffing their animals; and we had no means of locating Janet. Following the advent of the lamb, even Bethan and Megan had gone silent; and now he was gone away somewhere, we didn't expect to hear from Tubby. Things seemed to have come to a natural end, but I knew Mark still hankered after it. He looked anxiously at the post every morning, rushed to answer the phone, and assiduously read his emails first thing. He was like a love-sick teenager: he wanted someone suddenly to come up with some clues, and he wanted me to declare undying love for him. Neither was going to happen.

Now, reading through what Mark has written, I can see what a sod he makes me look and in many ways (apart from the obvious), I suppose I am – but I'm not *that* bad, and seeing Mark creeping about day after day looking miserable – or, even worse, pretending to be jolly, really got to me.

I decided I must do something, but it had to be done in my way, on my own, so I could share it with Mark if anything came of it but, if it didn't, he wouldn't have got his hopes us. In that case, I'd just have to come up with something else to cheer him up. (You see, I'm quite a nice guy, really!)

So I made a plan: I would give the investigation one more

go. I would go and see Carol. I'd had a look through some magazines for another bridge holiday to cheer Mark up, and it struck me how expensive the Tunisian Bridge holidays were – and two weeks long! Well, she'd be back now, and she might have something interesting to say. Even if she wasn't the murderess, she might know a thing or two from all her poking into other people's business. And I had another hunch: I wondered if it wasn't Carol who had put the frighteners on Tubby. In terms of character, she was the most likely person to have sussed something out. But I wasn't going to tell Mark any of this because he would want us to go together, and, as I say, I preferred to go on my own.

So I rang her up to see if she was back, and when I heard a smug little "This is Car-ol;" (she had this irritating way of saying it) "how can I help you?" I put the receiver down. She was definitely back, then; but I preferred to take her by surprise. Next Monday I took a day off work, and although it would be a risk, driving eighty miles without knowing whether she'd be in, (and I would be doing just the same as Mark when he went to see Tubby), I don't mind driving. Anyway, if I got there in the morning, if she wasn't there, I could hang around for a bit, find something to do, and then try again later. It would be nice, actually, to have a bit of space; I don't mind my own company.

I told Mark I might be home late, extra work had come in etc.. I could see he didn't believe me, just by the way he said quickly, "Oh right, I'll expect you when I see you, then." To show me that he wouldn't ask any awkward questions.

Driving down gave me time to think about things – starting with me and Mark and the thorny question of our age difference. When I was sixty Mark would be over eighty, and I thought what a miserable old git he would be – but then I'd probably be a bit past my sell-by date, too. So it wasn't any good dwelling on that.

I moved on to what Mark proudly used to call 'our investigations' before it became a taboo subject. If I was honest, I couldn't really see anyone from GrandSlam Bridge as a murderer. Bearing in mind that Lady P. had been killed drinking a glass of poisoned whisky brought by a member of staff, it seemed pretty obvious that one of the hotel staff was responsible – probably with no intention of murdering her; probably for more of a giggle, thinking it would give her the runs when she was on her way home, or something.

So what was I doing going down to Carol's?

And what exactly was I going to say to her? 'Excuse me, Carol, would you mind telling me whether you killed Lady P.? You see, I think you have something of a criminal mind, because you went rummaging through the Skorski bag. Plus I think you're ready to take a risk, because you were seen in a state of undress on your way to have it off with Lewis. Plus nobody much likes you. In fact, you're pretty much up there with Lady P. herself in the unpopularity stakes.' Not really the route to success.

I opened the window and lit a fag. Seriously, could she have done it? Lady P. was always having a go at her, and on that last night she had been pretty nasty. Could Carol have thought 'this has been a pretty crap holiday one way and another, let's have one bit of fun?' Then goes back to her room, prepares a glass of poisoned whisky – er, never mind about where she got the poison from – waits until she sees the girl heading towards Lady P.'s room, distracts her in some way, and switches the glass?

Yes, it was ever so vaguely possible, but any one of us might have done the same – why her? What did we *know* about Carol? She was unmarried, perhaps divorced, I didn't know. Perhaps the key to the Tunisian holidays was a relatively flush ex-husband.

I rehearsed a speech: 'Oh hello, Carol, I hope you don't mind me calling on you like this, but I was coming this way and... Could I come in for a few minutes and talk about this nasty Lady P. business? Tubby was very upset and wanted to find out if anyone could throw any light on what happened.

I'm sure myself it was a heart attack, but Tubby asked Mark and me to look into it because – well, of course he didn't want the police or anything, just hoped to get his head round it all, so he asked Mark and me... We've spoken to everyone except you and Janet, because we knew, obviously, you and Janet weren't involved... but just so we can say we've spoken to everyone...?'It wasn't brilliant, but something along those lines would do.

When I got to Carol's road (Petunia Place, how bloody typical) I thought it was a pity Mark wasn't with me because if we'd played guess the house, we would both have got it spot on: a row of diddy little bungalows, and hers the one with 'Home Nook' in front of it. I parked the car and got out, but even before I rang the bell I had the feeling there was nobody in. I was right, not a soul. I don't give up easily, so I went off into town and found a Starbucks, had a coffee or two and then went back; still no sign of life.

Now, of course, I thought what a fool I'd been not to tell her I was coming, and now there was no need to make my little speech, I wanted to say it. I drove off and went and sat in a pub for a bit, determined to give it one more go. And the third time I was lucky – not in finding Carol, but someone else.

As I got out of the car and started off for the front door, a large woman (about half the size of Megan or Bethan) of about fifty in a pink track suit, came out of a door down the road, all excited.

"Are you the police or the press?" I was a bit surprised, but am good at being cagey, so I smiled and waited.

"It was me she was with, it was me who got the ambulance." She clearly couldn't wait for me to start asking questions – and I was happy to play along.

"I don't know what you mean. Has Carol had an accident?"

"You could say that," she answered, revelling in making me wait.

"What's happened, then? I'm an old friend of Carol's, you see and..."

"You're not a reporter then?" Slight disappointment.

"Not exactly. What's happened?"

"You had better come inside and let me tell you all about it."

The bungalow and the woman stank of cheap scent, but this was a small price to pay for the information. I refused a cup of tea and went into a lounge where you couldn't move for the biggest three piece suite in the world. There was a needlework picture of a poodle on the wall, I wondered if she would like the address of Dear Absent Friends.

"Of course, I was very surprised when she asked me; we aren't friends, only neighbours, and we all keep ourselves to ourselves here, but there she was asking me in. I'd never been inside before; of course she knew me from when I deliver the Church magazine (not that she came to Church much), and we say hello when we meet in the street and pass the time of day, you know how it is... 'Oh, Olive,' she said... 'I've had such a lovely surprise, and I want you to come and have a cup of coffee and share it with me...'

Olive did a good take on Carol's little-girl voice, "*I suspected she wanted to show off about something and, being me, I guessed what it was. People often say I've second sight.*"

She crossed her pink legs and I nodded from out of the middle of one of the sofas.

"Well, there was this big box of chocolates on the table, very showy, with a huge bunch of tulips on it. She likes anything fancy, as I expect you know – like those frilly blouses, although personally... but of course you're her friend." She shot me a glance. I began to wonder if she thought I was Carol's toy boy.

"Very prominent it was on the table, and she made a big show of bringing the coffee and putting it down next to the box. Well, personally, I think a nice biscuit goes better with a cup of coffee, but of course she wanted to show off about the chocolates.

'I've asked you in to stop me being selfish,' she goes. 'I've just eaten received these delicious chocolates that a dear friend has sent me,' and she a big drama of opening it up and started on about the 'dear friend' – obviously wanting me to ask who it was. Well, I knew it would be a man because I had a suspicion she was keen on gentlemen – never been married; tried too hard, I'd say, but I mustn't go on about your friend. But I *did* wonder perhaps if that was why she came to church – when she did come, because I could see her looking round when the rest of us had our eyes shut, praying." I didn't ask how Olive had managed to see, but I put it down to the second sight.

"You're not a church-goer yourself?"

"No."

"However," she went on, and I could see that she was enjoying keeping me in suspense and airing her old grievances, "I expect you want to know what happened next." I nodded.

"Well... she offered me a chocolate, but I wasn't going to humour her, and said 'no thank you. I am on a diet.' Oh, and I'm so thankful I did. I think God must have been looking after me, anyway, she helped herself to one and then another; and then she said 'I expect you want to know who sent me these?' But I wasn't going to humour her; I said, certainly not; I wouldn't want to pry other peoples little romances. 'Oh,' she said, 'this isn't a little romance, this is a big one. I shouldn't be surprised if you soon found yourself busy doing the flowers for a special occasion at the church.'

"I said when I did the flowers was on the rota, so I probably wouldn't be doing any special occasion flowers, and Mrs Gibbons usually did the non-Sunday flowers." I could see that Olive was quite a match for Carol.

"But of course, she was desperate to tell me, and she had just started about meeting him in Italy, when she began to choke and retch, and off she rushed to the toilet. Well, of course I didn't like to interfere, and I sat there waiting for her to come back – well, I must have waited for ten minutes, and then I called out, 'Carol, are you all right?' And when there was no answer, I went to see what was happening, and there she was slumped over the toilet and not answering. Of course I knew what I had to do." She paused and waited.

"What did you do?"

"Dialled 999 – and I must say this for the ambulance service, they were there in three minutes, which I was thankful for because I didn't know whether she was dead or alive."

"And which was she?"

"Alive, just, and they took her off – hardly bothering to ask me about it, but they took the chocolates for examination. You see" and her voice lowered, "it's my belief that far from there being a gentleman wanting to marry her, there was a gentleman who had had enough ... which, although I don't like saying it, doesn't altogether surprise me."

She looked at me as pleased as anything.

"But you don't know who the gentleman was?"

"No, only that she had met him in Italy, and ... Well, I did see a 'With Love' card on it and 'a little surprise for you' written on it. Well, it was certainly that, wasn't it?"

She gave a laugh and confirmed my suspicious that she was every bit as much of a bitch as Carol.

"I couldn't really make out the name; it was in funny flowery writing, but I could see it began with an L. Maybe Len, or Lenny or something." I digested this.

"And how is Carol now?"

" They said she was as well as might be expected." She sounded a bit disappointed, then she brightened up, "but hospitals always put the best face on it, don't they? It's their job."

"And you rang the police?"

Olive looked aggrieved again.

"Yes, I did. The ambulance people said they would see to it, but I didn't take any notice of that. I rang the police straight away to tell them all about it, but you know what the police are like; they sent some young policewoman round – I doubt she could even spell chocolates – and although I've phoned them several times since, I can't get anything out of them. Which I think is a disgrace, seeing as I am the chief witness, don't you?"

"Did you give the card with the L. on it to the policewoman?"

"Yes, I did – and very rude and insinuating she was too, just because I found it in a drawer." She must have seen the look on my face because she went on, "I wanted to be as helpful as I could."

"When did all this happen?"

"Only the day before yesterday."

"And have the police been back? I mean to Carol's house?"

"I couldn't say; I don't spend my time spying out of windows."

I asked her the name of the hospital. She said St. Giles, and they were funny over visiting. She had made a point of phoning the local paper, who had said they would get the story from the police. "But," she brightened up, "they said if anything came of it, they might come and interview me next week, maybe take a photo. I haven't been in the paper since my daughter got married." I got out of the sofa and tried to make my getaway. She didn't want to let me go.

"What did you say your name was?"

I was tempted to say Lenny, and I could see she was miffed when I said John. How did I know Carol? Oh, I had met her in Italy, had I? What a strange coincidence.

I eventually got out of the house into the car, the whiff of perfume pursuing me, and as I drove off, I lit up and breathed in the pure essence of fag smoke. There was a lot to think about. I considered heading for St Giles, wondering if they were 'funny' about people in general visiting, or whether it was just Olive. But I got on the wrong road (the *Satnav* was in Mark's car), and changed my mind. I mean what was I to say to Carol? "Oh hello – I haven't brought you any flowers, just wanted to know whether you had any ideas about who poisoned you and, while I'm at it, did *you* poison Lady P. by any chance?"

But it wasn't just that, I mean the awkwardness of it all. I expect I could have thought of something, but no, it was the fact that I wanted to go back to Mark and give him all this – like a present to say sorry – and tell him I wanted the two of us to decide what to do together.

I turned round, put my foot down and headed back home. I turned up the music and sang along with it and I imagined just how happy I was going to make him.

"Mark, guess what?" I'd say, and then he'd smile and come over to me and we'd have a bit of a cuddle, and then we'd enjoy the latest discoveries – together.

Chapter 15: Still John talking

As soon as I walked through the front door I knew something was wrong; you know how you do, without knowing why.

"Hi," I shouted, "Hi, Mark, I'm back; got something to..."

I went into the sitting room, and there on the floor, a glass of whisky knocked over on the floor beside him, lay Mark. Even as I was bending over him, feeling his pulse, listening to his heart, and seeing there was a bottle of Scotch half empty on the table, somewhere at the back of my mind a voice said: "The poisoner has struck a third time."

He groaned, turned over and mumbled, "God, I'm going to throw up."

He did, with knobs on, but after I got him cleaned up and into bed, I knew he was going to be alright. I also worked out that whoever the original poisoner was, he or she had not poisoned Mark, and that actually the person who had poisoned Mark was me. I realised as I lay at his side, breathing a faint smell of sick, but Mark's sick I could stand because it belonged to Mark, and the smell of a live Mark's sick was much, much better than the smell of Olive's perfume.

Mark likes a drink – well, we both do; we're not alcoholics or anything, but booze is very much part of our lives. Mark doesn't drink spirits much, he's mostly a wine drinker – but good wine, never anything under a tenner. Me, I'll drink anything; not beer particularly (I have to be careful with my weight), but I do like spirits, particularly vodka. But if Mark gets low, then he starts to drink, and if he's really depressed, he'll head for the Scotch – and that's what had happened today. I saw it all as I turned to look at his grizzled, balding head.

He knew I wasn't working, knew that I had lied to him, thought about how we could no longer talk to each other –

let alone, trust each other; got to wondering about what I was doing, who I was with, and started drinking, drinking until he passed out. I had to accept I'd done that to him, simply because I was too stupid or lazy, to sort things out, and to think things through.

I had a lot of explaining to do; and it seemed to me that as I lay there listening to him snoring, that somehow Mark was right and this Lady P. business was all mixed up with our relationship. Perhaps if we could get one right, the other would work out as well. Then I went to sleep too.

The next morning I brought him some weak tea and toast. He didn't look at me, but said ' thank you' in apathetic sort of voice, and drank the tea. I stood by the bed, wanting to say all sorts of things, but all I could think of was:

"You don't want to get dehydrated."

"No," he said.

"You feeling better then?"

"Yes, thank you."

"When did you start on the scotch?"

"I can't remember."

I felt that I wasn't making much progress, so I went outside to have a fag. When I came back he was sitting in exactly the same position staring in front of him. I had had enough of this.

"For Christ sake, Mark."

"What?"

"What do you think I've been doing?"

"I have no idea."

"You think I've been fucking the whole of Warwickshire, don't you?"

"Very possibly."

I looked at him exasperated, and he went on looking at a spot to my left, as if he didn't see me. I grabbed him by the shoulders and saw him wince – either because he couldn't bear me to touch him or, more probably, because he had one hell of a hangover. I let go, disobeyed rules, and lit up, and then sat down on the end of the bed, and slowly began telling him what I had been doing the day before. At first he pretended not to be interested and went on staring at the wall, but when I mentioned Carol's name he looked up, and when I said I'd gone down there he said ever so sadly,

"Why didn't you ask me to come with you?"

I kind of went through all the reasons in my mind, but somehow it seemed just too difficult to explain them, so I didn't. Instead, I went on telling him about the visit. As I talked – Olive … the chocolates … the police … an ambulance, I could see he was increasingly confused, and didn't know which way to jump: he wanted to go on being angry with me, but he wasn't sure whether I had done anything to get upset about, and he was beginning to think that I hadn't been screwing the whole of Warwickshire – or at any rate, not yesterday. He was also (as I *knew* he would be) very, very interested in all these new developments, and wanted to know more, but, at the moment, would have died rather than ask me. So he made a business over pouring out the last of the tea and staring into his teacup, and I said, "so what are we going to do next, then?"

It was the 'we' that did it; he looked up from his stirring and said in a 'what- a-silly-question' sort of voice, "go to the hospital, of course." And I knew it was all alright again
.

He began to get out of bed, knocking the rest of the cold tea over the duvet, "but I'm going to have a shower first."

"Go and have your shower," I said, sniffing, "but we're not going anywhere until we've decided who sent the chocolates."

When he was all sweet-smelling again we went and sat out in the garden next to Mark's tomatoes, because it was a nice, warm, sunny morning. Mark kept his dressing gown on because he quite fancied himself in it, and because he was beginning to enjoy being poorly, and probably banking on getting me to make lunch.

"Who sent the chocolates?" I asked, as if I hadn't thought about it at all.

"Well," he said and he began to smile the way he does when he thinks he's put one over on me, "you think it's Lewis, don't you?"

"You think I'm stupid or something? Just because Olive says the chocolates come with a card signed by someone whose name begins with L, I think 'Aha, it must be Lewis because Lewis begins with L.' That's what you thought – or, rather, what you thought I thought."

"Not at all, I credited you with much more sense, I thought you'd think 'If you're going to poison someone you don't put your signature to it." He picked a tomato and held it out to me. I shook my head and he put it in his mouth and spoke with his mouth full of tomato. "So do we now think that whoever it is who wants to poison Carol also wants to frame Lewis?"

"No, now we think: why did he or she want to poison Carol, and was it the same person that poisoned Lady P.?" Mark ate his tomato and waited for me to continue – after all I'd had longer to think about it than he had.

"What I think is this: whoever poisoned Lady P. was being blackmailed by nosy, expensive-holiday-affording Carol. And maybe it wasn't just lust that made her go off to Lewis's room that night; maybe she wanted to have a good poke round his bedroom after he'd finished poking her and see what she could find!"

Mark was happy with that, so happy that he bit into another tomato which I could see was unripe. Still, better not to say anything, I thought.

"Now," I said, "let's go about this logically for a change: Carol blackmails Lady P.'s murderer, and the person she blackmails decides to do her in by sending her poisoned chocolates…"

"How do you poison chocolates?"

"Don't know, come to that later, but they have to make sure she's really pleased to get them and will eat them. Now this person knows..."

"... that Carol was after Lewis, so if it looks as if the chocolates come from Lewis, she will eat them and pop off from some fast working poison, like Lady P.."

We sat and looked at one another rather pleased. Then I said: "You shouldn't have eaten that green tomato; you don't want to eat things like that after the sort of night you had."

But I was only saying it to give me a moment to work through the next bit: "hold on, wouldn't she be suspicious? I mean, Lewis, according to Megan, gave her a right old bollocking. Wouldn't she wonder why should he suddenly turn round and send her chocolates?"

But Mark had an answer for this. "Maybe the chocolates are only part of a whole deadly campaign. Perhaps the murderer has been working on her for some time – maybe he's written a letter saying how sorry he is, and how much he now regrets what occurred, and how much he fancies her, after all. Maybe he's even been *meeting* her."

" You mean it *was* Lewis." He shook his head.

"No, because why send a card with his name on it? Why not send a letter or card earlier saying you were going to send some chocolates and then send them anonymously later."

"Ah, but perhaps he ... she ... did! After all, Olive found the card in a drawer – not with the chocolates."

"Yes, but it's still too dodgy, the chances are that she'll keep the card, and if she's found poisoned, it won't be too difficult to put two and two together."

"Perhaps it's a double bluff," I said. "Lewis counts on *not* being suspected because he's signed the card with a big L. As you say, who signs their name to a murder?"

We looked at one another, and then I said, "No that's a bit too clever."

"So we're going back to saying that someone – probably Lady P.'s murderer, tried to murder Carol and frame Lewis?"

"Because he or she was being blackmailed by Carol."

Mark thought about this and then he said, "Yes, it's a double whammy really. Lady P.'s murderer uses Lewis as a means of getting Carol to eat the chocolates, and to frame him at the same time for her murder, thereby ensuring that his or her murky secrets go to the grave with Carol."

"Let's think who knew that Carol fancied Lewis and that Lewis had it in for her?"

"The Skorskis knew that she had tried to have it off with him."

"No, they didn't," I lit up thoughtfully. "They only knew that she had put on her seduction gear; they didn't know who she was after. Could old Skorski have seen where she was going? You are the one who did all the sketches and stuff at *Il Sole.*"

"I rather doubt it."

"Then there's Simon. Lewis might have told him when they were in the bar that night."

"I don't imagine they talked about much except teaching, that, and bridge, are the only thing they had in common."

"Well, Simon might have *guessed* she fancied Lewis, and if Carol was blackmailing him for Lady P.'s murder, he could have sent the chocolates."

"But Simon is about the only person who had no motive for murdering Lady P.," Mark objected.

"Well who else then?"

"Megan and Bethan both knew Carol fancied Lewis because Megan had overheard the scene… and we come back, yet again to the mysterious death of Bethan's husband."

"And the fact that they send presents to people by post…"

"It would have rather pointed the finger if it had been a leg of Irfon's lamb that had done for her."

"And we only have Bethan's word that she got the poisoned whisky from a waitress. It's so much simpler if Bethan killed Lady P. because she had upset Megan. Say Carol had seen this, and had blackmailed her. We assume Bethan doesn't mind a bit of bloodshed – think of the side of lamb, and the husband in the gulley."

"Irfon butchered the lamb," I said.

"And we don't want it to be them. Let's move on to someone else."

"Back to Tubby?"

"Tubby didn't know about Carol fancying Lewis."

"Well, we don't *know* that he didn't... and, now, listen, what we were talking about before – why was Tubby suddenly so anxious for us not to go on with the investigation? Answer: because he was being blackmailed by Carol. She was telling him to get us to shut up."

"Okay, but it's back to the old problem – why did Tubby stir things up in the first place if he'd murdered Lady P.. Why not let sleeping dogs lie?"

"Talking of sleeping dogs, let's go back to the Skorskis," I said.

"No, we've dumped them; let's think laterally."

"The Macalisters?"

"They wouldn't have known that Carol was after Lewis."

"Lewis might have told Janet – after all, she replaced Carol as his partner."

"Ah, wait a minute, John. Do you remember when I phoned Carol a couple of weeks ago, before she went to Tunisia – she already knew then that Lady P., had been murdered, and when I asked her how, she said she'd heard it from the Macalisters at a bridge do. But she paused before she said their name; maybe she was calculating if it was a good idea to let us know she'd been in contact with them? I mean, if she wanted to go on blackmailing, she would want to keep our suspicions away from them. Yes," he continued to think aloud, "I wonder: if she did meet them at a bridge week-end – after Italy, I mean – and somehow something clicked and she realised one of them, Trevor or Isabel or Janet had done it, that could have been the point at which she started blackmailing them. If so, it was one of them that sent the chocolates... and it could be that Janet's mysterious disappearance to London is connected."

"Maybe, although there's no more reason that they should have murdered Lady P. than anyone else. But, you're right; we'll put them on the list of possibles."

"Now another thing: how did Carol know who'd murdered Lady P.? *We've* been trying to find out for long enough; how did she know?"

"I'm not sure... but do you remember when we were waiting for the minibus in the foyer the next morning, she was about the last person to arrive, and she was very full of herself. Could she have been having a final snoop round and uncovered some piece of evidence?"

"I do remember her making a point of saying something like we hadn't seen the last of her, that she wanted to keep in touch with people. It could have been a threat."

"So what have we found out? I wish I hadn't eaten all those tomatoes."

"I did tell you." He began stroking his stomach, but I ignored this attention- seeking behaviour; he'd had enough sympathy for one morning.

"On the likelies list we have got: Simon, all the Macalisters, Bethan and Megan, possibly Lewis. In fact everyone except us and the Skorskies, oh, and Carol herself. In fact," I realised, somewhat gloomily, "we aren't any further on than we were before the whole Carol thing. And when we talk about likelies, do we mean the likely murderer of Lady P. or the attempted murderer of Carol? And do we mean that the two perpetrators are one and the same?"

"I don't know," said Mark, "but I do know where I am going now." And he wasted no time in getting to the bathroom.

While he was dealing with the combined effects of whisky and green tomatoes I went to get the post. There was one very interesting letter.

I waited for Mark to re-emerge and we read it together.

Elsinore

Dear Mark,

Thank you for your kind invitation to join you for bridge.

I have thought some time about your visit and have wondered what to do for the best. I think we were not as welcoming to you and John as we should have been and I apologise. Nor were we as honest as we might have been. Oh no, don't think I am going to confess to murder, none of us know anything about that, but we could have given you Janet's phone number. I do not know her address; that is why I am writing to you now. I should like you to go and see Janet – I know she liked John and used to talk to him when they were both outside having their cigarettes – and I think she might see you, particularly as you have such a good (?) excuse for visiting her. I take it, you are still engaged on your investigations?

You see, it is rather difficult to explain, but Janet and her step-father do not get on, and I would ask you not to enquire into the reasons which go back a long way. Janet would prefer me to leave Trevor, but as I do not wish to do so, she regards me as being firmly in his camp rather than hers, and has decided to sever all links with me. If I phone her, she simply doesn't answer. As you'll appreciate, I love her very much and I think she loves me, but she does not want to talk to me, or to visit, and I worry whether she is alright. I thought if you went, you could see how she was, and then let me know –without, of course, telling her that that is what you are doing. I hope you won't think this underhand, I just want to know that she is happy.

I look forward to hearing from you,
With regards,

Isabel Macalister

The mobile number was enclosed.

"Whatever shall we do next?" said Mark who looked as green as his tomatoes. I couldn't help grinning at the way the crafty old devil had begun the togetherness bit again.

"What are you smiling about?"

"Nothing. Let's make plans."

We decided to prioritise: Carol was more important than Janet.

I had wanted Mark to have the treat of ringing the hospital but I had to do it on account of his greenness. I got nowhere, though. What was the name? Which ward? You don't know what ward? What is she suffering from? Food poisoning? It might be Granville Ward. It wasn't. I had to start again.

It might be 'Sackville Ward'. It wasn't. I tried again.

It might be 'Wyatt'. Was I a relative? No. Could I try later, they were very busy.

"What it is, of course," I said slowly, "is the police. They've told the hospital not to let her talk to anyone."

"Surely they would want to know who was trying to contact Carol."

"Actually, Mark, we haven't really thought this through, have we? I mean if the police are involved, where does that put us? Aren't we accessories after the fact or the act or something? Hadn't we better keep out of it, at least until we know if she's alive or dead?"

"Do you think we ought to tell the police?"

"Tell them what?"

"Well... I suppose about Lady P.."

"The first thing they'll want to know is why we haven't told them before – if it is the case that another murder has been attempted they're not going to be particularly friendly about that." The more I thought about it, the nastier it all seemed. "And, come to think of it, *we* could be suspected of poisoning Carol."

"Why? Oh, I see, being the sort of guys who like taking the justice into their own hands."

"And there again, Tubby particularly told us not to interfere."

"Yes, but he was the person who started it all in the first place. We were only trying to do what he wanted!"

We sat and contemplated all the complications of telling the police.

"So," said Mark, putting on a very poor police imitation, "although you thought Lady Prettyman had been murdered, you decided not to go to the police either in Italy or in England, and although you had found at least ten suspects, you decided to keep this information to yourself. I wonder why that was, Mr Page? Nice house you have got here; must have set you back a bit. Like chocolates, Mr Page?"

"I don't know why you choose me," I said, somewhat narked. "I should think they'd be more interested in you."

"Because I shall probably be dead by then," said Mark setting off for the bathroom again. "Poisoned by green tomatoes."

"I'll probably be accused of that as well."

One way and another we thought we wouldn't go and see Carol just yet – but there was nothing to stop us giving our old friend Janet a ring.

Chapter 16: A new Janet

John wrote that well, didn't he? A nice sense of narrative, I thought, even if he has some funny ideas about me!

I listened while John phoned Janet – as Isabel said, he knew her better than I, and he got hold of her straight away. We had decided he should tell her as little as possible, certainly nothing about Carol, and nothing about her mother; just enough to intrigue and make her to want to see us. Remembering her usual miserable demeanour in Italy and her general air of angst, I didn't expect more than a grudging agreement. I was quite wrong; she didn't sound a bit like her miserable old self, she was positively bubbly:

"Lady P. murdered? I don't believe it! Oh, not murdered – but, well, might have been…. Golly, I wonder who? Am I a suspect? Oh, how disappointing! No, I won't say anything to anyone; don't see anyone, well, not that lot anyway. Hey, how did you get my number…?"

I gesticulated at John, but he didn't need my help. She didn't wait for an answer, but continued in her new-found bubbly fashion, "I tell you who ought to be locked up…"

"Who?"

"My stepfather… anyway, you're coming to see me – and Mark? Send him my love. Where do I live?" she laughed joyously. "In the worst possible bit of London, right in the heart of drugsland, I love it. When are you coming? I've got a surprise for you… No, I'm not going to tell you, just wait and see."

"Well," I said when John had put the receiver down, "what do you make of that?"

"It sounds to me," said John, "as if little Janet has got herself a boyfriend." We looked at one another.

"Lewis?"

"I can't see him living in 'drugsland' – bit of a change from The Gingerbread House and anyway he would have told her all about it all."

"Maybe they're just vaguely seeing each other. Perhaps

she's just in Stratford East some of the time."

"Well you could hardly describe Lewis as a boyfriend; he must be in his late sixties."

"Perhaps there's plenty of sex in the sexagenarian," I added rather smugly, "Some sixty year olds can still get it up."

John said there was undoubtedly some truth in this assertion – except he didn't phrase it quite like that.

"And if they are that close," said John returning to a state of gravitas, "Lewis would have told Janet about Carol's advances, and so *she* could have sent the chocolates, sort of jealous, but actually I don't think she murdered Lady P.. She sounded pretty surprised."

"But Lewis might have thought she did, which is why he didn't give us her number. And another thing, he's not been in touch with us except that one letter, or shown any interest in the investigation, which is odd because he seemed interested enough at the time"

"I can't really see Lewis having it off with her if he thought she was a murderess."

"Sex is a funny thing," I said.

"I can see you're feeling better."

"Absolutely. I think green tomatoes must have aphrodisiac properties. I looked at him expectantly, but he was in one of his killjoy moods.

"If what you were doing in the bathroom earlier is an aphrodisiac property, I'll do without them, thank you."

Driving down to London we had a bit of a twitch about Carol.

"We really ought to have gone and seen her," John said suddenly, but I don't suppose they'd have let us in." This comment jogged my memory:

"Do you remember that bit in 'The Godfather' where Marlon Brando's lying in hospital and there are guards everywhere and they're trying to get in."

"Who? The guards?"

"No, no, no, the others, the enemy, I can't remember what

they're called."

"And do they?"

"Do they what?"

"Get in."

"Yes." I thought about this a bit more, and then revised my opinion. "No, I don't think they do." This remark seemed to annoy John and he took his eyes off the road quite alarmingly.

"Don't be so irritating, it doesn't matter what happened in 'The Godfather', but it does matter if someone shoots Carol."

"I should think they're more likely to poison her. Anyway I thought you were all for getting rid of unpleasant people. That's what you said about Lady P. when you thought Tubby had killed her." This harmless remark seemed to make John even more annoyed.

"Look, Mark, I don't know why you are pretending to be so thick, but if anything happens to Carol, we're in a lot of trouble, big, big trouble."

I felt a little chilled by his words, but I also felt irrepressibly happy: John was mine – at least for the moment, we were doing this together, and I felt very sanguine about the investigation. Once we had seen Janet, everything would fall into place. Carol would be alright, I knew she would – and we wouldn't be investigated by the police.

"Either Carol is already dead, or she's alive and will certainly tell the police all about it. They they'll go off and arrest whoever's done it, or she'll decide to keep quiet about it and not spill the beans. Either way, it's nothing to do with us."

"I hope you're right."

"And," I had another happy thought, "she doesn't know what we've been up to, so she won't tell the police about us."

"She does know because the Macalisters told her."

"Well, we didn't tell them much because we didn't know much. We were just pandering to a whim of Tubby's." I did a little whistle. John was so unimpressed with my whistle that he drew into the side of the road and stopped the car. He lit a cigarette and sat in silence. I didn't like the silence.

"What do you want to do, then? "I asked. "Shall we just forget Janet and go to the hospital instead?"

Suddenly he smiled; one of the delightful things about John is his transition from grumpy to nice.

"No. We're so deep in now, I can't see that a visit to the hospital will do any good, but maybe it's best we don't mention the chocolate stuff to Janet." Hey, do you think Lewis will be there at Janet's?"

And so the crisis passed.

When Janet had said she lived in the worst bit of London, I thought she was joking; she wasn't. Foul-smelling litter spilled out of torn plastic bags and lay in disgusting, sodden heaps on the pavement, shops were boarded up, hooded youths clustered in silent groups. Janet lived next door to a massage parlour above an empty curry house, also boarded up.

"I don't fancy leaving the car here," said John glancing in the direction of three shaven-headed youths sharing a dubious cigarette and a girl with purple hair and a skirt above her knickers. We decided to negotiate. We reached a deal: they got twenty quid down and a tenner when we got back, if the car was untouched. The youths intimated that we could have the girl – literally, thrown in if we wanted. Apparently she liked it over the bonnet of a car. We acknowledged their kindness but said we were prevented by pressure of business.

The door was all bolted up and the bell was broken. We hammered, and the youths suggested we break it down and volunteered their services. It was a nasty time, waiting, particularly as the purple girl came over and started kicking at the door and spitting near my shoes. Hell hath no fury like a woman scorned. However, all was well, there was a sound of bolts being drawn back and Janet appeared, but a Janet like we had never seen before: instead of the scraped back hair and the shapeless top, here was a girl with – and I was taken back to words I had heard before, but couldn't immediately identify – 'hair all down her back', wearing jeans and a tee-shirt with a plunging neckline and a big smile on her face. I must say she looked very good, I simply wouldn't have recognised her. John smiled.

"Are you the surprise?" He asked. She laughed, the sort of laugh that people do when they are relaxed and happy, a sort of post-coital laugh.

"No, he's upstairs."

Ha! I thought, no surprise for us, Janet, we've already sussed out your lover! But as so often, I was utterly wrong.

The surprise was lying on the sofa, surrounded by cans of lager, watching a very loud game of football. It was called Gino.

He didn't bother getting off the sofa, merely glanced up at us, said something, I imagine, ribald, in Italian to Janet, and went on watching the deafening match.

"Real Madrid," said John ever versed in the arcane mysteries of football. Gino raised his can in acknowledgement, but made no further attempt at sociability. If the morose Janet was now bubbly, the smiling Gino had also undergone a reverse.

Perhaps Janet sensed something of my thoughts, for she commented, "Gino doesn't like to be disturbed when he's watching football. We'll go into the kitchen." I thought it would be difficult to disturb Gino in view of the noise emanating from the television.

There wasn't much sitting room except for the television and Gino's sofa, and the kitchen was a sort of alcove off it. It might be a love nest, but it certainly wasn't a luxurious one, nor was it very clean. She sat us down at the kitchen table, which bore the sticky remains of some spaghetti and went into the bedroom to get a third chair.

"I can't offer you much to drink," she said, coming back with an ancient battered Lloyd Loom chair, "because the kettle's broken, but there's half a bottle of Frascati, but I forgot to put the cork back in, so it's probably off." She laughed happily, nothing fazed her. We said we were quite all right, thank you.

"Have you come down specially to see me? Am I the chief suspect?"

"No, we had to come down to see some friends of

John's…"

"I'm sure they don't live round here," she said. "Go on, I am your chief suspect really, aren't I?"

"I'm afraid not; you seem much too jolly to be a murderess."

She sighed luxuriously, and began twisting up her hair into a sort of bunch. "I am terribly, terribly happy."

"Where shall we start?" asked John. "With you or Lady P.?"

"Oh me, I'm dying to tell you all about everything, but I'll have to go back a long way."

Oh dear, I thought, she is going to tell us all those things that her mother didn't want told – but still, it might have a bearing on everything else.

"It's such a relief to be able to talk about things now. I never could before, I mean before Gino." She had a lovely voice and as she sat there twisting up her hair she looked like some Renaissance picture. I couldn't think why we had never noticed before what a beautiful woman she was. A shout issued from the sitting room, someone had scored a goal. Janet shut the kitchen door.

"That's better, she said. "Now we can hear ourselves think."

"Start at the beginning," said John. Janet began clearing away some glutinous spaghetti plates and started talking nineteen to the dozen.

"Daddy died when I was a baby – Mummy doesn't talk about it much, and I think she had a really hard time bringing me up on her own without much money. We never did much except watch television, and there was this presenter on a children's programme that I used to watch and I got a sort of crush on him, like little kids do. So Mummy wrote to get his photo for me, and I don't know how, but we got asked up to be part of a studio audience to meet him and, well, it all took off from there. He was really taken with Mummy and they started seeing each other – Mummy was really very good looking then… she doesn't look too bad now, does she? And he was quite successful then, so it seemed quite a good thing for her to marry him…"

"Weren't you awfully jealous? I mean it was *you* who had the crush on him."

She got up and tipped the remains of the spaghetti into the bin and stuck the plate on top of a lot of other stuff, into the sink.

"Well, that's the funny thing, when I saw him in the flesh, I didn't like him any more. He was sort of podgy and his bottom was too big, and his hair was greasy and he smelt of smelly aftershave – you know how men smother themselves in it when they haven't washed themselves properly?"

I said I hoped John and I weren't guilty of such behaviour.

"Oh no, gays are really clean, I mean you have to be, don't you?"

I wasn't sure that I liked the implications of that, but I let it pass. John was grinning.

"So I didn't like it really when he came to live with us, and I wished Mummy had never written off for his photo. Anyway, then his contract wasn't renewed and he did a lot of 'resting'…"

"And the money dried up?"

"No, that wasn't a problem; he's always had quite a bit stashed away. And to be fair, he's not mean. No, there was another problem."

She untwisted her hair and let it fall on to her shoulders, and began gathering it into a bunch.

"He began touching me up." She said it in a very matter of fact sort of way, as if she was saying that he spent too much money on fast cars. I was appalled.

"Oh, Janet, how dreadful."

She started wiping the table with a very unhygienic-looking cloth:

"He didn't rape me or anything, but he was always watching me, and always coming into my bedroom and putting his hands under the covers; God, it went on for years."

"Did you tell your mother?"

"No, I didn't. In the first place he kept saying it was our

secret. Well, I didn't think it was our secret really, but he made me feel if I said anything it would upset Mummy. And then I was a teenager and all screwed up, but one day I went mad at him, I suppose I was about fourteen and I think I scared him because he stopped after that."

"Didn't your mother ever guess?"

"She did later because I sort of went off the rails while I was at uni – drugs and things, but no sex. I couldn't bear the thought of the hands, and then later I had a sort of nervous breakdown."

"What about the police?" asked John. "He could be put away for years."

"Well, it wouldn't be fair on Mummy. I think she still likes him, in spite of everything."

It seemed a rum sort of do to me. "Why are you telling us now?" I asked.

"I wanted to explain why I was so bloody when I was at the hotel."

"I can't quite see…."

"Well, after I had this nervous breakdown thing, I got better and was going to leave home, but before that I wanted to spend some time alone with Mummy. The Italy holiday was just going to be the two of us, but then he announced he was coming, and I was so angry. All the time I kept thinking, "How dare you come barging in, spoiling everything," – and in the middle of all this I met Gino and fell in love. But he was so handsome and always talking to the Italian girls, and I was afraid everything would go wrong again. But…" she ran the cloth under the tap and turned and gave us a dazzling smile, "everything was all right. He loved me and he had always wanted to work in England, for the experience, you know, and so here we are!" She beamed.

We both smiled at her, and I thought, well, whatever has happened to her and whatever the future holds for her, she's happy now, in all this squalor (I looked at the sink and the overflowing waste bin), and how wise she is to snatch at this bit of unexpected joy. Perhaps that's as much as any of us can hope for, a bit of imperfect happiness every now and then.

The cause of the happiness then came ambling into the kitchen and opened the fridge to help himself to another can of lager. He smiled happily. "I am Italian, but I like much better German lager."

He certainly was very good-looking; a sort of younger John, and I quite envied Janet. He went over and kissed her.

"She is looking very beautiful, yes?"

"She certainly is."

"It is I who make 'er beautiful."

"Sit down, Gino, and hear all about Lady P., you remember Lady Prettyman?"

"Yes, the ugly one, always rude, I never forget her."

"She died at the hotel! John and Mark think she might have been murdered."

" I 'ope she suffered much pain; it is better for such women to die. Now I want to finish the match before I must go to work."

I thought of one of our many theories: that Gino had engineered Lady P.'s death. Here was our chance to ask him to provide a motive, but somehow I didn't think he would have produced this cheerful piece of callousness quite so glibly if he had been guilty.

"What do you do, Gino?"

"I am waiter in a club in the West End. I 'ave very smart uniform."

"He looks amazing in it."

"I show you before I go."

"Now tell me all about the murder," said Janet.

John started on our agreed version: how Tubby had called us to the room, but we had kept quiet about it on Sammy's advice, but how later Tubby had contacted us and asked us to make some discreet investigations.

"But why did he think she'd been murdered?"

"He thought the whisky had a funny smell," said John quickly, not wanting to go into the Bethan bit.

"Then why didn't he say so at the time?"

"Because 'e is small, fat stupid man," shouted Gino from the sitting room. It was, I felt, as good an answer as any.

"I suppose he was in shock," she said.

John explained how we had decided to see various members of the GrandSlam Bridge party. He started with a bowdlerised version of our two encounters with Megan and Bethan; he didn't mention the Irfon saga.

"Bethan thought we were accusing her – which of course we weren't, and Megan came all the way to our house to defend her."

But Janet wasn't very interested in the Welsh ladies.

"Did you see Mummy and *him*?"

"Yes, we called in briefly.

"How was Mummy?"

"To be honest, Janet, she didn't look terribly good. I think she worries about you."

"Well, she needn't…. and was he being all dramatic about and showing off."

"I suppose you could say that."

"I wish we could fit him up with the crime and get him put away. But that wouldn't do Mummy any good. Anyway, I don't think he did do it, he's cowardly and feeble – all men like him, are."

"Someone said they saw him rushing off down the corridor on that last night. But then," John added boldly, "someone saw you chasing off with a bottle in your hands too."

"You see," she said grinning, "I said you suspected me."

"And what answer do you give?"

"Oh surely you can work this out, two famous detectives like you? No? Well, I was chasing off to find Gino; it was still all touch and go whether he would agree to come to England… I was so worried and upset in case it was the last time I saw him, and Mummy knew something was going on and she didn't approve, but she's not strong enough to go dashing about down corridors, so she sent *him*." Whenever she referred to Trevor she managed to imbue the word with loathing.

"But of course he was too stupid to find me, I saw him go panting along, so I nipped into a toilet and waited until he had gone past."

"Where was Gino's room then?"

"Oh, he had a room in the basement, I used to go there because it was safer. Who else have you seen?"

John told her about Lewis and his gingerbread house.

"Oh, I can just imagine it. He's a real sweetie, Lewis; he was ever so kind to me, all the time I was being so miserable because of Trevor and scared of losing Gino, god, I was and so jealous every time he spoke to anyone else! Oh, I was in a state."

"You didn't tell Lewis anything. I mean anything you've told us?"

"No, I was too miserable to talk to anyone and anyway Lewis is quite…." She started twisting her hair again. "He's very proper; I don't think he would have liked to talk about all this."

"You're not smoking!" said John suddenly.

"No, Gino doesn't like me to. I don't miss it, but you can, John, Gino won't mind. Here, have an ash tray."

She pushed a dirty saucer in his direction and John lit up and said, "You know, you're right, Lewis is very proper. Did you know Carol had gone to visit him in her nightie and he threw a wobbly?"

"No! Really? Oh, that was why we switched partners and Carol got poor little Simon. I did rather well out of that, then."

I didn't think she was pretending, and nor did John when we discussed it later: she didn't know, and if she didn't know, she wouldn't have sent the chocolates. She stopped twisting up her hair and the 'hair hanging all down her back' thing came back to me again. I had to ask.

"Janet, I know you said 'poor little Simon', but you weren't trying to hide something, I mean you didn't…. before you met Gino, you didn't have a thing with Simon, did you?"

"Simon?" She looked genuinely puzzled, "what do you mean?"

"You didn't go to his room? Only Skorski saw a girl with long blonde hair leaving Simon's room."

Janet became convulsed with laughter, and at that moment Gino appeared in a white shirt, waistcoat and tight back trousers, and posed by a dirty saucepan.

"I am beautiful, yes?"

"Bello, bellisimo," said Janet and went over and kissed him on the mouth. Then she said something in Italian, presumably about Simon. Gino also laughed and replied in Italian.

"What does he say?"

Gino considered. "I say I think 'e has not much inside 'is trousers."

Well, as John and I agreed later, all four of us in the kitchen were pleasurably aware that Gino in his uniform could not be subjected to the same criticism.

"Whoever it was coming out of his room, it wasn't me," said Janet, "and I should think she had a pretty disappointing time of it."

"Well, you say that," said John, "but Mr Arbuthnot-Jones says Simon has a very sexy girlfriend."

"Not sexee like my girlfriend," said Gino.

"Who's Mr Arbuthnot-Jones?"

So we told her about our visit to Simon's school, and how upset he'd been because she Lady P. was his Aunt and had been the only person who had any feelings for him, and I finished by telling her Lewis' account of their game of bridge.

"Well," said Janet cheerfully, if Mr Arbuthnot-Jones can't tell hearts from diamonds, maybe his account of Simon's girlfriend isn't so terribly accurate."

"Okay, but going back to this girl coming out of Simon's room…"

"But this wasn't on the night of the murder, was it?"

"No."

"Well, then why does it matter?"

Gino was frowning at a spot on his waistcoat.

"Janet, you make clean for me."

Janet obediently got up and began rubbing at Gino's front with a damp cloth; I had an uneasy feeling that John wouldn't have minded changing places with her.

"He might have been making a plan with this girl – if he wasn't having it off with her. A plan about murdering Lady P. maybe," I finished feebly.

"But I thought you said he liked Lady P.? Gino, stand still!"

Gino was amusing himself by moving his pelvis to and fro as she rubbed.

"Well, yes, but let's just suppose. Gino, did any of the waitresses have long blonde hair?"

"No, sono neri, 'ow you say?"

"Brunettes?"

"What all of them?"

"Si, this is why I like Janet, belli capilli."

John wasn't convinced. "The girl at reception was blonde."

Gino laughed insinuatingly. "Pia like real men, not your Simon."

There was an awkward pause, as it probably occurred to all four of us that Gino spoke from experience, then Janet said, "you had better go and take this off, Gino and I'll iron it before you go to work." She looked at him anxiously.

And John quickly continued with an account of our visits.

She couldn't get over the Skorskis profession. "They really had a stuffed poodle in a basket, and you thought it was alive?"

"Mark did," said John. "He's a bit thick, really."

Gino returned, in a pair of Ralph Lauren boxer shorts, carrying his trousers.

"These I like." He grasped a piece of the shorts in each hand, "they give me room for me."

"Yes, indeed." I said.

John blinked a little, but he concentrated on the matter in hand – I mean the investigation – Lady P..

"I mean," said John doggedly continuing, " you don't think it could have been anyone from the hotel?"

" Was there anyone in the hotel who would have liked to kill Lady P.?" I put in.

"Si." We pricked up our ears.

"Who?"

"Tutti, everyone wish 'er dead, everyone 'ope she die."

"Right," said John.

"Anyone in particular?" I asked, I thought John deserved a break.

"Yes, I tell you, I wish 'er dead, Pia wish 'er dead, the manager too, 'e 'ate her, and,...." He stretched out his arms, "all the waitresses and men at the bar."

"Was there anyone who didn't hate her? Was there anyone who liked her?" asked Janet, getting out the ironing board.

"No, everyone 'ate 'er." And so saying he retreated to the television.

"Well, if we turn our attention to the English contingent, I daresay their verdict would be much the same," I commented.

"I didn't hate her," said Janet testing the bottom of the iron, "I just thought she was an ugly old cow who was rude to everyone, but if you looked like her, I expect you would want to be rude to everyone. She wasn't poisonous – like Carol, for example."

"Yes," said John lighting up. "Simon said Lady P. once said something to him about being ugly, to try to cheer him up."

"We keep coming back to Simon," said Janet setting to work on the trousers. "Aren't there any more interesting suspects?"

"Well, who do you think it was, Janet, who hated her so much that they were prepared to kill her?"

"Hmm," she held the iron poised and then plunged it down on to the trousers. "What about Sammy? You don't seem to have thought about him. Lady P.'s language could be awfully racist. I know Sammy always laughed at everything, but it must have been very hard to take."

Gino's head appeared round the door;

"That Sammy I like very much, always laughing, giving lots of money, fucking boys in the kitchen."

"Yes, well," said Janet holding up the trousers and looking at them critically.

"Actually," I said, "it can't be Sammy. There's something we haven't told you." And I related my meeting with him in the strip joint in Soho.

"And what else are you keeping to yourselves?"

"Nothing," I lied. She gave me an old-fashioned look,

"I don't think I believe you, but never mind, I'll tell you who I think – I think it could have been the Skorskis, because of that awful row on the last night. Don't you remember - she called Karl a cheat?"

"Well, she was probably right!"

"Yes, "Janet began to warm to her theme, "I remember Claire standing up and saying Lady P. had spoiled everyone's holiday. And I think she even have said something like the world would be a better place without people like her. I could see there was something exciting going on because we had just finished playing, and oh yes, Claire started saying she was a pig, or something and started going oink oink, and then he started going oink oink oink, and then Tubby chimed in saying, "Oh, you mustn't say that," and she yelled out 'Tournament Director!' and Sammy went over and poured oil on troubled waters, and made Lewis and me go over and play instead."

"But it doesn't really sound like something you'd go and kill her for."

"Perhaps you're right. I'll just run the iron over the rest of Gino's uniform, because he needs to go soon and I need to get it ready."

When she came back I asked her if she had any more suspects.

"Yes, I can see Carol quite happily murdering Lady P.."

"Why do you say that?"

"Well, in the first place Lady P. was always putting her down, making her look small. You know, telling her she was a hopeless player, suggesting her clothes were vulgar – that sort of thing. Carol didn't like that."

"Well, who would?"

"Mmm, but she had that sort of sly way of pursing up her lips as if she was storing it away. She wasn't to be trusted, either; once I thought I saw her poking about round the Skorskis while Claire was asleep by the pool."

"Yes, Karl said that."

"And, well…" She looked up guiltily and then spoke while she busied herself with Gino's jacket.

"She was nosy, always trying to wheedle things out about you. She came up to me in the bar once and said, 'You don't seem very happy, dear. Perhaps it's your parents?" And I didn't say anything, and she went on, 'but of course, he's not your real father, is he…?' in a sort of insinuating way, and I thought, how does she know he's not my real father? And then …," she looked up from the jacket and then looked down again, as if she wanted to avoid meeting our eyes. "I think I might have just said something about, well, what I was telling you just now about Trevor, because I'd had a few drinks and I felt miserable, and I could see Gino flirting with that girl behind the bar."

Neither John nor I made any comment, and obviously relieved, Janet continued. "Anyway, it made me think afterwards that she's not a nice person at all. I even wondered whether she might blackmail people – have you ever wondered how she affords all these holidays? You don't get much working in a shop, I can tell you."

She thumped down the iron. "There, that's done," she said and smiled. For a moment I was tempted to tell her about the chocolates, but mindful of John's words, I remained silent.

The television went off in the other room and Gino appeared. "You 'ave car, yes? You take me to West End? 6.30 I must be at the club."

John is braver than I and said we weren't planning on driving into London, but would take him to the tube station, and suddenly everything was hustle and bustle and our time was at an end. Gino was ready with his uniform in its case, and was giving his lady a long goodbye kiss. I think both John and I were a little jealous.

"Keep me posted," she called as we started the descent

down the dirty stairway.

"Janet!" said John hastily removing his hand from something sticky on the banister. "Phone your mother and tell her how happy you are; that's all she wants to know, really."

"I might."

As I looked back up at her, I saw her leaning over the stairway, presumably to catch a last glimpse of Gino, her hair hung over the rail on the landing as she bent her neck.

"Rapunzel, Rapunzel," I thought. What a difference! I would never have recognised her as the same girl."

Amazingly, the car was still in one piece although the hooded youths hadn't waited for their tenner. John took advantage of the journey to the tube station to question Gino again.

"Did the staff at *Il Sole* know that Lady P. was dead?"

"Si, we know. Signor Lucca tell us."

"Signor Lucca?"

"The manager."

"Did you think she might have been murdered?"

"No, why we think it? And 'e tell us to not talk. So we not talk. It is not good to make angry Signor Lucca."

"But surely…?"

Gino leant forward from the back seat.

"Dead people not good for 'otel, and 'e say don't talk or nobody come to 'otel and we lose job, so we don't talk."

"And were they're really no blondes on the staff? I mean blondes with long hair?"

"No, I Gino would know that. But there are many guest, some have long biondi hair. One night I see girl with long blond hair leave hotel late."

"On the night Lady P. was killed?"

"No, not then, before then.

"And did you recognise her?"

"No she was a long way and going fast. Here is station, now I go. You 'ave nice car; one day I also have nice car. Ciao."

"Bit of a funny family, the Macalisters, if you ask me," John commented when Gino had got out and we were once more on the road."

"I wonder whether Carol had a go blackmailing Trevor."

"Could have."

"Poor Janet," I said. "I hope Gino doesn't see her as the means of attaining a nice car." John was quite shocked.

"You're so cynical, Mark. I think he's very fond of her – in his way."

"But there's not much future in it, is there? And I can't help thinking he'd heard Trevor boasting about how rich and famous he was, and thought if he could latch on to Janet, he might be set up – and when he finds he can't, he'll go back off to Italy, and Janet will be desperately unhappy again."

"Well, it's no good worrying about what might happen to them. We need to worry about us. I think you should phone the hospital." He gesticulated (very rudely) at a driver overtaking him.

"When?"

"Now."

"All right. I don't want you making signs like that at me!"

So I phoned and got through to Saville Ward.

"Carol Daly? Carol who? Oh yes, she's gone."

"Gone!" I shrieked in a falsetto tone." Do you mean she's…?"

"She was discharged this morning." The voice was full of reproach. I breathed a sigh of blessed relief and shot a look at John to say, 'what were you making so much fuss about, then'?

"Is she quite better then, I mean she doesn't need to stay in any longer?"

The voice developed an edge:

"We do not send patients home unless we are fully satisfied with their recovery. Miss Daly was anxious to be home and her friend came and picked her up first thing this morning."

"Olive," said John, "you got there at last!"

"Well, aren't you a bit happier now?"

"I certainly am. I think we'll go and take some flowers tomorrow."

Chapter 17

We are surprised to meet Laurence

The next morning we sat down in the study and were very businesslike.

"You ought to put all the information on your laptop, and have a proper database," said John.

"Yes, yes, but not today." I hate computers and I knew that when John said 'we' he meant me. "Today we're going to see Carol, and if she's just out of hospital she's sure to be at home. She may be all feeble and in bed, and we can attack her at her most vulnerable."

John gave me one of his looks. "There's only one way that Carol wants to be taken advantage of, and I can't see either of us doing that. Anyway, we'll need to be very careful: don't forget she's already had a go at us about asking questions and dropped in the 'libel' word. I'm not sure going to see her is a good idea after all. Do you want some coffee?"

Always ready to drink coffee, rather than actually get to grips with things, I nodded.

"Why should we be visiting her anyway? What reason have we got?" John questioned from the kitchen. "And do you want a chocolate biscuit?"

He came back with the packet and sat down. "You've been at these, haven't you?"

I declined to answer this question, and replied to the earlier one. "I shall say we are calling in on our way to see friends…"

"The Rooneys in North East Bath?"

"Very possibly – I understand that they've moved again. So we have just come to say we hope she's better…"

"And, by the way, how come you got poisoned?"

"Something like that. And then we'll say…"

"Correction, *you'll* say."

"I shall say…" I was on a roll, I was not going to be put

off, "how we'd heard rumours…"

"Who from?"

"Oh, I can't remember now, we've seen so many…"

"… dear absent friends?"

"Exactly."

"And has she done any good blackmailing recently?"

"I shall play it by ear," I said loftily. "Please pass the biscuits."

"Don't eat them all, then."

"I haven't noticed you being particularly abstemious."

"Before you start using any more rude words, let's work out what we think. I'll get a bit of paper. Why is there never a pen anywhere in this house?"

We had a short break to enable us to find the required equipment, and John sat himself at the desk looking studious.

"Right then, someone tried to kill Carol because she had discovered the identity of the murderer of Lady P. and she was blackmailing them. We think the murderer knew that she had been after Lewis, and so sent poisoned chocolates indicating they had come from him, so she would think she was in with a chance after all, and would eat the chocolates."

"Very succinctly put."

"Now, who do we think that person might be? Are you writing this down?"

"No, you're the one sitting at the desk. I shall continue theorising."

"Is that a long word for doing nothing?"

I ignored this. "We think the most likely suspect is Simon because he probably knew that Carol was after Lewis, but on the other hand, it seems unlikely that he murdered Lady P. because he was about the only person in the world who liked her. Are you writing this down?"

"No, this would be better set out in a proper form on the computer."

"On a spreadsheet?" I know nothing of computers, but had heard the term.

"No," said John patiently, "not a spreadsheet." He abandoned the attempt at writing and began doodling – he's rather good.

"We think it could have been Lewis because he didn't like Carol and his name starts with L, but he didn't have any reason to kill Lady P.. Plus, if you're going to murder someone you don't tend to indicate it's you by signing your name. Your turn."

"We think it could be Bethan or Megan because they both knew that Carol was after Lewis and thus could have used the chocolate trick.

Both of them, and particularly Bethan, who goes in for killing husbands and sheep, disliked Lady P.."

"Are we ready to cross everyone else off the list, then?"

"No, not necessarily. Let's see: we don't think Janet knew that Carol was after Lewis; neither do we think she killed Lady P.."

"Why not?"

"Because we like her." I stared at him defiantly, and continued. "We also don't think Trevor and Isabel Macalister knew about Carol's fancying Lewis, and although Lady P. was moderately rude to them, we don't think she was rude enough to make them want to kill her."

"Right. Do you know what this is?" He held up the paper for my inspection and I peered.

"It's Tubby's parrot." I said triumphantly, "and what *about* Tubby?"

"We don't think that Tubby knew about the Lewis thing, and we don't think that Tubby killed his wife, because if he did, why did he start stirring things up?"

"But," I interrupted, "he might have been blackmailed by Carol to stop stirring things up any more."

"Fair enough."

"We think – nor are we alone in thinking – that the Skorskis might have killed Lady P.; in particular, Karl."

"Why him?"

"Because we are wildly politically incorrect and think foreigners capable of doing anything. But on the other hand we don't think they knew that Carol was after Lewis, so wouldn't have known about putting an L on the chocolates."

"But they might have put two and two together after we'd gone, because don't forget Karl had seen Carol in her negligee."

I acknowledged this with a cursory nod and continued: "Gino is also foreign, so a prime suspect, but we don't think he killed Lady P. because he was too busy having it off with Janet. He was also unaware that Carol was after Lewis."

"He might have done; hotel staff always know everything. One of them might have seen Carol prowling about and told Gino."

"Nevertheless, we don't see him sending the chocolates because he wouldn't have known the address … and for a thousand other reasons."

"Next!"

"Now there's Sammy."

"Reasons?"

"Sammy knew everything – he might well have known about Carol, particularly if Lewis told him when he asked to switch partners. He may also have had enough of Lady P.'s racist remarks. Remember too that Sammy and Carol have both been in Tunisia – she could well have been blackmailing him there. In fact, do you remember how she said in a meaningful voice, something like being amongst…"

"… Dear absent friends?" John got excited here, got up and stood half way in and out of the French windows so he could be aided by nicotine and continued: "Wait a minute… as party organiser and Tournament Director, Sammy could walk about the corridors – and he was one of the few people who could have said to the waitress carrying the tray with the whisky, 'Lady P. has asked me to change her drink.' Plus Sammy was the one who got the whole business hushed up in Italy along with the manager."

"This is a good theory. I am tempted to say, a strong theory…"

"Don't be pompous. But it makes sense, doesn't it?"

"Except, why did Sammy go out of his way to involve us instead of just ignoring Tubby?"

"Because," said John unkindly, "he knew we would

bugger everything up."

"I don't think that's true!" I was hurt. "And anyway, it was still easier to fob Tubby off."

"But it does make sense."

I thought about this. "The thing is, I don't think Sammy cared about Lady P.'s rudeness very much; certainly not enough to risk being accused of murder. And he didn't *need* to murder her; he'd be shot of her when she went home the next day. Think how he was always laughing."

"A front."

"And another thing, of all he people who switched the drinks, Sammy is the most easily identified because he's the Tournament Director, and he's black. Any of the staff would identify Sammy straight away."

"Hmm." John was deflated at having his nice new theory shot down and began blacking in the parrot. "In fact, we are just back where we started: anyone could have murdered Lady P."

He screwed up the piece of paper and chucked it in the wastepaper basket.

"Except Carol."

"Unless she sent the chocolates to herself."

"And poisoned herself."

"Ah, but she didn't kill herself, did she?"

"But why should she, what would be the point."

"To avert suspicion from herself, make people think she was…"

"That she was blackmailing someone? And anyway, what people? Let's face it, there was only one person who was worried about Lady P.'s death, and that was Tubby – and now even he's stopped being worried."

"Perhaps she killed herself," said John glumly.

"Yes, very likely, suddenly realising how ugly she was and how everyone hated her."

"Or died of a heart attack, after all."

"But she died after drinking whatever was in the glass, and you're the one who first thought it was suspicious."

"Perhaps I imagined it."

"Oh, come on," I said, "time to go and visit Carol."

"Am I expected to take another day off work?"

"You've got loads of holiday due. Shall we take her some of my tomatoes? Then she really will be ill."

We didn't take any tomatoes, but we stopped off at a Motorway Services place and bought some nasty cheap flowers. We had just rejoined the motorway with about thirty miles to go when John exclaimed,

"Jesus, look, Mark!" Coming towards us in the opposite lane was an ancient black Daimler, and painted on the side I could see the words *DEAR ABSENT*, and craning my neck as it went past I read the words *FRIENDS*. Inside I was sure I could see Fifi in his basket, but the vehicle was going at a fair old pace.

"Well," I said, "the quick and the dead."

"Perhaps," said John, "the Skorskis sent the chocolates, and have gone off hoping to pick up the body for embalming."

"They would have done better with Tubby's parrot," I said, but neither of us laughed; somehow the sight of the Skorskimobile had lowered our spirits. Even the weather, which had been bright and sunny seemed to change; the clouds rolled over, the sky turned grey and a fine drizzle began to fall.

"Do you realise, said John after some ten miles had passed, "we don't have a single shred of evidence about anything?" We sat in silence. Finally I decided to cheer John up with a new theory.

"I think the Skorskis took Fifi to Italy with them, hidden in Karl's little bag. Carol saw him there and told Lady P. and Lady P. mocked Karl, then, in revenge, he poisoned her with a healthy dose of embalming fluid."

John laughed and suddenly everything was all right again. It even stopped raining.

"I bet 'orrible Olive will be there," he said as we turned into 'Petunia Place'. But here he was wrong.

"Just the sort of house she would live in," I whispered as we stood outside, waiting for her to open the door.

It opened. You could have knocked both John and me down with a feather.

"Tubby!" I shrieked, feeling my voice going falsetto with surprise. "What on earth are you doing here?"

"Who is it?" trilled a familiar little-girl voice from behind his shoulder.

"Um," said Tubby. Had he forgotten our names again?

"Well, hel-oh," said Carol beaming from behind her blue-rimmed glasses. "Now what are you two big boys doing on my doorstep? Are those lovely flowers for me? Aren't I the lucky one!"

"I'm so glad you've recovered," I said, stupidly, brandishing the cheapo blooms.

"Why don't you come along in?" She took time off from the beaming to give us an appraising glance. "Have you come all this way just to see little me?"

John was even more gob-smacked than I was, but eventually managed to mutter something like, "Hello, Tubby."

Carol was quick to put him right.

"We have quite forgotten about Tubby, haven't we, dear? His real name is Laurence."

Oh yes, I thought, he told me that on the phone.

Carol gave a little laugh, "Larry to me. Aren't I a lucky girl? Larry, sweetie, would you find a little vase for me?" And the obedient Tubby went shuffling off.

John and I did some more gawping while one or two things began to jiggle about in my mind – mainly John's words about Sammy: 'he knew we would bugger everything up.'

John was the first to recover. "We were so sorry to hear you'd been ill. Olive said you had gone to *hospital*! Nothing serious, was it?"

"Oh, Olive!" she gave a girlish laugh, "she loves a drama!"

"But you were in hospital. Some chocolates…?"

"Oh, it was my own silly fault: Larry sent me a surprise present and I was so excited I just tucked in. Of course, I usually check, but it was such a lovely surprise, I forgot, and the chocolate had nuts in it. I suffer from a nut allergy, you see, it attacks my system. I have to be careful."

"Nut allergy," I said stupidly.

"Nut allergy," echoed John.

We hadn't thought of that.

"Poor Laurence felt so guilty, but I told him it was my own silly little fault. If I hadn't been such a greedy guts…"

Laurence/Tubby came stumbling back into the room, clutching the flowers and gabbling anxiously. I thought he had lost weight.

"Oh dear, no, it was all my fault, and you might have died," he turned to John. "I only wanted to give her a little surprise; I just thought I would send a little thank you gift, and I got the chocolate people to send, but," he concluded sadly, "I always get things wrong. Oh dear, oh dear!"

"But it's an ill wind, pet, isn't it?" said Carol brightly. Pet looked confused.

"I might not have become your fiancée so soon!" She aimed a triumphant beam at John and me. "As soon as he saw what he'd done, Laurence proposed at my bedside."

"I had to go down on my knees," he said feelingly.

Poor Tubby! John and I exchanged looks. Carol had certainly had her pound of flesh.

"And now…," Tubby continued.

"Yes?" I said faintly, wondering what new revelation would be forthcoming.

"I can't find a vase," he said hopelessly.

"You silly Billy!" said his light o'love, in a tone that reminded me of nothing so much as Lady P.'s parrot. And as I looked at Carol, I wondered if Tubby might come to look back on his life with Lady P. as a relatively happy time, in comparison.

We were told to sit down, and we sat.

"Go and put the kettle on, Pet," instructed the fiancée, "and you'll find a vase in the cupboard on the right."

"Now," she said, "I expect you two boys are wondering all about Laurence and me." She was absolutely right. We were itching to hear, and she was itching to tell.

"Well," she said sitting down rather heavily, and crossing her legs. I disliked her, but as I sat there opposite, I felt sorry for her; she could never have been a pretty woman; her nose was too big and her eyes too small, and, frankly, it wasn't the sort of face you'd want next to you on the pillow. She was rather on the stout side, and the legs now crossed for display were not good legs, but, I thought, like the rest of us, all she had wanted was to be loved, but – for whatever reason, probably because she wasn't a particularly pleasant person – love had eluded her. Perhaps she had hunted for it too eagerly, played her cards too soon, as in the case of Lewis. But now all her Sundays had come at once; of course Tubby wasn't exactly an Adonis, being short and stout and fussy and muddling, but he was a man, he was free, and she had netted him. She beamed round, making sure she had our attention.

"It must have been two weeks after I came back from Italy – not really a very good holiday, not a particularly nice selection of people, some of them really very peculiar." In a lowered tone, "You may wonder how I know, but I find people often confide in me. Some of their little secrets ... well." She gave us a meaningful look and continued.

"No, I tell a lie, it was just over the three weeks, and off I went on a bridge weekend in Daventry. I'm always at a loss without my bridge, and of course I was wondering who my partner would be – I've had some very unfortunate experiences with partners in my time, and wasn't I surprised to see Larry? The Macalisters were there too: Trevor and Isabel, he was looking very poorly I thought, but of course... and poor Janet wasn't there, she seems to have disappeared! Well, I do hope she hasn't... I'll say no more. Anyway, as Larry and I were there on our ownsomes, it seemed the most natural thing in the world for us to partner each other: two lonely souls together. But of course, I had no idea, no *idea* that poor Larry was a widower, and I was amazed, yes, and saddened to hear of Marjorie's passing."

She looked up, as if to gauge our reactions, and gave us a piercing look through her blue rimmed glasses, as if to challenge any assertion to the contrary.

John and I were still too blown away to react. Marjorie! When had any of us ever called her Marjorie? We would no more have thought of doing that than of calling Tubby Laurence, or indeed, 'Larry,' as this appeared to be the soubriquet that our dear present friend used. I was amazed at the confident way she had familiarised herself with the name and how freely she used it.

"Of course, Marjorie wasn't an easy woman…," and raising her voice: "The best coffee cups are in the high cupboard to the left of the cooker, Larry," then lowering it again, and casting her eye towards the kitchen from where the sound of falling crockery now emanated, "and perhaps between you, me and the bedpost, not the *most* suitable husband for my Larry, but.." brightly adding, "we're going to put all that to rights now, aren't we darling?" This endearment was addressed to Tubby as he came stumbling in with the cups.

And why was he stumbling? I asked myself. Ah! Of course, I knew there was something different about him: he wasn't wearing his glasses. I wondered why not, and as I was turning this over in my mind along with about a thousand other questions that Carol's remarkable coup had prompted, I suddenly realised why. It was vanity!

"I must say, and I'm sure you boys must agree, my Larry looks years younger, quite a boy!" Carol certainly had an uncanny way of reading your thoughts

And instead of squirming with embarrassment, our Larry looked as pleased as punch and peered at his fiancée, "mmmm," he went, making a repulsive and unsuccessful kissing sound with his lips. He had sacrificed his glasses for the role of young Romeo. I wondered whether he would buy some contact lenses.

"Now where had I got to…? This coffee's not very hot, darling. No, no, you mustn't go working any more, I'm sure we don't mind, do we, boys?"

I could see that John's thoughts were much like my own – if she calls us 'boys' again I shall throw Tubby's tepid coffee at her.

I sat examining Carol: she had had some highlights put in her hair and she was sporting a pink frilly blouse, a rather tight, shortish black skirt, and tight too were the shoes, pointed and obviously new. No wonder Tubby had to do all the running around, I thought.

Again, as if she read my thoughts, she chipped in with, "The hospital say I must try and rest after my ordeal."

"She had to have her stomach pumped," offered Tubby.

Carol gave a little frown at this; some things were obviously better not mentioned, but Tubby continued (perhaps in his mole-like state he couldn't see it). "And when I think it was all my fault, oh dear, oh dear, I can't think how it happened."

And he started doing what Tubby spent most of his time doing, twiddling his thumbs. Carol must have noticed it too, and I was gratified to see that it irritated her as much as the rest of us, because she said quite sharply.

"Don't do that, dear, pass the boys the biscuits."

So we sipped our tepid coffee from Carol's best cups while Tubby blinked and beamed and went 'mmm' when he thought we weren't looking, and listened to the rest of the story.

"Of course Larry was very, very, sad, for when all is said and done, and far be it from me to pry into the marriage of another – even if the other is my own intended…" and the hand was extended to display what I should have noticed earlier, an expensive-looking diamond ring. (Although, remembering Tubby's general tight-fistedness, I somehow doubted it *was* expensive.)

"…. but of course as I said to Larry at that very first meeting, we can't always be looking to the past, we must be brave and look to the future." I thought perhaps the bravery was all on Tubby's side.

"And she asked me to go to Tunisia with her," said Tubby.

Carol gave another little frown. "I'm sure that was your idea, darling, not mine."

John had a question about Tunisia. "I thought you were going to Tunisia much earlier. I'm sure Lewis said you were off quite soon after Italy."

"Lewis!" Her eyes glinted angrily behind the blue-rimmed glasses, "I hardly think I would have told him my plans."

"But you were going earlier," said Tubby, "you told me you would rearrange your plans, so we could go together."

Hah! I thought, Tubby was nailed as soon as his widowed state was made known.

"I never mind how much I inconvenience myself, if it's for the benefit of others. And of course I looked on it as my duty to give succour to Larry in his bereavement – as we are bidden to do in the Gospel. I am a very keen churchgoer, and you will be too, darling. We shall have a very important service to go to soon!"

Tubby twiddled and looked anxious and dropped a biscuit on the floor.

Carol paused momentarily, there was obviously an awkward bit in the story to be got over. "Of course Larry told me – we don't have any secrets from each other – that he hadn't been quite happy about Marjorie's ... the way in which she died. He was terribly in shock, poor lamb, hardly knew what to think, and he told me he had even asked Sammy about it, and then you two boys so kindly offered to help..." The eyes behind the glasses (not sacrificed for the sake of youthfulness) glinted – slightly anxiously, perhaps?

"But of course, we all know perfectly well that poor Marjorie had sadly succumbed to her old heart trouble, don't we, pet?"

What heart trouble was that, I thought? Wasn't it your Laurence who had heart trouble – or fancied he did?

"She passed painlessly away, like a little ripple on Lake Como." She leant over to John, "Larry finds this little expression very comforting,"

John made a noise like a retch, but Carol was undeterred. "Of course, I knew and Larry knew really, that everything had been done just as it should. It was no good Larry reproaching himself and going on wild goose chases. 'Darling,' I said, 'you must tell John and Mark to forget all about this silliness…'"

"Yes, yes, I did, didn't I?" said Tubby, eager for praise. "I telephoned, and I told you, didn't I, I *insisted* that you stopped talking to people?" He attempted to look stern. "You have stopped, haven't you?"

"Absolutely," I said. But this wasn't enough for Tubby.

"And you," he said turning to John, he had obviously forgotten his name again, "you haven't been doing any more *investigating*?"

"What do you take me for?" said John, ambiguously.

"Of course there's nothing to worry about, darling," said Carol. But Tubby still needed convincing. "I don't want any trouble."

"No we don't want any trouble," said Carol and the eyes looked from one to the other of us pointedly.

"No sweat," said John easily. "We only saw a few of the party and nobody suspected foul play."

"Foul play!" She gave a little laugh, "of course they didn't. How could anyone think anything so 'orrible?"

I remembered how in Italy Carol's refined tones tended to slide under pressure. But she was soon back on course and continued with her account of the path of true love. Actually, it seemed to me that there were a number of lacunae between the meeting of the two lonely souls – 'dear lost friends', in fact, and the present state of engagement. However comments like 'a little meal á deux, 'a walk together among the flowers', suggested a clever Carol-contrived series of circumstances, cemented by a certain degree of bullying and… sex? We knew Carol was, as they say, up for it, but Tubby? Well, perhaps he was – after all, most of us are, and Tubby was, after all, an uxorious man – had he not advertised in *The Lady* for a wife? Easily malleable, perhaps he was the kind of man who fell in love with whoever offered themselves to him. He hadn't, after all, seemed actively unhappy under the reign of Lady P., just a little anxious, and anxiety seemed to be the keynote of Tubby's personality. Perhaps all he had needed was Carol saying "poor dear Larry', or rather 'my poor dear Larry' for him to cast away his glasses (and how vulnerable he looked without them), and abandon himself to married life. Had it been like that? Or had there been a very sinister difference …?

As I accepted another cup of tepid coffee, I longed to be alone with John to hear his thoughts. Because, after all, it might not have happened like this at all… but Carol was still spinning her tale.

"And when Larry's sweet old parrot passed away, it seemed as if a new era of his life was beginning."

"A better era," corroborated the sycophantic Tubby.

Had they perhaps planned it together, the murder of Lady P.? My imagination began to take wing: had they perhaps met somewhere before, and had Carol then marked him down as potential husband material – if Lady P. could be made to disappear? Or had she won Tubby round at *Il Sole* and had they planned their murder together? No, because Carol had been after Lewis…. Ah, but perhaps, having failed with Lewis, she had turned her efforts towards Tubby. Had she prepared the poison? Had Tubby administered it?

Looking at Tubby trying to hand round biscuits, it seemed unlikely, but, of course, he had been in possession of his glasses then. Had Carol somehow managed to poison Lady P. without Tubby knowing? But was it really worth the risk? After all, what was the guarantee that the widowed Tubby could so easily be caught? It was an awful lot to risk for thumb-twiddling Tubby – even without his glasses!

And now things could turn out a little uncomfortably for her. Even if she hadn't killed Lady P. – and the more I saw her sitting there, the more I thought it possible she had – the last thing in the world she wanted was John and me raking Italy up again. She wanted a line drawn under it all, and a new Tubby – a Laurence, in fact.

I sat, considering, and I could see John considering too: was there anything else we could ask? Not really. Carol had put the frighteners on Tubby, and I doubted we would hear another word on the subject from either of them. Anyway, even if Carol got up out of the (rather grubby) sofa, stood up and announced that she had murdered Lady P., driven to it by raging lust for Tubby, what could we do? We had only gone into this for Tubby's sake, and now Tubby was the one who wanted it hushed up.

And yet, I thought, it was more complicated than that. (I could see Tubby gathering up cups and wondering what to do with them). Tubby's role in instigating our investigation had long faded away; we were in it for something else. I liked to think that the something else was a desire to discover the truth, although I feared it was something else: nothing more than a desire akin to finishing the SuDoku (which John is much better at than I), or the crossword (which I am better at) – simply a dislike of being outwitted. I decided I needed to talk this over with him.

"When is the happy day?" I heard John ask, with just the slightest hint of sarcasm.

"We haven't quite decided yet," said Tubby aka Larry.

"Ha!" I thought, "you haven't quite got it all your own way yet, Carol."

But I was wrong.

"The banns are going to be heard on Sunday week," said Carol.

"Oh," said Tubby, "I had forgotten that."

Carol gave a merry laugh. "Forgotten! He'll be forgetting his own name next."

"No," I thought, "Tubby won't forget that he's called Larry now – he won't be allowed to."

We made 'well, we must be getting along' noises, and I sensed relief on Carol's part: she had sent those simple poofters off on their way; no more trouble from them! But I felt Tubby was sorry to see us go; I imagined we made a welcome change from an unmitigated diet of Carol. However, it transpired there was a much more potent reason: he was conscious of falling short in his duties and feared he would be getting into trouble again.

"I had better get back into the garden," he said. I was

tempted to ask if he was burying another parrot.

"Carol's given me some little jobs to do," he explained.

"Larry loves gardening," Carol added. "I'm afraid I've had to let it go, I'm not a great gardener, too busy with other things. The church takes up a lot of my time."

"Eat your heart out, Olive," I thought!

John went and peered through a net curtain. "You've been very busy," he said, "you've done a lot of cutting back."

"He's been very naughty," said Carol, "having his bonfires out there." She gave a little giggle. "I hope we shan't be in trouble with the police."

Tubby stood peering and puffing. "I like a good bonfire," he said. He was obviously proud of his handiwork, and saw it as a proof of his masculinity, for he continued, "it's man's work. Too much for Carol. Takes a lot of muscle."

I caught John's eye: stout little Tubby was hardly an icon of the body beautiful. We all went over to the window and stared out at a mass of twisty black-berried stems piled up ready for Tubby's next manifestation of masculinity.

"Gets everywhere, doesn't it," said John conversationally.

"What does?" I asked. I had never seen John as a horticulturist, but he is full of surprises.

"Belladonna," he said, "usually called deadly nightshade."

There was a long pause, then Carol said, "Fancy! I never knew that."

"Belladonna," said Tubby, and the thumb twiddling began again.

"Well, we must hit the road," said John who, I felt, was enjoying himself.

"Perhaps we shall be receiving a wedding invitation." I said coyly, but neither of the betrothed pair answered. Carol waved goodbye merrily but Tubby followed us to the car.

"You didn't say anything to anyone, did you, about… you know?"

"Certainly not," lied John, cheerfully.

Tubby stared doubtfully after us as we got into the car, but not for long. The sound of "Larreeeee" rent the air, and he trotted back before he got into trouble.

"Well!" I said. John lit a cigarette and started up the engine.

"Sometimes we get things a big wrong," he said and burst out laughing. I joined in, and the car positively shook with Sammy-like peels. John started the engine and, as we drove, we chewed over the whole interview.

John was of the opinion that Carol hadn't set her sights on Tubby in Italy, but simply that luck had been on her side, and she had met Tubby by chance at the Bridge Day in Daventry.

"That's not to say she didn't murder Lady P., though," I said.

"No, true."

"Nor that she isn't a blackmailer. Do you think she considered blackmailing him, and then saw marriage as a better option?"

"But that would mean Tubby had killed Lady P. and quite frankly…"

"No, you're right, and in fact there's no reason why she should have blackmailed anyone when you come to think of it. All that going through the Skorski's bag was probably sheer nosiness."

"What fools we were to think someone was pretending to be Lewis, we should have thought of L for Laurence – he did tell us."

"I bet she killed the parrot!"

"Poisoned it with belladonna."

"How did you know about belladonna?"

"Boring gardening programme while you were being sick after that whisky."

"You don't really think…?"

"That Carol took an armful of belladonna to Italy with her and poisoned Lady P. with it? No, I don't, but I'll tell you something, Mark," and John, alarmingly, took his eyes of the road to gauge my shock, "I do think Lady P. was poisoned with belladonna."

"Why?"

"It dilates the pupils of your eyes, and now I think of it, that was what was so weird about Lady P.'s face. Don't you remember when we saw the body, her eyes were all huge and staring."

I was unimpressed. "So would yours be, if you'd just been murdered."

"Yes, I suppose. Well, just an idea. Maybe we're too hung up on poison – after all, Carol wasn't poisoned, and I don't imagine the parrot was either."

"Well, I'm not so sure about that. Just imagine, Tubby – sorry, Larry – invites her over for a romantic twiddling, and the first thing she hears as she walks through the door is a voice screeching, "Tubby, you old fool!" So she resolves to put an end to all that, and next time she goes over, she takes a handful of black berries with her."

"Or maybe Tubby takes a handful back with him from the burn up, and puts it in with the cannabis or whatever it is that parrots eat." Anyway, that's typical of us: we're always getting side-tracked; the bloody parrot is irrelevant."

"Well, you never know."

We felt disinclined to formulate any theories, we just tossed the occasional thought to each other:

"Didn't Tubby look different without his glasses?" John said.

"Yes, much younger, more sort of vulnerable, like a little girl."

"Well, he's got a big girl to look after him now."

"How silly we were with our theories about the bogus L and the poisoned chocolates."

"It was that bloody Olive that put me on the wrong tack," said John wrathfully, "I bet she knew all along there was nothing the matter with Carol and just wanted to stir things up and make herself important. All that worrying I've done about the hospital and the police…"

"Never mind," I said, "think how unhappy she'll be when she hears the banns go up on Sunday."

"Not as unhappy as Tubby."

"I don't know. I think in a sort of way he's up for it."

"I can't imagine Tubby being up, can you?"

"Some things don't bear thinking about!"

John reached down and put a CD on, and because he was in a good mood, it was Mozart which he doesn't much like, but knows I do.

The night was coming on and I felt one of those sensations of great happiness that you get sometimes at unexpected moments: John and I were driving along together – having been made total fools of, and having solved nothing, but we had laughed together and nothing else mattered; all that mattered was the two of alone in the night. I put my hand on his thigh.

"It's all that thinking about Tubby with a hard-on that got you excited," he said.

"Tubby?" I said, "Laurence to you, mate."

Chapter 18: Two Sad People

The next day was a bit of an anticlimax: John got up to go to work muttering about how nice it must be to be retired and lie in bed all day, which, actually, was terribly unfair because I had got up specially to make him tea and toast.

"I hope you'll have solved everything by the time I have got back," was his parting shot, as he went off through the door. "Or at least," he added, coming back in and wagging a finger at me, "set up a database."

I smiled noncommittally and thought to myself, 'I have got to the age of sixty-one without databases (and what exactly, are they anyway?) and I shan't be starting now.' Nevertheless, I switched on the computer and had a look at the emails. If only I had done so a couple of days before we might both have been saved a great deal of worry. From Sammy:

"Hi, you two!

Did I tell you about Tubby and Carol – all down to Uncle Sammy's Lonely Hearts Club bridge holidays in Tunisia, I reckon. He hasn't wasted any time and she was in for the kill, bumper supply of frilly blouses. I don't think she got the ring on her finger then, but I daresay she has now. Anyway, neither of them wanted to hear about Lady P. dead or alive, so just as well you didn't waste any time sleuthing. Well, I suppose you didn't, cos I've not heard from you lately, and one thing's certain, neither of them are going to waste any time over it.

Now I'm sending everyone I can think of, and certainly everyone from GrandSlam who was at the Italy thing, an email or whatever, to get you all come to Sammy's Benefit Bridge Day. It may go under another name, but the fact is Tunisia was a bit expensive – I was more than generous to the local youth (not half worth it, though). So, I'm inviting you to spend fifty quid each, and visit the lovely picturesque

Cotswolds and play bridge with your dear old friends…"

"Dear Absent Friends," I thought.

There was a form to download and some maps of the area; the date looked all right – about three weeks ahead, and I accepted for both of us, writing out a cheque for £100, which I doubted I would see my fifty from. It would be a splendid opportunity to observe everyone; the question was, did we want to tell Sammy what we had been up to, or not?

I re-read the email and took stock: was there any subtext to it? Was Sammy saying in effect, 'I don't know how much you've found out, but whatever it is, just forget it'?

And if he was saying that, *why* was he saying it? Was it just that Tubby and Carol had told him to forget it and to tell us to forget it, or was there some deeper motive? I made a cup of coffee and began to ruminate.

If Sammy was guilty … but there was the same old problem. If Sammy was the murderer, goaded by Lady P.'s racist remarks, why had he stirred it all up quite unnecessarily? Even if Tubby had gone whingeing on at him, he was so malleable, Sammy only had to be firm and tell him there was nothing anyone could do – and indeed, there wasn't! There was no evidence of anything – that had been our problem all along. And besides, Sammy didn't really take things to heart; as long as he had enough cash for some sharp clothes and a few boys, he wasn't really bothered about anything much. Add to that the fact that he had managed Lady P. superbly, and always got the better of her, I couldn't see Sammy as the murderer. And, now, if he was, why on earth would he go out of his way to get all the dear absent friends together?

I came to the conclusion that there was no subtext to Sammy's email – apart from the fact that he was charging us over the odds for this bridge thing, because he was strapped for cash – and even that wasn't a subtext, it was bluntly there in front of me on the screen!

So should we tell him all we had discovered? Tell him about everyone we had seen and all their little secrets –

Bethan's husband dying in mysterious circumstances, his treatment of Megan, the Skorskis bizarre trade, Janet's new romance, Simon's miserable existence bullied by his pupils, and Trevor's groping, our own abortive trip to *Il Sole,* the death of Tubby's parrot, the belladonna in Carol's garden? Should we spill this all out?

I would consult John, but I felt he would feel the same: in a curious way all these people, whatever they had done – or not done – *were* 'dear absent friends.' Just as the Skorskis must take pleasure in regarding Fifi in his basket, and wanted him left like that, so John and I…. well, we weren't quite like the Skorskis, god forbid, but for the sake of the analogy, we ought not to rip open the carefully preserved exteriors, it simply wasn't our business. I felt rather solemn and went off to make some fresh coffee. Then I switched off the computer.

When John came home I presented him with the ethical problem. John, unlike most people, is quite bright and sharp when he comes back from work, and he was buoyed up by Sammy's Bridge Day.

"Very generous of you forking out, Mark."

"Hmm." I felt that perhaps John was not the right person to give ethical judgements after all. And, in fact, when I did ask him, he took a very different viewpoint from me.

"You go through life and you collect a lot of baggage and sometimes it gets a bit smelly, and if you've got things that are smelly, either you do something about it – or other people will."

"But these people are our friends."

"No they're not, they're just people we've met, and if we've opened up cans of worms, we'd better find out what to do with the worms."

"Do you want us to tell Sammy everything, then?"

"No, I'm not saying that," he swung his long and shapely legs on to the sofa, the latter so much admired by Bethan, the former by me. "No, I don't see any need for that, but if we get pissed one night and it all comes out, that's no big deal either. And some things need telling… have you done anything about contacting Isabel?"

"Well, we told Janet to phone her."

"I think we ought to let her know Janet's alright."

"And tell her about Gino?"

"No, not unless she asks. Just tell her Janet's okay, and why doesn't she phone her? I'll do it now, if you like."

I was glad he was volunteering, but he got off lightly because neither of them were there, so he left a message. But he was in a practical mood.

"What we need to do is make a list of unanswered questions. Which reminds me: have you started on that database yet? Silly question."

"Let's think of some unanswered questions. I'll jot them down."

"Have you got your quill pen?"

"Well, there's the mystery of Simon and the blonde girl who was in his room. Was she a prostitute, or was she in a plot with him to kill Lady P.."

"Even though he had no reason?"

"Listen! Was it his girlfriend from England? The one Arbuthnot-Smith…"

"Jones, not Smith. The one Arbuthnot-Jones so admired?"

"Even though he can't see properly."

"I thought we were talking about unanswered questions, not why they weren't worth asking in the first place."

"Okay, well we haven't seen Simon, or Lewis for that matter, for ages. He never replied to my invitation to come over and play bridge – which is unlike him, as he is such a particular man. Perhaps we should try again; it might be useful to talk to Arbuthnot-Jones."

"Well, as he's stone-deaf..."

"Never mind, put him on the list: 'What Jones didn't tell us.'"

"Shall I put down what Sammy did with those boys in Tunisia?"

"Probably not relevant."

"Where Carol buys her frilly blouses…"

"Who killed the parrot…"

"We're being silly. One thing that did occur to me was whether Carol found anything of interest when she rummaged through that bag."

"Claire Skorski's handbag?"

"Or his."

"We're not likely to discover that, and I imagine Carol's blackmailing days are over, don't you?"

"Another unanswered question."

"Do you know…," said John helping himself to a vodka tonic. "Want one?" I shook my head.

"I think we aren't asking the right questions," he continued. "I think we ought to go right back to the original scenario."

"Meaning?"

"Well, let's assume for the moment Lady P. was murdered by a glass of poisoned whisky – possibly with belladonna in it, which started off on a tray carried by one of the hotel staff, a girl with blonde hair. If the girl hadn't put it there, someone else had: how did it get there?"

"Well, I suppose Gino tells the barman what the orders are and he puts the glasses on trays, and gives them to the waitresses to take up."

"Yes, but Lady P. had *had* her goodnight drink already; it's that second drink offered by Bethan that poisons her – and we don't know where that came from. Logically, Mark, and I know you don't want to hear anything against her, it makes sense to say that it came from Bethan – or even Megan – or the two of them together, because if it didn't, how would anyone get the drink on to this blonde girl's tray."

"I suppose they would distract her in some way."

"What? 'Oh, excuse me, just put that tray down, so I can swap that glass for the glass of poison in my hand.' Very likely – and anyway, who *was* the girl?"

"Another unanswered question."

"Here's another: where did the poison come from? Who takes poison with them on holiday?"

"Janet's a biochemist and Skorski has his embalming fluid. I don't see you writing all this down."

He shook his head impatiently (he looks incredibly sexy when he does this).

"Yes, someone – well, it could be Skorski – who has already decided to commit murder; who knows that Lady P. will be there."

"Like Simon? It's beginning to look a bit black against him."

"Not necessarily; we all got a list of names and addresses before we went. Someone else could have seen Lady P.'s name, someone who had met her before – and wanted to make sure they didn't have to meet her again."

"But we never heard that anyone on the holiday *had* met her before."

"Sammy might have done – on a previous bridge holiday."

"They neither of them ever said."

"Why are Sammy and the hotel guy so anxious to hush everything up? People have heart attacks all the time; it's not the hotel's fault."

"My guess is the manager's worried because of Lady P.'s title. He thinks he'll have trouble from the Great and the Good of Inghilterra – or perhaps he thinks one of his staff might have done something – perhaps he's done it himself: 'Gino, givea this nice drinka to the English lady with the longo naso; I give her nice sleep.'"

"I wish you wouldn't try and do accents. What about Sammy, why does he go along with all this?"

"My guess is that he owes the manager money or he's had one ragazzo too many."

"And what about...?"

"Let's go to bed," I said.

The next morning I looked at the list and felt depressed by it: I felt I was unlikely to make much progress with any of the unanswered questions and besides, it was a nice day and I didn't feel like sitting indoors crouched over a computer.

I rang Jeremy to see if he wanted to play bowls; he didn't, so I was forced to think again, and it occurred to me that it was just the day for a nice drive in the country. How pleasant to be offered lunch at the Gingerbread House, and afterwards call in on Simon and have a look for Arbuthnot-Jones.

I decided against ringing first because I felt like going now, and didn't want to be put off, so I decided I'd just arrive on Lewis' doorstep and claim I'd gone to get some picture-framing done (I had once had dealings with a man in Worcester), and was calling in on spec.. Of course he might not be in, but at least I'd made an effort. I felt busy and rather pleased with myself: John shouldn't think me idle just because I wasn't busy with databases.

I arrived at the Gingerbread House in under an hour and was delighted to find Lewis at home – but it was not the Lewis I knew.

Perhaps the defining characteristic of Lewis had been his smartness, a smartness that tended towards the dapper, which, I suppose was why John and I had originally wondered if he was gay. Even toward the end of the fortnight's holiday at *Il Sole,* when the rest of us were beginning to look decidedly dog-eared, Lewis remained immaculate, his shirts crisp, his trousers, (even those that were linen) uncreased and unspotted, his hair firmly combed across the bald patch, no shadow upon his chin, and his whole person smelling pleasantly fresh and clean. Lewis had always looked as if he had emerged from the ministrations of a personal valet.

This was now markedly not the case. My mouth opened and shut but, after all, you can't really say to someone you don't know very well, 'I say, why do you look so shabby?' But shabby he was: the shoes lacked polish and bore traces of mud, he wore an old sweater and the trousers looked as if they should go to the cleaners.

Perhaps he read my thoughts, for he said, "How very nice to see you, Mark; I'm afraid I'm not fit to be seen; I've been in the garden, tidying things up before the winter takes over. Can I offer you some coffee?" But the voice sounded weary and I surmised I wasn't going to be offered lunch this time. Nor was I invited into the elegant sitting room with its dominating portrait that I glimpsed through the open door.

This time I was taken into the kitchen; and although it was a very different kitchen from Janet's, I felt there was something a bit hole-in-the-corner-ish about being put there; after all, there wasn't even Gino's football to escape from. However, as he busied himself with the business of choosing coffee beans and grinding them, I felt the return of the old Lewis.

"Have you come to make a citizen's arrest?" He asked, extracting the ground-up beans, "or is this merely a social call?"

"No, I had to go into Worcester to… er… get some pictures framed and I thought I'd drop by."

"Really?" I had forgotten that the Headmaster always spots the lie, but he didn't pursue it. "Would you like some cake? The WI have been very good to me lately."

I accepted the cake, but I thought as he bent down to get the tin out from a low cupboard, how aged he looked; his movements lacking that perkiness that was so much part of him. He straightened up and made an obvious effort to be polite.

"Tell me all your news; you have the air of one who wants to tell all."

"Well," I said, "there is so much to tell, I hardly know where to begin."

"You had better emulate Alice and start at the beginning."

"Well, you know we went to see Simon, because you've played bridge with him."

"Yes," he looked rather severe. "I think you rather upset him – as I warned you, might be the case."

"Well, I'm sorry about that, but at least it made us realise that he was actually fond of Lady P. and so unlikely to have killed her."

"And what else have you been doing?"

"We went to Italy."

"And what was your purpose in doing that?"

"Well, I…"

"What did you learn?"

"Well, I had a look at the layout of the rooms."

"And did anything strike you?"

"Not really, should it have done?"

"Mark, you are the detective, not I. Would you like Victoria sponge or coffee cake? The Victoria is a day or so older?"

I settled for the Victoria sponge, Lewis ate nothing, and the coffee bubbled away in an old fashioned percolator.

"Well no, nothing much struck me. I had a look at the Bridge Room but it was full of stored furniture, so it didn't stir my mind with old memories. But I tell you something: I had an interview with the manager and he made a big case for everything having happened quite normally – nothing fishy at all – and finally he tried to bribe me. What do you think of that?"

It was, of course, hopeless to try and impress Lewis with my advanced detective skills.

"An interview? Where was this held, in the bar?"

"Well, yes."

"And can I guess the nature of the bribe? A free Scotch?"

"Strega," I said sulkily, "two."

"Ah. And was that the extent of your exertions?"

I thought back over our ghastly abortive trip, and it struck me how little I could remember, except how miserable it had all been, and how horrible it had been coming back, when I had believed I was losing John. Really, I thought, the anxiety and unhappiness over all that, had quite driven the purpose of the trip from my mind, and now I thought of it, it all seemed totally senseless. So I thought I wouldn't linger on it, but should tell Lewis about our other, possibly more fruitful visits, starting with the least suspicious of our suspects and leading up, as I hoped, to the trump cards of Tubby and Carol. I started by telling him about the trip to the Skorski's taxidermy emporium, but he just sighed and looked weary and unimpressed, even when I told him that Claire Skorski had seen Carol going through her bag.

"That doesn't surprise me."

I was about to tell him I knew all about her seduction attempt, but there was something a little intimidating about him as he sat opposite me drinking black coffee with, what I felt, was a sardonic air. So, instead, I said, "Skorski let slip that he saw a blonde girl coming out of Simon's room."

Even that failed to impress him. "And where was Skorski at the time? Up three storeys at the far end of the corridor? I very much doubt he could see anything of the sort."

"It was possible – just. We put it to the test," I said proudly, but Lewis didn't follow that up either.

"And what other adventures have you had since your return?"

"All sorts; I'm keeping the best to last. I would have told you before, but I got no reply when I phoned you – several times."

"Very remiss of me, I'm so sorry. I've been... busy. Please, tell me the rest."

I had intended telling Lewis everything, from Megan's rape, Bethan's husband's mysterious death, to our suspicions about Lewis himself, and the poisoned chocolates, but as I went along recounting the visits of Bethan and Megan, Lewis courteously refilling my cup with his (excellent) coffee and pressing me to more cake, I found myself summarising and omitting. I hardly know why, but I got the impression that he only listened in order to humour me, and that he was no longer interested. It was also clear that, for some reason, he had cooled towards me, and he hardly enquired after John at all. I should have picked up on this before, I reflected, when my invitation for bridge and my phone calls remained unanswered.

So now I merely skimmed the surface. I told him nothing about Bethan's and Megan's visit except that John and I both believed that Bethan had taken the glass off the tray in the belief that it was Lady P.'s goodnight drink, and that she had not put it there herself. I expected all sorts of questions: why had the Welsh ladies come to visit us? How did we justify these assumptions, and so on? But he didn't ask anything.

"I am sure you have your reasons for exonerating the Welsh ladies," he said, thereby implying that we had, as usual, based our conclusions on little more than intuition, but I felt he was letting me get away with it. For whatever reason, he had ceased to interest himself in it all – rather like Tubby, I thought ruefully – although in Lewis's case there was, of course, no Carol.

He was, however, mildly interested in the Janet and Gino ménage, and surprisingly censorious.

"Oh," he said looking up in that sharp way he had – one, I daresay that had struck fear into his pupils hearts, "I suspected something of the kind during our time at *Il Sole*." I was rather irritated at what I considered Lewis' know-all attitude.

"Why was that, Lewis?"

"I caught her looking at him several times, and I saw her walking about at night in a rather purposeful way." He gathered up our plates abruptly, "I think it a great pity that a nice young girl should behave in this way."

I asked a bold question:

"And what, may I ask, were you doing, that you saw her wandering about?"

Lewis sighed and I thought we had been wrong about his age: he was easily seventy, only the careful grooming deceived.

"I sleep very badly, Mark. I have not been able to sleep properly since my wife died, and after those terrible last weeks when she was in so much pain, I thought I should never sleep again. She and… one other have been what made my life worth living; on your own there's not much really, however much you pretend to the contrary. So if I can't sleep, I wander about a bit. Can I give you so more coffee?"

Was this a satisfactory explanation – and dare I ask him about the 'one other'? Would this be the key to everything. But, come to think of it, why should this 'one other' be connected with GrandSlam Bridge? Probably an old flame who had disappeared long before the wife.

"Yes, thank you, Lewis." I accepted some more coffee, "I'm so sorry to hear of your unhappiness." I paused and cleared my throat, it seemed a little unkind to cross-question a man when he's just told you about his wife's death, but it was now or never.

"I suppose you didn't see anything interesting on your nocturnal wanderings at *Il Sole*?"

"Not really. As I say, it did occur to me that Janet was going to visit Gino because I saw her going down the stairs to the basement area where I presumed most of the staff had their quarters."

"Why do you think their living together is such a bad idea? Janet was obviously desperately unhappy in Italy and Gino has made her sparkle! That can't be all bad, can it?"

"Have you finished with your cup? I am afraid I am a rather old-fashioned sort of person – I don't like what is, I believe termed 'casual sex'. I believe if one loves, one should marry, and I believe in fidelity. However, I shan't inflict my reactionary views on you; I'll offer you some pragmatic ones instead. From what you say, it sounds pretty sordid there. I don't suppose there will be any money forthcoming from the parents. I imagine Isabel depends on Trevor and I shouldn't think he will be very keen on subbing them – certainly not after the way Janet used to behave towards him. I suppose she will get what she deserves – disappointment."

I thought this was a pretty harsh viewpoint and I wondered whether to tell Lewis about the childhood abuse of Janet by Trevor. However, it had been told in confidence, so I decided not to. I didn't feel it was something I would find easy to talk about with Lewis anyway. I decided to change the conversation.

"I've kept the best bit of gossip to the end."

He sat down and smiled; I felt I was to be humoured: "Ah, now, who haven't we discussed? Let me see: ah, Tubby and... hmm, Carol White."

"Now," I said smiling, "not even you, Lewis, will guess this." And I told him all about it, although of course I did not say that we thought he or Simon might have sent her the poisoned chocolates."

While I was talking Lewis began bustling about the kitchen, washing up the cups and drying them vigorously and putting the remains of the cake back in its tin. He even got out a little brass handled brush and pan to tidy away the crumbs from the table.

"Well," I concluded, "what do you think?"

"I think," he said putting away the brush and pan into an immaculately tidy cupboard, "that the whole thing is immensely ironic."

"How?" Lewis paused for thought. "Well, Tubby has the good fortune to lose one harridan of a wife and almost straight away puts his head in the noose and chooses another."

"I don't think Tubby likes living by himself…" And then, of course, I realised what a tactless comment that had been had been, and I hurried on, "because he advertised for a wife in some magazine, didn't he? That was how he got Lady P."

"No, I believe she advertised for a husband."

"Well, it came to the same thing."

He began wiping the table vigorously. "She may not get him in the end; they aren't married yet."

"She was talking about putting the Banns up."

"Poor Tubby! Let's take a turn in the garden before you go… I am sorry I can't give you lunch."

He led the way and something made me turn for a last look at the kitchen with its gleaming green aga and elegant hanging copper pans, and it struck me that there was something different about it, something missing… but what, I didn't know. We only passed through the kitchen briefly on our last visit, and it could have no bearing on Lady P.'s death.

Outside, all evidence of the summery idyll spent in the garden had gone. Instead, a pile of branches had been hacked back, a number of beds prepared for autumn sowing and the area around the apple tree cleared, I supposed for spring bulbs. Perhaps Lewis' weary appearance was simply due to an old man overdoing his gardening.

A thought suddenly occurred to me: "do you have any belladonna in your garden?"

He looked at me, I thought rather sharply. "I don't believe so. Why do you ask?"

"Tubby was clearing it out of Carol's garden." He

suddenly smiled.

"Aha! I see, you have Tubby and me as partners in crime, leagued together in smuggling belladonna to Italy with the purpose of poisoning Lady P. and installing Carol in her place."

I felt rather foolish, "it was just something that John and I talked about, belladonna, I mean, not you."

Lewis led the way down the path. "I rather assumed your investigations had come to a natural end: Janet and Gino paired off, Trevor and Isobel left to enjoy their retirement undisturbed, the Skorskis busy with their taxidermy, I with my garden, Simon his teaching, and Tubby and Carol prepared to lie on whatever bed they have prepared for themselves. And you and John as close as ever, of course."

He stooped to pick up stray plant label. "After all, you can hardly carry on indefinitely if Tubby does not wish you to do so. I would imagine Carol will have something to say, if you do. If you do not intend calling in the police, I should have thought it was better to call it a day, wouldn't you? As you said at the beginning, there can be no evidence; you have looked into things – in your own way, quite thoroughly, and you know no more now than you did at the beginning. You gave it your best, and one wants to avoid being obsessive about things when they can't lead anywhere – don't you think? "

I didn't think this entirely true, but I thought it best not to argue. However, I hadn't quite finished.

"I heard Carol was after *you!*" I said.

Lewis picked a clump of grass and wiped his some mud off his shoe. "Who told you that?"

"Lots of people!" I enjoyed being, for once, in possession of knowledge Lewis didn't have and which he might want to hear. Somehow, I felt I liked him considerably less than I had previously.

"Let me see… oh yes, Megan or Bethan probably overheard our little tête à tête."

"And Karl Skorski saw her setting off in her negligee."

He turned to me abruptly, "I think we have heard enough

about Carol."

"Why do you dislike her so much, Lewis?"

He bent down and picked up a fallen apple. "Would you like some fallings? It has been a very fruitful year; they are excellent bakers, and I have more than I know what to do with."

I declined the offer and rather bravely repeated my question about Carol, but Lewis was already on his way back into the house to get a polythene bag, as if he hadn't heard my refusal of the apples or my question about Carol.

I looked across the garden to the beautiful view beyond. The meadow had now been ploughed and lay in even, undulating brown ridges, the hawthorns were heavy with berries and from somewhere came the baaing of sheep. How calm and serene it all was; surely a man might pass the evening of his life happily here – and yet how little one really knew of others: their happiness and unhappiness, the agonies beneath the calm surface of perfectly ordered lives?

Lewis returned with the bag and began busying himself with the fallings. When he had half-filled the bag, he straightened up and said, "You ask me why I dislike Carol White, and I will try to explain. There are a few last apples left on that branch above you, I think you might reach them; you are taller than I."

He paused and watched my rather feeble efforts, and then he began.

"I was very much in love with my wife She was a wonderful woman, more of a girl, than a woman, unspoilt by... life, pure and good. We had no children and as so often happens, each became husband, wife, son and daughter to the other. There's an apple on that branch up there to your left, could you reach it? I adored her, and to see her dying in agony... I would rather have died myself a hundred times."

He turned away rooting about in some long grass, but I think it was only an excuse. "I regard her memory as sacred," he continued. "I miss her presence with me during the day, and when I wake in the night as I so often do, I think... oh, I am afraid you will think me a fond old man, I sometimes imagine that, were I to walk a little I would perhaps meet her again, see her, maybe catch a glimpse. Lake Como was where we went on our honeymoon; Lily loved Italy, and I tried to relive some of our times together, walking alone by the lake in the dark. I was preparing for such a walk that night when Carol came to my room, and for a moment, just for a moment, I thought the figure at the door was Lily… and when I realised it wasn't, but that it was Carol White, I was…" he paused, "… filled with anger against her – more than was justified of course, but it coloured my perception of her: a woman I already felt an antipathy for, with her infernal malicious gossip. That she should come, expecting… well … at such a moment… you must understand my dislike."

"Of course."

He straightened up, looked at me, and shook his head, "I shouldn't have told you this, and I wouldn't have done, but I… ah well" he handed me the bag, "Will these be enough for you? I think they should be sufficient for a crumble."

"Yes, that's plenty, thank you."

I felt embarrassed: it was the first time I had seen Lewis, as it were, exposed. However, he pulled himself together. "Now, Mark, I have taken up enough of your time."

The interview was at an end, and he walked me back to the car. We neither of us spoke; he, I suppose, thinking of his wife, and I reverting to my earlier reflections on the hidden miseries of people's lives. I was about to drive off when I remembered I hadn't asked him about Sammy's bridge day.

"Will you come to Sammy's benefit day? John and I are going? You could come with Simon. After all, you played your strange four with Matron and Arbuthnot-Jones. Actually I could ask him for you, I was thinking of calling in on the way back…"

"Before or after you have collected your picture framing from Worcester?" Once again I saw the old Lewis with a twinkle in his eye.

"Well, I…"

"I don't think I should call in on Simon; he really doesn't like being seen in the school situation. None of us likes to be seen where we do not shine, do we? And Simon is not happy there, he is unsuited to… schoolmastering. As I mentioned, he was very upset last time you called."

I nodded vaguely; after all, Simon had been upset about Lady P.'s death, rather than our appearance at the school. I *was* going to see him. Of course, Lewis knew that perfectly well.

"Just be kind, then."

"Of course."

I switched on the engine, and just caught Lewis' parting words:

"Don't forget those pictures, will you, Mark?" And he hadn't said whether he would come to the Bridge Day or not.

So I went to find Simon; I don't know much about school timetabling, but I reckoned if I was lucky I might hit lunch hour. The previous occasion when John and I had been there, the place had been pretty deserted. Not this time: there was obviously some sort of posh lunch going on, and the car park situated at the end of the impressive avenue of limes, was full of Mercs and four-by-fours. Getting into the school was a Fort Knoxian exercise: first I had to speak into an entry phone; "Please state your name and business." I stated my name and took so long to decide what my business was, that the voice said it was sorry, I had better try again later. I did: I said that I was Mr Hadley and I wished to see Simon Johnson *'about the books'.* I thought that would satisfy them. Did I have an appointment? No. Another long wait, but finally the voice conceded that I might be admitted and allow myself to be scrutinised, and the door was opened. The Receptionist, or School Secretary, or whoever she was, was actually quite nice.

"I'll see if I can get him on the mobile; I think he's on playground duty. I'm sorry but I'll have to ask him if he knows you, we have to be awfully careful nowadays with paedophiles and people. Oh, I'm sorry…" She was very young, pretty and inexperienced, and she ran her hands through her long blonde hair, "I didn't mean to imply… only we've got The Governor's Lunch today and everyone seeing to that, and they've left me to hold the fort. I just do photocopying and things normally. I'll see if Simon's there. One moment."

She finally got him and was trying to make herself heard above a cacophony of voices. I even thought I recognised the old cry of "Simon, Simonetta, we're coming to getcha." She turned to me apologetically, "He says 'what books?'"

"Just tell him it's Mark Hadley from GrandSlam Bridge."

She looked puzzled, "From what?"

"Shall I talk to him?"

"No, I'm not allowed to let anyone else use the phone." She spoke anxiously into it: "What did you say, Simon? He's called Madley... I think he's brought some books for Mr Williams' bridge building exercise." She turned to me for corroboration: "Is that right, Mr Madley?"

"Absolutely."

"Oh, that's all right, then. Where are you, Simon? In Little Court with the juniors? Okay."

She beamed at me. "Now I'll do your name badge." I think I'd made her day. While I was waiting for her to write out 'Madley' and place the slip inside two pieces of Perspex, I asked her if she also knew where I would find Mr Arbuthnot-Jones.

"I'm afraid he only comes out at night."

"Like the bats?"

"Bats? Oh no we don't play cricket at night."

"Why does he only come out at night?"

"Because he's very old."

I said I couldn't quite see the connection, but she explained quite patiently that old people sleep all day. I said that I knew old people who didn't, but she said, "Well, Mr Arbuthnot-Jones does." She leaned over towards me. "Actually, he drinks quite a lot; I think he has hangovers."

I nodded and asked her if she would like me to do the badge, but she said quite crossly that she could do it quite well, thank you. After a while I suggested that she insert the label from the bottom because that was where the opening was, and she said yes, she knew, thank you. In the end she put the piece of Perspex back in the drawer and handed me the paper label and a safety pin.

"That will do just the same," she said.

I replied that I was sure it would and could she tell me where Little Court was. She look puzzled and said that while she knew where it was herself, she wasn't very good at giving directions and she wasn't allowed to leave the desk, so I suggested she find someone to take me. "Like her," I said pointing to an important-looking bespectacled little girl who emerged through a door on the left. I couldn't have picked a more eager guide.

"I often take visitors," the small person remarked as she led me through a maze of corridors, "because I've got my Brown Certificate in People Skills. I am the only one in Upper IVa with a Brown Certificate and only Felicity Greer has got the Pink One." I said that I found that very impressive, whereupon she asked me whether I had gained any such certificates, and when I admitted I had none, I felt I had fallen in her estimation.

"That's the Great Dining Hall," she said as we traversed yet more corridors, "there's a very important lunch there today." And indeed I could hear the sound of animated voices; they were obviously doing themselves well.

"Does Mr Johnson teach you?" I asked. I fell further in her estimation.

"Oh no, I am in the A form, Mr Johnson only teaches C and D, he even…" And the voice reached heights of scorn, "…. he even does remedial."

"So you don't have him at all?"

"He sometimes does preps," She became confidential, "I think he has to do all the duties and things that the good teachers won't do."

"Isn't Mr Johnson a good teacher, then?"

"He's hopeless, he can't keep any order, everyone plays him up all the time."

"Perhaps he needs your certificate in People Skills."

The small person considered this point and finally

concluded, "I think it would be a waste of time him trying; he's much too soft, and anyway…" the light glinted on her spectacles… "it's very difficult. I got a special clap when I got my certificate because I got the top mark for Understandingness. Mr Johnson wouldn't even get a pass."

I said that it obviously wasn't given to everyone to achieve such eminence, but surely Mr Johnson must have his good points. The small person considered this judiciously:

"He's very hopeless, but he's quite kind. Once when I hurt my knee he was really nice and took me to Matron when Mrs Glover said there was nothing wrong with it, and Matron put a bandage on, so there was something wrong with it, and he'll always listen, he just needs to be a bit sterner. He's hardly ever stern, and you can see him getting upset, and all Upper 3b are really horrible to him. Paul Skorski used to be able to make him cry."

"Who? " I exclaimed, "who did you say?"

"Oh, a boy called Paul Skorski, but he was really horrible and cheated in exams. Do you know him?"

"No," I said thoughtfully, "but I may know a relation of his."

"I don't think he'd got any relations because he was foreign, but he's left now because England made him ill."

Before I could further my investigations into the mysterious Skorski who had left because of England's unhealthiness, we emerged into the light, and I immediately knew where Simon was, because that's where the noise emanated from. Looking at him there, small and alone, remarkable only by his big glasses, and surrounded by a hostile group of small people I thought of a scorpion surrounded by a ring of fire. Although, of course, I reflected, Simon was no scorpion.

It took him a while to see me, and when he did, I felt he was not overcome with joy; his bland face registered some surprise, and perhaps a glimmer of dislike.

"That's Mr Johnson," announced my important friend, "I will introduce you." Useless to declare this unnecessary; part of her certificate had included Introductions; indeed they had taken 15%.

Simon was actually very nice to her, and thanked her for being such a clever girl and bringing Mr Hadley – which wasn't easy for him to do, because he was beset with a gang of eight-year olds all shouting, "Sir, Sir, come here, Sir." The noise throughout Little Court was deafening, and the place resembled something out of Hieronymus Bosch: two boys appeared to be killing each other in the far corner, and a ritual sacrifice straight from 'Lord of The Flies' seemed to be taking place behind the climbing frame. Simon regarded it all with a sad, resigned air. The little girl seemed loath to relinquish her duties, and she asked whether she should take me somewhere else because "it's very noisy here, and people will get hurt soon." But I thanked her and said she had brought her task to a fine completion, and I could quite see why she had got her Pink Certificate, which made her very cross.

"I told you it was the Brown," she said, "anyone can get the Pink." And she went stumping off in high dudgeon.

"She said you had brought some books," said Simon, raising his thin voice against the roar, "but they didn't say it was you, they said some other name." He looked at me accusingly.

"Yes, I know," I shouted back, "but it was the only way I could get in."

He looked confused, either because he hadn't heard, or because he was wondering what I was really up to.

"Oh," he said looking nervously toward a small girl who was pulling another small girl along by her pigtails, "well, I don't know what you've come for." I could see it was going to be very difficult to engage in any meaningful conversation, particularly now an angry boy was shouting indignantly,

"Sir, he hit me, I think he's bust my arm." A group of interested spectators gathered round.

"Sir, will you get an ambulance? Shall I fetch Matron? Will he die, Sir?"

As Simon was wondering what action to take, the injured one got tired of waiting for justice to be done and ran off to exact revenge on his own behalf. Thankfully the sound of a bell was heard from afar. The result was amazing: a complete silence fell, and children shuffled themselves into long lines where they stood with their hands up.

"Upper IVa, dismiss," said Simon anxiously, and off marched Upper IVa as if butter wouldn't melt in their mouths. A similar process was undertaken with the rest, and eventually Simon and I were left standing alone in the playground with pieces of litter blowing about.

"They get Detention if they're late in," he explained. "They're meant to pick up the litter before they go, but I can never make them do it."

"Do you have to be somewhere now?" I asked.

"No, I've got a free period."

I wasn't sure what to do. Simon made no effort to move, except for picking up a few sweet papers. He didn't seem inclined to ask me to accompany him anywhere.

"I just came to tell you all the latest," I said, "I've seen a few of our fellow bridge players."

"Oh." He straightened up and began fiddling with his glasses and managed to drop the sweet papers. I was fed up with this.

"Could we go somewhere and have a cup of coffee?"

"I don't know."

"Come on, Simon," I said in a rather hectoring tone. He looked at me uncertainly and at last he said, "alright then, we'll go to my flat. Its just across from the gym, but I've only got a few minutes."

We walked in silence for a bit and then he said quite suddenly: "Have you come about the…murder?"

I laughed in what I hoped was a reassuring manner, "Oh no," I lied cheerfully, "we've given all that up and, anyway, Tubby has other interests now." And I told him about Carol. I couldn't really gauge his reactions because he was walking slightly ahead of me, but I could sense he was interested, and when I told him about the newly affianced Laurence, he made the same remark as Lewis.

"How ironic."

"What do you mean?"

He looked back at me: "Oh, I don't know. Poor Aunt Majorie, I suppose. I just wish she hadn't died."

"And poor Tubby too," I added.

"Yes, what a terrible life he'll have." Suddenly he gave a little giggle. "I expect he'll wish he really had poisoned those chocolates."

"Well, he's still in with a chance; the garden's full of belladonna."

"Belladonna? Is that what killed Auntie?"

"Who knows!"

"I suppose you could kill someone with belladonna."

"John and I secretly think Carol poisoned Tubby's parrot with it."

I had forgotten Simon didn't know about the parrot – either its existence or its death, but the story didn't seem to amuse him, only to sadden him.

"How terrible to hear Aunt Marjorie's voice after she'd died. It would have scared me to death." And that remark, implying as it did, a sort of afterlife for Dear Absent Friends, prompted me to tell him about the Skorskis, and that in turn reminded me of the boy Paul Skorski who had been 'made ill by England.'

"Was he any relation?" I asked. "That little girl said he cheated in exams, and I thought it might be an inherited trait from Karl." But Simon denied this quite vehemently; Skorski was a common Eastern European name.

I was about to enlarge on the Skorski theme by asking about the blonde that Karl had spied leaving Simon's room, and from there find out about the glamorous English girlfriend seen by Arbuthnot-Jones, but we had reached his flat and conversation was suspended.

I could not believe the flat. Of course, I knew he had come into money on the death of his father – probably quite a lot of money, since he had financed the holiday of Tubby and Lady P.. And it wasn't just that the eighteenth century furniture and display cabinet full of Sèvres (or at any rate, what looked to my untutored eye, like Sèvres) must have cost an arm and a leg, but that his taste was quite unlike anything I had expected. Again, it made me wonder if he was gay, because it was the choice of an extremely refined man of almost feminine taste: the walls were light blue with what looked like hand-painted birds, and the curtains a light silk with the faintest hint of pink in the weave. The chaise longue was flamingo in hue and the chairs blue velvet.

"Simon, how beautifully you've done it!"

And here in his own ground, his exquisitely chosen ground, he seemed to gain in stature, the eyes so small behind the glasses, seemed to shine.

"It's my secret… after school, to come back here. It's like coming to another life – when I'm not me any more." This thought (understandably) seemed to make him more cheerful. "I would make you some tea, but I don't think there's time. I mustn't be late back," and he glanced anxiously at the exquisite ormolu clock on the mantelpiece.

"You have beautiful taste!" I couldn't stop gawping, and I realised how rude I must appear, not just because of the gawping, but because of my evident surprise that the insignificant Simon could live in such an exquisite environment.

"Why have you come?" he said, standing fidgeting by the cabinet. And in an instant the new sophisticated Simon vanished, to be replaced by the familiar timid and weedy figure of the failed schoolmaster.

"Well, not to accuse you of murder," I smiled. "I had to go into Worcester, so I thought I would call in on Lewis and then see you as well."

Simon's little piggy eyes behind the enormous glasses blinked nervously. "But why did you want to see me?"

Why indeed?

"To ask if you were going to Sammy's benefit day; did you get an email? And now I've seen Lewis, I think you ought to get him to come. He seemed… well, not quite himself."

"Yes, he's very sad at the moment... I mean, would you like to sit down?"

I sat on the exquisite chaise longue, hoping that I would leave no smudge on its immaculate surface.

"So why is Lewis unhappy?"

He perched on the side of the sofa. "I don't think I can tell you that. It's something he doesn't want to talk about, and I think you should respect other people's secrets."

If I wasn't going to learn about Lewis, I determined I might as well learn something about Simon. I didn't have any compunctions about prying into *his* secrets, but, so it wouldn't be too sudden, I told him about Janet and Gino.

"I'm really glad, she was very nice… only not very happy. Sometimes people aren't, but I hope she will be now. I liked playing bridge with her, but Lewis didn't want to play with Carol, he didn't like her, so I had to play with her instead."

The ormolu clock struck a tinkly two and Simon glanced up at it nervously.

"I will have to go soon."

"You haven't said if you'll go to Sammy's bridge day."

"Oh, I don't know… perhaps. Do you think Carol will be there?"

"I've no idea, but at least you won't have to play with her."

"I… I… really, I must go now. I hate being late for things."

It seemed to me that we had only just come, and there was time to talk, but Simon was on his feet again. So we left the beautiful flat, which he locked very thoroughly behind him, and we set on back towards the school.

"I hear you have a glamorous girlfriend!" I attempted a roguish tone, one which was, as it transpired, particularly unsuccessful. He stopped in his tracks and stood quite still, and when he spoke, his voice became shrill with anger.

"Who told you that? How dare they, how dare they poke their noses in?" And then he set off walking again, almost at a run.

"I'm sorry," I said hurrying to keep up, "it was Mr Arbuthnot-Jones. I wondered if you might have met this nice girl in Italy…" I wanted to add 'since Karl Skorski said he'd seen a blonde girl leaving your room,' but courage failed me, and I didn't fancy a scene in case thousands of children emerged to view it. When we got to the gym, Simon stopped outside and I could see he was very upset. I was afraid he was going to burst into tears.

"Actually, I don't know why you came here. I can see you do think I murdered poor Aunt Marjorie, and now you start talking about the Skorskis and… other untrue things."

"I only asked about your girlfriend."

"Well, it's none of your business, coming here and prying, and asking Lewis questions, too. I'd rather you didn't come again… ever." And he set off up the steps into the main building, but instead of pushing open the heavy doors, he turned back again.

"I'm sorry, I didn't mean to be rude. I'm always on edge because… I'm at school."

"Please don't apologise, it is I who should be apologising, I have been very rude – and intrusive." And indeed I had: who was I to go pushing myself into other people's lives? Maybe the time had come, not just to bow out of Simon's life, but from the whole Lady P. business.

"Really Simon, I don't think you murdered your aunt. Actually, I think you were very fond of her, so please forgive me."

He stood there looking at me uncertainly and then he smiled. Oddly, he had a very sweet smile, if he hadn't worn those hideous great glasses and if his eyes had been a bit bigger, and his body more, well, manly, he would have been all right, but certainly school life didn't bring out the best in him. A sound like the crack of doom rent the air: the lesson bell had gone. A look of pain crossed his face, but when the noise abated he said very nicely, "Of course I forgive you,"

"Simon?"

"Yes."

"Why on earth don't you give all this up? You're not short of money, why not take a year out and do something you enjoy for a bit? Or am I being interfering again?"

"No, no. Yes, I might, but I can't yet. You see, I'm waiting to go into hospital."

God, I had put my foot in it again.

"I'm sorry, I didn't know, I hope it's nothing serious."

"Well, yes, it is really, but…"

Whatever it was, I wasn't going to learn. About fifty thousand children seemed to come pouring out of the door, none swerved to avoid him and he seemed to sway hither and thither on the tide before he finally disappeared into their midst.

I made my way back to Reception. It wasn't very far at all, and I suspected that my friend with the People Skills had not passed her Taking-Visitors-the-Shortest-Route Certificate. In spite of all the security precautions the Reception desk was empty, so I left my badge there and went out to the Car Park, and who should I see sauntering along with something of a rolling gait, but Arbuthnot-Jones, obviously risen early. He greeted me with bibulous enthusiasm: "Ah, Headmaster! Excellent lunch! Congratulate the governors for me!" I smiled weakly and passed on. Somehow I couldn't summon up the enthusiasm to ask him about Simon's girlfriend.

Chapter 19: I miss the funeral

"Where have you been, then?"

"Let me get a glass of something strong and I'll tell you… Goodness, you've bought a new sweater – and new trousers." I was somewhat aghast at this display of conspicuous expenditure, but I must say John looked particularly fetching in it all.

"Uh-huh, and before you start tut-tutting, let me tell you I've bought nothing since Italy."

"When you bought all that designer stuff."

"Not 'all that designer stuff', one jacket, and you spent a fortune at the bottega della Oxfama. Go on, tell me all about it. At a guess I'd say you hadn't finished the database."

"Indeed not."

"Nor started it."

"Doing something much more interesting: I went to see Lewis and Simon, and two more miserable specimens of humanity you couldn't hope to find."

I started with the Lewis visit and reiterated Lewis' changed appearance and his general air of dejection.

John sat silent for a moment, and then he said, "How was Sergeant?"

"Sergeant?"

"The dog, you idiot!"

"Ah" I said, "ah!" Then I added quickly," I knew there was something missing in the kitchen."

"Could it be that the Skorskis have missed out on yet another job?"

"Yes, you're right; no basket in the kitchen and he had dug up under the apple tree… Oh gosh, poor old Lewis! No more Sergeant, no wonder he looked so miserable. Still, I don't know why he couldn't say. I think Simon knew."

"Probably given him by the beautiful wife, last link with her and all that stuff. Anyway that would be why he was looking all scruffy and pathetic."

"You don't sound very sympathetic."

"Well, you know me, no time for dogs and children. Go on about Simon."

"Well, he was miserable too."

But John was equally unsympathetic. "Always said he was a wanker."

"John, I was thinking, maybe we had better not meddle any more…"

"Hang about, isn't that what I said weeks ago and you got all upset and thought I didn't love you any more and was having it off with all of Warwickshire?"

We had never openly discussed what I had thought after Italy, and the day he went to Carol's and found me passed out with the whisky – which is just proof that John knows me very much better than I know him. I looked at him and smiled and went over and kissed him.

"And you'll never guess who phoned me!" he said after I had finished making my demonstrations of affection. "When I tell you, you certainly won't want to give it all up – you'll want to get your deerstalker on straightaway."

"Who, then?"

"Guess."

I poured myself another glass of wine. I felt I'd had a long hard day and it wasn't getting any easier.

"It was Tubby offering you a job lot of belladonna?"

"Wrong… What's that wine like? I hope it's not like that other bottle we had from there?"

"I wouldn't be drinking it if it was. I expect it was Gino confessing to murder."

"Wrong. I think I'll have some then. Carry on guessing while I get a glass."

"Karl Skorski… Oh! by the way, I didn't tell you about the boy at Simon's school who was made ill by England."

But John dismissed this as a red herring.

"It was Irfon saying he'd taken a contract out on your life."

"Wrong! I'm not too sure about this wine."

"Well, don't drink it then; I like it. Anyway I give up."

"Isabel."

"Oh!" I felt this a bit of an anticlimax, "what did she want? Was she ringing to thank us for going to see Janet?"

"No."

"I can't play any more guessing games, John, I've had a long hard day."

"Yeah, it's really hard when you don't go to work."

"Tell me!"

"Trevor's dead."

"What?"

"There!" he said complacently, "I knew you wouldn't guess that."

"Trevor?"

John beamed: "It's good, isn't it, all the baddies get killed. Carol will be next, I daresay."

"What…? How…? I mean, was he really killed?"

"Of course. Janet sneaked off home and finished him off – with Gino's help."

I didn't believe him, but pretended I did, because he likes to be a tease, and I quite like being teased.

"Is she in police custody?"

"Well, I hate to disappoint you, but no, and Trevor wasn't killed either. Isabel said it was a stroke; he'd had them before."

"I suppose…"

"No. And it wasn't belladonna either."

"Is she upset?"

"Well, she sounded a bit upset… Oh, and she asked us if we wanted to go to the funeral."

"How odd! What did you say?"

"I said you'd go."

"Why not you as well?"

"You know I don't like that sort of thing, anyway I'll be at work."

"You could get time off, compassionate leave or something. When is it, anyway?"

"Can't remember; next week sometime – I wrote it down by the phone."

"I wonder why she wanted us to go?"

"Well, she said we had been kind going to see Janet, and she was going to ask several people from GrandSlam."

"I suppose Janet will be pleased. I mean he's got his come-uppance, hasn't he?"

"Playing about with little girls sends you to an early grave – that's why it's better to stick to boys."

"I say, John, do you think this means Janet will come into some money?"

"I don't know. I suppose it'll be left to Isabel. I can see you're still thinking it was a murder by Gino or Janet, but it really wasn't: he had a turn and died in hospital. We're in England now, you see, and there are autopsies and things if they're are any suspicious circumstances." He grinned. "I bet you don't want to give up the investigation now, do you?"

"Do you?"

He stretched out on the sofa showing off the new trousers to great advantage.

"Well, let's go through what we know, and then we can decide if it's worth going on with it or not."

"Talk me through it," I said easing myself into the sofa opposite; this was just the kind of thing I liked.

"We got into this because Sammy asked you to help Tubby find out who had killed his wife. At that point, Tubby was up for us helping and was sure it was Bethan because he'd heard her saying something about wanting to murder Lady P...."

"A little inaccurate, but I'll let that pass."

"But we thought it was unlikely to be Bethan or Megan, but that somebody, maybe a member of the staff at *Il Sole* or one of GrandSlam – perhaps Tubby himself had done it, and we muddled about trying to find out more – even going to Italy. But then Tubby pours cold water on the whole thing and we thought…"

"That someone had put the frighteners on Tubby."

"And in a way they had: Carol had told Tubby to stop it. So we suspected Carol, but were confused by thinking that Carol knew someone *else* had done it, and was blackmailing them…"

"But as usual we were wrong."

"So," said John almost as sternly as Lewis, "are we saying that Carol probably did it, and we can't get anywhere because Tubby won't let us? If so we might as well stop poking our noses in, eh?"

"Well…"

The wine was taking effect; I didn't seem to be able to think of anything useful to say, but John continued inexorably: "On the other hand, we're not at all certain that it *was* Carol – it might have been the Skorskis, or Trevor and Isabel, or Janet, or Gino or Simon, or Lewis."

"Or Tubby… or the manager of the hotel, don't forget he tried to bribe me."

"And if we are brutally honest we know no more now than we did at the beginning… Or Sammy."

"That's not quite true: we know more about their backgrounds and their characters."

"A lot of use that has been… Or Bethan or Megan. Or Bethan *and* Megan."

"The other thing is that there are people we like, and we don't want them to have done it, and people we don't like, who we would like to pin it on."

"Only," said John, "we can't pin anything on anyone because we haven't got any evidence and Lady P. is at the bottom of Lake Como. Let's open another bottle, I quite like this one after all."

"I like your new trousers."

"Are you sure it's the trousers you like?"

"Them too."

We opened another bottle and reviewed things.

"The thing is," I said as I poured the wine, "it would have been better if we'd stopped after Tubby told us to. I don't know really why we didn't."

"Like children in a sweet shop, told not to. So they nick the sweets."

"It wasn't just that, we really thought that if someone was trying to scare him, we ought to find out who it was."

"Well, now we know it was Carol, and we're not going to

do anything about it."

"The thing is," I said thoughtfully, "what we've never really addressed is what we would do, if by some miracle we *did* find out who had done it. I mean when we first went into it, the idea was – I suppose – to tell Tubby what we'd found out and let him deal with it. But now…"

"Call in the cops?"

"But would we? I mean, suppose it was someone we really liked: Bethan, say, would we really shop her?"

"Well, we'd have to if it was Bethan, because then we'd be thinking about the first husband and wondering if she was a serial killer… She might turn against Megan."

"Or Irfon. But supposing it was someone who had just wanted to kill Lady P. After all, you…" and I wagged a finger at him, "didn't shop Tubby when you thought he'd killed her."

"Yeah, that's right – but I was in shock."

"You weren't in shock later."

"Okay, okay, but I kind of think differently now. I mean, I don't think I like playing God and deciding who's bad and needs punishing and who doesn't. And if someone's killed once, they may kill again, and you have to think of the victim. People don't think enough about victims. Anyway, as we're never likely to have any evidence, even if we did shop them, they'd probably get away with it, and we'll go down in the police records as a couple of nutters who go about accusing innocent people of murder."

"John?"

"Mmm?"

"Would you shop me, if you'd thought I'd done it?"

"No, I'd blackmail you and then I could afford some nice shoes to go with my new trousers."

But would he? Some questions are best not asked. "I suppose we'd want to confront them with our knowledge and get them to confess, and tell them not to do it again."

"Mark!"

"Okay, that does sound a bit pathetic. Shall I come and sit over there?"

"Mmm, and bring the bottle with you."

"Let's make no plans at all," I said.

Who would have wanted to make plans about murderers when they were sitting next to John – who had been wearing his new trousers.

On 28th November, I arrived at the Church of The Holy Trinity carrying John's scrawled instructions and a bunch of chrysanthemums. It was, however, evident that there was no funeral going on, or about to go on. The church was completely empty except for the sort of man you dread to meet; what I think people used to call a 'holy Joe', a kind of pseudo vicar who likes messing about with incense and choirboys, and dressing up in silly robes like a drag queen.

Anyway, I had no choice but to ask him *why* there wasn't a funeral. All sorts of ideas were going through my mind: at the last minute the police had been called in – it had been a murder after all, and at this very moment an autopsy was being performed… Janet, Gino and Isabel were making statements… Connections were being made with Janet's childhood ...

Holy Joe was busy doing something with some hymn books.

"Excuse me," I said.

He gave a start as if I had disturbed him from some deep reverie, only I knew I hadn't because I'd seen him clock me when I had walked in. He bowed to the altar and came ponderously towards me, bald headed, white-robed and with a badge proclaiming him Head Church Warden. I felt an immediate and intense dislike for him; I wished *he* could have murdered Lady P. and I could be the person to shop him. He gave me the sort of holy smile that says, "I myself am saved, have a seat reserved next to Gabriel, can't be sure about you."

"How can I help you?"

"I was expecting to come to a funeral. Mr Macalister? I'm a friend..."

"Alas, no. Our dear friend was buried some days ago. I

myself was able to comfort the widow." He smiled a weak yet triumphant smile. Perhaps not choirboys, I thought.

"Well, it says here," I peered at my bit of paper, "28th."

"May I?" He tried to take the paper from me. I felt like saying, 'No you mayn't," but ever weak, I handed it over.

"Ah, I think you have misread it, I believe that is a 3 not an 8."

And of course he was right. John had scrawled it down and I had read it wrongly. How infuriating – all the more so that this pseudo god man should be able to put me right!

"How sad that you missed the service, a truly beautiful occasion for a dear good soul."

Yes, so dear and good that he had nearly ruined a young girl's life. I gave him a weak, holy smile like his own.

"If you'll just bear with me, I'll go to the vestry and obtain a service sheet."

"Oh no, please don't…"

But he was not to be put off: "It is most fortunate that I am here as it is only I and Father John, of course, who have the sacred trust of the keys."

Very slowly he walked to the vestry, obviously enjoying making me wait. I fished in my pocket and found a pound coin which I put in the Collection box. It was a horrid church; late Victorian gothic. I could imagine all too readily Trevor reading the lesson in loud thespian tones.

"I see you are admiring our beautiful church. Perhaps I may be permitted to give you a short tour?" He withheld the service sheet, and I wondered if I only got it on completion of the tour. However, remembering how he had got hold of my scibbled note, I practically snatched the service sheet from his.

"Thank you," I said, "but I am afraid I don't have the time."

"I thought you had come for the funeral."

Okay, Mr Clever, if you're going to have a go at me, I'll have one at you. "I'm afraid I'm not keen on Victorian gothic."

"Perhaps you are unfamiliar with it. I have had one or two

visitors who have had their eyes opened to its beauties; indeed, there is beside you a small pamphlet which I myself have composed under the kind auspices of Father John."

"Actually, I'm thinking of going to see Isabel…"

"Isabel? Ah, Mrs Macalister. Well, I speak as one who has some experience of visiting the bereaved, I should advise against too long a sojourn."

I assured him that my sojourn wouldn't be too lengthy.

"The Lord is a great comfort at these times," he said complacently, presumably implying that the Lord and Isabel were very cosy together and that while two's company, three is a crowd. He reverently lifted a kneeler and hung it on a hook, eyeing me keenly. "Were you a *close* friend of the departed?"

Aha, I thought, I've got you rattled. You fancy a little bit more comforting of the widow and you don't like to think of me stealing a march on you.

"No," I smiled, "I am much more a friend of Isabel's."

He looked sour and meditated a parting shot.

"You will be sorry to have missed seeing the Stations of the Cross. *Most* people find them very moving." He extracted a duster from a drawer of the pamphlet table and did a little mournful dusting of a pew end.

"Well," I countered breezily, "I must be moving."

"God's blessing go with you." He managed to imply that he doubted it would.

"Good luck with the dusting," I said.

I drove up the hill to 'Elsinore', half expecting to see a flag flying at half-mast, but there was no movement on the turrets and no car in the driveway. I thought it was probable Isabel was out or away. Bloody old church warden, I thought, I bet you knew she wasn't here. But she was, so there I was wrong again!

She wasn't dressed in black, although somehow I had expected her to be, thinking, I suppose of widows and weeds and things. Instead, she was wearing a flowing, blue denim skirt, a very pale blue cashmere sweater and a silver chain with what looked like a small Michelangelo's David. It looked vaguely familiar – I supposed she'd worn it in Italy. It occurred to me, not for the first time, that while Janet shared something of her looks, the mother had more: a quality that really lovely women have, a sort of awareness of their beauty, but lightly borne, nothing to make a song and dance about.

"Mark! How nice of you."

"I'm so sorry, Isabel. I got the dates muddled and I've missed the funeral. Can you bear more flowers?"

She smiled: "Come in, Mark, I'm very pleased to see you. Shall we go into the kitchen, do you mind?"

"I hope I'm not in the way, and I'm… so sorry."

"Thank you." She took me into the kitchen, (I never seemed to be invited anywhere else now, I reflected). "Would you like some coffee - or there's masses of food left over. What Trevor would have called the baked meats…" Something which might have been a tear glistened. No wonder I only merited kitchens, I thought, since all I ever did was to make people cry!

"I don't want to be a nuisance."

"You're not, I am pleased to have company…I haven't been on my own for a long time."

She was getting cake and ham, and other nibbly bits out of the fridge. I hardly liked to tuck in, but I was starving.

"Do you want to talk about it, or would you rather not?"

"Not, I think. Now sit down and help yourself."

"Will you join me?"

"Yes, I will. It's funny, you're not supposed to crave food when you're sad, but I feel I want to eat and eat." She sat down beside me, and I thought what an ice-breaker death is: last time all our conversation had been awkward and stilted. But then, of course, I suppose both she and Trevor had thought we were trying to fit them up with Lady P.'s murder. How long ago it seemed, and how inept we had been, John and I.

"It was kind of you to go and see Janet. She phoned me after your visit, you know."

"And she's been up for the funeral?"

The ham was delicious and I was wondering if it would be

disrespectful to the dead Trevor to take some more.

"Yes, she and Gino, and Gino's sister who is staying with them."

I thought of the tiny flat and wondered where.

"They were terribly sweet, Gino and his sister, they were in floods of tears, and they hardly knew him."

But not Janet. Isabel must have read my thoughts – both the greedy, and the suspicious, because she forked some more ham on to my plate.

"Mark, I wanted to talk to you, to… put something right. I don't know what Janet said about Trevor…" She held up her hand to stop me speaking, "but I think I can guess: she will have told you that Trevor had… interfered with her as a child."

"It's none of my business, Isabel. John and I wouldn't dream of..."

"Well, Mark, that's the trouble…"

"Trouble? I don't quite…"

"You see, it isn't true. Do you really think as the child's mother I would have been unaware of anything like that – and that if I had been, I would have stayed in the same house with such a man for five minutes?"

This was a bit of a surprise; my fork came to a halt half way up to my mouth.

"Well…" I didn't really know what to say, fearing to imply that either Janet or Isabel must be a liar.

"Surely you don't believe that?" Her eyes flashed with anger and I couldn't help thinking she might be rather passionate in bed. She got up to make the coffee.

"No, I…"

"Of course, you may not believe me, but Trevor would never have done anything like that in a million years. Trevor, well, he had his faults…" For a moment a smile crossed her face, as she thought of them: "his silly boasting and his everlasting play-acting, but he would never have done anything like that in a million years. Do you take sugar?"

" Um.. no. Thank you. But why did Janet…?" I was thoroughly confused.

"Well," she ran her fingers lightly through her hair which was elegantly done, I had noticed, in spite of all her grief. "When I married Trevor, I worried things would be difficult because, as I expect she told you, it was Janet who had fallen in love with him first. I imagined she'd be terribly jealous and so on – you know the way pre-pubescent girls are – but oddly enough, when Trevor and I got married, Janet didn't seem to care about him any more. I suppose he wasn't so glamorous close to." I thought of Janet's words about a big bottom and too much after-shave, and nodded.

"Anyway, she started taking an interest in religion – always doing things at the church: Christian Union Meetings, Crusaders, or whatever and, in fact, I encouraged her. But then it turned out there was this man… at the Church… who liked little girls."

I had a flash of insight. "It wouldn't have been the Head Churchwarden, would it?" She smiled and replied rather ambiguously, I thought, " Someone like him."

" I just wondered because when I went to the church I met this man, to whom I took an instant dislike."

Isabel shook her head: " isn't that strange! Well, we were never sure whether anything had actually happened – and we could certainly never prove anything, so nothing was done, other than pursuing other interests outside the Church. But the whole thing got Janet… a bit mixed up."

"But how did Trevor come into this?"

Isabel sighed and reached over for another cigarette,

"I spoke just now of Trevor's faults. Well, some were endearing, others less so." She must have seen a look on my face. "No, not little girls, grown women."

I thought back to *Il Sole* and I remembered how Trevor had looked at the girl in Reception.

Isabel continued. "Yes, Trevor was a serial adulterer. Of course, I minded, but I sort of got used to it after the second or third time – I accepted that was what he was like, and after all…" she looked up and smiled, she really had a lovely smile, little crinkly lines round the corners of her eyes. "Trevor provided us with a pretty good lifestyle in other ways. I had been very poor, as a... a widow, I didn't want to go back to that." She looked at me rather guiltily, "Does that sound awful?"

"It must have been very hard." I was trying to get my mind round all this.

"I was prepared to put up with it. I'm quite a stoical sort of person, really, but Janet wasn't – isn't, and unfortunately, once she had actually seen Trevor and this woman... You see, Janet and I had always been close after... I was widowed, and she's always been fiercely protective of me. So she hated to think that I was, well, being humiliated, as she saw it. Anyway, she decided to punish Trevor, and began making accusations; she realised from her experiences at the Church that men could get into a lot of trouble for that sort of thing. So she decided to pretend that Trevor... and she used to start making accusations whenever she suspected he was having a new affair.

"What did you do?"

"Well, I tried to be sensible and Trevor tried to make a sort of joke of it... Can I fill your cup up? No? Well, you can imagine, that wasn't a very good idea."

Poor Trevor! I had thought him a very silly man with an inflated sense of his own importance, but he hadn't really deserved all this. Or there again, perhaps he had; why couldn't he have been content with the beautiful Isabel? Why go after all these other women? Perhaps, after all, he was conscious of being a rather inadequate sort of person, and simply wanted to prove himself her equal. I tried to imagine it all: Isabel, cool and elegant, desperately trying to be understanding, Trevor histrionic and full of bluster, other people poking their noses in.

"Didn't you have the Social Services and people creating trouble?"

"Well, no, don't forget this is going back fifteen years or more, before the media and everyone latched on to child abuse in the way they do now – and fortunately, no-one believed her. She was inconsistent, and even accused Trevor of being in her bed when he was in the States. She had counselling and so on, and then it seemed to get better and eventually she went to University and everything seemed to be going well. She even found a very nice boyfriend and all was well for some years. But then the boyfriend left and, to cut a long story short, Janet had a nervous breakdown and ever since she has been in and out of all sorts of places.

"But why did she tell John and me this story? I mean surely she must have put this all behind her ages ago?"

"I don't think she ever really got over whatever it was that happened in the church, and I don't think she knows the truth herself now – I do think she convinced herself about Trevor." Isabel smiled, "And I suspect she quite likes the attention it brings. At *Il Sole* she got angry because Trevor had to go and have a thing with that girl Pia from Reception, and Janet wanted to punish him again… She was furious because the holiday was meant to be a kind of bonding thing, for us all to get back together, one happy family, and I suppose she told you and John to get her own back on Trevor. Oh, Mark… let's not talk any more about this."

"No, of course not."

"And now, of course, she has met Gino."

I was expecting her to say that here was another disaster, but I was wrong.

"I like Gino; he makes her very happy, I could see that when they came up for the funeral."

"But, Isabel. Forgive me, will it last? I don't want to be cynical, but doesn't he perhaps see your family as a … well, a …?" She stood up.

"Then that is what it must be."

"What do you mean?"

"Do you mind if I smoke? I know it's silly and Trevor, bless him, helped me give it up, but now… he isn't here any more and it doesn't matter now."

"You mustn't say that."

"No, of course not. What was I saying? Oh yes, I think Gino *is* fond of Janet, and I also think he is rather ambitious, but he doesn't have any skills except his experiences as a waiter. Now, it occurred to me, why shouldn't they start a restaurant – or even a hotel."

"Where? In London? It would cost a fortune."

"No, not in London. Here. Literally here, in this house."

She stood up and smiled. "Shall we take our coffee into the sitting room?"

"You haven't eaten anything, Isabel, and you said you were hungry."

"Come on!" she had a puckish twinkle that was very attractive. "What do you think of my idea?"

"I think you should put yourself first."

"Now there we disagree. Can I offer you a small glass of something with your coffee – there's a rather nice Armagnac that we brought back from Italy? Trevor likes… liked it."

She went over to the cabinet. "You see I may have given you a wrong impression. It wasn't all doom and gloom, Janet's problems, well, they were like an illness really, a recurring illness which sometimes got better. We actually had some very happy times together, and things got better when Janet went away to school – oh, dear, that sounds awful, doesn't it. But there were good times; sometimes Janet forgot about being unhappy and hating Trevor, and he was very fond of her. You see, we couldn't have any children of our own, and he wanted to be the perfect father, that's what made it all so sad. And I think, if Janet could take this house now and make something of it – whether as a hotel or restaurant, well, in a way that would be a kind of tribute to Trevor because it was his house – he owned it; I had no money at all when I married him."

"Has she told Gino everything?"

"If she has, he never said anything to me."

She handed me a glass of the Armagnac; it was quite delicious, and she sat opposite me with her legs elegantly crossed. She lit another cigarette and the smell scented the air and gave the room a slightly exotic feel.

"Will you have a glass yourself?"

"No, I don't think so; I used to drink rather a lot, perhaps too much, but now I seem to have lost the desire for it. It's funny, isn't it, how life plays all sorts of tricks on you?"

"Where would you go if you made the house over to Janet and Gino?"

"I don't know; perhaps abroad. When I was young, before I met my… first husband, I loved sitting in hotel foyers, watching the world and longing to be part of it."

I wondered what she meant: did she sit there waiting to be picked up? She was, I felt, a woman with a past, but was she a woman with a future?

"I think you should be very careful before you hand over the house. I certainly think you should get everything arranged legally, so if things were to go wrong…"

She laughed, "It's very nice of you to be concerned, Mark, but you don't need to worry. I may be fond of my daughter, but I'm not stupid either."

She was, I thought, an enigma. I didn't know what to make of her: had she loved the irritating Trevor, did she love Janet? What sort of ménage á trois had it really been?

I had some strange thoughts as I sat in the green sitting room with its Garrick prints and leather bound books of press cuttings, with everything comfortable and convenient, and this beautiful, somewhat mysterious woman, opposite. How would it have been if I had not been gay, if instead I had continued a lover of women and married such a one as this? Would I have been happier living as it were within the kindly approbation of straight society, saying, not 'This is John' or – horrible word – "this is my *partner,* John," but "This is my wife, flesh of my flesh, this is my child, bone of my bone, this is my home with its photos and its memories which I shall pass on down the family tree …" I didn't know; who, after all, is perfectly happy? And I was happier than most, I had as my lover a man who was to me, husband, wife and child, and who could ask for more than that? Of course I said none of this, and for a while we sat in companionable silence.

"And now," she said, "you must tell me all about your investigations. Have you nailed your murderer yet?"

What should I tell her? I felt disinclined to launch into all the ramifications. I was warm and comfortable and the Armagnac slipped down easily. Outside the French windows the cloud had lifted and a watery winter sun shone over the remnants of an Autumn garden, the odd dahlia raised a crimson head and a few final gold leaves fluttered down and aligned themselves with the others in sodden heaps.

I think I told her little. I drifted idly from tales of one dear absent friend to another, very much as the smoke from Isabel's cigarette (she smoked Gitannes) drifted from one part of the room to another, and she sat quietly on the sofa, smiling gently. I assured her that our investigations were over, abandoned as pointless, and I chatted about Simon and Lewis, Megan and Bethan, the Skorskis, and I told her about Tubby and Carol. But, after a while, I realised that she was not listening to me at all, but was away in some far-off place in the past where she had once been with Trevor… or her first husband (of whom she never spoke), her daughter, or, and I somehow felt this the most probable of all, away with one of those many men that she had met years and years ago in the foyer of some foreign hotel, when she was young and willing and eager.

"I'm sorry," she said suddenly, "I haven't been concentrating properly. Who did you say had done it?"

"No one," I said, "or at any rate, we shall never know who."

Then she said an unexpected thing:

"Perhaps you will say Trevor did it; then the case would really be closed, wouldn't it?"

I have no idea why she said this, or what sort of response she expected me to make. I was hampered at the time by being unable to decide whether she was a sort of distillation of perfect womanhood, or quite a smart cookie with her eye on the main chance. I thought my best tack was indignation.

"I wouldn't dream of saying or indeed, thinking of the sort. Just because Trevor was falsely accused by Janet, it doesn't mean that I would … indeed of everyone – yourself and Janet excluded, I can think of no-one less likely to have murdered Lady P.."

"Thank you," she said, "I am so glad." She paused, "he was a very good man, you know… and very dear to me."

Tears welled up in her violet eyes, and I felt I must take her in my arms.

"There, you mustn't cry, my dear."

I had a very strange feeling as I held her there against me – I suppose it was a sort of reminder of my mis-spent youth, but I also felt an uncomfortable sense of danger, the reasons for which I couldn't fathom. Gently I disentangled myself. She looked at me for a moment, with an expression which I couldn't identify, but she was soon mistress of herself again.

"I think I'd like to be on my own now."

"Will you be all right? Is there someone you'd like to come and be with you?"

"No, thank you, Mark; I think I'll go for the Garbo option."

"I don't like to think of you here on your own." It was quite true; I felt that she should have someone with her; after all Trevor had only been buried a few days before, and, well, shouldn't her daughter be with her? Perhaps she read my thoughts.

"Janet will come up again soon, I daresay… very soon when I tell her about my restaurant idea."

Mother and daughter, was there much love between them? How should I know?

"And I expect William will be coming up."

"William?"

"The guy you met in the church."

"But I thought he reminded you of the man who…"

"One sees things differently after a passage of years."

Does one? Does one view differently a man who reminded you of someone who had possibly interfered with a little girl, and that girl your daughter? Perhaps this William *was* that man; she had been remarkably vague about it all. Would you really want him sniffing around after your husband had just died. Or … and I thought of a beautiful young girl sitting alone in a hotel foyer, did Isabel want sex just as much as her husband? Did she look for it anywhere? Had she thought even me worth a go?

"You mustn't be judgemental, Mark, particularly as…

well, I am very lonely without Trevor."

"Yes, of course."

Suddenly I wanted to be gone; suddenly the gay world seemed a much more honest and… honourable world than that of heterosexuals. John and I had both bought sex – a lot, but we had it without this nasty baggage of mawkishness. We didn't have any truck (or indeed fuck) with what was mean and ugly.

"Well, all the best, Isabel. Don't worry about seeing me to the door. Just take it easy."

She smiled, a little absently, I felt. Perhaps she was already planning how to present herself to William. Somehow I doubted he would be bringing the sacred trust of the vestry keys with him.

Chapter 20: Who would you push?

"I think you fancy her," said John.

"Do you?" I thought how odd it was that after the many times I had been jealous because I thought that John was lusting after someone else, I had now made him jealous, with my description of Isabel!

"You sound as if you do."

He was cooking supper (for a change). It was some sort of stir-fry thing with lots of cashew nuts and prawns.

"Put it this way… If I was straight, I think I would have done."

"Can you grate some ginger? Did you believe her about Trevor and Janet."

"Of course."

"Well, I don't. I think Janet told us the truth, and I think that your friend Isabel…"

"She's not my friend."

"…that *our* friend Isabel wanted to clear Trevor's name. I wouldn't trust him. I can just see him touching up little girls."

"De mortuis…"

"Eh?"

"He's dead, John."

"Yes. Well."

"Anyway it doesn't matter."

"No, but it goes to show that you can never trust people. Look at all these statements the DAFS have given us. We'd like to believe that we've been told the truth, but the fact is that everyone has probably lied to us."

" 'What is truth, said Jesting Pilot?'"

"Don't be so fucking irritating, and haven't you done that ginger yet?"

While I didn't seriously think that John thought I fancied Isabel, I could see that I'd got him a little rattled. I can't say I was unhappy about it.

"And how come you muddled the date of the funeral? I know I wrote it down right? "

"Well you know how bad your handwriting is…"

"Okay, I can't understand foreign quotations and I don't know about jousting pilots, and I can't write, not having had a superior education at schools like yours and Simon's…"

"John, calm down; I will admit that it might not have been your writing, it could conceivably been my bad eyesight, after all Willy Wanker at the church seemed to think so."

"Hmm." He was a little mollified. "I think I might put another chilli in this."

"No."

"No?"

"No." So he put another chilli in, just to assert himself. I liked that.

"When you told her that you thought her family were very unlikely murderers, did you mean it?"

"Yes, I think so; I think they were …..are a pretty peculiar family, but I can't see why any of them would have murdered Lady P., can you?"

"No, but I think it's interesting that either Janet or Isabel is a liar."

"It looks as if it all might end happily for Janet, if she and Gino get the house."

"I should think he'll get his hands on the money and clear off back to Italy. Let's eat."

He had been right about the extra chilli; the stir-fry was quite delicious, but then, John is right *most* of the time.

"I wonder if she'll come to Sammy's bridge thing."

"Who? He had his mouth full of rice, "Janet or your friend? Didn't you ask?"

"No, I forgot."

"That's the next excitement, then, isn't it, the next opportunity to meet the DAFS."

"Well, yes, I suppose it is."

He looked at me quite gently: "I think it should be the last, the last time we do all this, afterwards I think we should get a new project…"

"What had you got in mind?"

"Macrame or Faith-healing."

"Ah."

We sat in silence, the only sound being that of chomping jaws.

"I wonder who will be there?"

"I wonder."

"I would think not Bethan and Megan, too far to come. Probably the Skorskis…"

"You know," John said, "I was thinking about Claire Skorski and what she said about being upset by Carol going through that taxidermy bag. Well, other than the fact that it was bloody nosy of Carol, why should Claire be upset? Taxidermy is a perfectly respectable way of earning a living. What else could there have been in the bag for Carol to find?"

"Hmmm. I don't know."

"I don't know either, but you know how we always reckoned he cheated…"

"Oho, you mean like infa-red glasses."

John looked miffed. "No, not exactly, but, well there might have been something…"

"Maybe, but I don't actually think Carol went in for blackmailing on any large scale. I think she just liked the power of being in the know."

"There were all the expensive holidays. How did she afford them?"

"Oh, I don't know, people often have all sorts of hidden savings."

"I wish I did."

We continued eating and John finished up the rice with the last of the stir-fry. I looked at him rather reproachfully.

"I'm compensating for not having any hidden savings," he said.

I thought I would change the conversation, not because I had any that were hidden from John, but because money can become a rather sore point between us.

"If you were on a desert island, who would you least like to have with you there, I mean amongst our dear absent friends?"

"That's a tricky one."

"Put it another way, if you were in a balloon with them, who would you push out first?"

John stacked up the plates. "No pudding, it'll have to be fruit."

"Lovely. Now, who?"

He laughed, John has a joyous laugh; it's not in the Sammy class of laughs, but it's lovely. "Obviously Megan and Bethan, otherwise the thing would crash land straight away."

"And then?"

"Well, I'd like to get rid of Simon because he's so weedy, but being small and weedy is probably a good thing if the balloon is overcrowded, so, let's see…"

"Well, go back to the desert island.

"I'll have gorgeous Gino? I could spend many a happy month alone with him"

"No, he's not a DAF."

"Megan and Bethan wouldn't be nimble enough to go hunting, and nor would Tubby without his glasses…"

"Like the fat boy in *Lord of the Flies*."

"I can see Karl Skorski being good with a knife."

"But he might use it on you. No, I think what I'm actually asking is whose company would you prefer… and you can't have me."

"What makes you think I would choose you, huh? Well, unlike you, I'm not a fan of Lewis, don't like Simon, and couldn't stand either Tubby or Carol. You couldn't have Bethan without Megan. Trevor's dead and Isabel would be trying to get into bed with me. Claire Skorski would never stop talking and he wouldn't do any talking at all, so I suppose it would have to be Janet. What about you?"

"Me? Oh, I'll have Sammy!"

I had some grapes and John had an orange; he's the only person I have ever known who dissect and eat an orange as tidily as it were a chocolate one. When I had finished admiring his dexterity, I asked: "But is there any correlation between people we dislike and people who might have done the murder?"

"No, because I dislike nearly all of them."

"Perhaps Lady P.'s death is like the murder on the Orient Express, and they all did it."

"Including us?"

"Oh yes, we were insulted by the number of times Lady P. called us poofters, so you hatched a plot with Tubby and finished her off while I went downstairs and colluded with the manager and his brother."

"That's pretty much on a par with the rest of our theories," said John.

Nothing much happened then until Sammy's benefit day – Megan and Bethan sent us a postcard from the Golden Valley, asking us if we were going, because they thought they might, if we were, (which I regarded as rather flattering). Bethan added that she supposed poor Tubby wouldn't have a partner, which reminded me that quite a few people were going to be surprised if Tubby turned up with Carol. As well as the DAFS, there were all the other people on the GrandSlam bridge holiday who had left the day before Lady P.'s death.

Unexpectedly, an email arrived from Lewis asking us if we knew whether Carol and Tubby were going, because, if not, he and Simon might go. I said I didn't know; why didn't he ask Sammy?

There were no other communications, unless you count a glossy flier that arrived from the Skorskis offering us a cut price deal: two stuffings for the price of one and, of course, as I remarked to John at the time, the Skorskis didn't know about the Tubby-Carol thing either. So altogether we were looking forward to quite an eventful day and, of course, one could always depend on Sammy to make it go with a zing.

Chapter 21:
Sammy's Bridge Day and 'John the Poisoner'

It was immensely plush: flunky types took our coats and two very smart young ladies conducted us to The Oak Room. They obviously had certificates in People Skills, both the Pink and the Brown; they hoped our journey had not been too tiring and apologised for the hold-up on the motorway, as if they were personally responsible.

"Will I be able to smoke anywhere?" John asked, a little ungraciously, I thought. Indeed yes, he might relax on the balcony of The Marlowe Room, because although the hotel was obviously concerned about the health of its visitors, they were also equally anxious to cater for the requirements of individuals. It was, apparently, their intention to make sure that their visitors' every wish should be satisfied – but they seemed to clear off pretty sharpish when they saw me about to ask another question.

"I wonder how Sammy will make money out of this?" queried John.

As soon as we entered the Oak Room, the answer was obvious – it was absolutely seething. I couldn't immediately see any DAFs, but there were more than a hundred well-heeled looking punters.

"One hundred times fifty quid," I said sotto voce.

"They'll expect a good feed," John said sotto voce.

"I bet it'll be finger foods," I hissed back.

"Hellohoh." It was the retired Admiral whom we had met at *Il Sole*, but who had flown home before the fateful night. He was, as before, accompanied by his miniscule wife. John always claimed that the Admiral had found her in a locker in the course of a naval inspection and as there was no space left for tidying her away, he had married her instead.

"Been playing much bridge, have you?"

"Much bridge?" echoed the tiny wife who was clad from

head to toe in a rather unfortunate shade of green.

"I'm afraid, hardly at all."

"Never mind, never mind."

"*Never mind*," came the squeak from below decks.

"Good holiday, that one at the *Sole*, eh?"

Obviously they knew nothing about Lady P., and who were we to tell them? But there was a continued muffled squeaking, a sort of nervous twittering from under the gunnels, and we all three bent our knees and lowered our heads as if to re-enact a scene from The Navy Lark.

"There was a lady… I think she had a title, a funny name, yes, Lady Prettyman, I wonder whether she will be coming today?"

"We hope not," said the admiral straightening up again, and I remembered there had been exchanges of cannon fire across the bows during bridge sessions at *Il Sole.*

"You needn't worry," (John is given to straight-talking). "She's dead."

"Ah!" said the admiral, "shouldn't wonder if the husband did her in. I'd have done it myself, given half a chance."

"Yes," came a triumphant little voice from below, "no more doubling three no trumps where *she's* gone." John looked quite shocked and I thought what a pity it was that the fleet had left the day before Lady P.'s death; they would have made cracking suspect material. But before they could deliver any further comments, they were engulfed by another couple, ninety if they were a day. The din was enormous as dear absent friends and despised attendant enemies greeted each other, cups and saucers rattled, middle-class voices boomed and blue-haired ladies shrieked. We fought our way over to the table where the coffee was.

"Chocolate biscuits," said John, "that'll cut into Sammy's profits." A familiar hooting greeted this, the rich unrestrained laughter of Sammy himself. He seized John and kissed him with enthusiasm, he kissed me too, but I felt the enthusiasm was rather more restrained.

"No more sleuthing, then?" This was an ambiguous remark, but one, I felt that implied injunction.

"Oh no," I said "the bridegroom-to-be put a stop to that."

"Man," said Sammy, "when I look at Tubby, I thank the Lord I'm gay."

I peered around the room for DAFS and thought I could make out the Skorskis standing by the door at the far end of the room, but I couldn't see any other familiar faces.

"I take it they're not coming, Tubby and Twinkletoes – I know Lewis said he wouldn't come if they were." Sammy looked a mite sheepish and then grinned broadly. "But who was I to turn away a couple of old friends?"

"Oh, Sammy!"

"They weren't coming, honest. Tubby phoned and said so, but she phoned a couple of days ago…" Sammy did a very good imitation of Carol's tinkly tones: "Oh, Sammy, you wouldn't have room for two little ones, would you? I've managed to persuade his lordship after all."

John shook his head, "I don't reckon much on Tubby's chances, do you?"

"Sweet Fanny's buttocks," Sammy agreed cheerfully, and swivelling round, he gave a great hoot of delight and reached out his arms, "Doreen and Jessica, my darlings, it must be three years!"

"Sammy goes a long way back," said John. We stared out over the crowd.

"Look!" said John. "It's Simon and Lewis and look! They've brought Matron and Arbuthnot-Whatsit."

But before I could digest this latest development, what had seemed an impenetrable crowd began to give in the middle, and as I was wondering what superhuman force had caused this Red Sea parting, my question was answered: like a pair of tanks in the face of enemy fire, Megan and Bethan made their inexorable progress, clearing humanity from their path through sheer bulk and skilful use of handbag. Bethan took me and Megan took John and, as huge arms encircled me, I felt I was undergoing a primordial experience, like being returned to Mother Earth.

"Boyoes," said Bethan, "I am pleased to see you." She took a large white embroidered handkerchief out of her bag and wiped her face. "There's a fair few folk out there." Megan lingered over John and released him with reluctance. I reflected that everyone took longer over kissing John than me.

"We loved the lamb," said John politely.

"Yes, I've brought some fliers," said Bethan. "You wouldn't mind recommending us, would you?" Perhaps after all, the half lamb had not been a bribe, but a sales tactic – like the Manager of *Il Sole*, or even the Skorskis bargain stuffings; just sometimes I wish I could be loved for myself. Anyway, I couldn't wait to tell them about Tubby and Carol, and rather meanly wanted to get in with the story before John.

"You'll never guess what's happened," I began. John said he was off to the Marlowe Balcony for a fag.

"I hope you get there in one piece," I said as he embarked on the business of beating a path through the encroaching crowds. "Now listen! "I said, turning back to Bethan and Megan – and out it all came. I got a gratifying response from the Welsh ladies.

"Dear God," said Bethan, "she's not wasted any time."

And Megan, whom I had in fact always suspected of being the deeper thinker of the two said slowly, "I wonder whether she put the poisoned whisky on the tray? I shouldn't wonder if she had her eye on him all the time."

"And to think," said Bethan seething with rage, "he went about telling everyone I'd killed Lady P.."

"Well, not exactly, Bethan.

"Well, he made you two think I had, and all the time he'd plotted to kill her himself along with that Carol."

"Actually," I said, "I don't think she was out to get Tubby. Remember how you told me she had set her sights on Lewis?"

"I shouldn't think anyone would make Tubby their first choice," agreed Bethan.

"She calls him Laurence!" I said.

"Laurence!" Bethan imbued the name with a terrible searing scorn, "I should think he'd be better off with Tubby."

"I shall pretend I don't know anything about it," said Megan.

"That's a good idea," said Bethan, "then we can make a great thing of saying how much he must miss his wife."

"Mind you," I said, "I do feel sorry for Tubby. I should think he'll have an awful time with her. He'll get not a moment's peace with Carol poking her nose into everything."

"She'd worm out anyone's secrets," agreed Bethan. But before I could pursue the import of this remark, Sammy called for quiet in order to make an announcement - which he did with his usual aplomb. He was thrilled to see so many old friends (dear absent friends, I thought), and he knew we were going to have a marvellous day. People could now begin taking their seats, either with their partners or as a four, if they had come as a four – but, no, you needn't worry if you hadn't come as a four or even as pair: Sammy could arrange that in a blink of an eye. The important thing was for everyone now to proceed through to The Shakespeare Room, ("third on the left out of here") and to sit down. There would be sixteen boards played before the delicious buffet lunch (I had been right), and twelve boards after lunch. Steady now, he didn't want anyone hurt in the crush.

It was when we got into the Shakespeare Room that I thought perhaps Sammy's 5k wasn't going to be earned so easily after all: he was surrounded by a seething throng of hyperactive bridge players, jostling each other and asking him questions: where should Winifred sit, they hadn't got another couple, where were the toilets, and where was the bar? Kathleen always sat north and Geraldine couldn't stand draughts, Harold had to have a chair with arms and Mary-Anne must sit with her back to the window. Anna thought the cloths didn't look quite clean, and Mrs Jaggers thought the cards should be new, and were there any large printed cards for her husband?

Bethan, Megan and I found a table somewhere in the middle and sat down. I peered about for John wondering if he had finished his fag and how would he know to come to the Shakespeare Room, and should I go and find him? Megan and Bethan were also peering about.

"Well," said Bethan disappointed, "I can't see Tubby and Carol, can you, Megan?"

"No, Bethan, I can't," and nor could I; perhaps after all, they weren't coming. It would, I reflected, take a lot of courage on Tubby's part to admit that he was going to marry Carol – all the more so, since most people didn't even know Lady P. had died! Ah, here was John, looking amused.

"I've just seen Lewis and Simon; they *have* come with Matron and Arbuthnot-Thingy," he said sitting down.

"Where?"

"In the corner, there." And indeed they were: Arbuthnot-Jones beaming all over his face and Matron with her golden beehive piled even higher than before. Neither Lewis nor Simon looked very happy about it.

"What on earth made them bring those two?"

John shrugged. "You've seen the Skorskis?"

"Goodness, "said Bethan looking up from filling in her card, "the whole world is here. "I wonder whether the Macalisters are coming." And then of course I remembered they didn't know about Trevor's death – or about Janet, either, but this time I thought it only fair to let John do the telling.

Sammy was just about winning: he had everyone sitting down bar a few stray grumblers muttering beside the fireplace, and he was bracing himself to get things going, when there was a commotion at the doorway as a figure in a frilly pink blouse positively bounced in. Here was Carol, accompanied by the small, round, figure of Tubby, twiddling his thumbs as if his life depended on it.

"There they are, Megan," said Bethan, "she's got her frills on and he's lost his glasses."

They made their progress towards Sammy, triumph in her every step and anxiety in his every twiddle.

"She wanted to make an entrance," whispered Megan.

"I wonder she's not struck down," said Bethan. "There's no doubt in my mind but that she killed Lady P.."

"Oh Bethan, mind what you say!"

"Mind what I say!" exclaimed Bethan, "Don't forget he accused me of poisoning his wife! I shan't let him forget that."

Carol was beaming all over her face: "Oh, I'm afraid, we've complicated all your arrangements, Sammy; what annoying people we are!"

I craned forward to see how Sammy would deal with the situation, but nothing was a problem to Sammy. He had a spare couple who would make up the tables, (and indeed there were a couple of boyish-looking Sammy-friends), he was delighted to see his friend Carol in her stunning pink.

"Pink!" muttered Bethan who was also eagerly trying to catch what was being said. "I should have thought black would have been a better colour."

Carol was having a good look round to check that everyone had noticed her arrival, but Sammy swept them both off to a far table, wafting them away under the gusts of his laughter.

Now we were all settled, and Sammy would personally shoot anyone who wasn't. A polite gust of laughter – Sammy could do no wrong. All East-Wests were to move down seven tables; this was very simple, they were to add seven to their existing table number and find the correct table, so if they were now at Table 3, they should look for Table 10 and so on. Now another great upsurge took place, sticks were brandished and voices raised: "We should be here, what are you doing in our places?" John and I were East-West, and Megan and Bethan sat north-south ("We don't like moving more than we can help."). I wondered what would happen if Bethan got Tubby, perhaps Sammy would do some laughing. John and I moved up our seven tables and we got May and Mavis.

"We haven't been playing very long," said May, or it may have been Mavis – they were hard to distinguish since both were nervous bespectacled sixty year olds in muted shades of beige. They hadn't understood how to fill in the conventions card, but they assured us they played like Mrs Ramsay had said at the classes.

"Basic Acol?" asked John who likes to get things straight. They thought so, yes, they were sure that's what Mrs Ramsay had called it. Mavis hoped we weren't very good players, May said she thought we were. She added that they didn't like taking risks, they preferred to make a contract than to bid too high. John said should we start, seeing as everybody else had? And suddenly there was silence.

Nothing concentrates a man's mind, we are told, like the thought of being executed the following day. Well, next to that, I'd put the first bridge hand of a day that people have paid a hundred quid for.

They weren't risk takers: on the first hand they settled for two diamonds – which they made with four overtricks – John had a Yarborough and I had a two queens, so we were rather happy with the result since we guessed most oppositions would bid and make a slam. On the second hand they were bolder and made three clubs: that time they had twenty-seven points and should have made three no trumps; so on the next hand John and I took a gamble: bid and made four spades with twenty points, but then got carried away on the fourth hand and bid a rash four hearts with just nine points in his hand, and unsurprisingly went three off.

May said that it just showed how it was better not to bid too high and Mavis said she wouldn't have bid at all on that hand. John looked rather cross; he doesn't like being told he's wrong. Then conversation flagged and I had a good gawp round. We were all quite tightly wedged in, but my eye was caught – perhaps I was thinking of Bethan's comment about Carol: 'she'd better have worn black' – by two very elegant, darkly clad ladies. I am rather short-sighted, though (and, like Tubby, I am rather vain and feel I am more attractive to my partner without glasses), but I thought they had a look of Isabel and Janet. John who turned to see where I was looking, commented only, "I see your friend the widow has turned out."

"Indeed, along with your desert island companion."

And there they were! It needed closer inspection, but looked to me as if they had both had new wardrobes, and that

Janet who had first changed from dowdy bridge-holiday Janet to sexy Gino-lover, had now metamorphosed into Janet the elegant heiress. And there was Isabel, not too grief-stricken to turn herself out smartly. Was she looking beyond holy Willy Wanker for something a little more mainstream? They were playing North-South, so I had hopes of catching up with them later.

Now it was time to move on, Mavis said she was sorry they 'had beaten us,' but she expected we would do very well 'considering'. I edged John forward before he could say they had given us three 'tops' and ask 'considering what?'

We were now rather more centrally placed, with the Navy behind us, and Carol's girlish tones somewhere in the near vicinity, but I could hear nothing of Tubby; perhaps he daren't speak. I reflected gleefully that the admiral and his wife knew nothing of the dramatic events, and I hoped I should overhear some commiserating before the next hands were played, but alas, Sammy was a hard taskmaster and there was no time for idle chatter.

And now we had our work cut out. We were paired against a youngish couple (and of course, when I say youngish I mean from the position of my advanced years, so I suppose they were actually in their late thirties). I remembered them from *Il Sole* and I didn't much care for them – and nor did John. They were like many childless hetero couples who rather turn in on themselves; I don't know why it happens, because it doesn't happen to gay couples who are happy to develop interests outside themselves. But as I write this, I wonder if I am being entirely honest, for while it is true to say John has other interests outside me, I don't know that I have many that don't involve John. I suppose there are my bowls with Jeremy, but really he's another Arbuthnot-Jones, a duty rather than an interest.

Anyway, here were Stewart and Jacqueline; he is very tall and angular and she has very short carroty hair and freckles and is immensely thin. I once heard Lady P. telling her that she looked as if she could do with a good square meal, and asking him if he had got more bones in his body than other people. John had made the mistake on our first night at *Il Sole* of calling her Jacky, and Stewart had taken him aside afterwards and asked him if he would please not shorten Jacqueline's name, because they only allowed their very close friends to do that, they believed names were very meaningful things. John had replied in that case he would be careful not to call him Stew, but that he was welcome to shorten his name or Mark's, if he liked. They didn't seem to care for us very much after that, and anyway kept themselves to themselves. We used to watch them doing exercises together in front of the pool every morning at 8.30am on the dot, and then they went for a walk, he carrying her bag and she his. John had once stood next to him in the loo, having a pee and said he had an extraordinarily long and thin penis – like a knitting needle, he said. I found them rather frightening; if they hadn't gone home the day before Lady P.'s death, I should have thought them strong candidates for the murder. However, they were very good players and gave no quarter.

"I see you're still playing strong twos," said Stewart rather contemptuously. "As you may remember, we play weak twos and five card majors."

"Stewart and I also do Jacobs," said Jacqueline.

John smiled brightly. "Thank you for telling us that, Jackie."

We both enjoyed the expression of pain on their faces. Our triumph was short-lived, though; they managed to make a very difficult three no-trumps against us and even got an overtrick.

"Well done, darling," said Stewart, "you did play that well."

"It was your brave bidding, darling."

They bathed in each other's smiles.

"I think we had better get a move on," said John irritably.

"We play very quickly," said Stewart.

"Yes, we do," said Jacqueline.

This time we managed four hearts, but so had those who had played the hand previously.

"A flat board," said Jacqueline.

"You could have made an extra trick if you had finessed the eight of hearts," Stewart informed me.

"I noticed that too," said Jacqueline.

"I expect most people will make the extra trick," said Stewart.

"I am sure they will," said Jacqueline.

However on the next hand they made five diamonds but had only called three.

"Pity you didn't call game," said John unkindly.

"It wasn't really there," said Stewart, "you shouldn't have allowed us to make the fifth club."

On the fourth board I played one no trump and went three off.

"Bad luck," said John.

"You shouldn't have been in no trumps," said Stewart.

"One heart was the contract," said Jacqueline.

We had played the boards in record time.

"Did you know Lady Prettyman had died?" I asked in the lull that followed.

"What a tragedy!" said the extra-boned Stewart.

"Yes," said Jaqueline, "and poor Tubby. I should so much rather be the one to go than the one left behind."

I turned to John, "Would *you*?" I asked. I really wanted to know.

"No," said John.

They both looked very shocked.

"Some things don't bear thinking about," said Stewart and he gave his wife's hand a little squeeze.

"Well, Tubby's found solace in the arms of another now," I said. Since John would have preferred me dead to dying himself, I was going to be the one to spill the beans. Stewart and Jacqueline gave a double shudder, and I was about to fill in the details when a tinkly laugh reminded me that the 'one left' was sitting practically behind me, opposite the solace-bringer. I thought I had better change the conversation, but it was time to move on and I hadn't been able to overhear anything!

Our next move was an improvement, geographically at least; we found ourselves placed with the Skorskis. He was still accompanied by his mysterious small bag and looked as murderous as ever, while Claire seemed to have had her hair done for the occasion. At least, it had obviously seen a person with a scissors since the new style consisted of a number of uneven tufts and surprising projections; however, there her efforts had ended, she wore the same top that she had worn most of the time at *Il Sole*. I was looking forward to imparting the gossip about Tubby and Carol, although I wasn't sure how much of the Macalister gossip John and I should vouchsafe. However, I was to be disappointed, for Claire immediately bent over the table in excitement, and even grabbed hold of a bit of John's jacket to ensure his attention.

"I say, I say, did you know, there's Tubby going to marry that Carol. She's got a ring; he's going to marry her."

"Oh," I said disappointedly. "How do you know?" I was miffed that John and I, chief harbingers of the DAFS' news, had been done out of our announcement.

"Bethan told me. You remember Bethan, Welsh lady, friend of that other Welsh lady, they come from Wales? Remember them, do you? Well, I think it's disgusting, and," she continued, pointing at her husband, "… so does Karl, don't you Karl? You think it's disgusting, don't you, Karl?" But Karl was not as loquacious as he had been in his own home surroundings, and merely nodded, he was busy extracting something from his little bag.

"And it makes you think, doesn't it? It made me think, you know about that murder. I said to you, didn't I? Told you when you came to us, came to our house, I wonder if she did it, killed Lady P., got her with poison. That's what I wondered and so did Karl. Mind you, I don't make any accusations; no I don't, you learn to be careful in business, you have to be careful." She drew breath. "You got my flier? I sent you a flier." John acknowledged receipt of the flier, and added he didn't think we could make use of one stuffing, let alone two. This evoked an angry response from Claire.

"Don't use that word, we don't use that word. People think it's only like stuffing, it's not, is it, Karl?" Karl conceded with a nod that obviously indicated it was something very different.

"The skill takes years to learn, it takes years: all the materials you need to use; you have to work with all sorts of specialist chemicals …"

John gave me a look and glanced meaningfully at Karl's bag.

"Yes," I telepathised, "probably carried it round Italy with him on the off-chance there was a bit of poisoning or stuffing to be done."

As Claire continued to explain the complications of taxidermy, I continued to wonder whether Carol *had* found something incriminating in the Skorski bag and if so, whether it was belladonna. Suppose….I stopped my conjecturing abruptly since the tone of Claire's voice (I had ceased to listen to the words) suggested that she needed appeasing, but John had already got in while I was still wondering how to interrupt the flow.

"It was a pity Lewis didn't know about your… business. His dog's just died and he's pretty cut up about it." John met with instant success: what kind of dog was it? What breed was it?

John, being a man who doesn't do dogs and children, looked at me.

"A golden retriever, I think."

"Oh, we could have done a lovely job, couldn't we Karl; we like a big dog. Oh, we could have done a lovely job with a big dog like that." Karl's nod conceded that a lovely job might well have been done.

"It was a bit mangy," said John, "I reckon you would have had your work cut out." No doubt he was mentally comparing the task to that of Fifi, I thought. His comment provoked an outburst from Claire, and even Karl was moved to speak: "Mangy eez no problem."

Claire explained several times that it even made the finished article better than new, through a sort of hair-transplanting operation. Apparently the dog would be as hirsute as if it had been a puppy. I looked at the strange tufts on Claire's head and wondered whether some such abortive attempt had been made there.

"It eez amazing," added Karl, and we judged that this pronouncement must certainly add weight to Claire's assertions, "vat a deeference ze 'air make, and vith zee golden 'air, ze dog look like zee new dog."

I thought it might be rather disconcerting to have your dear absent friend hanging around, not only dead, but looking ten years younger. However, all these interesting thoughts had to be put aside because the booming laughter of Sammy decreed it was time to devote ourselves to the cards.

And I must say I did wonder about John's magic glasses theory, for how was it that Karl knew my king of spades was a singleton when he only had a doubleton himself? And how did he dare go into no trumps with a void in clubs unless he knew that Claire had got six? Why did he risk letting John in with all his diamonds by finessing the eight unless he knew that I had the ace? Of course, he *could* just be a very good player. Whatever the rights and wrongs of Karl Skorski's play, they did very well against us: we got a 'middle' and two 'bottoms', and the last hand was passed out, which gave us time for more gossip.

I told them about Trevor's death, and as I spoke I was worried that John might be tempted to make some crack about mummifying poor Trevor, but he took the opportunity to go off to the balcony of The Marlowe Room. And, like the Tubby business, Claire knew about it already, and had even spoken to Isabel.

"Of course," she said, "I knew he had a bad heart; he was always taking pills. I often saw him taking pills for his heart." So here again was another direction for our suspicions! And hadn't Isabel herself said as much: 'perhaps you will say Trevor did it, then the case would really be closed, wouldn't it?'

"And Janet's living with that Gino – you know, the Italian waiter, going to run a hotel, they say; run a hotel! People don't know the difficulties of business, do they Karl? They think it's easy." But Karl was engaged in some complicated recording of his score. Claire was of the opinion that it wouldn't last anyway; bound to come to an end with a foreigner. I hardly liked to point out that she herself had taken this risk – apparently successfully. Suddenly another thought came into my mind:

"You don't have a relation with a son at *The Heathward House School* near Worcester, do you, only…?"

This apparently innocuous enquiry produced an instantaneous response from both of them: Karl's head shot up from his calculations, and Claire burst out, "Karl's nephew, and it's a good thing he's not there now, poor little thing, it's a good thing he's not there now." Fortunately she didn't seem interested in finding out where my information had come from – it seemed a bit complicated to explain. I reflected that it had not been a tactful question, bearing in mind my guide's assertion that he had cheated (a family trait?), and that he had been expelled.

"Hah!" said Karl and looked more murderous than ever.

"Perhaps boarding school life, didn't suit him?" I said anxious to get to the bottom of this and remembering that 'England had made him ill.'

"No, it didn't; it made him ill. He nearly died there."

"Well," I said brightly, "Perhaps the lady who saved his life is here."

"Eh? What do you mean? What…?"

"Vat are you saying?"

It was then I made a bad mistake.

"The school matron is here," I said wondering somewhat late whether imparting this knowledge was a good idea. Well, in for a penny, in for a pound.

"Simon has brought her along with another teacher."

"Simon?"

"You know Simon Johnson who was at *Il Sole*."

"Does he teach there? Is he a master there?"

"Well, yes." It was surprising that they hadn't known this, but then Simon was so shy that there was no reason why he should have volunteered the information.

"Where is that matron?" asked Claire, standing up to get a good all-round view of the room. I knew this must be serious because she only said it the once.

"Vere is she?"

I could see the back of the beehive in the far corner. "Over there," I said, "with the hair, by the door." But as soon as I had said it, I realised that it probably wasn't a good idea to divulge this knowledge.

"Ha!" said Skorski seeing her immediately, and no doubt recognising the hair tower. He got up, drew himself up to his full five foot two and, pointing a finger in the direction of the door, he roared out,

"There eez ze poisoner."

Then John walked in through the door. On his way back from his fag.

A hundred or more people stopped playing bridge and stared.

I have seen John in many moods of distress, anger, puzzlement, irritation, but I have never before seen him look so utterly bewildered. I have to say, as he faced the gawping crowd he turned white. My heart went out to him – despite his not wanting to die for me. Then a lot of things happened at once. I got up, Claire pulled Karl down and I heard the words, 'business' and 'careful'; people began to turn from staring at John to staring at Karl, and indeed at me. John said, "um," and started walking back to the table, and I fancied I saw the Admiral stand up and brace himself to relive Trafalgar; but of course, we had counted without Sammy.

I have heard silence mentioned as a weapon, people often talk about the power of silence, but it is nothing beside the power of laughter. Sammy's laughter rumbled, and then it grew and expanded like a giant balloon until it filled the whole room; and it continued until he had the whole room laughing with him; nobody had a clue what at, but such was the power of Sammy's laughter that John got back to the table, Skorski sat down and Matron remained intact – although I noticed that the beehive didn't move, an indication perhaps, that she was lying low. Sammy's intelligent, indeed gorgeous smoky brown eyes flicked here and there, and when he stopped the laughing, he began to talk about arrangements for lunch – which I thought very clever, because no matter how excited and curious people are, they always put their appetites first, so while there was a small amount of muttering from people who hadn't finished playing, attention was diverted – and eventually dissipated, because now John was back at the table he was sitting right next to his accuser, apparently quite happily. The crowd was disappointed.

"What was all that about, then, Karl?" asked John still looking rather white, "Who am I supposed to have poisoned?" But as Claire and Karl and I all started to offer quite different explanations at the same time John looked even more bewildered than before.

"I know how Bethan felt now," he said.

I tried to piece together the accusation against Matron, and it wasn't easy because you couldn't really understand Karl who tended to lapse into some unintelligible Eastern European language (I have never actually discovered what his nationality was), when emotions threatened to overcome him, and Claire seemed only to have the story at second hand anyway. It *seemed* that the boy (a nasty piece of work, I felt), was suddenly taken quite ill while he was in the San with something minor: Matron claimed he had sneaked out and nicked something out of the school laboratory, but the Skorski father, (the brother of Karl, or perhaps the cousin) claimed that his boy would never have done that, and that Matron had poisoned him.

The whole thing seems to be complicated by the fact that the school were pretty anxious to get rid of him anyway, and the poisoning seemed to bring matters to a head. A compromise was reached whereby the boy left because 'boarding school life didn't suit him'; I daresay money changed hands too.

"I shouldn't go accusing Matron again, if I were you," said John when the story had come to an end, ('and it was dreadful, wasn't it Karl, shocking, it was?') "particularly here among all these people."

"You have to be careful when you're in business," I added craftily. We left it like that because time was getting on, and we could see we needed to get into the lunch stakes. Sammy had again been clever: seeing there were an awful lot of people and they would all have to help themselves, he said those who wanted drinks should go to the bar, and those who wanted to eat would go to the Conservatory where food was laid out. Such people, we gathered would be provided with water. Thus he had divided us up into the boozers and the mean.

"You get the food and I'll get the booze," said John.

"They might not serve you," I said.

"I'll risk it," he replied.

Carrying two plates wasn't easy – as John had foreseen when he volunteered to do the drinks run, particularly as you had to fight to get into the queue and maintain a place there. Eventually I gave up on loading them separately and stuck one under the other and loaded up the top one. John likes his food so there was something of an Eiffel Tower effect as pieces of pork pie swayed aloft above precarious piles of sandwiches, quiche, and the rest. It was all rather embarrassing as I looked extremely greedy, and in fact, I heard Jacqueline glance at the plate and whisper to Stewart, "I hope not everyone takes so much, darling."

And then seating was at a premium, and some people carried their spoils back to the bridge room, but I had my thoughts of second helpings and a retreat would ruin any chance of that, so I found a couple of spaces at the end of a long table and positioned myself by May and Mavis. Next to them, one each side of the table spreading over their chairs sat Bethan and Megan, and next to them Mr and Mrs Admiral. There was one space at the far end.

Suddenly Tuby, aka Laurence hoved into view. He, like me, had drawn the short straw and was carrying two plates, and I noticed a piece of beetroot fall off the side of one of them. He looked lost and bewildered – not quite the Lothario we had witnessed on the previous occasion. Now he stood looking round for seats, but without his glasses he was at a disadvantage. If only he'd had his hands free he could have had a comforting thumb twiddle.

Then Carol arrived on the scene and sitting herself down on the one remaining seat remarked, "Just room for a little one." She reached up and grabbed one of Tubby's plates and set to, leaving Tubby to fend for himself. However, the gods were kind to him because Mavis and May got up saying they weren't big eaters and were going for a little walk – they had found the morning very tiring. Actually, I could see exactly why they were going: John had returned from the bar carrying a bottle of Côtes de Rhone, and who wants to sit next to a poisoner?

"Is that all you got?" he asked ungraciously, looking at his plate on which I had put the lion's share of the spoils.

"Ssh!" I said. "This should be interesting."

Carol sat gobbling at the other end of the table, holding her hand up from time to time to reveal its sparkling adornment, and as nobody had much to say, she kicked things off.

"What a nice lot of people here. It can be such a lottery, the sort of people you meet at these things, can't it?"

Tubby was staring glumly at his plate. Perhaps, I thought, he couldn't see what was on it, or perhaps he was just fearful of the situation in which he found himself. If so, he was right. The admiral, perhaps detecting the glumness, put on a kindly expression and cleared his throat:

"I'm so sorry to hear of your loss."

"Yes," came a tiny voice from below decks, "we all think it so brave of you to come here today." Carol looked up sharply.

"Very good of you to partner him," said the Admiral nodding down towards Carol who looked immediately and pointedly towards Tubby. But if she was expecting support from that quarter, she was to be disappointed. Tubby went on staring at his pork pie.

Then Bethan took a turn. "Yes, Tubby, particularly brave as I know you found it very difficult to come to terms with what happened to Marjorie."

Well, I thought, Bethan must be innocent, otherwise she wouldn't risk bringing this up now. Was she really convinced that Carol had done it?

"I expect you miss her very much," added Megan from behind a pile of sandwiches.

"Such a strong person too," said the Sub-Mariner. Tubby's look of abject misery encouraged the Admiral.

"You will get over it, in time. Time is a Great Healer, but you mustn't expect too much too fast; these things take time."

All this emphasis on time encouraged Megan, who said gently... (was Megan's general air of gentleness quite what it seemed, I wondered?): "Oh yes, nobody but the most heartless could get over such a dreadful thing quickly."

"And I'm afraid to say," said Bethan with her mouth full of sausage roll, "that there will be plenty of eager ladies about, willing to take advantage of you."

"Don't you take any notice of them," said the Admiral stoutly. "You tell them you're very well off as you are, thank you."

All this time John and I sat meekly eating our quiche, saying not a word, but covertly looking to see what Carol would do. We could see indecision writ large on her face. At the Admiral's homily about Time The Healer, she looked as if she might say something, but after Megan's crafty intervention she opened her mouth only to post in a slice of tomato. Tubby had finally managed to locate a piece of Scotch egg and looked at it very studiously. I wondered whether either John or I should say anything, but then quite suddenly Tubby turned to me and burst out, "Tell them! You had better tell them. Say something before *she* does."

Only then did it strike me how halcyon those days with Lady P. must seem now to Tubby; what golden days when there was only Lady P. and the parrot to worry about. And, really, when you came to think about it, how very much more frightening Carol was than Lady P. had ever been. Yes, Lady P. had been rude and unpleasant, but it had been a kind of surface rudeness, there hadn't really been any underlying malice in her. Perhaps even her rudeness had become exaggerated because of her unfortunate appearance. Perhaps, after all, she hadn't been such a bad old stick; hadn't she gone out of the way to be nice to Simon when he was unhappy as a child?

But as to Carol….there really was *nothing* nice about her. *Had* she been the killer of Lady P.? I certainly wouldn't have put it past her.

"I think," I said, and because it was the first time I had uttered, everybody turned and looked at me: Tubby, Carol, the Admiral, the Admiral's wife, Megan, Bethan, even John. "I think you should know that the lady at the end of the table is engaged to be married to… (I toyed with 'Laurence' but it seemed too complicated)… Tubby, here."

There was a silence. The Sub-Mariner made a little squeaky noise and then the admiral cleared his throat.

"Ah!" he said.

Everyone looked at Carol and then everyone looked at Tubby, and then everyone looked at Carol again. But Carol wouldn't have been Carol if she hadn't risen to the occasion. She gave a bright smile.

"I began as a sharer in grief, and I have ended as a sharer in joy."

The only trouble was that Tubby didn't seem to be doing much of the sharing. At last he managed a watery smile and then he clasped his hands and twiddled his thumbs. For a while nobody said anything at all, although we were all agog to see who would break the silence. Eventually the Submariner spoke.

"Is it to be soon, the wedding?"

I thought this a very sensible question, one that I wanted to know the answer to myself, because when we had last seen them there was talk of the banns being read. Both Tubby and Carol spoke at once, Tubby appeared to be saying something to the effect of not over his dead body, while Carol obliterated his words with hers.

"As soon as we can – I owe it to dear Laurence."

"Who's Laurence?" asked Bethan, although she knew

perfectly well. "Is he another of your conquests?"

A groan came from the end of the table. "I said we shouldn't have come, I knew it would be like this."

"Come along, darling, don't be silly," said his fiancée, but there was an acid tone to the word 'darling'.

"Oh dear, oh dear," said Tubby.

"Pull yourself together, man," said the Admiral. There was another silence.

Suddenly Bethan asked quite inconsequentially: "Where are your glasses, Tubby?"

"I expect he prefers not to see too clearly," said Megan, who was showing a new confidence.

"Like Oedipus," said Bethan displaying surprising erudition. "He blinded himself when he realised what he'd done."

It was at that point Carol lost it. I can't say I blame her; she'd had a lot to put up with, and her lover had not shown himself to be a flower of English chivalry. She turned on Bethan, no doubt venting on her all the rage she felt against Tubby.

"If I was you, Bethan Thomas, I should be very careful what I was saying on the subject of husbands. Oh yes, I know a thing or two about that – and we all know who saw Lady P. last, and who handed her a glass of poison. You've got me to thank that you haven't been investigated by the police!"

"I think, my dear," said the Admiral turning to his wife, "we'll go and get some fresh air." He nodded vaguely in the direction of John and me. "We'll hope to see you at the Bridge table."

"Now just you listen to me. I don't know what makes you think you can speak to me like that…" began Bethan, standing up and lunging towards Carol. Alarmingly, Megan seized a plastic knife, but their combined bulk prevented violence, and Carol jumped nimbly out of the way.

"I'm going outside," she shrieked at her lover, "and you'd better come too, or you can have your ring back."

It was a kind of lesser re-enactment of the Skorski episode, lesser, because fewer people were about, some being in the bar and some in the bridge room, but the effect was the same: everyone turned to gawp at the retreating figure of Carol, and then took a turn gawping at Tubby.

"Oh dear, oh dear," he said.

Interest too, focussed on Megan and Bethan, as the latter glowered with rage and literally shook with fury, while Megan's plastic knife sent a palpable frisson of delicious terror throughout the assembled company. It seemed to me that Megan was by no means quite as meek as I had thought, and I wondered who was actually responsible for Megan's husband ending up in the gulley. If Megan did that, well, Lady P. was a piece of cake. Perhaps, after all… But now John asserted himself.

"Here," he said, putting his arms (as far as they would go), round the shoulders of the objects of terror. "We're going to go outside for a bit and get away from all this." And meekly as the lambs on Bethan's farm, they lumbered after him.

I was left alone with Tubby.

"She's a terrible woman," he groaned. "She would come, she would come, and I knew, I knew… Oh dear, if it hadn't been for the chocolates…"

"Chocolates?" I said. "Do you mean the ones you gave Carol?"

He peered hopelessly at a piece of cucumber. "I'm sure there weren't any nuts," he said mournfully, "because I asked at the shop specially. It was only a little box." He gazed sadly down at a piece of pork pie, took a stab at it and missed. "If only she would let me wear my glasses." And indeed he did look bereft without them; the glasses had given him a kind of authority, not much, but a bit.

"And it was only because I felt so guilty about those chocolates that I proposed. Well, I didn't really propose; I don't know how it happened."

I let him mumble on and began to build up a picture of what had happened. Carol had eaten a nutty chocolate in the presence of Olive, and had herself taken off to hospital, but whatever the truth about the nuttiness (or otherwise) of the chocolate, the outcome was not very serious: she had been kept overnight and discharged in the morning. Tubby even gave the impression that he thought it was Carol, rather than the hospital, that had insisted on the overnight stay. He was then bidden to her sickbed and the engagement was arranged.

"I didn't mind at first," said the sad fiancé. "She was very nice to me when I met her at a Midlands Bridge Day, and when I told her about poor Marjorie she said she was going to Tunisia and wouldn't it do me good to go too – to Sammy's Bridge holiday there? She even said she would put off her visit for a week or two so we could go together. It seemed a good idea and we had a nice time there," he sighed, and I reflected that Carol's negligée – or lack of it, must have finally come into its own.

"But I didn't really want to go on seeing her afterwards. The mistake I made was sending her those chocolates," he concluded pathetically. "I don't want to be married now."

"Well," I said, embarking on the rest of John's food, "you don't *have* to marry her." He shook his head sadly.

"Why *did* you send her the chocolates?"

A look of embarrassment came over Tubby's face:

"To… er… say thank you for… er… giving me a nice time."

Poor Tubby! What a heavy price he had paid for Carol's sexual favours! However, Tubby's angst provided a marvellous opportunity for investigating further.

"I suppose it was Carol who told you to stop investigating your wife's death?" He nodded sadly, but managed to locate and spear the elusive piece of pork pie.

"Why did she do that, Tubby? Why did she stop you wanting to find out the truth?" He swallowed the pork pie and peered into his waterless glass.

"She said she wanted me to forget all about being married before, to forget about Marjorie and think about her instead. She couldn't bear me to talk about Marjorie, and then, poor Albert…"

"Albert?"

"Our parrot."

"What happened to Albert?"

"I think she poisoned him. One day he was fine, and then after she'd gone... he went too; I sometimes wonder if she poisoned herself too with those chocolates, just to get me to marry her."

I thought this very probable and wondered why neither John nor I had thought of this before.

"Could she have poisoned Marjorie?"

"I wouldn't put it past her," he said sadly.

"Do you think Marjorie *was* poisoned, or do you think it really was a heart attack?" Tubby reached for the water jug, but it too was empty.

"I don't know, I don't want to think about it. I thought Bethan had done it, but I wasn't right, you say."

"No, Bethan definitely didn't do it," I said firmly, but of course, I didn't really know that. "What we think probably happened," I asserted stoutly, "was that a member of staff... your wife wasn't always very tactful, you know... put something in her drink, probably not meaning to kill her, just get their own back."

For a long time he sat staring at his plate in silence, then he got to his feet. "I must go and find her," he said, "and stop her being cross." And he went stumbling off to meet his nemesis.

For some time I sat there thinking about murderers: somehow I couldn't see Tubby as one, and although Carol seemed to be pretty free with poison when it came to birds, would she really have been far-sighted enough to poison Lady P. on the off-chance of getting Tubby? Somehow I didn't think so – but why had she stopped Tubby's investigations? I would have thought finding out the culprit would have been right up her nosy street. Well, perhaps after all, she was simply jealous of Marjorie's intrusive presence and wanted to get rid of it – along with Albert. Ah well!

I gazed about me and looked for familiar faces. I thought it would be nice to see Janet and Isabel, Simon and Lewis or even Arbuthnot-Jones and Matron, but I couldn't see any of them. Probably, I reflected, Matron had wisely hidden herself away from the wrath of the Skorskis. The only familiar faces, both of which were hovering near, were May and Mavis.

"Excuse me," said May, or it may have been (no pun intended) Mavis,

"We have been a bit anxious, we've never been on a Bridge Day before and we wondered if they were always like this? You know... violent?" She gave a shudder. "There was that man sitting at your table this morning accusing your friend of being a poisoner – which we are quite sure he's not, because we thought he was a very nice young man; and then there was a lot of funny laughter, and now this lady has been shouting at that gentleman... I thought we would ask you because you seem to know all these people, but I must say Mavis and I find it all very strange."

I assured her that Bridge people weren't all murderers, but that some of them could be very odd. Mavis said they didn't think they would do any more bridge, and actually she had wanted to do genealogy but the classes had been full up. I said I thought they should persevere.

"Look how you took John and me to the cleaners," I said, generously referring to the last hand.

"Yes," she said proudly, "that was the only top we had."

I felt this such a blow to my amour propre, that I beat a hasty retreat, and went off to find John who was, as I suspected, on the Marlowe Balcony. It was all very cosy, as not only were Megan and Bethan there, but Janet and Isabel too, and they were all, except Janet, smoking.

"Well!" I said.

"I haven't had a cigarette in years," said Bethan,

"Nor me," said Megan,

"But we've been under so much provocation at the hands of that woman..."

"Bethan has been telling us all about it," said Isabel. She looked terribly attractive, in a black tunic and trousers, her hair was swept up in what I believe is termed a chignon (it appeared a little more blonde than I remembered it), and round her neck was the delicate silver chain with the tiny Michelangelo David suspended from it. I wondered if it had been a present from Willy Wanker, but decided it was much too tasteful – and expensive – for a Holy Joe present. Janet too, looked good, also in black and with her hair in a plait down her back, she looked like a younger version of her mother.

"Fancy her accusing Bethan!" said the indignant Megan.

"She was obviously just feeling guilty," said Janet, "I shouldn't worry about it."

"What do you mean guilty?"

"Well, I meant getting engaged to Tubby, but I wouldn't put it past her having done in Lady P.."

"Oh darling, you shouldn't say that," said Isabel, but not very indignantly.

"All right then, but if we're talking about engagements, Carol's not the only one to have a ring to show off," and she held out her hand.

"Wow!" said John and gave her a big hug. Lucky Janet!

"Well, I hope you'll be very happy," said Bethan.

"And so do I," said Megan, but I did rather wonder how they viewed matrimony, Bethan's husband having proved a far from satisfactory mate, and Megan never having had one at all.

"Many congratulations," I said, "and may I kiss the bride to be?"

"Of course you can." And as I took her in my arms, it quite took me back to the days before I had discovered boys, and I had had to make do with girls – and if I'm honest there had been a fair bit of 'making do!'

Janet rattled away with all the callousness of the young, after all none of us were likely to enjoy the sweets of matrimony ourselves, and poor Isabel had been recently deprived of such sweets. But she was so joyful that you couldn't begrudge her joy; she was so happy and Gino was so happy and Gino's sister who was still staying with them (where?) was so happy, and Gino's mother was so happy, and all Gino's family were going to come over to the wedding, and even my old friend, the Manager of *Il Sole* had been invited, and it was going to be in the local church which had a very interesting history (very, I thought, thinking of

Willy Wanker), and of course it would have to be a quiet wedding because of Trevor having died, "and," she looked at John and me briefly, "I've probably said all sorts of silly things about him in the past, but actually he wasn't too bad." She glanced at her mother; perhaps the hotel idea was contingent on Trevor getting a good press, or perhaps she was really sorry about it all. All this, I reflected, would need some discussing with John since he had maintained that Janet had spoken the truth about Trevor.

"It's a shame, really, that he can't come to the wedding," she added – for good measure. And afterwards they were going to have a honeymoon in Italy and then they were coming back to turn *Elsinore* into a hotel and restaurant.

"We can supply you with fresh lamb," said Bethan, quick as a flash, "… which reminds me, Megan, we haven't put out the fliers, we ought to get them out on the tables before the afternoon session starts."

"Sammy said he'd make an announcement, and we thought you and John could put in a word of recommendation," said Megan.

"I shouldn't ask John," I said, "he's got a reputation as a poisoner."

"Get along with you," said Megan who was growing quite bold. "I've never heard such a lot of silliness." And off they went to promote Welsh lamb.

"Yes, what was that all that fuss about poisoning?" asked Isabel.

"It's frightfully complicated," I said.

"We'd much rather hear about the wedding," said John who obviously didn't feel up to explaining it either.

"Well, there is something else," said Janet, "only I didn't want to say it in front of Megan and Bethan, in case they were disapproving, like Welsh people are."

"Darling!"

"I'm going to have a baby!" She patted her stomach, "look you can see it's there already. Gino's so thrilled. Of course, he wants a boy, but Mummy and Gino's sister want a girl, and I don't mind what it is, but I hope it looks like

Gino." We proffered more congratulations, although actually I was getting quite weary of all this good fortune.

"So you see," said Isabel turning to me and smiling, "I don't think I shall be disappearing abroad after all. I think I shall be the new nursemaid." Before we could get bogged down in nappies, the sound of laughter was heard to pervade; Sammy was telling us it was time to start the afternoon session. So, as at the sound of the school bell, we all got up and started back.

"I never told you about Gino's sister, did I?" said Janet as we made our way back.

"Yes," I said, "she wants a girl." I was rather bored by all this.

"No," said Janet, "not that…." But at that moment we were separated by the crowd, and as Sammy was giving instructions I missed the news about Gino's sister. Sammy still maintained order, but I thought I detected a note of weariness in his voice: We would find a couple of fliers on the tables which his old friends from the Italian GrandSlam Bridge holiday had asked him permission to put there, and while he had never been stuffed himself (and he fluttered his eyelashes meaningfully, so that a few of the more daring laughed), he knew an excellent taxidermy service would be provided; on the other hand he had certainly tasted the delicious Welsh lamb (which must have been a lie, since nobody ever got Sammy's address), and so, he believed had other people here present – "haven't you Mark?" (Wisely he refrained from mentioning the poisoner.). Obediently I stood up, gave a watery smile and rubbed my tummy – exactly like Janet, I thought afterwards.

The fliers reflected the characters of the originators: the Skorski flier was obviously composed by Claire, as it told you several times over what an excellent service it was. There were pictures, too, among which I recognised Fifi in his basket. Bethan's flier showed her beaming beside a sheep, and Irfon brandishing a knife, rather in the manner of Megan at lunchtime.

"I don't think we shall be taking advantage of either of

these two offers," said the unpleasant man sitting north at our table.

"No," said the wife whom John later referred to as Mrs Bling, so bedecked and emblazoned with jewellery was she. "I think it lowers the tone having this sort of thing thrust on you." She clinked at me. "Do you play much bridge?" But without waiting for a reply, continued, "we do; we play seven days a week, three bridge clubs and social, five card majors, weak twos, Roman key-card. Shall we start?"

She had long scarlet finger nails and flicked her cards into place. He threw each card down contemptuously as if it was a nuisance having to play with such amateurs as ourselves. So it was a great delight when we got two 'tops' off them. They didn't like it a bit and as we moved on, we left them arguing furiously:

"I can't imagine why you didn't take the trumps out and run the diamonds," she clonked.

"Because I didn't have enough trumps."

"Well, you insisted on playing in spades, I offered you two other suits…" And the necklace made a dangerous in-swing across the table.

I looked across the far end of the room where I could see Lewis and Simon sitting in silence waiting for the next pair to come to their table; neither of them looked very happy. I was wondering again why they had come, and why on earth they had brought Matron and Mr Arbuthnot-Jones.

And then we got Matron and Mr Arbuthnot-Jones

"Hello," I said, "do you remember us?"

Neither of them did, nor were they any more interested in us when I explained where we had met. I got the impression that they had had rather a liquid lunch: Arbuthnot-Jones burped comfortably and seemed to be engaged in loosening his trousers.

"Hey!" said Matron interrupting my explanation and turning to John. "Why was that funny little man accusing you of being a poisoner, this morning?"

John was clearly taken aback and rather at a loss what to say, since he hardly liked to deny being accused himself, only to point the finger at her.

I came to the rescue. "His name was Skorski," I said. "His brother had a boy at your school." Even then Matron seemed none the wiser, but her hand shook a little as she patted the beehive.

"But why did he say you were a poisoner?"

"It wasn't me; it was you," said John who had obviously had enough of this. "He thought the boy got ill in the san or something."

Arbuthnot-Jones gave a loud burp.

"I do remember something," said Matron doubtfully, and then she burped too.

"We have had an excellent lunch," remarked Arbuthnot-Jones, who appeared to have his flies undone. "Young Simon took us into the restaurant; none of your buffet rubbish. A very good Claret."

"He's come into money," said Matron. "No, not *him*" – this to John in case he had thought she meant the flasher. "No, Simon; he's very generous with it, and he brought us here today," she raised her voice, "didn't he, Cuthbert?" Cuthbert smiled, oblivious to Matron's words, but he looked severely at John.

"I am afraid I do not hear good things about you," he said shaking his head and frowning terribly. "No, indeed I do not. I am of the opinion that you have had your hands in Matron's medicine cupboard."

Sammy announced that we were to play the new boards as soon as possible.

"Thank God," said John loudly, so loudly that Arbuthnot-Jones leant over and gave John a slap on the arm, "and there's no need for that sort of language, young man," he said.

"Shall we get started?" I suggested. "I think we are getting behind."

Matron said it would be a p..p…p..pleasure, and promptly dropped all her cards on the floor.

"Cuthbert!" she cried, her eyes turned downwards to retrieve the cards. "Your flies are undone."

We were, I felt, attracting a lot of attention. A woman on the next table shouted out for the Tournament Director, and Sammy came over, the smile a tad strained.

"Those people are causing a disturbance," she said pointing as much at John and me, as our opponents, "and it's the same man who caused all that trouble before lunch." I got the feeling that Sammy was a little tired of laughing and didn't begrudge him his 5k.

"Man," he said reproachfully, shaking his head at John, "you're giving Sammy some grief today." Then he picked up Matron's cards and made us take an average. We got on to the next hand. Arbuthnot-Jones played four hearts, which took him a very long time, especially since three of the hearts actually turned out to be diamonds. I looked at John and he shook his head. "Say nothing," he mouthed.

Matron and Arbuthnot-Jones got a top. Matron peered at the scorecard.

"Fancy," she said, "nobody else played in four hearts."

They let John and me play an innocuous two clubs, but then A-J nodded off.

"He's very old," said Matron, "at least a hundred."

We got Sammy to come and give us another average. Then we sat there in silence, waiting for the tea break, with the old man snoring softly. Matron closed her eyes, looking as if she had gone the same way, but she suddenly came to with a jolt and said," I remember that boy you were talking about." We pricked up our ears.

"He was a bad lot, and caused me all sorts of trouble."

"What happened?"

"He was skiving off in the San," she said, "and I said there was nothing wrong with him and he was to go back to class. So he said in that case he would make sure there *was* something wrong – he was a very rude boy, and he took a bottle out of his pocket and before I could do anything, took a big mouthful. And then, of course, he began to vomit, and I had to get the doctor, and then the parents – foreigners – made a fuss, and I got into trouble for not keeping the medicine cupboard locked, although I was sure I had.

Anyway, he left. I think he'd been cheating in an exam and doing other things. We were all glad to see the back of him." She nodded and burped.

"Well, that was his uncle making that fuss this morning."

But Matron had lost interest. "Come on, Cuthbert, wake up! It's time for tea." She got him to his feet and did up his flies.

"We've had a really nice day; it was kind of Simon, wasn't it?" She smiled and turned to John. "Do you think we've won a prize?" John said he thought it very likely, and Matron, beehive bobbing merrily, led the old man off. But not before he'd wagged a finger at John.

"No more of your nonsense, young man," he said.

"I don't think I've ever caused so much trouble in my life as I have today," John said defensively. We thought we wouldn't bother fighting for tea so we sat gossiping at the table.

"Why on earth did he bring them?" asked John.

"I think he's very kind," I said. "Perhaps that's part of his trouble, why he's so ineffectual."

"I think he's pathetic," said John.

"I think he and Lewis are very good people," I said staunchly, "much better than us. We would never have brought Matron and Mr. A-J to anything."

"Speak for yourself." said John, "Who was it who allowed him to make four hearts when most of them were diamonds?"

"Oh, look," I said, "there's Carol, and it looks as if she's heading for us." There she was, cup of tea in hand, waving a playful finger in our direction.

"I wish everyone would stop pointing their fingers at me," said John." First it was Skorski, then Arbuthnot-Jones, and now Carol."

"I'm surprised she wants to speak to us at all," I said. "I wonder what she wants." Up she came, all frilly blouse and girlish smiles.

"Oh there you are! I've been looking everywhere for you boys. May I join you?"

"Well, Carol," said John without committing himself,

"what do you want?" She sat herself down.

"I just thought I must come and put things right; there was such a nasty little scene at lunch, wasn't there? But you see when people become engaged to be married there are all sorts of little stresses and strains that people… like you two, don't know anything about…" She gave a saccharine smile and took a sip of tea. "The conversation was so very unkind to poor Laurence. I'm not complaining about the unkindness shown to yours truly by the Welsh… I was going to say ladies, but I am afraid I must say women. But of course, although I don't know the truth – I'm not one to pry into other people's business, as I'm sure you know, but I have a feeling there was something very odd about Bethan's marriage. And poor Megan, well who knows what goes on there?" She took another sip of tea and looked smilingly at us. I was wondering what the point of all this was.

"And of course I noticed you, Mark, sitting and talking to Laurence, and I do hope he didn't say anything silly under the pressure of grief." She looked at me rather nervously, but I didn't feel inclined to allay her fears. She sighed loudly and continued, a little less confidently, I felt.

"If only you knew how Tubby has agonised over those chocolates." She paused and then, as neither John nor I made any comment, continued, "and how he has begged and begged me to hurry the wedding along, and I have to say, 'now Laurence we must grieve properly for Marjorie. We won't put the banns up this week.'" I wondered how Tubby had managed that one.

"Of course, poor Laurence had a number of suspicions about Marjorie's death – he may have mentioned them to you…" Still John and I sat silent, and I felt she would soon get rattled.

"Of course there was nothing to be suspicious about, the poor dear died from a heart attack, as we all know, don't we? But it's natural, isn't it to be looking for causes when a dear one dies?"

"And then there was the parrot," said heartless John.

She looked up sharply but was equal to it. "Yes poor little

Albert, another sad reminder of Marjorie gone. But, as I was saying, it was quite understandable for Laurence to imagine funny things, because quite frankly, boys," she leant forward and I inhaled eau de cheap roses (perhaps she had the same source as Olive), "I don't like saying it, but there were some very odd people on that holiday…" She gave a little laugh. "Sometimes I think only Laurence and I were quite… normal."

"I thought most people were perfectly nice," said the mendacious John.

"Ah, perhaps you aren't quite as sensitive to people as I am. I have always had a sixth sense ever since I was a little girl, and it wasn't just being sensitive. I'm afraid I came to know that some people were… not quite the sort of people you expect. I think if Sammy had been a little more careful… but of course I'm not blaming Sammy."

"What was wrong with the Macalisters?" asked John bluntly.

"Well, I'm afraid I shouldn't like to give away any confidences and I don't like to speak ill of the dead, but I think that Trevor's relationship with his stepdaughter was a little… unusual, and although she is getting married, well, a girl from that background marrying a waiter – not that it will last. I'm afraid Trevor's money is the big draw there, as, of course, it was for her mother. And to be quite honest, between you, me and the bedpost, I suspect that Isabel was little better than she should have been when she was young. I shouldn't be at all surprised to learn that our little Janet was born out of wedlock."

I gulped, wondering where on earth Carol got her information from. Really, Tubby should have gone to her in the first place (before his sexploits) and not wasted his time with Sammy or John and me.

"And who else do you think had a sinister double life?" I asked.

"Now, Mark, you are having a little laugh at me! I don't mind, I am very good at laughing at myself, and of course I am not saying that everyone was odd on that holiday, after all you and John are... *nearly* normal, but I am afraid many people... Karl Skorski, for one was a very peculiar character."

"How do you know?"

"I once picked up something for him that he dropped out of his bag... I'm always tidying up after people, and although I expect he uses all sorts of odd things in his line of business, it did seemed strange to carry a bottle marked 'toxic' like that about with him on holiday..."

"Ah, yes!" I thought. "Where did the Skorski boy get his poison from? Not from Matron's locked cupboard, but from his uncle's little bag?" But John had had enough.

"I am going out to have a fag," he said, "and you can dish the dirt on me to Mark."

Carol gave a little shrill laugh, "Oh, you mustn't think that, John, I never have a bad word for anyone. Although I was a little bit hurt at lunch that you two boys didn't stand up for Laurence and me." She looked up grimly expectant. I supposed the real point of her coming over was to cast suspicion on the other DAFS, and now she was trying to evaluate how successful she'd been, but when John walked off and I said nothing; she got up and offered a parting shot.

"Of course, I realise it's hard for you two boys, missing out on these things that we normal people regard as true God-given sacraments."

"We get by," I said.

The last hand of the afternoon was uneventful: we played against a man with a very loud bridge tie and a thin wife called Esmeralda, and came about middle on each board. And then it was all over.

Bridge players are funny people: they are prepared to sit all day playing cards, but once it's finished, they are anxious to be gone. This was a case in point, many rushing for the door muttering about 'getting the car out,' without even bothering to stay for the result. Esmeralda and Mr Tie said they must get back because it was Bridge Night at the club; I saw Lewis with Simon shepherding Matron and Mr A-J out, and Janet and her mother disappeared without trace. The Skorskis gathered up spare fliers and he put them in his little bag, while May and Mavis fled as soon as they could. Some of us, however, were made of stronger stuff: Bethan and Megan plumped themselves down and hoped for glory; I saw Jacqueline and Stewart holding hands and looking expectant, and Carol had made Tubby stay, and sat smiling at everyone who passed.

It was at such moments that Sammy came into his full glory: the leather trousers shone and his gold jewellery glistened and his laughter filled the room. Would we like to know the results? Well, would we? "Yes," we roared like kids at a children's party, and Sammy told us. The admiral and the submariner won North-South, and who should be the East-West winners but his old friends Mark and John? I thought of the hand against Matron and one or two others where we hadn't exactly covered ourselves with glory. Was it a fiddle, a sweetener from Sammy? Never mind, who were we to complain? Mr and Mrs Admiral got a bottle of wine and John and I drew the short straw and got a box of chocolates. Sammy won't go broke on prizes, I thought. I let John collect the chocolates.

"Well, Sammy," I asked as we finally left, "are you a rich man now?" He threw back his splendid head and his body positively rippled.

"Man," he said, "I am the richest man in the world until tomorrow."

A thought struck me: "How did you stop Skorski attacking Matron?"

"Matron? Who's Matron? I thought it was John he was after. No? Well, I told him I'd stop the fliers if he whispered again."

He reached into a box and pulled out a bottle of gin. "Give that to Lewis's two friends." he said, "It's the wooden spoon. If you don't see them, drink it yourself."

"Hey, Sammy..." said a nubile-looking boy helper.

"Sugarplum," he said, "I'm all yours."

It was time to leave. On our way to the car we passed

Simon ineffectually helping Arbuthnot-Jones into an ancient, but perfectly preserved Morris Minor. He looked up and smiled, he had rather a sweet smile: his cheeks dimpled and his eyes shone brightly behind his enormous glasses.

"I'm sorry I was rather rude when you came to the school."

"You weren't rude at all," I said, "and you invited me into your beautiful flat." He looked embarrassed and went trying to fold the old man into the car. I wondered if I should ask him if there was any news about his operation, but decided against it. Matron waved merrily from her seat next to him.

"Here," I said, "you did win a prize after all."

"Mother's ruin," said Arbuthnot-Jones, reaching out for it with both hands.

Then Lewis opened the window and beckoned me over.

"I shall add my apologies to Simon's," he said. "I am afraid I was far from welcoming when you called; my dog had just died and I was rather upset. Well, very upset. So please forgive my discourtesy."

"There was none," I said. But further embarrassment was saved by Arbuthnot-Jones finally falling into the back seat and pointing at John who was skulking about with a fag.

"A hundred lines and a good thrashing!" he shouted out, but Lewis started up the engine, and off they went. I had a feeling they were all pleased to see the back of us.

Chapter 22: We are extraordinarily clever

"You're not bad for an old 'un," said John.

I always think life is a bit like climbing up a mountain: pretty hard most of the time, but occasionally you reach a kind of plateau, a grassy knoll, as it were, where you take off your boots, have a sit down and a look about you, and a sense of peace descends leaving you feeling pretty damn good. Well, that's how I felt now. We had got back from the bridge day and decided to forget about it all. In fact we had a good meal, lots to drink, and watched one of the DVDs that I had purchased all those months ago when I so fatefully bumped into Sammy in the Soho sex shop. It was funny and quite arousing and the aftermath of our viewing very pleasant – which is what John meant by his cryptic comment. We lay comfortably in our very large double bed and ranged amicably over the day's events.

"Who do you think will drink the gin?" asked John. "Matron or Arbuthnot-Thing."

"Both," I said, "they'll have an orgy. They'll invite Lewis and Simon along and Arbuthnot and Lewis will take turns with Matron, and he'll forget all about the wife."

"Who'll Simon have, then?"

"His sexpot girlfriend, of course. Oh damn, I never followed that one up after he was so touchy about her, I should have asked Matron."

"Too late now." We lay quiet for a bit and then John said,

"Well, at the end of the day, who did it?"

"Probably one of the staff," I said regretfully, "but I'd like to think Carol."

"Do you think she'll get Tubby to marry her in the end?"

"I'm afraid she will."

"Yup, I think she will too."

"She really is a horrible woman," I said, "gathering up the dirt on everyone."

"I wonder what she's got on us."

"It's funny, you know John. I was thinking earlier she was

really much more unpleasant than Lady P., oh I know she could be bloody offensive, but that's as far as it went really – she was just a rude, ugly woman. She wasn't malicious in the way that Carol is. Really, if anyone had to be murdered it should have been Carol."

John sat up like a shot.

"*What* did you say?"

"I said......"

"Mark!"

We looked at each other.

"No, it couldn't... could it?"

"Yes... now wait... don't interrupt... suppose the victim was meant to be Carol! Suppose..."

"You are saying that someone meant to kill Carol, but killed Lady P. by mistake."

"Yup."

"Well!" I said. "Why didn't we think of that before?" We basked in our amazing brilliance for a few seconds. Then I said sadly: "Not easy to kill the wrong person though, particularly when they are behind a door with a number on it. It seems to me that if you're going to kill someone, you make sure you've got the right person? If you know that the person you want to kill is in room X, you don't go to room Y." I might be the one with all the extra degrees, but John is the one who sees to the heart of things.

"Don't forget that it wasn't the murderer who went to the room, but the waitress. She was the one who went to the wrong room, it was she who made the mistake."

"But they all must have known Lady P.'s number, she was always shouting it out."

"Mark, I need a fag." It was against house rules, but the situation warranted it. He lit up and spoke slowly: "Well, perhaps she was a new girl. Bethan said she didn't recognise her."

"Surely a new girl would be extra careful to take it to the right room."

"Now, wait a minute," said John. "You did your fancy plan of numbers when we went to *Il Sole*, that morning when you were so crotchety…"

"Me?"

"Where have you done with it?"

"Ah!" I said.

"You see if only you'd done that database. Can't you remember what you've done with it?"

"Not immediately, I'll look tomorrow."

"Well, do you remember anything odd about the layout of the rooms … what I'm getting at… yes, was Carol's room near Lady P.'s?"

"I can't remember," said Mr Useless.

"Can't you remember anything?"

"Yes, I can, I can remember that the numbers were in a sort of Gothic lettering, so, actually, it would be quite possible to confuse the numbers."

"Yes, you're right, the numbers weren't at all clear, so … now wait, you got the dates of the Macalister funeral muddled because you couldn't read my writing. What was the date you went?"

"Twenty-eighth, I think… Ah, I see, the actual date was the twenty-third, and I got the three and the eight confused because they're both curly."

"Go and find your bits of paper!"

"Bits of paper?"

"Those sketches that you did."

"But it's cold, the heating's off." I took a look at John's face: "Oh, all right then, but I'll have to put some clothes on."

"I'll turn the bloody heating on."

There was a heap of stuff in my desk. I went through it, but couldn't find anything. It was, of course, John who eventually found my bits of paper– inside a zip-up compartment in the suitcase. I was pleased to see there was a bag of euros there as well – although I didn't think it was the right time to be commenting on this.

"What *is* all this crap?" asked John, staring at my assorted diagrams critically.

"Well, I um…"

But John got there before me. "Oh, I see, that must be the

Skorskis bit on the fourth floor, and that's... oh, here it is, here's our corridor. What number were we...? Ah, 320 and Lady P. was... 333 and Carol was... 338."

"So 338 gets mistaken for 333, but why? I mean it's easy enough to confuse 333 with 338 on their own, but if you are walking along a corridor you can't help noticing that 337 comes after 336 and 333 comes after 332. I mean you look at all the numbers as you walk along."

"The corridor lights were on a timer thing and kept going off so you get confused." But he didn't sound totally convinced.

"Let me look at that piece of paper," I said, "Ah, look John, all this is very interesting, yes, I remember now. It took a long time to walk down the corridor because some of the rooms are suites, so they take up the space of two rooms and so you get into a muddle, thinking you have passed more rooms than you have, and with the numbers being gothic lettering..."

"Yes, but the staff must have been used to that."

"I've thought of something simpler."

"Yes?"

"The murderer wrote down the room number on a slip of paper; after all, that's what usually happened for the goodnight drinks; it was only Lady P. who used to shout out."

"Yeah and the girl was in a hurry, or an idiot, like you about the funeral, and didn't read the number right." I thought about this and then I said sadly.

"But it would be too risky because he or she could be identified straight away afterwards."

"But they weren't identified, were they?" said John. "I reckon what happened was just what the murderer counted on, the thing being hushed up."

"It still seems too big a risk."

"Well, said John rather irritably, "we've been all through this before, and have established that we don't know exactly how it was done, but can we just assume for now that it *was* done, and move on and work out who it was and why they did it?"

"It's funny, isn't it," I said, "that we were so sure it was Carol, and now – if our theory is right – she is the one person who can't have done it! Oh, and Tubby, of course."

"Let's go through the suspects." John had begun to be very serious and methodical. "Let's start with the least obvious – I don't fancy the Skorskis... I must say it's a bit nippy."

"No, I'm with you there, because whoever wanted to kill Carol was obviously being blackmailed or intimidated by her in some way, and all she could say about the Skorskis was that they were taxidermists – although she did say something about him having had a chemical of some sort with him."

"Yes, but she couldn't have known exactly what it was, and anyway there's no law against carrying stuff like that around."

"Okay, cross the Skorskis off the list for the moment." I got up and did a bit of foraging round in the cupboard.

"What are you doing now?"

"Putting a sweater on because I'm bloody cold."

"I thought that one had gone to Oxfam years ago." I looked disapproving; "I like to get the wear out of my clothes."

John shook his head and continued: "What about Megan and Bethan. Carol knew something about Bethan's husband's death because she started on about it when she lost her rag at the lunch."

"But there again, even if she did, she could only have picked up a hint of something from eavesdropping on their conversation..."

"Yeah, and it was over and done with twenty years ago. Even if there was a police investigation, Bethan was obviously cleared. It's not something worth killing for."

"Remember how hot-tempered she is – remember Wales," I spoke with feeling.

"Yes, but that's it, she's hot-tempered, she not a forward planner."

"Well, what about Megan then? Remember how she rushed to Bethan's aid, coming all that way to our house. She actually confessed to it."

"Well, I suppose it's possible, but don't you think we would have picked up some vibes? After all, we did spend the day with them and they didn't seem very worried."

"Well we'll put a question mark by them," I said snuggling down under the duvet.

"What about Simon? She was always having a go at him over the bridge table; he can't have liked her very much."

"But do you kill someone for criticising your card play?"

"Card play brings out the worst in people," said John, "I often feel like killing you when you do stupid things. I did this afternoon when you let Jacky and Stewart get you down in three no trumps."

"But you spared me, and actually Simon wasn't a very bad player, he wasn't much worse than she was."

"It isn't very warm, is it?" he said and followed me under the covers.

"Well then, he was irritated, driven to distraction by being unfairly told he was awful."

"No, don't be stupid. Perhaps she knew something about Simon…"

"Like the girl coming out of his room."

"Come off it, Mark, in this day and age everybody is in everybody else's rooms, and certainly in Carol's book I should have thought it would have been a plus – I mean that he was capable of having it off with someone. And, quite frankly, I can't see Simon having any dark secrets, can you?"

"There's his operation. He didn't say what it was."

"If people don't talk about their operations, it's because it's something like wisdom teeth or in growing toenails, and they think people are going to laugh at them. Or something big and they don't talk about it because they're scared."

"Okay, Simon is another question mark. What about the Macalisters?"

"Well, Carol wormed something out of Janet about Trevor, and any of the three of them could have been anxious to shut her up: child abuse and you're in prison for years. But, then, if Janet made it up…"

"Still nasty."

"I wouldn't put it past Isabel to do it. I think there's quite a lot we don't know about your friend."

"I wish you wouldn't call her 'my friend'."

"Well you had that cosy little afternoon with her."

"You know, it's odd, I was thinking about her the other day…"

"There you go…"

"And I had a feeling that I had met her somewhere before…"

"You had, you met her at *Il Sole*."

"Ha ha!"

"Perhaps Trevor did it after all. Didn't she suggest that to you?"

"Only as a joke."

"Funny sort of joke."

"Maybe she knew Janet did it, and dead old Trevor was a useful dumping ground."

"More question marks, then?"

"Yes, but I don't think they did."

"Why not?"

"I just don't."

"So much for logical deduction" said John.

"Well, I shall move on to the next suspect."

"Who is…?"

"Sammy."

"I can't see one reason why Sammy should have done it. Okay, he was always up to stuff, but Carol wasn't really very clever, and Sammy was; he'd have turned the tables on her with a laugh. He wouldn't have needed to kill her."

"So that leaves Lewis."

"You've always wanted it to be Lewis, haven't you, John."

"Only because I think he did it."

He got out of bed and went off to have a pee. We seemed to have reached an important point in our deductions, so I went off too and made a cup of tea to clear our brains.

"Why do you think Lewis did it, John?" He stirred the tea

and took a gulp.

"In the first place – you've put too much sugar in – in the first place, he's like Sammy: he's clever, much cleverer than the others, and I reckon he could have worked out a way to do it. I thought that, the day we spent with him at his house, I felt he was toying with us, laughing at us. He's spent his life running a school and he knows how people work"

"But he gave us advice on how to proceed with our investigations."

"Yes, but was it any good?"

"Oh, I see what you mean. Yes, and he tried to stop us going to see Carol, saying she was in Tunisia – which she wasn't. Was he scared that she knew something incriminating about him – even that she'd worked out it was her whom the poison was meant for?"

Unexpectedly, John shook his head. "No, Carol *was* going to be in Tunisia, she put it off for Tubby, if you remember. Lewis also told us not to go and see Simon because he'd be in a state with the beginning of term. Again, he was absolutely right, so I don't think that's it. But what he *did* do was try and scare us off, don't you remember all he had to say about libel and stuff? So the only people he said we should go and see were the Skorskis, because he knew that we just would go on farting about wasting time there – and he was right again."

"Well, okay," I said reluctantly. "Let's say it was him."

"Why?"

"I've thought about that quite a lot." I felt rather hurt; I didn't know John had been devoting his time to secretly thinking about Lewis and not telling me.

"I'll tell you why: I think he has a big hang-up about sex. There was that funny remark he made about his wife being 'untouched' – I reckon he never had her, and made her into a kind of a saint, the perfect woman – everything connected with her was holy. Don't forget, he took her picture on holiday, and there's that huge portrait in the living room – and I think the whole seduction bit by Carol made him see red. Yes, I think he's sexually very odd – we couldn't decide, remember, for a long time if he was straight or gay. I think he's neither, I think sex disgusts him, and he can't stand the thought of people having it off. I think he dislikes us too, by the way.

"No, no," I said hurt.

"Look," John continued, "he's used to being the one to discipline other people, handing out prizes and punishments, perhaps he regards himself as God Almighty." I listened in silence, and I had to admit it sounded very convincing, but I was sorry because I had always liked Lewis. I sat on the edge of the bed and thought.

"Well?" he asked

I sighed, "Yes, you're probably right."

"You reckon?"

"So what do we do now?" I asked. It was something we hadn't really discussed – what we would do if we found who had done it. I suppose because it had always seemed so unlikely that we would discover the truth.

"I think we go and talk to him," said John.

"We could simply do nothing, after all there isn't any evidence, as I'm sure he'll be the first to point out."

"There's something you've forgotten, Mark."

"What?"

"Well, he wasn't successful, was he? He might try again."

"What are you saying?"

"He might well have another go at Carol."

"Well, he's had plenty of time since he's been back, and he hasn't."

"I still think we warn him that if anything happens to Carol we go to the police."

"That won't be much comfort to her if she's done in – nor to us if the police find we've been hiding evidence."

"But that's just it; we haven't, because there isn't any!"

"Right," I said, "when are we going?"

"ASAP, and I think we tell him we're coming, but not why."

"I shall say we're having some pictures framed in Worcester," I said displaying my extraordinary subtlety. "He'll know what I mean."

"Do you mean to drink his tea or coffee or whatever?"
I thought about this.
"No," I said.
"Nor do I," said John. The whole situation was so exciting that we got under the covers and made the most of it.

Chapter 23: I have a remarkable dream

He was engaged in pulling up the last of his hollyhocks that grew so picturesquely round his front door; he looked relaxed and quite his old elegant self: a tweed jacket, pale green shirt, good trousers and expensive-looking, well-polished brogues. He straightened up.

"Ah, here you are. Isn't it a beautiful day!"

Suddenly I felt the full embarrassment of the situation. Here we were, visiting a man whose hospitality I had enjoyed on more than one occasion, in order to tell him he was a murderer and to threaten him with exposure. I reminded myself of Lady P.'s agonised corpse and told myself that murderers are not nice people.

"Come along in," he said. I must say John looked as awkward as me. Lewis smiled, "I haven't made tea," he looked from John to me, smiling. "I thought one of you two might prefer to do it." I found myself thinking, "Yes, but you might have put something among the tea leaves!"

"Perhaps later," I said.

"Of course."

He led us into the tiny, spotless sitting room with its vases of fresh flowers, and the inglenook dominated by the portrait of his wife. She wasn't, I thought, a beautiful woman, in fact she looked rather like Carol, but the overriding effect was of 'the angel in the house,' quite literally, for she was wearing a floaty white dress with some sort of tulle round the shoulders which gave the impression of embryonic wings. I thought she made an extremely uncomfortable presence. Lewis must have caught my look for he commented, "I feel she is still with me, the portrait is so lifelike." Neither John nor I knew what to say: it certainly seemed that suave Lewis had the upper hand, quiet, unruffled, and absolutely confident.

"Won't you sit down? I think I'll put the gas fire on, I used to always have a proper fire, but old age forces compromises on us."

"Lewis!" said John suddenly; like me, he couldn't bear

the suspense.

Lewis held up his hand, "Just a minute while I master the intricacies of the remote control. I sometimes think our ancestors had an easier time of it without all this technology, but I daresay you think me a bit of a dinosaur." I had thought of Lewis as many things, but not a dinosaur.

"Now we are all comfortable," he remarked as the gas plopped into life and the flames leapt up."

"Lewis…" John began again, but hardly seemed to know how to go on.

Lewis was, however, quite willing to make things easy for him: "You should have put the handcuffs on me back in September and saved yourselves a lot of trouble." He smiled, "I did admit it then, you know."

John was tired of all this. "We want to know what happened." He dropped the bombshell: "Why you killed Lady P. instead of Carol?" Lewis sat back.

"Ah, you worked that out. Well done!"

"Just tell us how you did it," said John.

"And why," I added.

"Well," said Lewis sitting back and crossing his legs, "I don't know that I can tell you much that you don't already know."

"Just go through the sequence of events," I said.

"I am more than a little curious about the present sequence of events. If I tell you I poisoned Lady Prettyman, intending the poison for Carol White, do you make a citizen's arrest or do you simply read me the riot act? If the former, I doubt whether I shall go to the gallows, as I shall simply deny it – unless of course you have taken the precaution of hiding a tape recorder in those well-designed trousers of yours, but I rather doubt that," he glanced at John – needless to say, not at me!

"And after all, what police force – Interpol or whoever – wants all the trouble, when nothing can be proved? I believe you said three doctors had written a death certificate, giving the cause of death as a heart attack. Will you not, perhaps, look a little foolish six months on, accusing an elderly retired

Headmaster of murder?" Neither of us could immediately think of anything suitable to reply. Then I said, "Why did you end up murdering the wrong woman?"

Lewis turned and adjusted the lace antimacassar behind him. "I have always been regarded as rather an efficient sort of person. Now it looks as if you have come to tell me I am an arch bungler."

"Is that what distresses you the most – not killing someone, but killing the wrong someone?"

Lewis leaned back. "Let's not be melodramatic about this. Of course I didn't mean to kill anyone – a mild bout of diarrhoea, at the most, was what I hoped for. Of course, I should have preferred it to be Carol rather than Lady P., but both were fairly unpleasant members of the human race, and probably we're better off without Lady P. Carol most certainly must think so," he smiled, "though possibly not Tubby. Are you ready for some tea now?"

"Just tell us how you did it."

"But, my dear fellow, you know! None of it was very complicated. It was simply unfortunate that the waitress confused Room 338 with 333."

"But weren't you worried that the girl would identify you?"

"No, not at all. In the first place, I thought at worst, Carol would get a stomach upset, and nobody was likely to come chasing after me because Carol was slightly unwell. Anyway, we would all be gone from the hotel. And, let's be frank, to nubile, blonde waitresses of that age, old men like me all look the same: dull and sexless. They have eyes only for young men – and, goodness, what sluts they all are!"

I felt this last comment was the only one spoken with any real passion.

"When did you realise what had happened?"

"Not until you told me. I heard Tubby had been taken ill, but naturally I didn't connect that with myself, and nor should I have. As I understand it, Sammy put up an excellent smokescreen – although quite why he did so, I don't like to imagine. I had no idea that Lady P. had died until you told me."

"But weren't you appalled to see Carol the next morning, alive and well?"

"No, not really, I assumed the glass had never got to her, or she hadn't drunk it, or if she had drunk it, it hadn't done her any harm. I think I was rather relieved. It was a foolish action on my part anyway; the result of drinking too much in the bar with young Simon."

"But what made you do it? What was the trigger, as it were?" He looked thoughtful, and for the first time he seemed hesitant and more unsure of himself; then he glanced up at the portrait and seemed to gain strength from it.

"I thought Carol White an unsavoury woman from the moment I first met her and I was sorry Sammy asked me to be her partner. However. I thought she might improve on acquaintance. She did not. She revolted me. You see, I have rather unfashionable ideas about sexual behaviour, and I found her flaunting herself at me in her frilly blouses… unpleasant. When she came to my room, I was sickened by her, and what made it worse for me, was that in features she was not unlike my darling wife who was so pure and good, and who would have died rather than behave in such a manner. Carol's behaviour was tantamount to an attempt to pollute my wife's memory. I could not bear to be near her afterwards and I asked Sammy to change the partnership. Oddly enough, I liked Janet and I thought – mistakenly, as I now know – that she was an innocent girl with some unresolved problems; I didn't imagine her chasing after Gino was more than a lonely girl's search for some company of her own age; I did not think her a slut like so many young girls nowadays." He paused and virtually shuddered: " it is horrible to think of women going into men's bedrooms in search of…" I was not going to be put off by Lewis' priggishness.

"Simon had girls in his room, didn't he?"

He looked momentarily surprised and then said, "I know nothing of that." He continued: "When I ran my school, any sexual impropriety was dealt with immediately by expulsion.

I believe in living cleanly..." He looked up challengingly at us, "...chastely, and I am, to be honest, rather homophobic... Please don't misunderstand me, I think you are both charming, delightful, I enjoyed your company on holiday and when ..." (he gave an ironic smile) you were kind enough to visit me, but I should prefer it if you... resisted the promptings of your nature. I think the world would an infinitely better place if more people chose to live as Lily and I."

It was the first time I had heard him pronounce his wife's name and it reinforced the feeling of horror I was beginning to feel for this cold, inhuman man. I glanced up at the portrait and wondered what sort of life he had condemned poor Lily to: wearing her white dresses and deprived of sex. I looked up at her again, but she gave me no clue as she stood there with a smile on her bland face."

"Carol seemed to soil everything," he continued sharply as if somehow he had intercepted my thoughts and wished to deflect them, "she even intimated that Trevor Macalister had had an unnatural relationship with Janet. Naturally I didn't believe it, but it left an unpleasant taste."

"But you failed to kill her. What is to stop you making another attempt?"

He relaxed and laughed, "John, how many times do I have to tell you? I didn't intend to kill her in the first place, just give her an uneasy night. I certainly have no designs on her life now." He smiled broadly. "If I had, I think I would leave it to Tubby, poor man! Now, what about some tea, and you can tell me what you propose to do with me. Shall I get ready for the station?"

We declined tea, and I added, "You know perfectly well that there's very little that we can do with no evidence, but if anything does happen to Carol..."

Lewis smiled, "You have my word."

But John has a very strong innate sense of justice and he wasn't happy. "You seem to have got off very lightly; at the very least you have a responsibility to say you are sorry and somehow make amends."

"A good point; you would have made an excellent Headmaster, John. What would you like me to do. Give some money to charity?"

John thought, "I don't know what I think. What do you think, Mark?"

"I think," I said, "that it is not right to commit murder and that Lewis should suffer, but equally, I believe that he does."

"How?" asked John abruptly.

"Mark is right. You may be headmaster material, John, but Mark is more empathetic. He knows that the loss of my wife is a daily torment. While I had Sargent, it wasn't so bad. I could bear it; I even used to imagine that once he had come into the room, she would come in afterwards, all flushed from their long walk. She loved taking him for long walks, she went out for hours when I was busy during term, and in the holidays I used to go with her too, but I wasn't such a good walker, I used to get tired." I tried imagining them together, Lewis urbane, but severe, and Lily walking and walking, as if her journey was never-ending.

"And then Sergeant died, and I am afraid I was most unwelcoming to you, Mark. I was distraught. 'What a foolish old man,' you will be saying, but it felt as it the last link had gone. I buried him under the apple tree…" He was struck by a thought, "…and that dreadful Skorski woman – someone must have told her at the Bridge Day – all she could say was what a pity I hadn't told her." He gave a poor imitation of Claire: "'We could have done a lovely job, a lovely job, make him look like a puppy, like a puppy.' I told her poor Sergeant was twelve, eighty-four in our years; well, you saw him, he was a dear mangy old thing… and all she could say was, and his voice rose in a falsetto 'lovely thick hair, it makes all the difference,' as if that could bring Sergeant back to life!" We were both silent.

"I beg your pardon; I have bored you long enough."

"It has hardly been boring," I replied.

"I suppose it is too much to ask that you keep this afternoon's conversation to yourselves? I should like to appear at the odd bridge table without being pointed at – like poor John was, by Skorski – whatever was that about?" Neither of us felt like enlightening him.

"I'm not making any promises," said John.

Lewis smiled. "Nor am I. I should not hesitate to sue you for both for libel if I felt idle talk had defamed my character in any way." And at that he stood up, as if we were dismissed.

"As you know, Lady Prettyman's death was due to heart failure, and indeed this was vouched for by the Italian doctors; you told me yourselves, if you remember."

We got up.

"Goodbye," I said, but I did not offer my hand. John said nothing.

"Well, he said, "if you're sure you'll not have tea…" He paused on the doorstep,

"One thing: I wouldn't bother Simon at the moment if I were you. He's going into hospital next week – it's rather major, I'm afraid. Perhaps he told you."

"Yes, we did know."

He watched us as we crossed the road and got into the car, a small dapper figure in his beautifully-cut, elegant clothes, dead-heading the last spray of autumn roses.

We never saw him again.

Going back in the car, we both felt deflated.

"All that work for nothing, really," I said.

"It wasn't work at all, we just did it like playing golf or something."

"Do you think he really would sue us?"

"Probably; we had better not say anything to anyone."

"Not even to people like Megan and Bethan? I mean surely they're owed the truth."

"Not even to them. "

"What do we say if they ask, then?"

"That even clever guys like us can't get to the bottom of everything." He was right; we had had enough hassle; we drove along in silence.

"He was right, really, wasn't he – Lewis, when he said he

had nothing new to tell us. He didn't really tell us anything we didn't know already."

John took his eyes off the road for a moment and looked up.

"Two things bug me: first, who is this blonde waitress? We never saw a blonde waitress, Gino denies that there were any blonde waitresses, and yet Bethan and Lewis both specifically describe a blonde. Also, why does he never want us to talk to Simon? What do you think it is, this 'major operation'? Cancer?"

"I don't know," I admitted, "And I just said I knew about Simon because I didn't feel like talking to Lewis any more."

"Well, as he's admitted it, there's nothing more we can do now." He turned back to concentrate on the road. "What shall we do with all our spare time?"

"Play bridge?"

But somehow neither of us felt much like it.

Arriving home was depressing, too; always before, it seemed to me, there had been the expectation of a new clue, a new avenue to be explored, but now we knew all there was to know there would be no more little excitements. However, as so often, I was wrong: there was one – an invitation to Janet's wedding.

"It's a church do," I said. "I wonder if Willy Wanker will be there?" I turned it over; Isabel had scribbled on the back, 'Janet and I are coming your way next Tuesday, any chance we might pop in for a cup of tea about 3.00? We've a favour to ask from Mark.'

"Probably going to touch you for money; that's why she's been making eyes at you," said John glumly.

"No," I said ignoring the provocation, "they've got pots, but we shall have to buy a present. What shall we get?"

"A plant for the garden."

"What sort of plant?"

"A nice healthy bush of belladonna."

I could see John was feeling down, just like me. I should have to cheer him up. And I did. I cheered us both up – in the most unexpected way, next morning at the breakfast table.

I was half way through my piece of wholemeal (added extra grain) toast when I remembered it.

"I had the most extraordinary dream last night."

"But you never dream," said John tapping at his boiled egg in a discouraging sort of way.

"How do you know?"

"Because you would tell me all about your dreams, if you did – at length."

"Well, I am going to tell you about this one now." John yawned and poured out some more coffee.

I was undeterred. " Well, I was at *Il Sole* doing my reccy on the rooms, just as I did that time when you were so nasty…"

"Me? Nasty?"

"Horrible. Anyway, there I was feeling confused because the rooms didn't seem to have any numbers at all, and suddenly down the corridor racing towards me like the hound of the Baskervilles, is Lewis's dog, but as it gets nearer it starts standing on its hind legs and I can see that although its body is all mangy, its head is all flowing with long blonde hair, you know like the Skorskis said…"

"Yes, yes."

"And not only that, but it's wearing Tubby's glasses, and I remember thinking 'Ah, that's why he doesn't wear his glasses, because he's given them to Lewis's dog because it's so old, about 84; how kind…'"

"As dreams go," said John, "it doesn't sound as if it was the sort to give you nocturnal emissions."

"And then I saw Skorski with his little bag and he said, "Ah, you see vat a difference ze golden 'air and ze glasses make," but then he seemed to change into Bethan, and began saying how she was going to provide all the meat for *Il Sole*."

"Was I there?" asked John.

"No, I think you were somewhere else, being disagreeable."

"And then what happened?"

"Well, nothing really. I woke up." I was a little deflated

by John's obvious lack of enthusiasm; I thought it had been rather an amusing dream. John said nothing and went on banging at his egg, and I helped myself to some more toast. 'Miserable sod,' I thought. I began to ruminate on the origins of my dream: I had thought about Lewis' dog because he had gone on about it, and then Tubby and Bethan had come into it because…Then John said, "Wait a minute!" John always says this when he's thought of something."What did you say Skorski said?"

"I can't remember now," I said sulkily. "Something about the hair and the glasses… It was obviously because of what Lewis told us about Claire saying that she could make a lovely job of the dog. She said it to us too…"

"She didn't mention glasses."

"Well, of course she didn't because…"

But John wasn't listening to me, he spoke quietly to himself: "Tubby looks different without his glasses… and it is very difficult to see without glasses when you're used to them."

"I don't understand what…"

"And Skorski turned into Bethan?"

"Well, you know how it is in dreams."

"I'm not thinking of dreams," he said.

"John, what are you talking about?"

John brought the spoon down on the egg (fortunately it was finished) with a crash and bashed it into pieces.

"We have been two of the biggest prats in the world, and I'm… going to have a fag."

"Just tell me."

And then he did. He had the fag as well. For a while we sat in silence, then he said: "Phone call, do you reckon?"

"You're the one who's good at accents," I said.

He grinned, "Welsh or Scottish?"

"Oh Scots, I think, it sounds honest; that's why they get them to do the voice-overs. We'd better go and see him as soon as possible."

"Oh no, we'll go and see *her*," he said, "this wee bonnie lassie."

"Och aye," I said.
It all went like clockwork.

Chapter 24: The sad plight of the blonde

The blonde stretched herself out luxuriously on the *chaise longue*; she was perhaps, a little overdressed for receiving afternoon visitors, wearing a long, pink, décolleté satin dress and rather large pink satin shoes; her thick blonde hair hanging seductively about her shoulders and her eyes shining brightly behind impossibly long eyelashes.

Well, actually, none of this is quite true because I have used the wrong pronouns. You see, the blonde was not a woman – not yet. But now with his make-up and, of course, without his enormous thick glasses on, he could easily have passed as a woman.

"My name is Simonetta," he simpered, looking at us for our approval. "I have been very worried," he continued pointing a toe in my direction, "about the colour, I wanted more of a salmon."

"Simon," I said, "I think that's the least of your worries."

"I hope you're not going to be nasty to me," he said coquettishly.

"You better hope again, then," said John. Simonetta sighed and something of the old sad Simon was visible in his features.

"It's me that should be nasty: you lied and cheated, ringing up saying you wanted to meet me because I was so pretty." He turned accusingly to John, "it was you that pretended, wasn't it?"

"Yup."

"And if I'd known it was you, I wouldn't have let you in." He looked suddenly guilty. "Oh dear, I shouldn't have let you in – I said I wouldn't."

John and I perched on the antique French chairs and took stock of the situation. Of course, it should have occurred to me on my last visit that the room was really a boudoir. I wondered whether he had managed any seductions there? Somehow I doubted it. John looked around unimpressed: "We want you to tell us all about the murder," he said giving a strong emphasis to the word.

Simonetta shook back his hair, perhaps in an attempt to win us over with his sexual wiles.

"We know Lewis didn't do it," I added, "and we know you did."

He looked pettish. "I told Lewis, he needn't protect me, but he would insist on looking after me. I really didn't want him to take the blame."

"We want to know what happened."

He pouted. "I don't see why I should tell you anything. You're not policemen, just nosey-parkers."

"Because," I said, "you shouldn't let Lewis take the blame for something you did." A look of confusion crossed his face and I could see the old Simon, the schoolmaster manqué.

"No, I suppose I shouldn't, but Lewis said I wasn't to talk to you, not even let you in, and I wouldn't have done if I hadn't been expecting a nice gentleman. I got all confused when it was you, and anyway now you know I did it."

"So what happened?"

His hand went up to his glasses, but then he remembered he wasn't wearing them, and somehow this seemed to dispirit him.

"It all went wrong and I killed poor Auntie Marjorie." There was a silence and he brightened up,

"You didn't guess about me at the hotel, did you? I thought you might have done afterwards when you told me Mr. Arbuthnot-Jones said I had a girlfriend." He looked coy. "It was me, you see, not a girlfriend. I get dressed up sometimes here, and I used to go out late every night after the bridge in Italy; it was such fun. When I have had my operation I can do it all the time, it will be safe then. I shan't have to worry about people finding out; I was afraid some of the children had at school because they used to chant "Simon, Simonetta, we're coming to get her."

Of course! Only I had assumed it was 'getcha'.

"Just tell us how it happened," said John, "we're not police and we aren't going to tell them, but you need to come out with the truth, just the once."

"Yes, but Lewis said I mustn't say anything to anyone, and specially not to you because I would get into trouble, and just let him deal with it."

"Why should he shoulder the blame?" This was something neither John nor I had been able to understand when the whole Simon thing had first hit us, but John obviously felt that this was a question best dealt with later.

"How did it start?"

Simon said nothing so John turned and gave him one of his looks – in his way, I thought, he's every bit as scary as Lewis. Obviously Simon thought so too.

"I need to think." He sat up on the sofa, taking care not to crease his dress, and crossed his legs. He was wearing shiny tights – at least I hope they were tights, somehow the thought of suspenders was even more horrible.

He couldn't seem to decide how to start so I prompted him: "Carol had found out about the cross-dressing?"

He frowned, "I don't like that expression."

"But she had found out?"

"How had she found out?"

"Well," she came to my room one night after bridge… I don't think she was trying anything on. After all," he simpered, "I'm not that type, and she said afterwards, she had come to discuss our card play, but I wasn't there because I had just nipped out to the bathroom down the corridor – there was a better mirror down there – and she must have seen me, because the next day she began hinting and insinuating and giggling, and I was afraid she'd tell everyone…"

"And did she?"

"No, I don't think so. I think she liked being the only one in the know."

"Has she tried to blackmail you?"

"No, I've told you, she just liked knowing – that was why I wasn't particularly worried. I didn't think she would bother with me any more after Italy. It wasn't until Lewis said…"

"What did Lewis say?"

"What you said. That she might blackmail me."

"When did he say that?"

"It was after that last bridge and Lewis said come and have a drink, which was very nice of him, and I was quite happy to, because I wasn't going out that night because we had to get up early and, anyway, I'd packed up all my things. People don't usually ask me to for drinks, so I was pleased, and we had lots to talk about, both being teachers. I hadn't really spoken to him before that evening; well, I hadn't really spoken much to anyone, because I find it difficult to talk to people, and anyway I used to go out at night…"

"Just tell us what happened."

"I am telling, you mustn't be so impatient, you're like the naughty children in my class… We talked about teaching, and I told him how hopeless I was, and he was really kind and said things would improve and that he hadn't been very confident when he had started, and then I said how frightened I was of the children and particularly big boys, and I told him about the horrible Skorski boy, and how I had had to be very careful to make sure Karl and Claire didn't connect me with him, in case they were relatives or something. I mean that they didn't find out the name of the school I taught at, and I told him how the boy had made my life like hell and stolen from me and how it had caused so much trouble…"

"What did he steal?"

"My eye-brightener."

"Eye-liner?"

"No, silly, brightener; I like to keep my eyes looking sparkling, I expect you noticed them even with my glasses?" He looked at us coquettishly, but met with no response. "Well, I didn't tell Lewis what I used it for, I just said it was medicinal."

"Anyway I always had a phial of it with me, and that horrible boy took it out of my pocket and wouldn't give it back…"

"Couldn't you tell him…?" began John, then glancing at the pink creature on the sofa, he added, "No, I suppose you couldn't."

"No, I never got it back, and I had to send for some more, and then later he went into the San pretending to be ill to miss

Latin, and Matron said he wasn't ill, and he said he would make sure he was, and took a gulp out of my phial and started being sick. Matron got into trouble because he told the doctor that he had got it out of the Matron's medicine cupboard. Of course, I knew what must have happened straightaway, when I heard about it afterwards. He was quite ill, you see."

"Did you tell Matron what had happened?"

He shook his head, "I was too frightened. And then he got expelled anyway." Perhaps he saw John's look of contempt for he added: "But I have always been very nice to Matron since. I play bridge with her and Mr Arbuthnot-Jones, and I bought them lunch at Sammy's bridge day."

"And did you also think it necessary to be nice to Arbuthnot-Jones?"

"Well, I think he might once have seen me, because he said something to you about a girlfriend, didn't he? Sometimes you see, I slipped out of my flat dressed nicely, but I wasn't really worried about him, because he can't see properly anyway; he just made up the bridge four."

"And what was this eye-brightener made of?" I asked.

But John answered for him. "Belladonna."

"It's very good, look at my eyes now."

He turned his little piggy eyes towards me and I went back to the main subject: "And you told Lewis all this?" He looked confused and began to slip his foot in and out of his shoes. "Yes, I think so, I'm not sure."

"What else did you talk to Lewis about?"

He looked sulky, but whether this was because he didn't like the question or because we hadn't complimented his eyes, I didn't know.

"Nothing much."

"Did you talk about Carol?"

Simon fiddled with his blond locks and said crossly: "Yes, but we only talked about her because she came into the bar. I think she wanted to make up to Gino or one of the barmen, but they weren't interested, so she had a whisky and went away again. She ignored Lewis and me, and I said to Lewis that I didn't like her because she was always prying into things and saying nasty things about everyone, and Lewis said he hoped I hadn't given her any reason to spread rumours about *me*. I had drunk two gin and tonics by then, and I can't really take alcohol, so I started telling him about my other life. And then Lewis said he wouldn't put it past her to make trouble at the school. I didn't like to think of that."

"What happened next?"

"Can I have a little drink of water?"

"No," said John.

"You *are* mean." He paused and John nodded towards me: "You ask the questions," he said.

"Carry on," I said to Simon, "what happened next?"

"I don't think I'm going to tell you any more, I've talked to you when Lewis said I shouldn't, and he'll be cross with me."

"I can't see why Lewis should waste his time on you."

Simon started gathering up his hair, rather as Janet had done when we sat at her kitchen table.

"Lewis walked me back to my room because I was a bit tipsy. I thought he might like to stay for a bit, but he said he was tired and so we said goodnight, and he went off to bed, and then I thought about how Carol could blackmail me, and I thought, 'Why don't I stop her?'"

"Poison her?"

"I didn't really mean to kill her."

"But then you wouldn't have stopped her."

"Well, I just thought if she got a bad stomach ache she might think it was me and be frightened and leave me alone."

"Why should she think it was you?"

Simon looked confused and he did some more fiddling with his hair, "Well, I don't know really, and I'd drunk all that gin."

"So what did you do?"

"I decided to pretend to be one of the hotel bar staff and take up the whisky to her." He looked at us somewhat defiantly. "I got dressed up…"

"As a waitress?"

"Oh, I always take my black skirt and white blouse with

me, then I can be all sorts of things. First I put on one of my wigs…"

"You were taking a tremendous risk."

"Yes," he smiled proudly, "I was very brave, wasn't I?"

"But suppose she'd recognised you?"

"Well, I thought about that and this was why I was so clever…"

"Why?"

Now he looked more confident, as if he knew exactly what he needed to say: "well, you see, if she did recognise me, I would just say I thought she would like to see me properly as a lady, and I had brought her a drink to say goodbye. And if she didn't, I would pretend to be the waitress and just say it was from Gino. I thought she'd like that."

"But weren't you afraid that if she got ill she would say it was you dressed as a waitress?"

A crafty look came over his face.

"No one would believe her, I mean, it's not very likely, is it? But just to be safe the next morning – you know how we had to be ready at four – I went out to the dustbins outside and got rid of all my things. It made me quite sad, but I knew I had to because the dustbin people always came about six and used to wake me up, and then they would take all the evidence away."

"What about Lewis?" I said. "After all, he knew the truth about your cross-dressing; he might have sussed out what had happened."

"Lewis is my friend," said Simon proudly; "he wouldn't have given me away."

"So what happened? How did you get it all so wrong?"

"Well, I was quite scared, but I thought I'd be safe, because I'd often dressed up in Italy and nobody ever recognised me. In fact…" he gave a little giggle, "once you both walked past me in a bar."

So much for our remarkable powers of detection!

"And when I got to the third floor – and I knew it was 338 because it was on her key ring when we were playing bridge – but the corridor stopped at 328, and when I turned the corner, the light timer went off. Then I got a bit confused, because the rooms were all on one side, for the nice sea view, I suppose, and there weren't odd numbers any more, and of course I didn't have my glasses on, and I hadn't put my contact lenses in, and I thought 'Oh dear, which one is Carol's room, which one is 338?' and I was just starting to try and make out the numbers when I saw Bethan and I remembered hearing her say in the Bridge Room that she would take a recipe or something to Carol's room, so I thought that must be Carol's room with Bethan standing outside. The number looked like 338, and I had to make a decision to go and do it now, or not at all, because I was getting a bit scared, and so I thought, "Yes, be a brave girl and give it to Bethan and then *she* can give it to Carol."

"But then Bethan would get the blame."

"Yes, I suppose she would."

"Didn't you care?"

"But you see, I thought we would all be out of the country by the time all the trouble started. I mean everyone would just think it was a tummy thing – nobody would think anything of us."

"Didn't she recognise you?"

"No, she looked very cross and preoccupied; I think she was concentrating on something else. I suppose she'd gone to have a row with Auntie about her being rude to Megan, but I didn't know that then." He smoothed down his dress and smiled as if he had done something clever. "I did it very well: I went right up to her on my high heels and I said, "For the signora, dentro, please," just like a real waitress, then I just let her take the glass off the tray and I hurried away as the lights turned off."

"And the result was you killed your own aunt."

"She was a cousin, I just called her auntie."

"And how did you feel when you saw Carol alive and well the next morning?"

"I was a bit shocked, but then I just thought she hasn't drunk it after all and anyway…" he looked sheepish, and very ludicrous in his pink satin, "I didn't think I'd put very much belladonna in because I was a bit scared when it came to it."

"So you didn't mean to kill her, after all?"

"Yes, no... Stop asking me questions. Actually, I must have put a lot in after all because I found the phial was nearly empty the next day, but I don't remember it all properly, and I'd drunk a lot of gin... whisky... Are you going to tell the police?"

I ignored this. "So when we came and told you about your aunt's death, that was the first you knew about what had happened?"

"Yes, when you said that, I couldn't believe it, at first. I didn't know what had happened – why she had died, I mean – but then when you went on talking, I worked it out, and I felt so sad..."

"Sad!" John snorted.

"Yes, sad," he turned to me as if to get me on his side. "I don't know why he's so horrid to me; it could have happened to anyone. I was sad because everyone hated her, but she was very kind to me – you know I told you she was good to me as a boy, well, I didn't tell you the whole truth. In fact, she found me dressed up in girls' clothes when I was about thirteen, and she said 'Life's unkind, isn't it? I should have been a man and you should have been a woman; never mind here's a tenner.' It was nice of her, wasn't it? And that's why I paid for her and Tubby to have a nice holiday," the voice died away, "but instead of doing that, I killed her." And the bright little eyes glistened with either tears or belladonna.

"Didn't you wonder afterwards why she hadn't contacted you, and didn't you try and find out if Tubby was all right?"

"Well no, we weren't very close, and then I was cross and thought how rude not to write and thank me for the nice holiday. And then I got a note from Tubby just saying she was dead, and she had been cremated, and I thought fancy not asking me to the funeral, after I had been so kind, so I didn't contact Tubby again."

"And you never heard again from Carol?"

"No, and I was cross about the Bridge Day, Sammy said she wasn't going." He looked up for reassurance. "You won't tell the police, will you? You said you wouldn't?"

"We don't have any evidence," I said. A silence fell.

"But," I continued, "we want to know why Lewis is taking the blame for all this?" One of the greatest puzzles in the whole business seemed to me to be why the upright Lewis should go perjuring himself for a little wimp like this.

"Yes," said John. "How come suddenly Lewis is telling you what to do? How did he know what had happened?"

"I told him."

"You told him?" I was astounded. "Why? When?"

He sighed, "Do I really have to go through all this? You see, I promised Lewis…"

John decided to take over. "Yes, that's what we want to know: why were you involving Lewis?"

Simon pouted, but one look at John's face was enough to get him talking again.

"After you'd come telling me all about Auntie, I got very worried and I rang him up and said I was very worried about something."

"Why? Why Lewis?"

"Because you had been talking to him, and because he had been kind to me that night and I wanted someone to talk to."

"And what did he do?"

"He was really kind and told me not to worry…"

"So you ring him up and say, 'Hey, Lewis, do you remember me from Italy? Well, I killed Auntie, and now people are asking questions. What shall I do?'"

Simon looked cross and he tossed back the golden locks. "No, of course it wasn't like that and I didn't tell him over the phone. He said he could tell I was upset about something, and he would drive over… so he did, and I told him."

"And I suppose he said, 'Oh, jolly bad luck, Simon, but don't worry, people commit murder every day, and often get the wrong person. Don't you worry your pretty little head about it, I'll take the blame.'"

Simon wriggled a bit on the sofa.

"Or perhaps," said John quietly, "you offered him a bit of

your inheritance to sort things out for you?" This was something that we had discussed driving over, but Simon looked so shocked at the suggestion that now it seemed unlikely.

"Oh no, Lewis isn't like that; he's very proper. He was very angry with me when I told him."

"So what *did* he say when you told him?"

"Well, he thought for a bit, and asked questions, and then he sort of sighed and said I had done a very bad thing, but he supposed in a way it was his fault because it was after we had talked about Carol in the bar and he had said she might blackmail me, that I began to be afraid of her. Then he thought some more and said he was old and life didn't hold much for him because he'd lost his wife, but I was young and when I'd had my operation I could start a new life, so he would sort everything out. If the worst came to the worst, he would say he had done it, but I mustn't talk to you, or anyone ever. But now I have. Do you think he will be cross?" A look of the old, anxious Simon returned.

"Everything will be all right now, won't it? Now I've told you. And there won't be any police, will there? Lewis said there wouldn't if I did what he said, but I haven't, have I? I've talked to you – but I wouldn't have done if I hadn't been confused by you pretending…"

He looked up anxiously from the folds of satin and I saw there were great wet patches under the arms. Suddenly I felt disgusted with the whole thing: his lack of any responsibility for what he'd done, his ineptitude, and his pink satin and his pretty little room. It's people like him, I thought, who cause all the world's problems. I still couldn't for the life of me understand why Lewis should have taken so much trouble over him; I would have left him to sweat it out. After all nobody is responsible for the effects of a casual conversation in a bar. But now I wanted to get way from it all, be outside in the fresh air.

"Come on, John," I said, "let's go." Okay, I knew there were unanswered questions, inconsistencies in what Simon had told us, loose ends to follow up, perhaps moral lessons to be preached, but I had had enough, I got up and John followed me to the door. Simon got off his couch and stood twisting his hands together and I thought what a grotesque sight he was.

"You won't do anything or say anything, will you? Not now I've told you, now I've confessed?"

We walked over to the door and I had opened it, and was about to go out when John turned round, went back into the room and sat down. Now, about fifteen years ago when I fell in love with John, it was, if I'm honest, with his body. I didn't expect – God, this makes me sound arrogant – that he would ever be my intellectual equal, but I was wrong. AS time went on I began to realise that his brain was in many ways sharper than mine; more and more often he surprised me, sometimes stunned me with his acute insight. Now was to be such an instance.

"Come back in, Mark," he said. He turned to the pink creature who was busy removing his high heels, and he said: "Except it wasn't like that, at all."

I thought I had better sit down too.

"Yes, it was," said the creature in the pink satin, the hair straggled over his shoulders; he couldn't make up his mind whether to put the shoes back on.

"Lewis set you up," said John quietly. "He set you up to kill Carol in Italy, and he set you up to protect him back in England."

Simon dropped the shoe he was holding.

"What do you mean?"

"Pull your skirt down. Sit down and listen and I'll tell you what happened and you can stop me if I miss anything out."

Simon went pale. "He said I wasn't to say, it was all for me really. Please don't tell him, you won't tell him… I did it all, the poison, I mean, it was my idea…"

"You! A creature like you couldn't have thought of a plan, couldn't have done anything… shut up and don't interrupt."

Simon and I sat spellbound as John began to speak, and as he spoke I saw how everything fitted into place. (I was terribly proud of him, but a little bit of me wished that I had thought of it first). He stood up and began pacing about as if the action of his body helped his brain. "You are sitting in the bar with Lewis and he gets you talking. You tell him about your handy little phial of belladonna; perhaps you tell him about the cross-dressing at the same time. Yes, I think Lewis gets it out of you…" John went into a very good imitation of Lewis's rather clipped tones: '…What was the medicine that the boy took from you? Belladonna? What was that for, Simon? Isn't it used to dilate the pupils? I wonder why you were carrying that round with you? To make your eyes sparkle like a girl's? Let me get you another glass of gin, Simon.' Then Carol walks in and Lewis gets an idea, or… I dunno, maybe he had the idea already, because now I think of it I suspect he had already sussed out the cross-dressing, he was pretty observant. Had he?"

"Yes," he whispered, he sat, an oddly grotesque figure with his legs apart, the satin clinging to them. "He told me that he had seen me go out one night… he used to walk round late, he couldn't sleep… because of his wife or something, but I don't think…"

"Yup, Lewis already had the idea, otherwise he would never have bothered to ask you to drink with him. Perhaps he had bought his own poison already and perhaps your mention of the belladonna was just a Christmas bonus, I don't know, you can tell us in a minute. Anyway, Carol walks into the bar and Lewis starts feeding you with titbits and gets you worried…"And as John began to go into his imitation of Lewis, Simon actually began to shiver. "'Of course,' says Lewis, ' you know Carol has been spreading rather nasty rumours about several members of GrandSlam… Trevor and Bethan, to name two, for example, and I daresay she has something on the Skorskis… Goodness knows what she will do with the information about *you* back in England… I do hope she doesn't intend telling your colleagues at school, the damage she could do doesn't bear thinking about, does it? Almost makes you feel like pouring that little phial of belladonna into her drink, doesn't it, ha ha! What a pity that you've left it too late, no way of doing that now, is there,

Simon? Oh, you have thought of a way? That's very clever of you, what is it? Let me guess your plan: you dress up as waitress and take it to her room? But that's much too risky, isn't it? Not a good idea. Let's talk about something else, shall we? No, no Simon, it was just a joke, but, on the other hand, no one could deny that in many ways you'd be doing a really kind thing, Simon, not just kind for you, but helping the Macalisters and the Skorskis and who knows, perhaps she had something on Mark and John, you will be pleasing me too - she behaved in a most offensive way to me! Good luck, Simon.'"

I was gobsmacked, as much as by John's grasp of Lewis's psychology, as by anything else; but Simon had been trying to interrupt with various twitterings all the time John had been talking. Now John folded his arms, sat back and let Simon have his say.

"It wasn't, it wasn't like that! He didn't set me up; he was kind to me, he wanted it for my own good. He was sorry for me, he was only thinking of me.

"So, I'm right, Lewis did suggest it all to you."

Simon began twisting his hands. They were very small and he had painted his nails. Now he looked pleadingly at John. "He didn't set me up, it was a sort of joke, really, he joked with me because he liked me."

"Joked with you about killing someone? 'Why don't you kill Carol, that'll be a laugh?'"

"No, no, I got it all wrong, I always do. Lewis explained afterwards, back in England, I mean, when I phoned him, that I hadn't understood he wasn't serious, that he didn't mean me to do anything." He clasped his hands and looked like a child repeating a lesson. 'That's why I mustn't talk to anyone,' he said, because I'd get it wrong. But he knew a way of putting everything all right again, but it was rather complicated and I mustn't tell about our conversation in the bar." He looked towards John for approval: "And I didn't tell you all those things you said, did I? I only told you a little bit about the conversation."

Admitting the crime didn't seem to matter to him; what

mattered was to find a way of proving that Lewis hadn't set him up. We would never get to the truth while he trusted Lewis.

"Lewis didn't like you," I said. "He loathed you: you disgusted him, anyone sexually 'aberrant' or who shows any ordinary desire for sex is disgusting to Lewis. The fact that you dressed as a woman would have nauseated him; he thought you and Carol both deserved punishment, and he was a man used to meting out punishment. If you got caught and jailed, all well and good. You were a cat's paw."

Tears were beginning to form in the bright little eyes.

"That's not true!" Then he brightened up: "If it was true, he wouldn't have said he'd done it, he would just have told you it was me –which it was."

Ironically I could see that he was now actually anxious to claim responsibility, just so he could still believe in Lewis. John sat with his arms folded saying nothing, but I was working it out and spoke my thoughts out aloud.

"No, he couldn't risk us coming to talk to you again, because he could see that you wouldn't even be able to tell a good lie. He realised you would let out the secret of the waitress; you might even tell us how he had fed you the idea – which is more or less what you have done. However, if he told us it was him, admitted to doing it, while making sure we don't know how it was done, he is quite safe, because there is still no way of explaining how the poison got to Lady P., we would just have to accept that he had done it, but we wouldn't be able to do anything about it. If we start gossiping we look very foolish because we can't explain how he did it, and he could very well call our bluff and threaten us with court action for libel. It was a clever way of putting an end to our investigations and stopping us coming to see you."

"It wasn't Lewis who did it, it was me."

Suddenly I saw how it had been.

"But it wasn't you, was it? Why did he go to your room? It would have been much simpler and safer for Lewis to tell you what to do, and then go back to the safety of his room. Why didn't he do that?" I turned to John. "Surely it would have been safer to leave Simon to it?"

"Would *you* leave him to it?" replied John. But for once I was ahead of him. "It was Lewis who poisoned the whisky."

"Yes," said John slowly, "you're right. Is that what happened, Simon?"

"My name is Simonetta," he announced, with a sudden burst of bravado.

"No, it's not," said John brutally, "it's Simon until you've gone under the knife, and only Simonetta afterwards – so long as they manage to cut off the right bits. What happened?"

The creature wriggled. He stroked his hair, smoothed his dress and put on his shoes, but we waited and he had to speak: "He came up to my room because I said I would show him my pretty clothes."

John looked at him amazed. "You really believed he wanted to see *that*?"

"The reason Lewis came up to your room," I said, "was to provide you with a glass of whisky, otherwise how did you come to have a handy glass of whisky in your room to put your belladonna in, and a tray to stand it on."

"Yes," said John, "that was worrying me. Did Lewis bring the glass up?"

Simon was always at home with factual questions and he was actually quite eager to explain. "It was his own glass of whisky; he just happened to have it with him and it was very lucky that he did... Well, I don't mean lucky, but otherwise I wouldn't have been able... But he told me not to say."

"What happened when you got to your room?"

"I showed him my phial, and then I told him he could watch me get dressed if he liked... I thought it would be a little treat for him. I began getting all my things out, and I'd just popped to have a pee, when Lewis said he was feeling tired and he was going to go back to his room, and... He said he would leave it to me to put the belladonna in." He looked up, suddenly confused. "But now he says it was a joke, it wasn't like he was telling me to do it, and that's why I mustn't mention him. He just patted me on the back and he way. So you see it was me."

"While you were in the loo," I said, "Lewis wiped his prints off the glass with one of his immaculate handkerchiefs, then he added a great slug of belladonna, wiped that and left it right in the middle of the table. What you did now was up to you. If you didn't do anything, well, Carol lived to fight another day, if you did poison her, it was nothing to do with Lewis. He had merely, inadvertently, left his glass in your room."

His eyes opened wide: "Do you think he put some belladonna in first before me?"

It occurred to me that now Simon actually wanted to show that he had done it. So long as he could believe in his own responsibility, then he was somebody. But if Lewis had done it, he was just the same useless person who stood in the playground for children to torment.

"Course he did," said John. "He knew you wouldn't put enough in, and if all else failed, he wouldn't have minded if you drank it yourself."

"No, no!" He almost jumped out of the sofa.

"Listen, Simon," I said. "Don't you understand? Lewis set you up. It was he who poured belladonna into the whisky, and then he just left you to do the dirty work. Perhaps he wanted you to be caught."

Simon said nothing, but his mouth opened and shut; he knew I was right.

"Now," said John, "let's work out what happens afterwards. The next day we all wait for the minibus, and you have a little fright when you see Carol, but you get over that. Actually, you're not really surprised because you haven't put much belladonna in the glass anyway. Then you have a look for Lewis, but he doesn't take any notice of you any more, but you're not surprised, perhaps he's told you not to talk to him, or perhaps it's just that you're used to people dumping you. Then you go back to England and all is hunky-dory – or as hunky-dory as anything ever is at that school – until we turn up and you realise you've poisoned Auntie Majorie. Then, suddenly, things aren't so hunky-dory and you telephone Lewis..."

"Wait a minute," I said. "I bet he didn't phone Lewis - Lewis phoned him, maybe while we were having lunch. Do you remember, he was quite a long time in the kitchen after we had the main course, probably phoning to try and stop Simon seeing us. Did he ring you?"

"When?" said the pink creature.

"That day when we first came to see you. Did he have your phone number?"

"I don't know. One of the boys had hidden my phone, so I didn't get any calls."

"Actually," I said talking to John rather than Simon, "when we first went to the Gingerbread House and started asking questions, Lewis probably wasn't too worried, there was no reason why we should associate Lady P.'s death with either him or Simon. In fact, he was probably quite happy to have us bumbling round, confident that we wouldn't discover anything. So long as neither of us discovered that Simon was a cross-dresser and that Carol was the intended victim, he was quite safe; but still, he thought it might be just as well to ring Simon and tell him not to see us. Unfortunately, he got no answer – and do you remember, John, he tried to put us off coming here for a few days, saying something about Simon not coping at the beginning of term? So, he reckons all he's got to do is to stop us seeing Simon, discourage any further visits from us, and certainly not accept any invitations to play bridge. But then, while he's mulling things over, he gets a call from Simon telling him that we *did* come to the school, and have been asking questions, and he sees we've stolen a march on him. So he has to think again."

I turned to Simon: "He turns up on your doorstep, yes? What does he say? And what did he *really* say, not what you told us earlier?"

"He really did say what I told you earlier. He *was* thinking of me, he was." But the voice had lost conviction.

"He was thinking of himself and what a fool you were and how was he going to shut you up."

"And what else did he say? What haven't you told us?"

Simon flounced in his chair. "He said that I had got things very muddled and he had never said anything to me about Carol… But I am sure he had, things like John said, but he was angry and said I mustn't argue, I must understand that if he had said anything it was a joke and I should have known it was only a joke. However, he would take responsibility so long as I promised not to talk about it any more. To try and forget it ever happened, and that I absolutely mustn't say anything about my lady's clothes. He said if there were any problems, not to contact him, but that he would keep in touch – maybe we could have some nice games of bridge."

"Ah that explains the merry bridge foursome with Arbuthnot-Jones and Matron; a good way of monitoring things – which is why, I suppose, he came to Sammy's bridge day, to see what was going on with the DAFS: whether we had stirred anything nasty up."

Simon looked confused: "Dafs?"

"But then last week," I continued, "John and I called on Lewis and he had a nasty moment when we told him that we knew the poison was meant for Carol. But he was still okay because he realised that we didn't know about the cross-dressing, and he must have breathed a sigh of relief. All he had to do was to admit to the murder, but make sure we never discovered any evidence that would convict him. Then, I daresay, he called on you."

Simon said nothing, so John bellowed out, "Well, did he?"

Simon jumped; I think he was still trying to fit everything together and work out where he stood – whether it was better to admit that Lewis had set him up, or go on pretending to himself that Lewis had been his friend.

"What did Lewis say?"

He looked piteously at John, but saw it was no use. "He said he'd told you both that he had done it and that I mustn't talk to you under any circumstances …in case I got things wrong…"

"In case you told the truth, he meant."

"And he said if I did talk, he wouldn't be able to protect me any more and I would get him into trouble, too. And when you came I didn't mean to let you in, only I thought you were my nice gentleman, but I did try not to tell you everything, I did try, didn't I?"

"What else did he say?"

For a moment the little bright eyes sparkled with malice; at last he saw a chance to get his own back on us:

"He said you were both stupid, like queers always are, and didn't stand a hope of finding out the truth."

"But he was wrong," said John.

For some time the three of us sat in silence and I watched Simon's face – I can only describe it as dissolving: the eyeliner and mascara had started to run in little streams down his face. It was such a poor face too, it wasn't male, it wasn't female; it was the face of a complete non-entity. He raised a piteous face towards John, whom I think he regarded as the crueller of the two of us.

"Do you really think he just set me up... so I would get all the blame?"

"If anyone had to get the blame, yup."

"Do you think he really thought I was disgusting?"

"Yup."

"Do you think he would have been happy if I'd drunk the poison?"

"Yup."

He sighed a long sigh, so heartfelt that even John said afterwards he felt an atom of pity for him.

"Everyone always makes a fool of me: it was the same when I was little, and it's the same at school. And John fooled me, ringing up and pretending to be a nice gentleman who wanted to get to know me, but he didn't... and I thought Lewis really liked me and wanted to help, but he only wanted to help himself, and he made me murder poor Auntie."

Neither of us said anything, and then he looked up and added defiantly: "but when I'm Simonetta it'll be different, because I won't be a fool then. It'll be my turn to be beautiful and make a fool of other people."

John, it became suddenly apparent, had reached the end of his tether. He stood up and got out his fags.

"I don't usually smoke inside other people's houses because I respect them, but I don't see anything here to respect." He lit up.

"Whatever you do," I said, turning to Simon, "don't tell Lewis you've talked to us; don't even tell him you have seen us."

He had begun to shiver again. "What would he do?"

"I think he might kill you. You see, you are the only person who can give evidence against him."

"And, of course, he thinks the world is better off without people like you," said John mercilessly.

"Do you really think he would kill me?"

Suddenly the full horror of his situation seemed to strike him. He got clumsily to his feet, teetering on his heels, and there was a ripping noise as he tore the hem of the dress, "Please no! No. You must stop him, please stop him." He began to reach out towards me.

"Stop doing that. You are quite safe as long as Lewis doesn't know we have been here."

"But…but…"

"You have an alternative."

"Yes?"

"You could go to the police and tell them what happened."

You could see him thinking quickly; nobody is stupid when their life is at stake.

"No, no, they wouldn't understand, and Lewis might still get me. If he asks, I shall say I haven't seen you, I shall say you never came. Yes, he can't prove you came… You won't tell him, will you?"

"Why should we?"

"…And I shall give in my notice to leave the school. After my operation – it's only two weeks time – I shall go away, a long way away… I have my money."

"Where will you go?" He brightened up again; he liked questions he could answer.

"I have a cousin in Canberra; I shall go to her."

"What about your flat?"

"It belongs to the school."

"And all your beautiful furniture?"

A crafty look came over his face. "I should like you both to have it."

"No thanks," said John, "not our style. Give it to Matron – you owe her. Cheers." And, stubbing his fag out in a priceless Sèvres vase, "come on, Mark."

As we got to the door the creature in the torn, pink, sweat-stained dress looked beseechingly after us:

"I'm not really a murderer, am I?"

John looked back and spoke for both of us:

"You are nothing," he said.

Chapter 25: Isabel's Surprises

"So, what made you suddenly realise? I asked. "I mean that it was Lewis, all along?"

We were sitting in a rather horrid gastro pub – I had wanted to get straight home, but John said he needed a pint and I knew how he felt. We are neither of us beer drinkers as a rule, but I think subconsciously we both wanted to do something eminently masculine.

"Witches live in gingerbread houses," he said and got out his fags. One of the things, I love about John – or, I suppose you could say one of the ways he has a hold over me, and I don't mean that in a derogatory sense, is that while he has a pretty good idea of the way in which my thoughts tend, I am always surprised by his thought processes.

"What do you mean, John?"

"Well, as a kid, my auntie used to read me fairy tales and stuff, and I remember Hansel and Gretel scaring the pants off me. So when I first heard that Lewis lived in a gingerbread house, I thought 'Wow, that's scary…'"

"You didn't say anything to me," I said reproachfully.

"Well I don't say I went on brooding over it, I didn't really think of it again, not until…"

"Until when?"

"Well, all the time we were at Simon's and he was telling us about how Lewis was protecting him. I kept thinking, 'This is weird.' I know we'd thought maybe it was because Simon must have given Lewis money to keep quiet…"

"It was the best reason we came up with."

"But we both knew it wasn't likely – I mean, from what we know about Lewis, he'd have been only too glad to shop Simon and see him punished, so there must have been another reason."

He stopped and looked meditative – he looks wonderful when he's all lost in thought.

"I think I'll have another pint."

I went to the bar.

"So," he continued, as I returned with his pint and my orange juice, "where was I? Oh yes, the business about the girl being blonde – Lewis said that the waitress he'd given the whisky to was blonde, and Bethan's story backs him up, but Gino said there weren't any blonde waitresses, so that bugged me too. It was only when we were going out and I looked back and saw Simon standing there all small and pathetic, and I suddenly thought, 'Gretel!', because the funny thing is that, in the book, the one my auntie used to read, there was a picture of Gretel looking all pathetic, and…" he looked up from his pint, "get this: she was all dressed in pink frills with long blonde hair, and she couldn't see, but the old witch was about to push her into the oven." He turned to me, his mouth covered in froth and his cheeks flushed, "and then I knew that Lewis was the old witch in the gingerbread house who'd pushed Simon into murdering Lady P."

I shook my head in wonderment – as much as at how incredibly sexy John looked, as at the tortuous way he had arrived at the truth.

"Really," I said, "when you think about it, we found out that it was Lewis, not through any evidence, but because of your auntie's reading about Hansel and Gretel, and my dream about Lewis's dog."

"When you said that about the dog and its long blonde hair," he continued, "I remembered all the times people had gone on about hair making a difference…"

"Ah, yes, what the Skorskis told us at the bridge thing, 'Vat a deeference ze 'air make, and vith zee golden 'air, ze dog look like zee new dog…'"

"Don't try doing accents, Mark."

"…. And then Lewis repeated what the Skorskis had said, and then that came out in the dream… and there were other hair things: Janet looked different with her hair all loose when we went to see her at that flat… and," I added for good value, "there was matron's beehive." But John wasn't having Matron's beehive and rightly pointed out it was an irrelevance.

"It was *long golden* hair that made the difference."

"It was the glasses too; we saw Tubby looking different without his glasses, but we didn't think how Simon might look without his big black glasses…"

"Well, we should have remembered because he took them off once when we told him about his aunt."

"And we thought about Tubby not being able to see, but we didn't think about Simon not being able to see; we thought of Janet's hair, but not Simon's."

"And in my dream Skorski turned into Bethan, but really it was Simon turning…"

"We didn't think laterally; all we needed to do was to think dogs and hair. Even Fifi was a clue!"

"No more than Matron's beehive – both were aide memoires."

"Up yours too."

"Going back to dogs, it was Lewis's dog dying that made him vulnerable that day, made him tell me about his wife and Carol, and why he hated her. If he had been himself, he wouldn't have talked about it, he would never have given away so much evidence against himself."

"I bet he kicked himself afterwards."

"But it was my dream," I said proudly, "that brought it all together – the transforming effect of long golden hair, and the glasses factor."

"Before you sit there congratulating yourself too much," he said rather seriously, "we have to think what we are going to do about Lewis."

"Well, I'm not sure there's not much we can do – or in fact, need to do. There's no reason why he should think we've gone to see Simon: as far as he's aware we know nothing about the cross-dressing. And, just to make sure we don't cause any trouble, he mutters about suing us for libel if we step out of line. Besides, I think he's arrogant: he's told us not to go, so therefore we won't."

"That didn't stop us last time, the last time he told us not to go and see Simon, we went straight off there; he won't have forgotten that."

"Ah, but that's why he thinks we won't go this time,

because last time we went, we *did* upset Simon, and Lewis was shown to be right. And this time he's got even more moral high ground: there's poor Simon worried about his operation. I think he'll leave Simon alone. Of course, there's still Carol. I know he said he wouldn't have a go at her, but I suppose she might not be safe?"

"Well, he's had plenty of time since Italy to have a go at Carol, and he hasn't, I'm not going to lose any sleep over Simon or Carol; it's something else that worries me."

"I see what you mean, there's the moral question – should Lewis be allowed to get away with it?"

"I wasn't thinking about moral questions," he said, "I was thinking about us."

"What you mean? Ah, if Lewis *was* to find out Simon's spilled the beans, he'll have a go at us? Oh, I don't think he'd bother; after all, he's not really in any danger from us; even now it would be very difficult for anyone to make the crime stick – there isn't any evidence, only Simon's word, and a good defence barrister could do what he liked with him, Lewis knows that."

"You could be right... I don't much like this beer; I'm going to have a vodka."

I watched him walk over to the bar and I turned things over in my mind, not just the question of Lewis, but people's lives and whether anyone's ever done a survey on how loneliness contributes to crime. If Carol hadn't been lonely perhaps she'd have been less likely to pry into people's secrets; perhaps she wouldn't have gone after Lewis. If Lewis hadn't been lonely after the death of his wife, he wouldn't have been bothered about Carol, and if Simon hadn't been lonely, he wouldn't have been as vulnerable a target for Lewis – and he wouldn't have told us everything. Even the Skorskis traded on people's loneliness; was that was a crime too? How lucky John and I were to have each other... but then as I watched his delectable hips standing at the bar, I felt a cold wind blow as I remembered how I was in my sixties and he was in his forties. Untouched by the icy blast he came back and sat down.

"I was thinking as I was standing there waiting for that guy to be good enough to take my fiver, I don't think it's court cases and stuff that worries Lewis, I think it's the loss of his good name – people saying 'no smoke without fire' and so on; losing his reputation for – what's the word, pro something?"

"Probity."

"Yes, could be. I think he's an evil man. And if he gets to wondering whether we have actually said things to other people, he gets to thinking that it's time for a spot of headmasterly punishment again."

I sighed; this was all very unpleasant, particularly as we'd had such a successful day in other ways.

"We could go to the police," he said.

"Do you think we should?"

"I dunno – do you?"

"I don't know what we should do. If we told the police, we'd have an awful lot of explaining to do." I didn't really relish the thought of this.

He looked at his vodka in silence. "So what *are* we going to do?"

"John, I have no idea."

Suddenly, with one of his unpredictable mood changes he laughed. "Let's forget all about it for a bit. Here, I've bought you some of those poncey vegetable crisps you like."

I felt as if a huge load had been taken off my shoulders. "That's very kind. Did you have to take out a bank loan?"

"No, but I want to have the beetroot bits."

It seemed we had decided not to think any more about all these questions that day. And, in fact, Lewis' name remained unmentioned until the following afternoon – and by the time it was, Lewis seemed to me the very least of my worries.

"Who the hell's that?" asked John peering out of the window. I had a sudden terrible fear that it was Lewis with a shot gun – or even worse, Simon arriving in a ball gown, come to throw himself on our mercy.

"Who is it, John?"

"New BMW, don't recognise… Oh, it's Gino in his

shades, blimey! He looks … He's dropping them off. Oh, what a pity, he's driving off."

"Who?"

"It's the Macalister clan."

"Oh goodness, I'd forgotten all about them, and there's no cake."

"Your girlfriend will have to go hungry then."

"I wish you wouldn't…" but there was a ring at the bell.

Isabel was very elegant in cream and black, and Janet had a decidedly womanly look about her. Neither appeared particularly bereaved; in fact they seemed full of the joys of spring.

"What a lovely room!" said Isabel, "how beautifully you have done it; what pretty curtains!" I was rather pleased she singled out the curtains for approbation, John and I had had some disagreement over their choice and I had prevailed. Janet, however was less interested in our décor than in telling us all her news: had we seen the new BMW? Gino loved it. They had both given up their jobs and were living at Elsinore (together with Gino's sister), ready to get to grips with turning it into a hotel. And, of course, they were busy planning the wedding, and buying things for the baby.

The benefits of Trevor's money were obviously kicking in.

"Tea?" said John, rather tersely.

"Not for me," said Janet, "it makes me sick at the moment."

"I won't either, thank you" said Isabel; "we can't stay long. Gino's waiting for us with Daniella in the pub, I expect he'll watch the match and want to go as soon as it's over."

Gino had obviously established his position among the female Macalisters. There was a lull in the conversation and I wondered why they had come.

"We haven't got you a present yet, Janet," said John, "what do you want?"

He was still being rather ungracious I thought.

Janet smiled. "Let's go outside, John," she said, "like we used to on the balcony at *Il Sole*, when we used to bump into each other having a fag. The only difference is that you can still go on smoking and I mustn't now."

"It's a bit cold out there," he said.

"Never mind, I like fresh air, and you've got to indulge me because pregnant women have to be indulged."

"Does Gino indulge you?" I asked rather doubtfully.

"Of course; I am the mother of his son." She put her arm through John's. "Come on, if you don't want to go outside, let's leave these two oldies together and go and join Gino in the pub. I want you to meet Daniella."

"Hrm," said John. I wondered whether he was still jealous of Isabel and was imagining all this as some sort of plot to leave us alone – which, in fact, it was.

"Come on," she said, "or the match will be over." She had probably said the only thing that would have got John to budge; he grinned and admitted defeat.

"Now, tell me, Isabel," I said as the front door banged to, "why have you come, why is Janet leaving us alone?"

"She wants you to give her away at the wedding and is too shy to ask you herself."

I didn't think the new Janet was a particularly shy person, and I wasn't sure I wanted to be a participant in the wedding, so I didn't reply.

"Actually," said Isabel undaunted, "it was my idea really, so Janet said I should ask you myself. And I said, alright, but I wanted a few moments alone with you." She smiled a rather beautiful smile and leant over and whispered, "I think she thought I was going to seduce you!"

"Oh," I said. I began to feel worried: perhaps John was right – Isabel *did* have designs on me, and now she was being aided and abetted by Janet.

"So I told her it would be easier for us to discuss the arrangements á deux."

Now I felt very worried indeed – 'why me?' I thought? 'Willy Wanker would be more appropriate – or, perhaps not,' but I didn't voice my thoughts.

"I do like these curtains," she said.

"What is it?" I asked apprehensively.

Isabel sat back in the leather sofa that had been much admired by Bethan, crossed her legs and smiled seductively.

"I want you to cast your mind back," she said. "Right back to 1975."

"I don't think anything particular strikes me."

Now if she had said 1985 that would have been different, because that was the year I met John.

"You were attending a conference in Florence – something about the Renaissance, I think. You might have been running it, or perhaps you were giving a paper? Anyway, you were staying at the *Hotel Carpaccio*."

"Was I? Well, I might have been, I was always at conferences in the seventies… why, were you there? Did we meet?" I cast my mind back, but nothing suggested itself.

"I wasn't at the conference," she said. I felt enormously relieved, "… but I was at the hotel." My sense of relief vanished.

"It was your last night," Isabel continued, "and you were looking for fun, and your eye lit on a girl sitting in the foyer, well actually there were two girls, but only one was pretty, and to cut a long story – or perhaps a short story shorter, you picked her up, took her out to a nightclub and ended up in bed with her."

She smiled at me. "Remember?"

Well, no, actually I didn't. I was, I suppose, quite promiscuous then back in the seventies, not sure whether I was hetero or bi or gay, but doing the best to find out. Fieldwork, you might call it. Now, as I cast my mind back, I could see exactly what she was driving at, and I had a nasty feeling that she might be embarking on some obscure form of blackmail.

"I thought you might not remember," she said smiling, "because, after all, it was just a one night stand and you had a plane to catch the next morning; there was no commitment on either side, and the next morning you were gone."

"It sounds rather sordid," I said. I was beginning to feel very uncomfortable, but I was glad to hear there had been no commitment – on either side.

"No," she said, "it wasn't sordid at all; it was very romantic; he was a lovely man, and the next morning I found a little silver locket on the pillow; I think he had bought it in Reception before he left. It had a little silver David in it." She reached under her sweater, "rather like this."

And there was the silver pendent that she had worn on the day that *hadn't* been the funeral. I remembered admiring it, and I had thought at the time it was just the sort of thing I might have bought myself, if I was buying something for a woman. I had obviously been right.

"Jesus. Christ," I said.

"And nine months later there was Janet."

I put my face in my hands.

Isabel laughed; it was a nice laugh, a Sammy laugh.

"Don't worry, Mark, I haven't come to blackmail you or blame you. I have only come to ask you one small favour."

I looked up,

"Yes?"

"I told you; I want you to give Janet away at the wedding."

I began to panic. "Have you told her. Does she know I'm her father?"

"No, I haven't told anyone. I invented my cover story years ago. I have always been a respectable widow, and I intend to remain one. I have no wish to complicate Janet's life or my own."

I sat rather still, there was an awful lot to think about. Isabel sat quietly, waiting for me to speak, and at last I said, "Do you hate me now? Did you hate me then, afterwards…?"

"No, why should I hate you, Mark? I told you it was a one-night stand, no commitment on either side, and, in fact, you had even left your phone number, but I lost it. I wasn't particularly organised in those days…"

"If I'd known…" It didn't bear thinking about.

"But you didn't, and I didn't know how to find you; I didn't listen very carefully when you said where you lived – I could only remember it was somewhere in London. Anyway we were both sloshed." I didn't know what to say; I cast around for something appropriate.

"It must have been very hard for you, Isabel."

"Well, it was a big decision to have the baby, but no, not really. My parents were very good and we all adored Janet. We invented a husband killed in a car crash which I 'didn't like talking about,' and then I met Trevor."

"I must be honest," I said, "I don't really remember it… Perhaps I do remember something vaguely, I'm not sure, perhaps it will come back to me, but I'm surprised that I don't remember your name: Isabel is fairly unusual."

"That's because I called myself Izzie, and you thought I said Lizzie. I didn't correct you, I liked being anonymous too."

"Oh god, what a mess!"

"Not at all," she said quite sharply, "we both have a lovely daughter and we shall, no doubt soon have a lovely grandson."

"Er, yes," I said, the grandson bit only now dawning on me. Then a rather pertinent question occurred to me: "when did you first know – that I was the guy you… er, met in Florence. Did you know at *Il Sole*?"

"No, not a clue; it was that time when you had muddled the date of the funeral and came to my house. As I was sitting there, there was something – I don't know, in your gestures, maybe; perhaps your voice seemed faintly familiar… but even then it didn't occur to me. But when I saw you at Sammy's Bridge Day, suddenly I knew."

"Hadn't I told you my name in Florence?"

"Yes, you said Mark – I don't think we bothered with surnames. Mark isn't a very unusual name, you know; there was no reason on earth why I should ever connect you with the Florence all those years later."

I sat and thought; there seemed to be rather a lot to think about.

"I think I should like that cup of tea after all," she said. "Shall I make it?"

"No," I said. "I would like to be on my own for a bit, if you don't mind." And I went into the kitchen and filled the kettle.

I am not a very good person. I'm amiable and easygoing, and my life path has largely lain in pleasant places; I don't like hassle. Now I could see hassle, endless amounts of it. No doubt I should have been thinking how wonderful to have a daughter, how irresponsibly I had acted, how nice Isabel had been about it and lots of things like that, but in fact my initial thought had been how lightly I had got off. And after that I didn't think about Isabel or Janet at all, I thought instead, 'what will John say? Will he be upset? Will he think I want to go off with Isabel? Will he use it as an excuse to dump me? Do I have to tell him?' And then I thought, 'God! Does Isabel expect me to marry her?' I dropped the box of teabags on the floor, and the woman in question came into the kitchen.

"It's all right, Mark," she said. "I don't want to be Mrs Hadley!"

Isabel was, as I say, a very perceptive woman. "And, in fact," she continued bending down and retrieving the tea bags, "if I did, I shouldn't stand a chance. I don't think anyone could prize you away from John! And as for me, well, I shall become a full time Grandmother, because I suspect *one* of the grandfathers at least, won't be spending a lot of time at the cradle." She smiled at me flirtatiously – she really was an attractive woman, I could quite see how Florence had happened. "There again," she continued, "I might marry Mr Williams from the church – or perhaps I shall manage 'Elsinore', or there again, I might take off abroad and try my luck – you meet all sorts of interesting people sitting in hotel foyers."

I poured the milk into a jug; the sense of relief was enormous.

"And now," said this most sympathetic of women, "let's talk about something else."

I offered some faint disclaimer, but Isabel waved it away, saying, "No, we don't need to talk about it any more, not now, perhaps not ever, but both Janet and I *would* like you to give her away – after all otherwise it would have to be Mr Williams."

"Of course I will."

"I knew you'd come up trumps. Now, are you going to offer me some of those delicious-looking chocolate biscuits?"

We went into the sitting room. I felt quite numb – and I was still worried about John.

"I should very much like to hear about your investigations," she said.

"They are all over."

She accepted a cup of Earl Grey. Then she said a surprising thing: "It was Simon, wasn't it?"

"What makes you say that?"

"Well, Janet and I worked it out – after Gino's sister told us about the cross-dressing ... you did know about that, didn't you?"

"Gino's sister?"

"Yes, Janet tried to tell you at the Bridge Day, but you went rushing off."

"What did Gino's sister say?"

"Well, that she'd seen all these dresses and wigs when she was cleaning his room: she was a chambermaid."

I opened my eyes wide. "I wish we'd known!"

She laughed. "I believe you're more interested in this, than in discovering you have a daughter."

"Oh no." But I think she was right.

"She told Janet when she was staying at their flat. Poor girl, I think she's glad to be at Elsinore; she had to sleep in the kitchen at Janet's. I didn't go to their flat, but you did. Was it so very small?"

"Yes."

"So we worked out that Simon must have dressed up as a waitress and handed Lady P. the poison. I've no idea why. I thought she wasn't too bad to him, not nearly as rude as she was to the rest of us."

"It wasn't really Simon," I said.

"Oh, do tell!"

"If I do, you must promise not to tell anyone, not even Janet."

"Guide's honour."

I suppose I shouldn't have done, but I could see no harm in it. After all, she knew quite a lot anyway. I gave her a very compressed synopsis of events: how Lewis disliked Carol and saw an opportunity of getting rid of her; how he had set up Simon, who had taken the poison to the wrong room.

"But why did Lewis dislike Carol so much? I mean none of us particularly liked her – poking and prying about, and of course, she managed to get Janet to go on about Trevor. Was she blackmailing him or something?"

"No," I said, "it was really to do with his wife. You see, Lewis hates anyone who was sexually aberrant – or anyone who had sex at all, really. He seems to have this thing about female purity, and somehow Carol's seduction attempt seemed to sully the memory of his wife. Actually, when I saw the portrait of his wife I thought she looked a tad like Carol, so I suppose the resemblance made it worse. Then he was revolted by Simon's cross-dressing, and so he decided to use him to punish Carol."

Isabel sat there, quiet and elegant, nibbling biscuits and not interrupting.

"But don't say anything to anyone," I added anxiously, "I don't care about Simon, but I don't want any trouble from Lewis." And I thought of the conversation John and I had had in the pub, and a shiver ran down my back.

For a while she sat silent and I thought perhaps she despised John and me because we still hadn't done anything about Lewis, but actually it wasn't that at all.

"It still seems a very extreme action for Lewis to take," she said at last.

"Well, who can see into another's heart? As the poet says: 'The mind, the mind has mountains, /Cliffs of sheer, call them cheap may, who ne'er clung there.'"

"Gerard Manley Hopkins is all very well, but I still think Lewis has got off very lightly," she said quietly.

"Well, yes he has. John calls him a very evil man but, on the other hand, he hasn't got such a wonderful life left: he only loved his wife and his dog, and now they're both dead. All he can do is to gaze at Lily's portrait, sit there all alone worshipping the memory of his dead angel. Whatever he's done, he doesn't have much to look forward to."

Isabel sat quiet so I turned to her: "What are you thinking?" I asked.

Isabel put down her teacup and gave a half smile. "Lewis's wife was no angel." Would Isabel ever stop presenting me with surprises?

"What!"

"I think I had better tell you. Do you remember – well, you don't really seem to remember much about me at all, which is disappointing, but there it is. Well, when you picked me up in the foyer of that hotel in Florence, I was with another girl. I'd known her, although not very well, years ago at school, and I bumped into her again at an Old Girls reunion thing. We got talking, and I mentioned that I had always wanted to go on holiday to Florence. The upshot was, she said she had never been to Florence either and could she come too? I thought this was rather a good idea, even thought it might be a bit dull because she was one of those ladylike looking girls – always dressed properly and looking a little prissy, I thought. How wrong I was! Lily went on that on holiday to pull, and pull she did. I was, as you know, quite choosy, but Lily wasn't; anyone would do for Lily."

"Oh, Isabel, you're not saying…?"

"Yes, Mark, I am, and I haven't finished either. Now, it was a wretched sort of holiday because I did actually want to see Florence, but Lily was only interested in the inside of bedrooms, and I spent most of the time on my own. I was pretty lonely…"

"So when this guy picked you up…"

"Well, there was that aspect of it. Anyway, when I found I was pregnant, I told Lily and I remember this angel of yours saying, "Thank god, that happened to you and not to me! I'm going to make sure I don't get into a mess like that. In fact, I think I might just turn myself into a respectable married lady one of these days.'"

"And this was Lewis's Lily?"

"Now don't interrupt. Then she passed out of my life, and

oh, it must have been ten years later I saw her. Well, I didn't see her, I recognised her in a photo, and you're right, as she got older she did look a bit like Carol."

"You *saw* her?"

"I saw her photo; she was sitting in the middle of a school photo, next to the Headmaster – Lewis."

"You seem to remember all this very clearly?" I was a bit suspicious, if the truth be told.

"Oh yes," she said bitterly, "I remember all right: she had scrawled on the back, 'Darling Trevor, this is me with my legs together. I don't think you have seen that before, have you, Lover?' The words are etched into my memory."

"And Lewis never knew?"

"No! Trevor said she was scared of him finding out, and it all blew over – as Trevor's affairs always did. Of course, I was pretty upset, but it wasn't the first time… Anyway, he never said much about it except that he soon got fed up with her, but he did say that Lewis had never touched her – he had a sort of hang-up about sex – but that plenty of others had."

I didn't say anything, but I had a picture of the deluded Lewis, smartly turned out in crisp shirt and spotless cords, sitting night after night by the portrait. But then I had another thought: Lewis didn't sit by the picture in adoration, but lost in speculation. Where had his angel been on those long, long walks with Sergeant? Did she really share his views on the value of chastity? Just how lily-white was Lily? And, of course, it was Carol who had awakened these thoughts; Carol with her vulgar clothes and prying ways, but who, nevertheless, resembled Lily in feature – and perhaps not just in feature, but in her sexuality as well. That was why he hated Carol: she had planted seeds of doubt in his mind. But as long as he lived, he would never know the truth about his wife: had she been the angel of his dreams, or another Carol? Lewis had his punishment.

"Are you still listening, Mark?"

I came to with a jolt: "Yes… oh yes. How had she met him?"

"Trevor went to give some talks on drama at the school –

she stalked him." She got up and wandered over to the window. "Oh, look …"

And that was the end of that, for coming in through the garden were John, Janet, and a girl whom I took to be Gino's sister. They all appeared to be having a riotous time, and I thought with a pang that John might have enjoyed his time with Gino.

"Real Madrid 'ave won, was very good match. You 'ave meet my sister, she call 'erself Daniella, she speak very good English, even better then me."

"Oh Gino," said his fond fianceé, "you speak terrible English."

"Then you learn good Italian," he patted her stomach. "Italian baby speak Italian." But his sister had much more sense of occasion.

"Good afternoon, Mr Hadley, I am pleased meeting you."

"Darling, Mark has very kindly agreed to give you away," said Isabel addressing her daughter and brushing away some biscuit crumbs. "And," she turned to John, "I hope you will be one of Gino's ushers; there will be such a lot of Italian boys, we must have a few English ones."

"I like the sound of all these Italian boys," said John.

Daniella had obviously taken a shine to John; she smiled knowingly at me.

"He is so funny, your John," she said. I liked the 'your'.

"Well," said Isabel, "I really think we must be off. We'll be in touch nearer the time about wedding details."

And suddenly they were gone.

"Did you have a nice time with the merry widow?" asked John as we watched them drive off.

"Yes, thank you," I said. "Did you have a nice time with Gino?"

"Why on earth are you asked to give Janet away at this wedding. Is it some plot to get you off with Isabel?"

"No, in fact she told me she wouldn't marry me."

"Oh, did you ask her then?" asked John carelessly.

"No."

"Why did she say she wouldn't marry you?"

"She said – with great perspicacity, I thought – that no-one would ever take your place in my life."

There was a silence, then he said, "You seem to have been having a very cosy little chat. What else did you talk about?"

I told him about Lewis' wife and about Trevor's affair with her, but I didn't tell him about anything else.

Chapter 26: Trouble under the branches

"John?"

"What?"

"Oh, nothing."

"Why did you ask then? I need a bit of peace and quiet to do this."

This did not seem a very propitious start, and of course it was stupid to ask John when he was busy trying to fit the bits of Christmas tree together, but it was his own fault – the Christmas tree, I mean – because he had objected to a real one because of the needles. John doesn't really do Christmas.

"I imagine you were going to bang on about Lewis again…" He rummaged irritably around amidst a lot of plastic branches. "I wish we'd had a real tree now, or even better, no fucking tree at all."

I could see this wasn't a good time to start telling him about Isabel, and I didn't want to talk about Lewis either. Five days had passed since our visit to Simon, and ever since that discussion in the pub, we both knew that we ought to do something: contact Carol, tell the police, or even go and see Lewis ourselves. From time to time we discussed the options, but there always seemed more compelling reasons to avoid doing any of these things – particularly visiting Lewis: cowardice being the main one. We got to saying things like, 'We'd better play it by ear,' or 'let's not rush into things,' and so on. Furthermore, Christmas was on its way, and although John and I are not great ones for the festivities, it was a good excuse for pretending there were other things to worry about beside possible murders.

As the days had passed and we heard nothing from anyone (including Simon and Lewis), the sense of urgency seemed to pass. We even stopped saying we'd better not rush into anything, because we could both see we weren't going to anyway. I suppose we had sort of tacitly agreed to do nothing.

For me, the question of Isabel seemed much more

worrying: I simply had no idea how John would react, and I was scared to put it to the test, particularly with Christmas looming large in the form of an assemble-it-yourself plastic tree. I don't do DIY and, although he's better at it than me, it's not really John's forté, either. It puts him in a very disagreeable frame of mind.

"Chuck over a bit of newspaper; I don't want to get glue everywhere, do I?"

"I thought it all fitted together without glue."

He gave me a look, worse than the one he'd given Simon.

"Perhaps *you'd* like to do this fucking tree. But I expect you're too tired lounging around here all day while other people are at work."

I had, in fact, suggested that it wasn't a good idea to do it as soon as he had got home, but I thought I would refrain from pointing this out. I got up meekly and took him the paper – even though I hadn't read it, but I thought I wouldn't mention that either. Then there was a ring at the bell. We both looked up.

"I wonder who that is?" I twittered. I seemed to be good at making inane remarks that afternoon.

"Lewis disguised as Father Christmas."

Then a small treble voice piped up, "Away in a manager…"

"Away off my fucking doorstep," said the arborist, as he cut himself on a sharp bit of branch.

"Have you got any loose change?"

"No, and if I had, I wouldn't part with it."

I thought I had better go to the door, even though it meant me finding the pound coin.

And there in a huddle stood the Skorskis and a fat boy of about nine whom I felt instinctively was the troublemaker from Simon's school. Karl was, as always, clutching his bag, Claire carried a large plastic one, and the boy wielded a mobile phone. When he saw me he stopped, in mid 'asleep-in-the-hay'.

"Go on, go on" said Claire giving him a poke. "Sing some more, sing another verse, Marco."

"No," said the young Skorski.

"'As beautiful voice," commented the uncle.

"Happy Christmas," I said. "Come on in."

"Sure," said the boy.

"We can't stay long. I don't think we can stay long, can we Karl?" Karl shook his head, presumably to intimate that they couldn't.

"You haven't given me my money," said the Skorski scion holding out his hand. I ushered them in (I ignored the young Skorski), and John emerged from behind the tree and gave a horrible sort of grimace.

"They're easy to do, those trees. I can put one up in two minutes, no sweat," boasted the boy.

A glance at John's face made me wonder whether the child might be put to the test.

Now we were all inside, I had a good look at him, small and murderous like his uncle, but fat and oily on his own account. I felt that stealing poison would be a piece of cake to him; I wondered that he hadn't poisoned anyone else. Perhaps he had.

"Nice place you've got," said Claire. "Nice place, isn't it, Karl?

Karl touched the leather sofa. "Eez good quality."

Marco turned his attention to John's lighter, which was lying amongst the branches.

"No, don't you touch that, Marco. I said don't touch that."

She thrust the plastic bag at me. "Here, this is from Bethan; some lamb chops. Bethan sent you some chops."

"There was a leg too," remarked the odious boy, who was bashing at the sofa, "but Uncle Karl took it."

A momentary silence fell, but I remembered my duties as host.

"Have you been visiting Bethan, then?" I enquired conversationally, I indicated the mercifully undamaged sofa and even offered tea, but they wouldn't sit down, Claire stood peering about and Karl clutched his bag. The boy, meanwhile, walked about the room, picking up objects and examining them.

It appeared that they had been to see the Welsh contingent "in connection with business, working out something;" and had taken the boy with them "to give Karl's sister a rest; give her a rest, she gets very tired." I felt I could understand that, and I wondered whether the business had anything to do with Bethan's ability to push people into gulleys, but apparently not.

"Uncle Karl's going to stuff sheep," said Marco.

"Do not zay stuffing. Eez business to make pretty lambkins."

I supposed they must have got together over the fliers at Sammy's bridge day; I wondered how the business arrangements would work.

"So we had to come through here, come near your house, so we brought the chops – the meat – and we thought we'd tell you the news. Give you the news about…"

"… It was me that told you, I want to tell them," interrupted the youngest Skorski.

"Put my lighter down!" commanded John from among the branches. He was obviously failing the putting-up-the-tree-in-two-minutes test.

"'E 'eard on 'is mobile, very expensive machine," corroborated Karl.

I said I thought we should all sit down. And the news was certainly worth the pound coin that I reluctantly handed over in exchange for the lighter.

He was a loathsome boy. I longed to trip him up as he strutted round the room as if he owned it.

"My friend Mikey told me, he's still at the school, worst luck for him. He texted me and told me." He looked round conscious of his audience and casually picked up John's lighter again.

"Go on, go on," said the aunt.

"Put down my lighter," said John.

"You know Simonetta? That's what we called Mr Johnson. Well, he's run off. He didn't tell the school nothing, everyone thought he'd run off with Matron because Stuart Biggs saw Matron with a trailer taking all Simonetta's furniture into her flat, and then Tom Baker saw her driving him off in her old car, but she came back again."

"Eez bad woman, zat matron."

"And the school are mad at old Simonetta because he didn't tell them he was going."

"How does your friend know all this?" asked John, putting his lighter in his pocket.

"Matron told him. Matron said Simonetta had given her all his things before he went to Australia…"

"Australia!" John and I exchanged glances.

"And she's going to sell them all and go on a world tour and stop being Matron."

"It eez very good ting that Marco eez not there now; she eez bad poisoning woman."

"No, she's not." He picked up John's pliers and waved them threateningly at his uncle. "I told you and told you – I took the poison off old Simonetta; it was nothing to do with Matron, only I didn't want the school to know I'd pinched it."

"Eez no smoke vithout there eez ze fire."

"And Matron told Tom Baker that the reason Simonetta has gone to Australia is…" he looked round triumphantly, "to have all his bits cut off and be turned into a lady." He hooted with laughter and turned his attention to John's pliers.

"Eez very bad place."

"Well, Marco, "said Claire, "you don't want to believe everything you hear; people often tell lies, tell lies, I say. Uncle Karl and I know why he's gone, disappeared away, but we are keeping that to ourselves and not telling anyone. You can't be too careful when you're in business."

"I know anyway, 'cos I heard you talking. You think he killed someone with poison, and he's running away from the police, but I think he's too wet – and he'll be wetter when he's had his dick chopped off."

He turned to John and attempted a graphic demonstration of the process. John removed the pliers.

"Not use zat word."

"Anyway, we thought you'd be interested – like to know. Help you with your investigations. You like the chops? Good red meat."

"There was a leg as well, but Uncle Karl…"

"Don't be silly. I said, don't …"

"They're very fat, Bethan and Megan." He seized one of the sofa cushions, stuffed it under his sweater and walked around to demonstrate.

"Eez strange small man called Irfon, son of Bethan."

"No, Karl, he's Megan's son." She turned to me. "He's Megan's son, isn't he?"

"He belongs to both," said John attempting to up-end the tree. He had not passed the two minute test.

"I want to go now," said Marco. "It's boring here."

His aunt and uncle must have thought so too, because they seemed to take this as a cue for their departure. Karl clutched his little bag, and Claire, bereft of the plastic one (minus the leg), prodded at Marco.

"Come on then, I say. Come on."

And off they went into the night. From the window, I could dimly discern them getting into the side of the old Daimler with DEAR ABSENT… on it, and as they drove off I glimpsed Fifi in his basket. That's the last we shall hear of them, I thought – but, as usual, I was wrong.

"Jesus Christ!" said John as I came back into the room, "That kid's had my pliers!"

"He can't have done!"

"Where are they, then?" He was right, they had gone. "You see how right I am to hate kids."

"They aren't all as bad as young Skorski," I said.

"Pity Matron saved him," commented John as he put the tree in situ and regarded it. Then he looked at me and his face was troubled.

"I don't like the fact that Simon's scarpered, do you? Do you think Lewis paid him a visit, and we're next on his list?"

"I don't," I said stoutly, "I think Simon just got scared. If Lewis had been to see him, he wouldn't have had the opportunity to scarper: he'd be dead."

"If you think that," said John gathering up what remained of his tools, "we ought to go to the cops, because we're not safe, and Carol's not safe."

We both stared at the naked tree. One of the branches leant at a funny angle, but I felt it wasn't the time to comment.

"We'll go tomorrow," I said.

"Right." We both fell silent, neither of us relishing the prospect.

"Well," he said, "I may as well do the lights now. After all, we might as well enjoy them while we can. We'll probably be banged up for Christmas, if Lewis doesn't get us first."

Although I didn't think things were quite as black as that, I had to concede that our prospects didn't seem particularly rosy.

"Where did you put the lights?" John asked.

"In the big cupboard in the spare room."

He came back with an armful of lights and a tangle of wires. He had also found the box of chocolates we'd won at Sammy's bridge day."

"What were these doing in there?"

"I just put them in there; thought we could give them to somebody for Christmas."

"I wondered what I was getting."

"Don't be so silly." I felt rather out of sorts myself.

"Well, we'll eat them ourselves now; we shan't get offered many chocolates inside."

"I hope you don't suffer from a nut allegy," I said nastily.

John sat down and started opening it.

It was a big box and a pretty nauseating one – the picture, I mean. Some of the Skorski victims could have modelled for it – lots of kittens in a basket. I expect Sammy bought it as part of a job lot.

"I bet Tubby gave Carol a yukkie box like this." John said, wrestling with cellaphane.

"Well, it certainly wasn't as big. Tubby only gave her a tichy little box."

John looked up sharply. "How do you know?"

"He told me when I was talking to him at the bridge day –

when you went off with Bethan and Megan. I remember him saying it was only a little box and, anyway, he always struck me as mean."

"Wait a minute."

I waited.

"That awful friend of Carol's, that Olive; she told me it was a huge box and that's why Carol wanted to show it off."

We looked at each other.

"There must have been two boxes," said John slowly: "Tubby's and someone else's – and it was the someone else's that made her ill, although it came with the card signed L."

"Yes, but we have been over this before. One: if you're going to poison someone you're unlikely to put your name to it. Two: how do you get poison into chocolates, anyway? So, two: why wasn't she poisoned? *And,* three: if it wasn't a nut allergy, why didn't the hospital pick up on it?"

John thought about this and then he said: "If Lewis knew Carol had this nut allergy, all he had to do was to open the box and substitute nut chocolates for whatever was in there already, and send it off with a card signed L."

"Hang on! I don't think Lewis did put in the card with the L on it, I think he sent his box anonymously, banking on the fact that Carol would eat the chocolates anyway. I think the card with the L came with Tubby's box."

"Let's get this clear: Carol gets sent a small box of chocolates given to her by Tubby with a card signed L, and she eats them with no ill effects. The next day she gets a big box through the post with no card, and she thinks it's another one from Tubby, probably thinking, 'how bloody typical, he's forgotten to put a card in.' Anyway, this big box is the one she shows Olive."

"Yes, you're right, because didn't you say that Olive went through a drawer and found Tubby's card there – it wasn't attached to the big box?"

"That's right."

"And afterwards Carol keeps quiet about it, because even if she suspects the second box wasn't from Tubby, there's no reason why she should think the person who sent it should want to poison her. Most chocolates have nuts; she just thinks she didn't read the box carefully, and the ambulance people have taken it away, so she can't check. Also, she needs to make Tubby think it's his, so that he'll feel guilty and propose."

"But doesn't she wonder who sent the other box?"

"Perhaps she does, but there's not much she can do about it; the important thing is to make Tubby think it was his."

John opened up our kitten box to reveal a multitude of chocolates. He held it out:

"Fancy one?"

"Do you know, I don't think I do."

John said it was a funny thing, but he didn't fancy one either.

"Of course," he said closing up the box, "it might not have been Lewis."

"It has all the hallmarks of Lewis."

For about two minutes neither of us spoke, then John said:

"I think maybe we should go to the police tonight."

"Very well."

And then the phone rang. We were so hyped up that both of us jumped. John said afterwards he thought it was Tubby ringing us to say Carol had been poisoned again, and I thought it was Lewis, or Isabel. We were both quite wrong.

"Hello? Hello, this is Claire, Claire Skorski. We've just got home. Well, we've just got back… I thought I'd ring you, tell you – Karl's just sat down for a read of the paper, you know, the newspaper. Well, you remember that Lewis from the bridge – the one who was a headmaster? It's in the paper here: he's dead! Yes, found dead in his house. Suicide by the sound of it – nobody else involved, they say. Not suspicious, did it himself. It was the dog: he left a note about the dog, wanted to be buried with him, buried with him under an apple tree. People get very upset about their pets, very upset, that's why Karl and I provide a service, like doctors, medical. I said to Karl, if only we had managed to persuade Lewis about the dog we could have done a lovely job. We did offer, yes, we offered, and then he wouldn't have gone and killed himself.

We would have done it – good reduction, half price, I said. Anyway, thought I'd tell you. That's three gone from the GrandSlam: Lady P., him and that Trevor, and with Simon Johnson gone off to Australia – as good as dead. Didn't want to say much in front of Marco, in front of the boy, but you can tell he did it, that Simon, I mean, did the murder, killing Lady P.. Now he's gone to Australia, going off to another continent, fleeing from justice. I expect the police were on to him. But fancy him killing that Lady P.! You never know who'll be next. Makes you frightened to move about, doesn't it? Makes you scared. It's like Marco. Marco was poisoned by that Matron – the woman at the bridge, the woman with all the hair. Well, ever since that happened Karl never goes anywhere without his bag – full of antidotes, that's poison-stoppers, always has his bag, so if either of us get poisoned there's something to take. That Carol went rummaging through – disgraceful, I call it, shocking. Poor old Lewis, though; we liked him, played a good hand of bridge. Pity he hadn't been at that school, then there wouldn't have been the poisoning with Marco... Still. Forgot to ask you, slipped my mind, played any bridge? Have you played any bridge recently? We're always happy to play. You just give us a ring, ring us up..."

For some time neither of us said anything, then we both spoke together.

I said, "I think we can put off our visit to the police station."

And John said, "Can't see we need to tell the cops now."

The relief was so great that John laid down the tangle of Christmas tree lights that he had been nursing and went and got the vodka bottle and a couple of glasses.

"All the same," he said, "I can't see why he did it. After all, the dog had been gone a few weeks, you'd think he'd got over that by now. Do you think Simon shopped him?"

I sat so lost in thought that John had to virtually put the glass into my hands.

"Of course," he went on, "he could have realised we d

found out about the cross-dressing and was afraid we'd go to the cops. Or maybe he just felt guilty?"

In my mind's eye, I saw a rather beautiful woman sitting quietly opposite me on the very spot, in fact, where John was now sitting: 'I think Lewis has got off very lightly,' she had said.

"Hey, wake up! What is it?" I looked up:

"You know how we thought Lewis had got his punishment, because he would never know whether his wife really was the angel he thought her? Well, I think he found out."

"How?"

"I think Isabel sent him the photo – the one that Lily had sent Trevor. There would be no doubt after that, would there?"

Now it was John's turn to sit in silence. Then he said, "Wait a moment; if Karl read it in the paper…" and we both made a swoop on the glue-spattered pile that lay under the tree. John found it first.

DEATH OF RETIRED HEADMASTER

Retired headmaster, Lewis Roberts, was found dead in his sitting room yesterday evening underneath the portrait of a woman believed to be his wife. The picture was damaged and it is believed he shot at the picture before taking his own life. He left a note requesting that he be buried beside his dog.'

"Simon could have saved himself an air fare," said John at last.

"I suppose we murdered him really," I said.

"Balls; if anyone did, it was Isabel. Jesus Christ, I'm glad I'm not straight, when you think about the women we've met…"

"The female DAFS, you mean?"

"We thought Lady P. was a bitch, but in fact she was about the best of the bunch: there's Carol who goes about blackmailing people…"

"She didn't actually *do* any blackmailing: she just liked taunting people."

"That's worse. Then there's Bethan who probably murdered her husband…"

"I'm sure she didn't."

"And Janet who makes up stories about her stepfather abusing her…"

"She was only…"

"Then there's her mother, Isabel, who decides she'll ruin a man's life…"

"Isabel who decides she'll ruin a man's life…" The words went through me like a knife: was that what Isabel was going to do to mine?

"Well, haven't you got any excuses for her?"

"I suppose she thought Lewis ought to know," I said lamely. "Anyway, the men weren't much better: Skorski used to cheat and Simon and Lewis were murderers."

Isabel who decides she'll ruin a man's life… It kept running through my head: would John be even less inclined to forgive me if he thought my life had been mixed up with unscrupulous women like her – and contributed to producing more unscrupulous women?

"There's still one unsolved mystery," he said.

"What?"

"How that bloody kid nicked my pliers."

Chapter 27:
Last words from John –
under that bloody tree again

I am doing this last bit in case you've forgotten I can read and write, and because I wanted to; because something important happened to me.

Well, I thought that Mark was a bit down after the Isabel visit – I call it 'the Isabel visit' because that's what it was really, her making her presence felt. After all, Janet was in her thirties – okay, early thirties, but still no spring chicken – and I should have thought she could have come and managed to ask Mark about the wedding herself. However. Anyway, I ribbed Mark about it a bit, but he didn't seem to find it very funny, so I dropped it. And of course at the time there was the worry about Lewis: would he have another crack at Carol and, more to the point, would he have a go at us? And I wondered a bit as to whether Simon would manage to keep quiet, and would Lewis leave him alone, but I didn't say too much about that because I didn't want to get Mark any more worried, particularly as he seemed so edgy. So we stopped talking about it. And then, thank God, Lewis died.

After Lewis death I thought Mark'd perk up a bit – I must say, I did. I'd really thought we could get banged up, especially as it looked like Lewis *had* had another go at Carol, and we'd done nothing. Mark was a bit better after Lewis had gone, but he didn't really get much more cheery, and I thought maybe it was just a bit of a reaction to it all being over. And I told him, well, that's life really, isn't it – a bit of excitement and then back to normal. But it wasn't that, there was something on his mind – but he wasn't going to tell me, and I wasn't going to ask him, so there it was.

Anyway things lumbered along towards Xmas and that's

enough to get anyone depressed, Xmas is. We each bought a new suit for the wedding, and that was probably the biggest excitement in our lives. Oh, yes, there was one other excitement – Mark had his birthday and his priceless pot arrived. I couldn't find any belladonna, so I put some pansies in it! Even that didn't seem to go down very well; in fact he looked sadder than ever.

Anyway, just as we seemed to have lost all contact with the DAFS, one or two exciting things did start to happen. The first came out of me trying to cheer Mark up in a pretty pathetic way.

"Here," I said, as we finished supper, "what happened to those chocolates, the ones we won at the Bridge day that we didn't fancy before?"

Mark said he'd put them back in the cupboard so we got them out and pigged at them.

"Course, we'll never know for sure whether Lewis sent those chocolates to Carol," I said, "but we could do Tubby a bit of good. I bet he wouldn't make himself go through the wedding, if he didn't feel so guilty about the chocolates. It's because he feels so bad that he's, like, in Carol's power. I think we should tell him there were two boxes, and the nut ones weren't his."

Mark thought this was a good idea. And as there's no time like the present, we rang Tubby up – but he wasn't there.

"Perhaps he lives at Carol's now," Mark said, miserable as ever. "Perhaps he's even married her already." Anyway we left a message – explaining the situation, just in case.

Christmas came and we got a card from Bethan: a nativity scene, shepherds and so on. Mark said did I think it was an advertisement for Welsh lamb? We did get cards from other people, too – I'm just talking about the DAFS, but there wasn't a peep out of the rest of them.

Mark said "DAFS come out in the Spring," and, you know what? He was right. Well, it wasn't Spring exactly, but in the

New Year – January 3rd, I think it was, a postcard arrived from Canberra. It was signed Simonetta, and it said, 'It is very sunny here'. Which, as Mark said, could have meant anything. We also got an email from Sammy – not really Season's Greetings; more like looking for good cheer for the tournament director:

Hi folks,

How you doing? How do you fancy a world bridge cruise, snip at £5,000, nothing to rich guys like you!

I looked at the attachment: there were lots of photos of Sammy and his team – mainly pretty boys, but there was one woman.

"See any familiar faces?" I asked Mark.

"I can't see anything."

"Christ," I said. "You're getting like Tubby. Put your glasses on."

"Good God," he said, "it's the beehive! It's Matron. What's she doing there?"

I had a little read. "'Private masseuse'. She's bought her way in on Simon's furniture!"

Now normally something like that would have cheered Mark up no end, but even the thought of Matron drunkenly manipulating private parts didn't seem to make him any better. As I say, there was something on his mind, and I'd sussed out that the Janet wedding had something to do with it.

We were taking down the Christmas decorations – funny how things seemed to happen to us while we were faffing around with that tree. Mark was poking about taking off some horrible pink things at the bottom the tree, and I was on a step ladder doing the high bits of glitz. I looked down at him as he stood there miserably with a handful of baubles and I remarked that he wasn't usually so glum handling balls.

He peered up into the branches. (I had put one on crooked: he hadn't said, but I knew it had worried him all through Christmas!)

"Hello," I said, "can you see me? I'm the fairy at the top."

"John," he said suddenly, and I heard one of the baubles hit the ground. "If I had done something... something... I don't know... long before I met you and now there were... consequences... what would you do?"

"Depends what they were. Perhaps I'd send you some poisoned chocolates or top up your glass with belladonna."

"No, don't make jokes... Oh, John, come down off that ladder."

"No," I said, "I think I'll stay up here, then I can chuck icicles at you if I don't like what I hear."

And then he told me.

I must admit, I was surprised. Not that he had had it off with some woman in Florence; I'd known from the start that he'd had a lot of women before he found that he was gay. No, what surprised me was that he should think I would mind! True, I had ribbed him about Isabel, but she was in her fifties and if he had suddenly decided to start being bi again, I would hardly have thought she'd be the one to get the juices going again – and, after all, he hadn't exactly shown any signs of wanting to move to single beds.

"So what's the big deal?" I asked. I sat up there on the steps winding up a long strip of tinsel.

His face lit up rather more brightly than the lights I'd just taken off the tree.

"You don't mind? You don't think I want to go off with her or anything? You don't mind about Janet and... the baby?"

"No. Why should I?" Then I had a sing – like Marco, I have a beautiful voice: "'Grand-dad... lovely... that's what we all think of yooooooooooou...'"

Then I came down off the ladder.

There followed a short interlude among the baubles.

Well, I tell a lie: a longish interlude during which the angel got broken, but neither of us minded too much.

It was only afterwards I got to thinking.

"Mark, how much do you remember about Florence?"

"Well, to be honest, John, I don't remember it at all."

"Do you remember buying the locket?"

"It was the sort of thing I did."

"You know, you talked about Florence at *Il Sole*."

"What are you suggesting?"

"What I have always suggested: that Isabel has a lively imagination, and she has cashed in on what she remembered you saying at *Il Sole*. Even if you did have it off with her – which I doubt – who is to say Janet is your daughter? It might have been anyone she had it off with; after all Janet doesn't look like you. I think you'd find the merry widow would be very loathe to have DNA tests done – and why hasn't she told Janet? Mark, I think she's been leading you up the garden path. I think she thought she'd give it a whirl – nothing to lose, you might just be interested in her. But when she saw you weren't, she shrugged her shoulders. Probably made herself feel better by sending off the photo to Lewis. I wouldn't be surprised if she was looking for a hefty cheque for Janet too."

"Oh, John!"

"So you see what a fool you are to have worried so much." He nodded.

"I have never been so ready to admit to being a fool."

After a bit he said slowly, "I don't think that I want to go to that wedding and give the bride away."

"No." I said, "I think the Macalisters are a pretty peculiar lot. I think you should steer clear of them."

"But how can I get out of it?"

"I can think of a suitable person to give the bride away."

"Who?"

"Well there was a lonely widower, the kindly man who used to partner Janet at *Il Sole*, but sadly, he's no longer with us, so I have another in mind..." I did a lot of laughing.

"Sammy? But would he do it?"

"I am sure he would – at a price."

"£1,000?"

"Double it!"

Mark didn't have a problem with that. And, in fact, while I started trying to disentangle all the wires from the tree, he fired a little email off to Sammy.

"What shall we do about our wedding suits?" I asked. "Our shelling out for them is a bit like Simon going off to Australia. We could have saved the bother and the money. Perhaps we could take them back."

"I was thinking," he said in a funny awkward sort of way. "It seems a shame to waste them."

"Perhaps we shall get asked to Tubby's wedding," I said.

"No, and anyway let's hope that doesn't happen. I was thinking of another wedding."

I went on with the lights. "Is Arbuthnot-Jones getting married?"

"It wasn't exactly a wedding I had in mind," said Mark looking directly at me. "More of a civil ceremony."

"Civil ceremony?"

"John, I am asking you to marry me."

"Well, I said, "it's a good thing I'm not still sitting on the top of that ladder."

"But will you, John?"

He started towards me, then stopped. He thought I was going to refuse!

"Well," I said, "seeing as how I can't get Tubby, Lewis, Simon, Karl or Arbuthnot-Jones, I had better have you."

I gave up on the lights and a lot more baubles got broken. And just as I was in the kitchen opening the champagne, the phone went.

"Yes," I heard Mark say, "two different boxes. But this isn't a very good time, Tubby."

But he was not to be put off. I lifted up the kitchen

extension. "Are you sure there were two boxes?"

"Well, did you give her a great big box?"

"No, I gave her… quite a small box. I'm not made of money, you know."

"Carol was poisoned by chocolates she ate from a large box. So it can't have been your small box that made her ill."

There was a pause. "Then I'm not going to marry her."

It was the most definite thing I had ever heard him say.

"How will you get out of it?"

"I shall run away."

"Where will you go?"

"I… I…" The old twiddler was back; you could almost hear the thumbs going.

"If I were you, "said Mark, "I should go to Australia."

"Australia?"

"Canberra. A lot of English people go there."

"I might be lonely."

"Nonsense; I know an English lady who's lately moved there: Simonetta, lots of long blonde hair. I'll put you in touch. Must go, Tubby, ring you later – much later!"

"Do you think he'll go?" I asked returning with the bottle. I'm not good at pouring champagne; most of it went on the carpet.

"Wouldn't you?"

"Pretty much all the DAFS are paired off then, aren't they?" I said as I refilled the glasses, "us, Janet and Gino, Tubby and Simonetta, Megan and Bethan, the Skorskis, and I daresay Sammy doesn't go short. There's only your friend the widow…"

"She's got Wanker Williams from the church."

"Poor old Carol's the only one left."

"Well, there's Arbuthnot-Jones going spare, now Matron's dumped him. Anyway, she doesn't deserve anyone; if it hadn't been for her none of this would have happened. More bubbly?"

"Please. Where shall we go for the…. honeymoon, John?

Would you like to go back to Italy?

"No, we've done *Il Sole* – twice, and I hear Florence is full of tarts."

"Where, then?"

"Wait a minute."

"As long as you like."

"I should like to go to Wales," I said.

"Wales? What on earth do you want to go there for? You said you hated it."

"I fancy Irfon."

"No, you don't. Why Wales?"

"Well... when we went before and we went through all those mountains and that... well, you had a sort of look on your face, and I should like to see it again. Doesn't that sound pathetic?"

"You don't have to take me to Wales for that, John. As long as I'm with you..."

But before the violins start going, I'll stop.

We did go to Wales; it didn't rain *all* the time and Irfon gave us half a lamb to bring home.

And now we're living happily ever after.

Email from Sammy – one year later

'Prince' Sammy's Bridge Weekends at Elsinore Castle

Come and join 'Prince' Sammy at Elsinore for a luxury weekend of bridge and cosseting. Our elegant hostess Isabel makes us feel as if we are all old friends, and Masseuse 'Matron' is on hand to give special personal attention. Superb Italian cuisine (Italian chef and staff), with the additional benefit of the finest Welsh lamb (delivered fresh weekly by Irfon Enterprises). Unusual prizes, courtesy of Karl and Claire Skorski.

Read what some of our visitors have to say!

"Bridge events can be very frightening, but Sammy made us feel so safe. And we fell in love with Signora Janet's twins, John and Marco."
May and Mavis

"We came all the way from Australia and spent part of our honeymoon very happily here."
Mr and Mrs L. Smith.

"With an elderly husband and some dietary problems of my own, I have to be very careful, but my old friend Sammy made sure everything ran smoothly."
Carol Arbuthnot-Jones.

"We like to spend time just being together, and Sammy made sure we were never crowded."
Jacqueline and Stuart Clarke.

"My wife was particularly pleased with our prize, a delightful toy lamb."
Admiral Marlowe.

And Sammy says: "If only Elsinore had been like this in Hamlet's time, there wouldn't have been no tragedy!"

Come and share in the laughter!"
THREE DAYS FOR ONLY £1,500.

Lightning Source UK Ltd.
Milton Keynes UK
UKOW04f1005120116

266238UK00002B/13/P